Robert Elliot Wiese

THE ZOZER BROTHERHOOD

Published by

Loring's World Publishers
1342 Olino Street
Honolulu, HI 96818

Copyright © 1997 by Loring's World Publishers.
All Rights Reserved.
Printed in the United States of America.

Library of Congress Catalog Card Number 97-94189
    Loring's World Publishers
    ISBN NO. 0-9659387-0-0

Book Cover Design by Debra Castro,
INform Graphic Design, Inc.

Prologue

The procession slowly wound its way through the labyrinth of passages carved from the solid rock beneath the desert floor. The train of figures, all attired in gray robes which covered them from head to foot, chanted as they shuffled, trancelike, along the dark corridors. The reflected light from the torches that each figure carried bounced off the stark, irregular walls of the interlocking passages, giving the figures a pool of yellow light into which they melted as they pressed onward. Their chant echoed off the hard surface of the rock, all voices mingling to produce an undulating wave of sound. The scrape of their bare feet against the hard sandstone floor of the passages modulated the cadence of the chant; the effect on untrained ears was that of an unearthly moan flowing through empty chambers.

The queue of hooded figures continued forward until they reached a widening in the passage, a widening which created a room that had a corridor exiting from each end. There they stopped, grouping themselves in a circle around a raised stone altar located in the center of the room. The chanting ceased as one of the group stepped forward into the bright circle of light. He pulled back the hood which concealed his face and spoke.

"Brethren, we have a solemn duty to undertake this day. The omens bespeak the end of my days, and that it is time to take measures to perpetuate the Brotherhood. We of this highest anointed caste are prescribed to assure the

continuance of our Brotherhood, so as to further the work
our god, Zozer, commenced at the beginning of his reign.
It is for this purpose that the ceremony which we are about
to undertake should be dedicated. But hold! Before we
bring in the female, the instrument of our future, let us
hear the words of our brother, Imhotep. He has come to us
from the divine presence of Zozer, beloved of almighty
Ra. What he deems to say must be engraved into our hearts
as his words are the will of Zozer, to show us the path we
are destined to follow. Heed him well."

From beyond the circle a man stepped forward into
the blaze of light. This one was slight of frame, old in
appearance but imperious in bearing. The zealous gleam
flashing in his eyes caused all who fell under his gaze to
halt and attend his words.

"Oh holy and revered Brotherhood, I am come before
you now with grave words from our lord and master.
Mighty and Blessed Zozer has proclaimed that you here,
his extension beyond the heavens, shall inherit his eternal
blessings when the hour arrives for him to join the others
chosen of Ra. You here, seed of his loins, must take his
words and desires into all lands beyond our sacred Kemet,
and pledge that his memory is forever honored. As his
Chief Vizier and his Chief Builder, I come to you to say
our mighty Zozer is preparing to leave his earthly realm.
Already I am erecting his tomb at Saqqara, and should the
omens prove true, his human body will be laid to everlasting rest before the moon wanes, but his spirit will live with
Ra.

Keep his faith to your hearts, and never, under pain of
a horrible death, reveal what you do beyond the Brotherhood. Our revered Zozer must not be forsaken. So says
the Mighty and Blessed Zozer, Pharaoh of all these lands,
the glorious Black Land, sacred Kemet."

"You have heard the words of our brother, Imhotep. I repeat, heed them well. Now it is time for us to affirm our resolve, and to keep faith with the greatest of rulers. I, Semph, High Priest, am now ready for the act of perpetuation. Bring in the woman."

Out from the midst of the group, a small figure was pushed forward, hesitating at first to stand in the light.

The hood was removed and the robe dropped to the floor. Before all eyes stood a woman of exquisite beauty and regal bearing, holding her head high with defiance flashing in dark green eyes, flecked with gold. She stood before them totally naked, evincing no show of embarrassment as the torch light danced off the swell of her young breasts and firm thighs. Here was a woman who could command attention wherever she appeared. Standing with grace before this cadre of old men, her very presence brought a quickening of breath and a longing in their loins. The one called Semph spoke, his voice wet with desire.

"You have been selected from all the women of the Brethren to be our instrument of fulfillment. Your attendants have instructed you and have assured us that you have not known another man and that your time is nigh for you to bear young. Is this not so?"

"Yea, oh holy one. I am what the others call a virgin. No man has ever shared my bed. I am ready for the seed of the Brotherhood to bear fruit and I give myself willingly to the honor of perpetuating the memory of our mighty ruler."

"So be it, then. Make yourself ready."

After uttering these words, the high priest laid himself on the stone altar after removing the robe that covered his frail body. By the light of the torches, the attendants came forward with pots of vile-smelling pigments and proceeded to anoint his body. They drew multicolored, ab-

stract designs on his wrinkled skin, each design of which
was intertwined by a red line that commenced under his
chin and ended at his feet. There were yellow, blue and
green shapes spilling over his naked form and all were tied
together with that seemingly obscene red snake-form winding down his body.

Finishing this ritual, amidst the renewed chanting from
the on-lookers, the attendants turned their ministrations to
the woman. She yielded her young and supple body to the
touch of the brushes. Her pointed breasts were painted a
vivid blue with the color flowing down to her loins, circling the genitals. The effect was macabre. Their task
being done, the artists returned to the circle of the Brotherhood. The chanting rose in pitch, giving voice to their
passion.

With neither a glance to her right nor to her left, the
girl approached the altar. Looking through vacant eyes at
the prone figure lying on the stone slab, she mounted the
dais. She took his withered and inert phallus in her hand,
squeezing the limp organ slightly with her fingers. She
lowered her body to bring her face down to it and began to
caress the priest's manhood with her lips. Her attendants
told her she could excite the man this way, causing the
instrument to become rigid so that she might fulfill her
destiny. Gradually it stiffened, throbbing with pulsating
blood. The girl straightened, still looking at the shaft with
wonder, and pulled her body over the old man, straddling
him. She inserted his manhood into herself, as the attendants had instructed; however they had not prepared her
for the stab of pain that shot through her body, nor for the
flow of blood which seeped from within her, mingling with
the painted hair between her legs. She did not cry out from
the ache, believing this to be part of the ritual.

The pain eased somewhat as she began the thrusting

motion the attendants showed her, movements which were mechanical at first, but as the flood of desire filled her inner being the gyrations of her hips became more rapid. She felt waves of passion breaking within her loins, her breath becoming more in tune with the agony of pleasure she was experiencing. The attendants had not instructed her in this occurrence. The old man did not touch her body, giving himself up instead to the movements of the act. His climax came soon. He signaled the attendants to remove the girl, herself in the throes of awakened passion but not allowed to satisfy herself. The ordeal was over.

The old Semph rose, donned his robe, and addressed the group. "We have finished the act of perpetuation. Now it is in the hands of the gods as to the legacy of the act. Soon there will be forthcoming a new high priest of the Mighty Zozer, one who has the blessing of all who witnessed this conception. He shall be raised within the sanctity of these walls and when the time arrives for him to assume the role of leader, he, himself, will cut the throat of this woman who bore him. There shall be no other man for this woman to sully her body, the temple of our new high priest. It is for this reason she will now be taken into the desert, there to await her time for the glorious birth. Blessings on Zozer."

The attendants came forward and seized the girl with tender but firm hands. She surrendered herself to them willingly, realizing it was her destiny. They led her out of the caverns and transported her out into the desert where she took lodging at the nearby oasis of Messneh there to remain until the birth. She was called by no name, and the attendants paid her no attention, referring to her only as 'that one'. She did not want for things as her every need and desire was fulfilled.

However, the solitude and loneliness of the desert were

hard on the spirit of one so young who had been newly awakened to the joys of man. Ritual as it was, she nonetheless remembered the stabbings of her own passion flowing through her body when the old man's shaft filled the void of her loins. She was the chosen one, yet the yearnings she experienced and could not explain overwhelmed the soul. These feelings would not leave her even when Amun sank below the western horizon.

Her days were spent in the oppressive heat of the tent, anchored in the sea of sand surrounding the oasis. At night, with the coming of the stars, she lay on a blanket outside the tent, looking up to the heavens, praying to those stars. The air would be cooled by the breeze drifting down from the mountains far away to the north. Her loneliness grew with each passing day but still she remained captive of her faith, keeping count of her days marked on the trunk of a nearby palm tree.

Her thoughts were disturbing. She did not remember from where she came, or even her parents. The only recollections she had of her past were the teachings of the group who referred to themselves as 'The Zozer Brotherhood'. This was the only family she had and she offered no resistance to the future she now saw before her.

Yet, with a fear that would not be denied, she knew that there had to be something else out in the world, something the old priests had not told her. She could have no idea what that 'something' might be for she had no knowledge of any world beyond the endless sand. But still, with nothing to occupy her troubled mind during the long wait, the germ of doubt invaded her spirit. Oh, how she wished for enlightenment. If only the gods would answer.

During her eighth month, when she was big with child and knowing her confinement was nearing its end, she could not bring herself to remain a prisoner any longer. She could not give her child over to those men to train and to dominate. She had come to believe that her child should have a life outside of that place, away from the confines of an ideal that allowed no one to think of other things. She knew her life would be forfeited when the child grew to manhood and assumed the leadership of the group. This fact did not dismay her as much as the idea she could have no hand in the life of her child. This is what she had come to fear.

It was from this fear and discontent that she formulated a plan to leave the oasis as soon as she could. Where she would go or how she would get there, she gave not a thought. Her only desire was to leave the desert and to raise her child as her own.

Slowly, deliberately, she started to hoard scraps of food which she knew could be dried in the dry heat of the desert and would not rot. Water, however, was another thing. She knew from the talk of the elders that one could not survive in the desert without the precious water. And then there was her child. Would she have milk for it or would she be dry as were so many of the desert women? These were but a few of the reasons which made her hesitate.

The life of her child and the part she wanted to play in that life overcame the doubts. She forced herself to disregard her fears; she continued to gather her pitiful scraps of food until she felt there was enough for several days in the desert. She made her final preparations for the departure. She had not yet solved the problem of water.

The system of caverns which housed the Brotherhood lay below the desert floor in the natural depression known as Senuabut, which had been a flowing river, eons past. This harsh area was four days' journey by caravan west of the magnificent city of Membre, the capital from where Zozer ruled all of the land of Kemet. The pharaoh provided his secret society with all that was needed for its comfort. An underground stream fed the well and fresh food was delivered to the oasis of Messneh. The camel rovers asked no questions of those who received the supplies; the pharaoh paid well for their silence and ignorance.

The girl invoked help from the leader of the cameleers one day when supplies were delivered. She begged to be hidden away in the caravan, pleading for her escape. Her entreaties only fell on deaf ears, laughed at by the coarse men of the desert.

"Why should we risk losing a profitable venture for the sake of a pregnant woman? You have no gold, no jewels or anything of value. Even your condition makes you unfit for the slave market. No, you cannot come with us."

She was dejected but not defeated. Her determination to leave that place put into her mind the other plan, the plan she now knew must be followed. She would steal away into the desert with her meager supply of food and but a single gourd of water. She would try to find her way, unseen, to the east, toward the great river which the desert people called 'the waters of Hapi'. She prayed to the gods of the people for help in making good her escape, but herself doubting the existence of such gods.

When the moon was high in the dark sky and the cooling wind stirred from the north, the caravan prepared to leave, its business concluded. They preferred to travel the desert by night. Just as she watched the last of the caravan leave, a young camel driver approached her tent and after motioning her to silence, led her to his beast. Under the cover of darkness and the busy activity of departure, he hid the girl in the folds of the leather pouch draped over the haunches of the disgruntled and smelly camel. She had scarcely enough room, very little air, but here at least was a step to the outside world.

As the string of camels plodded their way out of the oasis she had worrisome thoughts of what might lay before her. She knew nothing of the outside. What were the people like? Would she be trading one prison for another? These doubts caused her to think that perhaps she had been too hasty in leaving. Perhaps she should have remained and made the best of the situation, but then, her former resolve returned. She was bound to find a better life outside no matter what it was like. She had no future at all in the desert. And so she kept to her decision and tried to think only for the well-being of her baby, now soon to come into the world.

When dawn came to the desert the alarm from the attendants reached the ears of the high priest. Livid with anger, furious at the attendants for having allowed the woman out of their sight, the priests of the Brotherhood convened a council.

"She must be found before the child is born," raged the high priest, Semph. "The supply caravan must have hidden her and taken her with it to the north. We must go forth and search until she is found. Bring her back, for she must deliver the child here in our sanctuary. It is to be my successor."

Another priest stepped forward. "What is prescribed in the event we cannot return her, oh holy one?"

"We shall continue to search until she is found, even though the search takes us beyond sacred Kemet. If she has delivered when we find her, kill both her and the child for they will be abominations to us and to our Mighty Zozer. Another instrument for bearing my successor must be brought to me at once while I still have my seed."

Semph stormed among the others, pausing now and then to pull at his garments in rage and frustration. Facing the group, teeth clenched in his anger, he cried, "If, for any reason, the woman and child escape our wrath, we must continue to seek them out, including all their inheritors, throughout the world and for all time until all traces of them have been totally erased from the earth. This Brotherhood, and our successors, shall now pledge our lives to accomplish this burden no matter where it shall lead."

The group closed ranks, chanting as they began the shuffling procession to the outer reaches of the caverns, out into the vast desert, to begin their search. The words of the chant were now different than before. The words now called for vengeance. "Oh Mighty and Revered Zozer, we pledge death and destruction to all who have broken faith with you. Hear, oh Zozer, we are one."

The caravan had traveled the entire night to reach its resting place. The camel drivers were joyous at seeing the palm trees in the distance as the sun rose in the east. Here they would camp in the cool shade of the oasis during the heat of the day, continuing their journey at nightfall. One of the camels was some distance behind the main body. The driver, Nemek, was keeping the pace slow so the ride would be less troublesome for the girl hiding in the folds of the coverlet. The other men had noticed the slower gait but said nothing as long as they remained in sight. They rolled their eyes toward the heavens, smirking at one another. Each suspected the cause.

"Nemek," the caravan leader called, as the last camel lowered itself to the sand, "you are a fool. Do you think the old ones back there will not find you? Already they come. They will kill her and you as well. And what about the danger you are causing us? The priests at Membre will stop rewarding us for making this journey."

"I am aware of the danger, Seneb," the young driver

replied. "But she implored me to take her along. We shall leave you here and take the way to the west through the Great Nothingness. The old ones cannot follow us there. When we are safely away I shall make her my mate and raise the little one as my own. Later, I shall rejoin you, if you will have me."

"Do what you will. However, Ra must be appeased. See to it at the first opportunity. If the old ones come upon us, we will tell them you turned to the east, to the great river where it touches the sea. You shall leave us before Amun dies in the western sky."

And so it was settled. Nemek led the girl into the shade and made her take some water. The long, swaying camel ride made her sick to the stomach, and her swollen belly heaved in torment. However, she willed herself calm, drank of the water, and lowered her body to the sand where she soon fell asleep. The boy looked down on her, marveling at her young beauty. She cannot be older than seventeen floods of the river, he thought to himself. Nemek was eighteen such floods.

After a time, the girl awakened. She rose up on one arm and saw the boy stretched out at her feet, lying in the sand instead of sharing the blanket. Her movements caused Nemek to open his eyes in alarm.

"Are you all right?" he asked.

"Yes, I am well enough now. You are very kind to look after me."

"What is your name? What is it you are called?"

She looked at him hard, partly in fear, then answered soft-ly. "I am called Nara. I do not remember my father or mother. The Brotherhood raised me, taught me their ways. It is the only life I have known until I left with you. I am very sad to have left but I must seek another life for my son." Tears welled in her eyes, overflowing down her cheeks.

"My name is Nemek," he told her. "I let it be known to the others that I am taking you as my own. Your child shall be my child. We shall be as one family."

"The Brotherhood will kill us both. We cannot escape their wrath." She shook in spite of the heat flowing in from the desert. "But I have no one else to look to for help. I will go with you and be your mate. I call on Aset and Urir to bless you and our new family."

"If you are well enough we must leave now. The old ones will be searching for you but they walk the desert sand. We will stay far ahead of them. The others here will lead them false. Come, we must leave."

The lone camel bellowed with rage at having to go out into the heat of the desert while the others remained by the water. Nara sat atop the beast, out in the open, covering her head from the sun. Nemek led the camel forward, prodding as the need arose. The forlorn couple took one last look at the comfort of the oasis then turned and resigned themselves to the perils that lay ahead.

When the sun god, Amun, lowered himself into the western sand, darkness descended on the pair but they dared not stop to rest. Nemek guided their steps by the stars. He had made many such journeys by the path of the stars; they were his special gods and he trusted them.

As they approached a dip in the landscape, known in these parts as the Great Nothingness, the new day dawned. By its light, they saw the haven of the last oasis before the beginning of the vast depression. They observed other camels at the water and their own beast increased its gait in its hurry to join the others.

Nara descended from the camel, grimacing in pain. "It is time," she groaned through clenched teeth. "My baby will soon join us."

Nemek supported her, leading her to the campfire. "Is

there one here who can help my woman? She is ready to be delivered." He shouted this to the group sitting by the fire.

From the edge of the fire one stood up. "Over here is the women's shelter. Let me take her there."

Rough, but caring, hands grabbed Nara, keeping her from falling. Together they made their way to the back of the campsite to the tent reserved for women. Inside, the desert matrons laid Nara down and with the skill developed by centuries of desert life, prepared the girl for delivery. They pulled her robe apart to clean the birthing area, using precious water mixed with special potions.

In the flickering light of the oil lamp the women were horrified to see the colored stains on Nara's breasts and lower body, stains which were yet vivid after so long a time. The women shrank back in terror as though demons from the underworld had come amongst them ready to mark them with the ritualistic designs. At last, one old crone inched forward, touching the misshapen body with tenderness.

"I have heard, as have we all, of such things. You must be one of the hidden ones, those we of the desert never see. It is said that one who is so stained must be destroyed else misfortune falls on the tribe. Tell us, is this so?"

Nara was weeping bitterly now. "I have run from those who would kill me and my unborn child. I will not cause you misfortune, unless those who seek me find me here with you. Help to bring my child into the world and I shall call on all the gods to be generous with you. We shall be gone from this place as soon as the baby is here. We can cause you no harm if no one knows we are here."

"So shall it be," the old woman whispered. "The ways of the desert are simple. We never turn away from one who is in need of our help if they cause us no harm. You will be safe here."

Nara's son was born later that night when the star-gods were high in their heaven. She called the child Menefee in honor of the great king, Menes, who brought all parts of the Black Land under one rule. A great omen, indeed. Little Menefee would grow strong and straight, a leader among men. Thus did Nara dedicate her man-child to Amun.

The family was gone from the oasis at first light. Their path took them around the edge of the great depression, always circling toward the north, seeking the safety of the mountains which dipped into the sea. The details of their trial were passed from mouth to mouth throughout the tribes of the desert. With each telling around smoldering camp-fires, the legend grew larger, until the names of Nara and Nemek were lost. Menefee stood alone.

Part 1
Chapter 1

Loring started to awake from his oblivion, slowly at first, then more rapidly as he became aware of his surroundings. The light in the room was brighter, almost blinding, aggravating the pain in his head. The sight before him was unreal, something one only reads about in cheap pulp novels. Gwen was on the bed, eaglespread and totally naked. She was trussed hand and foot, unable to bring her arms down or close her separated legs. She had something...silk panties...crammed into her mouth to keep her from emitting anything but guttural groans as she writhed on the bed. Her eyes were wide, almost exploding from her head. Sheer terror was telegraphed from every contour of her beautiful body.

"You will now tell us what we wish to know, Mr. Loring. Who are you working for, and what is the nature of that work? You will tell us now."

Loring was sprawled in a chair at the foot of the bed, tied so tightly that he could not even turn his head away from the stricken girl spread before him. The swarthy giant of a man standing over him continued talking.

"You must answer, infidel, else this insignificant whore will be sacrificed as was her traitorous ancestor." The man's malodorous breath punctuated his words.

"I don't know what you bastards are talking about. I'm just a historian, doing architectural research."

"We followed you here from Hawaii. We know that you spoke with the whoremonger who calls himself Claridge before you departed for this place. What is your business in this matter?"

"I don't know any of the details. I haven't met the people, other than Claridge. I have a meeting with them tomorrow. Now, let the girl go."

"Perhaps...in time."

"She has nothing to do with this...I just met her a few hours ago."

"The woman was hired. She was to get you here for us to question."

"I don't believe you. She never knew who I was."

"Did you think you had so much charm that she actually wanted you? No, my infidel friend, you had to be brought here for us to talk with: she merely served the purpose. She did her job well and she will get her reward. Now, who has hired you?"

Loring looked at the girl on the bed. She returned his stare, eyes still beseeching him for help.

"I told you all I know. The outfit that Claridge represented is called Zoser. Zoser International, and that's the truth."

The smelly giant spat on the floor, and turned back to Loring. "We know of this Zoser organization. Your searching in the past will uncover nothing they need. We are the chosen ones. We have the secret and you will not succeed in your feeble attempts to discover it."

The dark man approached Loring, tugging at the ropes that bound him to the chair.

"We shall leave for now, but take this warning to heart. Have nothing to do with the Zoser group. Return to Hawaii. Do not scratch the dirt in places where you do not belong."

Loring was surprised the man knew so much about him.

"Before we depart, we must give you one lesson to remember. Achmed, let us proceed."

Another man, one who had remained hidden in the deep shadows alongside the bed, approached. The girl lay rigid, eyes filled with the same loathing Loring felt for the two. The man carried a small box from which he took a stone container resembling a canopic jar and began to smear colors on the body of the woman. He painted her breasts a vivid blue, traced a wide red swath from around each breast and continued it down to her genitals. He colored her pubic hair the same vivid blue as her breasts and then held a table lamp over the bed to view the results of the obscene work of art. Loring could not take his eyes from the macabre visions that the painted form on the bed brought to his tortured brain. He struggled with his bonds in vain.

"Gwen, I'm so sorry," he said with tears in his eyes.

The nameless one then took something from inside his coat, held it up where the light from the lamp reflected its shadow on the body of the girl. It was a Turkish dagger, the type of dirk with a serpentine blade and a jeweled haft. Holding it aloft for a moment, the man uttered a phrase in Arabic, then plunged the knife into Gwen's left breast.

Loring almost passed out with the horror of the scene. The girl's body contorted with the initial thrust, then was still, the haft of the dagger continuing to quiver in the dim light of the lamp. Her blood flowed from the painted breast, mingling with the blue and the red pigments, bright red, at first, then darkening as it continued to roll down the body to the pubic hair where it pooled and started to coagulate. Loring prayed for oblivion.

The giant turned to him again. "Remember this,

Loring. Go back from where you came. We shall always be in your shadow."

Loring stared at the desecrated body before him. Sorrow for the girl he barely knew joined the rage he felt at having to witness such a bloodthirsty deed. In spite of his aching head, he forced himself to remain rational. There had to be some explanation for this horror.

He closed his eyes and tried to remember what had happened in the last twenty-four hours.

The British Airways flight from Los Angeles was making its long letdown approach through the thick overcast which obscured the rolling countryside north of London. As the plane passed through fifteen thousand feet the heavy layer of clouds faded away to scattered puffs of cumulus, giving most of the tired passengers their first glimpse of England. The 747 shuddered slightly as the massive aircraft passed through the thermals of air currents rising from the warmer ground. The pilot added power to maintain the glidepath speed. Heathrow Airport appeared some distance in front of the right wing as the plane started a slow banked turn to intercept the designated landing path.

From her central control station, a cabin attendant announced the flight's imminent arrival.

"Welcome to London Heathrow Airport. All passengers must report to Immigration for passport clearance before claiming their baggage. Those passengers holding United Kingdom passports will please proceed to queues One and Two. Please follow the signs to Immigration after deplaning. All of us aboard hope you had a pleasant flight and that you will fly British Airways again. Thank you."

Derek Loring remained in his seat, having no desire

to join the crush of eager people stampeding from the plane. His first-class seat was up forward, away from the surge. He knew the lines for passport check at Immigration would be long and slow-moving, and he was in no particular hurry to join in the crush since no one was scheduled to meet him this time. While he waited, he mulled over once more the purpose of the trip. He was still not quite satisfied, professionally, as to the reasons given for his selection. He was not overly modest, but he knew he wasn't all that renowned in his field to warrant such a plum of a commission.

Loring was an architectural historian and archaeologist who lived in Honolulu because of the wonderful climate and the laid-back way of life of the islands. He had written a few well-received papers on Mid-East cultures of antiquity which had been published over the past five years. His lectures at the University and other graduate schools on the Mainland were attended by enough students to enhance his reputation as a teacher. He had done some research for the government of Turkey about four years before, dealing with Islamic architecture and winning for him the Lister Prize in history.

This was the reason given by Zoser International when they offered him a commission to undertake a research project in Egypt. Joshua Claridge, a representative of Zoser, came to Hawaii for the purpose of retaining Loring to locate a remote structure of the pharaohs, dating from 1400 BC. Claridge invited him to visit London, all expenses paid, and consent to an interview with the directors of Zoser International. The full particulars of the project would be explained at the interview, and his fee would be negotiated if he elected to take on the job.

Loring saw no reason to turn down the invitation; it wouldn't cost him anything, and the idea did have a certain aura of mystery. Then, too, it would give him the opportunity to visit Marc and Veronica, very close and dear friends whom he hadn't seen for far too long. In spite of these pleasant reasons, he could not explain the uneasiness he felt.

The crowd was thinning out. Loring gathered his few things and started for the door, still prepared for a lengthy delay once inside the terminal. He nodded to the other straggler leaving with him, a man who introduced himself at the beginning of the flight, but kept to himself during the trip. Loring remembered the name he gave...Smythe, Wilfred Smythe. He said he was in the export business.

Loring's room was booked at the Regent Hotel in Picadilly. Except on those occasions when the Merricks insisted he stay with them, Loring used the centrally located Regent. The desk clerk recognized Loring and hurried forward to be of service.

"Will you be staying with us long, Dr. Loring?"

"I prefer to be called 'Mr. Loring'" he told the clerk. He always thought "Doctor" had such a pompous ring.

"A few days, perhaps a week." Loring was not at all sure of his future plans. The outcome of this trip would depend on the scheduled interview with Zoser International.

"We shall strive to make your stay noteworthy, however long you choose to stay." The clerk's broad smile was genuine as he handed Loring the key to his room, receiving in return the usual over-generous tip.

Loring picked up the late edition of the Times, glancing quickly at the headlines while waiting for the lift to his room. The elevator doors parted and several people exited the cab, spilling into the lobby, each intent on his own space. Derek felt a slight nudge from one of the milling passengers and he was about to murmur a quiet apology, when looking up, his eyes met the deep violet eyes of a very beautiful woman.

"Nadia? Nadia Shepherd! My God, is it you?"

The woman retreated a step, her hand rising to her mouth to stifle the cry of recognition. Loring gently took her arm and guided her away from the crowd. She responded in the graceful style he remembered.

"How wonderful to meet you again, Derek, and here in London of all places."

"Am I ever glad to see you! I can't begin to tell you how often I thought about you during these past four years. Can we get together to catch up?"

"Derek, I would love that. Let me ring you tomorrow."

"Great! I'm staying here at the hotel."

"I know. Now, look at me...crying with delight at seeing you. Damn!"

Nadia freed her hand from his and took a tissue from her purse. "I must be off. Until later."

His hands were damp with sweat...his and hers. He watched her disappear into the crowds along Regent Street and reluctantly turned back toward the elevators. Nadia had that grace of bearing that caused men to stare and moisten their lips in an imaginary romantic encounter, while women viewed her with open jealousy. She could be a threat to any woman. To him, her very presence was electric. Walking along the wide corridor to his room he remembered how delightful those few days in Istanbul had been, how comfortable they were with each other. And now, here she was again, in London.

The telephone was ringing when he opened the door. It was Joshua Claridge from Zoser.

"I'm happy to find you here in London, Dr. Loring. We look forward to meeting with you tomorrow. Can you be here around four o'clock? My associates and I will devote the remainder of the day to discussing the particulars of the commission we have offered you."

"Four o'clock will be fine with me, Mr. Claridge. I'm familiar with London so I won't have any trouble finding your office."

"Fine. I'm certain you have some pointed questions about the commission. I'm afraid I was rather cryptic in Honolulu. Then, there is the matter of your fee."

"We'll discuss my fee later, if you people have no objection. I'm more interested in learning the details of your project."

"I'm sure we will be able to fill in all the gaps to your complete satisfaction. Will you be doing the town tonight?"

"I don't think so. I'll probably get a drink down at the bar and turn in early. It was a long flight from Honolulu."

"That might be wise. Doesn't pay to overdo. Until tomorrow, then. Cheerio."

Loring hung up the phone and went about settling in. He had decided he would wait until after the meeting with Zoser before calling the Merricks. He wanted to be free to really enjoy the warm companionship of Marc and Veronica. He knew they would insist on knowing all about his being in England, and until he saw the directors of Zoser, he actually didn't know why he was here. He was really looking forward to a peaceful stay with his friends at Priory Farm before moving on.

After a soothing shower, he dressed casually and then went down to the bar. He wasn't hungry enough for an English dinner, but the thought of a couple of drinks appealed to him. He couldn't understand the anxiety he felt. He'd never had misgivings over a job interview before...why now?

A waitress approached the corner booth where he sat.

She was cute and perky, a bit on the young side. Loring guessed her age to be about twenty-five, certainly not more than that. She was wearing a skimpy, short outfit that fairly shouted out the charms skillfully concealed beneath. The girl placed a scotch and water in front of him and smiled warmly.

"This is from the gentleman at the bar. He claims to know you, sir."

Loring glanced toward the bar and saw a man waving to him, his raised glass a token greeting. Loring recognized him from the plane...Smythe, Wilfred Smythe. He nodded his thanks. Smythe left the bar and walked toward him.

"Good to see you again...Loring, isn't it? I hope you won't take offense, but I saw you were alone and took a chance on bidding you welcome. I remembered your drink from the trip."

"Thanks, Smythe. Here, sit down and join me."

"Much obliged."

"You mentioned on the plane today that you were in the export business. What do you deal in...art objects, things like that?"

"Nothing as exotic as that, old chap. Actually, I export fairly decent English wool and import fairly decent American dollars. Not a bad bargain, I must say. But you, Loring. What sort of work occupies your time? Not trade, I dare say. You don't look the type. I should guess you dabble in stocks and bonds, that sort of thing. Am I far off the mark?"

"You've no idea how far off the mark you are. I dabble, as you so aptly phrased it, in history, architecture and archaeology, and not always in that order. Pretty mundane stuff, if the truth be known. My idea of a great old time is to be up to my neck in ancient ruins, stumbling on bits and pieces of history, and conjuring up mysterious thoughts about those finds. Our ancestors were far less moral than mankind is today, but one hell of a lot more honest about their shortcomings."

"I say, doesn't the excitement of the search itself mean anything?"

"Not really. Oh, at first it does, but after awhile, it becomes just a job, like exporting good English wool. Still, there's nothing more stimulating than starting a new dig."

"Well, big sales meeting come morning. Nice to have met you, Loring. Have a good time here in London. Cheers."

"Yes, good night, Smythe. And thanks for the drink. Maybe we'll see each other again before I leave."

Smythe quickly left the booth. As he turned, he bumped into the waitress with enough force to knock her off balance. The tray of drinks she was holding flew into the air, ale and glasses and whiskey cascading over the nearby customers.

"You should bloody-well watch where you walk, girl. You could hurt someone. Clumsy twit." Smythe proceeded out the door, without a backward glance.

"Are you hurt, miss? Here, let me help you." Loring was at her side, steadying her. "That clod was to blame...this wasn't your fault."

"Thank you, sir. I'm quite alright. I only hope the manager doesn't dock me for these drinks."

"I'll speak to the barkeep, tell him how it happened."

"That's kind of you. I appreciate it. I must get this mess tidied up. Excuse me, sir."

The girl hurried to the other customers, wiping off tables amid her apologies. She was on the verge of tears, her eyes wet at the corners. Loring left the bar then, stopping to explain the accident to the barkeep, and to sign his check. He suddenly felt the need of sleep.

On his way to the elevator, he heard his name called. It was the desk clerk.

"Mr. Loring. There's a telephone message for you."

"Thank you." Loring angled over to the desk and was handed a pink message memo. The call was from Nadia. She wouldn't be able to ring him as promised. She called to tell him she would be away from London for the day but would reach him when she returned.

Loring walked aimlessly out into the bustling traffic of Picadilly Square instead of going to his room. He had counted on seeing Nadia the following evening and this change in the planned reunion, although temporary, awakened in him a heavy feeling of loneliness. The mass of people crisscrossing the Square only made his solitude more pronounced.

He returned to the hotel and went directly to his room. He knew it was foolish thinking on his part, but London had suddenly lost some of its charm. The telephone startled him out of his lethargy.

"Hello?"

"Mr. Loring? This is Gwen. You know, the clumsy waitress."

Loring was surprised.

"Oh, hello. How did you get my room number?"

"Well, I peeked at the check you signed. I'm afraid I didn't thank you enough for your help tonight. Would you think me too cheeky if I asked you to have a drink with me. I do owe you that much."

"Well, now, I don't know, Gwen. It's rather late and I have an important meeting tomorrow."

"I understand. Maybe some other time. G'night, sir."

"Gwen, wait!" Loring was still smarting over Nadia's

phone call. He came to a quick decision. "I'll meet you in the lobby. Give me five minutes."

"Oh, smashing! I'll be waiting."

Loring stopped long enough to put on a tie and grab his jacket from the back of a chair. Gwen was waiting by the Regent Street entrance.

"Well, sir, we meet again." She smiled broadly as he approached.

"Hello. Is everything all right? I explained the accident to the barman."

"Oh, yes. Everything is fine, thanks to you. How about that drink?"

"That's an invitation I can't refuse."

"To tell you the truth, I could use a large gin."

"Well then, it's settled. Let's try the pub down the block."

"I must warn you, I usually don't take up with brash Americans. You Yanks all take too much for granted."

"I'm not very brash, and I never take anything for granted."

She took his arm and they walked over to the pub. The bar wasn't crowded; theatre-goers were still in their seats in the various playhouses in the neighborhood. Gwen ordered a double gin, neat, and Loring opted for a pint of bitters. He picked up the drinks from the bar and carried them over to the minuscule table Gwen had captured.

"Well, here's to better Anglo-American relations," he said as he sat down beside her, unable to avoid brushing against her.

"Do you live close by, Gwen?"

"I have a flat in Chelsea. The tube gets me home in about thirty minutes. I say, what's your first name, Mr. Loring?"

"You can call me Derek. Derek Loring."

For the next hour it was just small talk with no serious conversation. Loring figured Gwen to be an uncomplaining member of that vast majority who had no real aim in life, going from day to day doing the same routine things to eke out a livelihood and not caring too much of what went on outside their own four walls.

After two drinks, it became obvious that Gwen was not too much of a drinker. The gin was starting to have its effect on her; her words were becoming a bit thick and slurred. He decided it was time to get her home before he had a drunk on his hands. That was one thing he didn't need.

Out in the cool evening air, she clung to his arm, becoming more rational as they waited for a taxi. She snuggled into his arms once in the cab. The ride to Chelsea didn't take long, and Gwen was almost sober when Loring paid the fare.

He half expected to find Gwen's apartment cluttered and very messy, with an unmade bed, dirty dishes in the sink, stale food on the stove and empty gin bottles strewn about the place. He certainly was not prepared for her immaculate and well-kept flat. She stood in the middle of the room, after taking his coat, and said in a rather softly modulated voice, "Please make yourself at home, Derek. I must get out of this ridiculous costume. I really don't like it at all, but the manager thinks men patrons will stay longer if I parade around half-naked. You'll find the makings of a drink over on the sideboard. I shan't be but a minute."

Loring stood, somewhat puzzled. Gwen didn't fit the image he had formed. While it was true she didn't give the impression of being an intellectual giant, she was certainly no cheap pickup. Her neat apartment was proof of hidden qualities she didn't broadcast. He went to the sideboard to prepare their drinks. He had no idea in what mode of dress she would reappear, not that it would make any difference. He had decided to leave as soon as possible. Just one short drink, then good night. He didn't hear the soft footsteps behind him. Whoever was there, hit him a sharp blow to the head, sending him to the floor with streaks of blinding light flooding the space behind his eyeballs. Then nothing, not even the scream of terror emanating from the other room.

Loring was abruptly brought back to the present. The sound of a door being splintered was muted in the commotion of running feet as the police swarmed into the flat.

Chapter 2

It was three in the morning when Loring returned to his hotel. His body was bruised and scratched; he ached all over from the rough treatment he received from the two murderers. The indications all pointed to the killers being from the Mid-East, he told the police. Their speech patterns, the unusual dagger used for the murder, and the one name they let slip out...Achmed...all had a Turkish origin.

The police had arrived thirty minutes after the killers left. Loring had tried but he still could not free himself from the chair. He remained immobile and resolved not to look at Gwen's body. In spite of this, he could not help but observe how peaceful the young woman looked in death. Gwen's color faded, making the obscene paint on her body more vivid. The bloody dagger protruding from her breast was the sole evidence of how violent her death was. Her struggles and terror remained only in his mind.

When the police broke into the apartment, they were horrified by the scene. The younger of the two constables turned ashen as he examined the dead girl looking for a pulse. He kept his eyes averted as best he could, murmuring softly, "Blimey, look at all this blood. I ain't never seen this much from one body. She's packed it in, that's fer sure. 'Ow's the other bloke, Terrence?"

" 'E's been knocked about some, but alive. Wait a moment while I untie them ropes. Now, there. You okay, Johnnie?"

"Yes, thanks. How'd you get here so fast?"

"Someone called the station house, anonymously. Claimed there was a dead woman up here. What the bloody-hell happened?"

The constable let Loring throw cold water on his face after the ropes fell away. Loring gave them his name and then began pacing, flexing his arms and legs to restore his circulation. He told them about the ambush he stumbled into when he brought the girl home. He repeated the questions the two killers hammered at him and their threat of future violence if he continued with his work. Loring told them he had just arrived in London on a business trip. In spite of all their questions, Loring felt the police considered him a victim as well, and were extremely polite and solicitous of his welfare.

Inspector Crimmins arrived a quarter of an hour later. Gwen's body was still on the bed, trussed and gagged. Nothing had been disturbed. Crimmins typified the British law officer most Americans expect from watching Agatha Christie mysteries on television. He was heavy-set, less than average height, and with bushy eyebrows tending to shade his dark eyes. His gray mustache drooped at the ends which emphasized a downward slope to his mouth. He wore a somber colored suit, rumpled and ill-fitting.

He approached Loring, who was nursing a large lump on the back of his head. He finally spoke, very politely and with a cultured, soft modulation to his voice.

"Mr. Loring, sorry to detain you. We do need whatever information you have. We intend to find the maniacs who could do such an unholy act, but we need your help."

"How can I help, Inspector?"

"Go over the details again, for my benefit. Leave nothing out. Any small detail can be vital in a situation like this. Take your time...we have all night, if you are feeling up to it."

Loring glanced up at the inspector, shook his head at the memories of the slaughter and replied, his voice trembling with anger and horror.

"Inspector, I have given all the information to the other policemen. However, if you insist, I'll go over the facts again for you. But please, have your men remove her body. I can't bear to look at it any more. If you need it there for further investigation, let's go to the other room."

"Of course. How stupid and unthinking of me. By all means, we should go into the other room. We might get you a strong drink. You look as though you could use it. Will you be all right?"

"Thanks, I am a bit shaky. A drink might help to settle my nerves."

"Quite so. Very understandable, I should say. Now, the details again, please."

Loring recounted everything that happened that night, from the time he picked Gwen up at the hotel until the police smashed into her flat. As each gristly detail came to mind, his voice quivered, conveying the feeling of stark terror he had experienced. In spite of what the killers had said, he fully expected to be murdered along with Gwen.

After his account of the killing, he told the inspector about his arrival in London. He tried to explain the nature of his work for Zoser International. The one detail he omitted was his meeting with Nadia. He considered that a personal thing which could have no bearing on the events in the Chelsea flat. He recounted the brief time he spent with Smythe in the hotel bar, including his bumping into Gwen.

Crimmins asked some pointed questions concerning various facts of Loring's story. "Do you normally accept commissions from people you don't know? Isn't that rather unusual?"

"Inspector, I did not accept the job. I merely agreed to come here and listen to what they had to offer. There were no strings, no conditions to the trip."

"I see." Crimmins seemed absorbed in thought for a moment, then asked, "Should you decide to accept their offer, mind telling me the extent of your fee? How much does this work normally pay?"

"I don't think that concerns you, Inspector."

"Please bear with me. It might be important."

"As of now, I have no idea. I'd have to hear the entire proposition and define the scope of the work. We may be talking about fifty thousand dollars, more or less. I did check out Zoser's credit rating. Dun and Bradstreet lists them triple A."

"Thank you for that. Mr. Loring, did you have any contact with persons other than the unfortunate victim here, and that Smythe fellow?"

"No, Inspector." Loring was undecided about Nadia. Then, reconsidering his position, he blurted out, "Other than the usual hotel people, no. However I did meet a woman I knew some years ago. I bumped into her in the lobby, right after I checked in."

"Could she have anything to do with this Zoser group?"

"I don't see how. But it has been four years since I last saw her. I do recall she once told me she lived in London."

"Mind telling me her name?" Crimmins was taking notes.

"Nadia Shepherd." Loring regretted having to bring Nadia into this mess. "Can I leave now, Inspector? I'm bushed."

"Certainly, sir. But don't leave London without first clearing it with Scotland Yard."

Before Loring could reach the door, Crimmins stopped

him. "Mr. Loring, please do us a favor. Don't attend your Zoser meeting with a chip on your shoulder. Give them every indication you are ignorant of what happened here. Find out everything you can and let me know the outcome. Will you do this?"

"I don't know, Inspector. Zoser has to have some connection with Gwen's death. The killers alluded to it. You expect me to act as though nothing happened?"

"Look here, Loring. If Zoser is not involved, an aggressive attitude on your part could jeopardize your possible project. If they are involved, they already know about the murder and your part in it. Please see what they have to say and make no reference to what happened here."

"Okay, Inspector. I'll do what you ask, but don't expect me to like it." Loring couldn't understand the inspector's position. Didn't the facts prove Zoser had some connection?

"I don't really blame you, after what you went through. But please do what I ask. Good night, Mr. Loring."

Loring threw himself on the bed. His head still ached. The overwhelming anger he felt when they killed the girl returned to color his reason. His thoughts drifted to the men of Zoser International. There had to be something strange and sinister about the organization. What was there about it that generated so much hate? Did Zoser condone such acts of violence? It would be difficult for him to be cordial at the interview, but he had given his word to Crimmins. He had to believe Scotland Yard had valid reasons for the request.

Sleep would not come. The look of terror on Gwen's young face would not leave his mind. A sudden grip of fear clutched at his insides. He recalled the attack on him in Istanbul four years before. The men who abducted him then insisted he reveal the identity of those who hired him to delve into the history of Islam. There was no reference to Zoser International then, but the questions they hammered at him had the same familiar ring. The fact he was doing some personal research didn't matter to his abductors. They believed he was involved in other schemes. Was there a tie-in, then and now?

He thought about Nadia. She was part of his past. Would the terrorists attack again, using her as bait? The sickening act of tonight was one he couldn't see happening to Nadia. If the murderers followed up with their threats, she could be in extreme danger just by knowing him and being with him. She had to be protected at any cost. But how could she be convinced of the danger? He couldn't very well tell her about the murder. Should he sever all ties to her, now, before the unthinkable happened? Perhaps she was already involved. Perhaps her being at the hotel wasn't an accident. How did she know he would be staying there? Loring fell into a fitful sleep. His dreams were horrible, fed from a mind filled with the events of the night.

He finally awoke well past noon. The message light on the phone was blinking. He reached for his cigarettes, lit one, and decided to have a shower before calling for his messages. Sleep had done nothing to restore his energy. If anything, it made him more somnolent. He needed that shower.

Loring took his time, letting the cold water splash over his aching body. He forced himself to put the past twenty-four hours out of his mind until he was dressed and called down for room service. When he answered the message light, the operator told him there had been two calls from Inspector Crimmins of Scotland Yard. He wanted Loring to get in touch with him as soon as possible. She gave him the phone number.

Crimmins was on the line as soon as the phone rang. He sounded a bit agitated, but still polite. "Mr. Loring, I believe we have a new development in the unfortunate happening in Chelsea last evening. Could you be ready in twenty minutes for my man to pick you up at your hotel? We need your cooperation with this latest event."

"Well, my meeting with Zoser is for four o'clock this afternoon and I don't want to miss it. If you can get me to the meeting in time, I'll do whatever I can."

Loring hung up and finished dressing. He wondered what could have bothered Crimmins so much and what help he could be to Scotland Yard.

He took the time to gulp down a few mouthfuls of hot coffee before he left his room and hurried down to the street, arriving just as the policeman drove up. Without a word except a polite, "Good afternoon, sir," they drove away.

Inspector Crimmins was waiting at a barricade erected across the entrance to St. James Park. He stepped over to the car as they drove up, extending his hand in greeting.

"Thank you for being so prompt, Loring. We have something here that you should be most interested in, if my guess is correct...two bodies, throats cut from ear to ear. From the looks of them, they answer the description of the two who murdered that poor girl last night."

Loring walked over to the spot indicated by Crimmins. Under a plastic sheet lay two bodies with contorted features. Their throats had been cut...neatly, with no sign of hacking. Professional looking.

"Those are the two men I saw kill the girl last night, Inspector. I'll never forget them. They even have on the same clothes. Look closely at the shorter of the two, the one called 'Achmed', and you should find some traces of blue and red paint. He was the one who colored her body."

"We already have. We did find the paint you mentioned. We were certain they were the ones, but we needed
you to make a positive identification. It appears the picture takes on a completely different aspect now, doesn't it?
We have the two murderers, but who killed the murderers?
Any ideas?"

"The only one I can think of is what you've probably
already decided yourself...the Zoser group."

"You're correct in that."

"Well, I'm going to find out what this is all about."

Crimmins looked at Loring sternly. "Look here,
Loring, remember what I asked you last night. Don't go
into that meeting with a chip on your shoulder. Don't let
them know you suspect them of anything other than what
they plan to offer you in the way of the research business."

Loring studied the lined face of the veteran policeman. He saw a professional, good at his work, who knew
the dangers of amateurs dabbling in police work. He had
to respect Crimmins' wishes and force himself to stay out
of it. Loring turned away from Crimmins, looking once
again at the bodies on the lawn covered with their own
blood. Justice? Retribution? His mind cleared.

"You're right, Inspector. I've no right to interfere with
your job. The way things are going, I'd get myself or someone else killed. You have my word. I'll go to the meeting
as though nothing out of the ordinary has happened. I'll
report back to you, personally, of anything I find out. Fair
enough?"

"More than fair, Mr. Loring. You do this for us and
we will see to it that not only are you protected, but informed every step of the way, provided such information
won't compromise my investigation, of course. My word
and my hand on it."

Inspector Crimmins extended his hand, grasping Loring's with a firm and friendly action. Loring was sure he saw deep understanding and respect in Crimmins' eyes. "If your man will take me to Sloane Square, I'll get to my meeting with Zoser International."

Thirty minutes after leaving St. James Park, Loring was at Sloane Square. He walked two short blocks to Zoser's offices, housed in a three story building which had seen better days. Zoser occupied the entire third floor. The reception area he entered was very austere, giving one the impression that the rest of the organization would be the same. A dour woman, well past fifty, took his name before announcing him. She escorted him through the heavy doors leading to the Directors Suite.

Joshua Claridge rushed forward to greet him, offering a strong, although damp, hand. Claridge was one of those Englishmen who had a perpetual flush, almost pink, and very blue, deep-set eyes. The shock of white hair and trimmed mustache belied his age. Claridge had obviously grayed prematurely; he appeared to be in fine physical shape.

"My dear Loring, please come in. These men are my colleagues. Brian Tupps is president, Dorian MacIvor is vice president, and George Wells, here, is treasurer. He will be the one signing your paychecks, if it comes to that. We are all eager to explain our needs for your talents. We hope you will start our project as soon as possible." Claridge was beaming, satisfied with himself.

"Gentlemen, this is Derek Loring, the well-known architect and historian from Hawaii. You know I just left those beautiful islands and I must admire his coming here to our unfriendly climate for this meeting. Shall we all be seated?"

"Dr. Loring, thank you for coming here for a detailed

explanation of our project," Brian Tupps stated in a voice barely above a whisper. "Claridge told you we wish to retain you for a commission, one you are well-qualified to take on. Your reputation precedes you, sir. Naturally, everything depends on our agreement as to your fee."

"Mr. Tupps, the fee can always be negotiated after I hear what this project entails." Loring noticed the quick, questioning glance Tupps threw over to Wells.

"Perhaps. I assure you this work is perfectly legal. We do not expect you to go against your ethics."

"Zoser couldn't pay me enough for that."

"Very well," Tupps said, then continued. "Let me begin by stating that what we discuss here is to be kept in strict confidence. This is one condition you must agree to.

"Zoser International is an acronym for the Zurich Office of Semantic and Ethnic Research. Our headquarters is in Zurich but we have branches in most major cities, worldwide. The prime function of Zoser is to research the language and backgrounds of persons who influence our society."

Loring interrupted. "Who benefits from this research? What, specifically, is done with it, other than curiosity?"

"Our clients are scholars, corporations, governments, all of whom might wish more data in order to evaluate their important decisions. We accept only those clients who are unable to obtain the information through their own efforts or resources."

"Okay. Now, what about your project, the one you want me for? What's it about?"

"Please be patient, Dr. Loring. I feel this preamble is necessary for you to understand our position.

"You recall that Anwar Sadat was assassinated in Cairo. President Mubarak's government publicly accepts the theory that Sadat was killed by religious fanatics over the Camp David Accords. Privately, however, the cabinet believes the assassination was motivated by what they term a vendetta. They believe there is something in Sadat's past which bears out this theory. The Egyptians want Zoser to uncover any evidence which might support the vendetta theory."

"You need a good private detective, not a historian."

"Again, Dr. Loring, patience. Hear us out before you jump to conclusions. Our staff has uncovered some hith-erto unknown facts regarding Sadat. We will turn our files over to you if you go along with us. We have hit an im-passe in our research. There must be further investigation into ancient Egyptian buildings and records to trace one remote branch of Sadat's family."

"I still think a good detective could do it, and for a lot less money."

"No detective has your expertise in ancient cultures. And money is not the issue. We have not been able to trace one name further back than 1400 BC. We want you to research the name back beyond 1400, all the way back to Imhotep."

"What will this name give you, if you find it?" Loring still couldn't understand why they needed him. "What is the name?"

"If we knew that, we wouldn't require your services. If the name can be traced, we suspect it will prove that a militant cult was responsible for Sadat's murder. Your work in this area provides the authority we need to publish that fact. Are you interested, Dr. Loring? This will be a quite a challenge."

"Before I commit myself, may I read what you have gathered so far? I promise not to divulge anything."

"You may have our files for twenty-four hours. Let me add that if you accept our offer, we will pay you one hundred fifty thousand dollars plus fifteen thousand dollars each month for expenses. We shall meet here tomorrow at the same time. Zoser hopes you will agree to this commission, Dr. Loring."

"I can assure you, I'll give it very careful thought. You'll have your answer tomorrow. Good day, gentlemen."

Loring left the conference table, headed for the door. He stopped with his hand on the knob. He turned back to face the men of Zoser. Loring wanted to see their faces, read what might be in their eyes. In Claridge's florid face he saw relief, as though he was glad the project was finally out in the open. MacIvor sat rigid, never having said nor done anything during the interview. His blinking eyes were the only animate thing about him. Wells was stoic, staring at Loring. Tupps had his handkerchief out, wiping the beads of sweat from around his chin. Loring smiled and left the room.

Settled back in his room, Loring kicked off his shoes, poured himself a drink and sat down to read the file. He was anxious to see what was so important. After the first few pages dealing with well known facts surrounding Sadat's political and religious background, the data began to appear detailed on one hand and very sketchy on the other. Facts concerning some generations of his family were steeped in hearsay, gossip, and questionable translations from old records. Other items were extremely well documented, showing meticulous research and evidence. It was natural to expect old records to be vague and quite mystical, but even so, the trace of one branch of Sadat's family was clear.

Loring realized he would have to authenticate the

known facts as best he could to see if he arrived at the same point of reference, which was indeed 1400 BC. Beyond that date, his findings would depend on how good his resources were, how thorough he could investigate and study the documents and the ruins. He would need clearances from government officials and museum curators. Zoser would probably be able to get him whatever permits were needed in that respect.

After finishing the file, he reread most of it, then decided to sleep on it before making up his mind. He was inclined to accept the commission; Tupps was right in stating that this would be a challenge. However, he not only had to rethink the project, but he had to have a talk with Inspector Crimmins. He placed a call to Scotland Yard. He knew Crimmins would still be on duty.

"Inspector Crimmins here." The sound of the firm voice gave Loring a lift in spirits. "What can I do for you?"

"Loring here, Inspector. Do you think you could come over here to the hotel? I've had my meeting with Zoser and we need to talk. Perhaps you could benefit from some observations I made."

"I have a raft of details that must be taken care of first. What say that I meet you at six-thirty? Would that be convenient?"

"Yes, that'll be fine. I'll be waiting for you."

True to his word, Crimmins showed up at the door at precisely six-thirty. Loring let him in then offered him a drink. "Or are you on duty, Inspector?"

"Mr. Loring, I'm always on duty, but I'll have that drink regardless. Whiskey, neat, if you please. This case has me coming and going. I think I deserve the relaxation."

He took the glass of whiskey and settled into an easy chair. Turning to Loring, he said, "Now, what did you want to discuss with me? Is this going to be for the record, or is it just between us?"

"Let's start by saying this conversation should be confidential, but I'm going to depend on your discretion as to that. I gave my word to the Zoser people that what they told me would not be made public for the time being. There are some things I can tell you that will not compromise any secrecy and they might have some bearing on this case. The broad nature of the work they want me to do I can and will reveal to you. I'll merely omit any telltale names. In that way, I can keep faith."

"Fair enough. Go on."

"First of all, I really don't trust them. They were hiding something from me. There's nothing I can pin this feeling on, but their manner of reacting to the interest I showed in the work was unusual, at least it was to me."

"Can you be more specific?" Crimmins sipped his drink.

"No, I can't. Perhaps your files contain some facts about this organization that could explain their hesitancy."

"We'll see. Please go on."

"They told me quite a story about why they wanted me to do some research for them. I think they could get the needed information regarding their project by their own staff. The files they let me borrow, I have them here with me, displayed unusual thoroughness by someone. Why do they want me? That's my first question. But let me continue.

"Besides Joshua Claridge, I met with Brian Tupps, Dorian MacIvor, and George Wells. They're the directors of the organization here in London."

"What was your impression of these men?"

"Tupps struck me as being very cold and shrewd, wanting to have things his way. MacIvor is crafty, never giving any indication of his feelings. Wells is a zombie...I don't believe he could go to the toilet without first getting permission from Tupps. Claridge is a blustery bag of wind, who thinks he's God's gift to the business world. Tupps did all the talking and he kept some bit of information from me."

"So you said. Go on, please."

"I don't have the entire story, but this is what I got. They claim to have a client...no name, as far as you're concerned...who wants the total biographical background on one of its former rulers, something to do with national security. I don't believe this. They were too casual about the whole thing."

"You said one of its former rulers. Are we talking about some country?"

"Yes. Anyway, if I take this job, I'll be going to Africa to search out what ancient records I can find. This could lead me back to the early days of civilization, to a man called Imhotep. What do you think I should do?"

"I can't rightly say. You have much more talent in the research end of it than I do," interjected Crimmins. "But there is something else you should know. While you were at your meeting, I looked up what we had on this Zoser group. Our computer gave us a cross-reference to MI 6...that's our equivalent of your CIA. I called over there to a friend of mine to see if their information could shed some light on our particular problem. My friend told me, in confidence, that they have nothing concrete on Tupps or MacIvor, but they do have a file on the fellow, Wells."

"What's he done, Inspector?"

"It seems he is not the zombie you believe him to be. The chaps at MI 6 knew of an operation Wells was tied to in Istanbul, about four years ago. There was some mention of political assassination, a group of fanatics, so it

seemed. MI 6 had some operatives on him, but the whole
thing blew apart and they lost him. They know he is here
in London, but they can't find anything incriminating about
Wells or the Zoser outfit."

"Anything else?"

"No, nothing significant...nothing you should concern
yourself with. Perhaps tomorrow shall bring some added
news. About the Shepherd woman...are you certain she
lives in London?"

"No, I'm not. I just remember she told me she did.
Why do you ask?"

"It isn't too important. We haven't been able to locate
her as yet."

Loring gazed intently at Crimmins. The inspector's
dark eyes were hidden by his bushy eyebrows which prevented Loring from seeing any message reflected in them.
He had a feeling that Crimmins was holding something
back, something he didn't want Loring to know. But the
information he reported about Wells was enlightening.
Now he knew why Zoser came to Hawaii after him. It
wants him to gather information on Sadat for reasons it
hasn't divulged, reasons which have some relation to his
research in Istanbul. Still, Zoser might be sincere, with
only Wells having a hidden agenda.

Crimmins broke into his thoughts. "From the tone of
your story, I gather there is something significant about
this Imhotep."

Loring walked over to the sideboard to freshen their
drinks.

"Imhotep was the master builder and the Grand Vizier
of the pharaoh in 2632 BC. He was the first to use stone as
a major building material. And, are you ready for this?
The pharaoh was Zozer, or Zoser, or Djoser, depending on
which authority and translation you read. Because of the

great work he did, Imhotep was elevated to the status of a god. It's anybody's guess as to what the connection is between the old king and this modern-day organization who wants me to go all the way back to the Third Dynasty looking for a remote family who may have been related to Anwar Sadat."

"Sadat?" Inspector Crimmins leaped from his chair.

"Yes. Under the circumstances, I believe you'll grant me this slight breach of privacy."

The look on Crimmins' face betrayed the thoughts that must have been pressing on his mind. He grabbed the phone abruptly.

"This has suddenly become too big for you and me," he said to Loring. "We need some higher level decision on this. Hello, Inspector Crimmins of Scotland Yard here. Let me speak with Geoffrey Hopkins. I'll wait."

Crimmins paced up and down the room as far as the phone cord would allow. He was agitated, there could be no mistake about that. "Hello, Hopkins? Crimmins. About that business we discussed earlier. It now seems that the game is in your court after all. This is the latest I have." Crimmins proceeded to relate the story Loring just told him, and how Loring sees Zoser having too much of an interest in the assassination of Sadat. "And Loring has told me he was innocently involved with the incident in Istanbul. What do you suggest he does now?"

After a while, Crimmins hung up the phone. "That was MI 6. Hopkins wants you to volunteer to continue your work with Zoser. He has known about your escapade in Turkey all along. The CIA told him. Your chaps are after the same thing, but have elected to stay in the background, letting MI 6 do the front work."

"I find that hard to believe. From what little I know, the CIA doesn't give way to anyone."

"I agree, but Hopkins told me to tell you that if you go along with Zoser, he will see to it you are covered every step of the way. He is sending over one of his operatives who will accompany you to Egypt as a translator if you decide to do this."

"Oh, great! Now I'm a spy."

"We don't wish to put pressure on you, but I'll be honest. We can't get far without you. This operative was part of the group who were watching George Wells in Istanbul and has a pretty good idea how he operates."

Loring thought for a moment, trying to get the churning butterflies settled in his stomach. He asked what, to him, was an obvious question.

"Wells knows me from Turkey; isn't it logical he knows all the operatives MI 6 had working in the area then? Don't you think they're cutting it a bit thin?"

"Those covert types here in London are as obtuse as your CIA. They should know what they are doing...at least I hope so, for your sake."

"Amen to that, my friend."

The inspector continued reviewing the murders with Loring for another quarter hour. He told Loring that Gwen's name was Thompson. It was an English family that went back for generations. They lived in Halston, a small town in Surrey. The family could offer no reason to explain why Gwen was mixed up with such people.

Loring wanted to know why the killers said her ancestor was killed in the same way. There wasn't any logic in their saying that unless there had been a similar case in her family. According to what Crimmins said, their investigation into her history turned up absolutely nothing. Loring offered another explanation: maybe the investigation didn't go back far enough.

"There's something else that bothers me, Inspector. The killers said Gwen was hired to get me up to her flat. She didn't know me from Adam, so it had to be Smythe who fingered me. The accident in the bar was a set-up — the girl only followed through with great feminine wiles. Am I right, so far?"

"It has certainly taken you long enough to figure out the obvious, Loring." Crimmins smiled at Loring in a rather sly way.

It was thirty minutes after Crimmins called MI 6 when there was a knock on the door. "That must be our secret agent," Loring said as he went to answer the knock.

"Hello Derek. I think you've been expecting me."

Nadia Shepherd stood in the doorway, her violet eyes aglow from the light reflected from within the room. She came in, closing the door behind her.

Chapter 3

Loring couldn't take his eyes off Nadia. She glided into the room confident and self-assured, nodding to Crimmins as she sat down.

"You must be Inspector Crimmins. I'm Nadia Shepherd. Mr. Hopkins briefed me to some extent, but I'll need a whale of a lot more than what I have now."

"You are Nadia Shepherd? No wonder we couldn't find any information on you." Crimmins' surprise was mirrored in his face.

"The mere fact you were looking for me gives cause for concern, Inspector. How did my name come up?"

"Just routine police procedure, Miss Shepherd. You had words yesterday with Mr. Loring, didn't you?"

"Ah, now it makes sense. The Chelsea murder last night. Is that it?" Nadia smiled at both of them.

"Yes." Crimmins' official tone melted a bit. "A nasty business, that."

Loring stared at Nadia in astonishment. Was it possible Nadia was the same girl he knew in Istanbul four long years ago? The Nadia he escorted through the Turkish bazaar, laughed with as they held hands, was not a secret agent. No spy would find such pleasure in simple things as walking through Topkapi Palace examining its treasures, or gazing with wonder at the splendor of the Blue Mosque. The Nadia of Istanbul did all these things. The woman sitting there smiling at him wasn't the same.

Nadia turned to Loring, her voice slightly on edge.

"Derek, aren't you going to say anything? Where's that sense of humor you always boasted about?"

"I don't know what the hell to say, other than 'hello'."

"Now that's very original."

"What did you expect, a song and dance?"

"Derek, don't be like that. This is serious."

"I am serious, damned serious. How was I to know you were a spy?"

"True, enough. We don't display signs around our necks for all the world to see. The Agency would call that quite counterproductive. And please don't use that word, 'spy'."

"Sorry, but you might have given me some hint back in Turkey."

"I couldn't do that, Derek, and you're intelligent enough to realize it. You were only a part of an assignment that had priority. I'm telling this badly, I know, but I'm trying to be kind."

"Am I correct in assuming you two have met before?" the inspector gestured to the two of them.

The tension was released. Loring and Nadia started to laugh.

"Your assumption is right on the money, Inspector," Loring said.

"It was in Istanbul, four years ago," Nadia added. "We'll tell you all about it later if there's time."

"Nadia," Loring interrupted, "can't you tell me what was so damned important in Istanbul? I just learned you were watching Wells. Why?"

"Both the CIA and MI 6 suspected that Wells was behind a planned assassination of the Foreign Secretary of Bulgaria who was in Istanbul on a state visit. We were informed of the plot anonymously, probably by Egypt.

Turkish security was informed but no one could find proof that Wells was ever involved."

"Where did I fit in?"

"The CIA felt the British should handle the matter and suggested we keep our eyes on you. They thought your research into Islamic history might uncover something out of the ordinary. Your reputation for accuracy would compel you to dig deeper for the truth."

"What did you think I would find?" Loring was puzzled.

"Everyone was counting on you to discover some secret association between the Turkish government and the Shah of Iran. We were told the planned assassination would be the catalyst to topple the government before a formal alliance with Iran could be signed. I was assigned to stay close to you and keep MI 6 apprised of your progress."

"Did I queer the deal by getting myself kidnapped?"

"When you were taken by those terrorists the whole caper collapsed. The police were everywhere and Wells got out in a hurry. After you were released, the only clear information we got was what the CIA told MI 6, which was damned little. I was called back to London after that."

"Right away?"

"Yes, the very next day. I've often wondered what it was you found that made those people take you the way they did. Evidently someone over there thought you knew a lot more than you did. Derek, what, exactly, did you find?"

"That's still a mystery to me. I didn't find a damned thing. I thought about it a lot these past few years and I always come up empty."

Nadia asked, "What happened?"

"I went to St. Sophia's to meet a mullah. When I got there, the mullah was nowhere to be seen but five local thugs were. They dragged me out the back way and took me to someplace in the old section of the city. They tied me up and kept asking the same questions over and over. 'Who are you working for and what are you looking for?'."

"How did you get away?" Nadia asked.

"Actually, I didn't. They kept me there for two days, then suddenly they took off, leaving me alone. Eventually I got loose and went back to the hotel, only to find you gone. Now you say you went back to London."

"That's not important. But this might be...who was the mullah you went there to meet?"

"Ibn Hassam el-Fazir. He promised to give me a copy of the original floor plans of St. Sophia. He told me the plans would show where a few unusual modifications have been made to the structure since the Turks converted the church into a Moslem museum. He said the government wasn't aware of some of these changes which had been made secretly."

"Derek, el-Fazir was discovered in a back alley behind the church the day after you were kidnapped. His throat had been cut and he was stabbed as well. The dagger was still in his chest when the police found him."

"My God! Did they ever find out who did it?"

"No, not officially. MI 6 believes Wells' group was responsible, but we had no proof. Sounds a bit like the murder of the Thompson girl, doesn't it?"

"So you people in the CIA and MI 6 believe there is a tie-in between Istanbul and Zoser?"

"Yes, a very strong link. All signs point to Wells being behind the Istanbul affair and Wells is now part of Zoser who wants you to dig into Sadat's assassination. Doesn't it make you a little suspicious of what Zoser is really after, seeing as how it employs Wells?"

"Hold on, Nadia. You're talking way over my head.

I'm not political, not in the least. These are things I leave to the experts. And I'm not an expert, not by a long shot."

"That's the whole point, don't you see? Who could ever suspect you, a scholar with impeccable credentials, of being anything other than that? We need you to use your knowledge, to break through any political doubletalk and find the real reason for Zoser."

Crimmins had been silent during this exchange. Finally, he leaned forward and addressed Loring.

"I can appreciate how you must feel, Loring. You most likely believe we are putting you in the middle, so to speak. I dare say, if I found myself in your boots, I'd turn my back on the whole mucking bunch of us and walk away."

"I'm seriously thinking about it." Loring addressed both of them.

"But, don't you see, the fact you are still here, torn between mixed values and loyalties, says it all. Let me clarify it somewhat." Crimmins continued.

"In the first place, those of us in the business of protecting our citizens from themselves, are generally very shortsighted. We usually see things as being merely black or white, leaving the gray areas to barristers and politicians. Every once in a while we are compelled to rely on persons whose views are not always as clearcut. This is one such case."

"I still don't see it."

"What Miss Shepherd told you is true...we need you. Scotland Yard has to solve the murders according to the law, and MI 6 must find out what Zoser is up to in the international arena. You are inside, so to say. By hiring you to do some research for it, Zoser has invited you into its parlor. No one on our side has ever had such a chance. I implore you, Loring, don't say 'no' until you have given it serious thought."

"I'll have to think about this."

"Please do. Now, I imagine you two have some private matters to discuss so I'll take my leave. Miss Shepherd, you must be perfectly frank with this man. Don't sugarcoat anything. Make sure he knows exactly what could be in store for him if he takes this on and things go sour."

"You can depend on that, Inspector. I'll be in close contact with the Agency in any event. You'll undoubtedly be hearing from Mr. Hopkins."

Nadia walked over to Crimmins and rested her hand on his shoulder. She gave it an affectionate squeeze, then added, "The Agency does concern itself with the consequences. Good night, Inspector."

When Crimmins left, Loring turned to Nadia. "When did you learn I was in London? Was it yesterday, in the lobby?"

Hesitantly, Nadia answered him. "No, we knew you were coming, knew about Zoser's man contacting you in Honolulu. We merely waited until you showed up."

"Why are you involved?" he asked quietly.

"Because I asked for this assignment. In some way I still feel guilty about what happened to you in Istanbul. I should have considered the possibility of something like that happening. I let my guard down and you had to pay for it. I wanted another chance to make up for my blunder."

"That's stupid thinking. How could you have prevented a bunch of fanatics snatching me?"

"There were ways, believe me."

"Did you ever think of contacting me in Honolulu?"

"Once. There was a period, about two years ago, when I was feeling very discouraged and depressed. I thought about you and was on the verge of ringing you up, just to talk. I had second thoughts, however, and decided to let you remain in my past."

"We did have a good time, didn't we?" Loring had to know if she had any other feelings for him, apart from the assignment.

"Yes, Derek, we did. I purposely let you think you picked me up in the bazaar. Actually it was me who set up that situation to make you do what you did. Surprised?"

"Not really. But after we met...the dinners and the sightseeing. That's what I mean."

"If you want the truth, yes, I did enjoy those outings. I came very close to forgetting why I was there. You made a very welcome and pleasant assignment. I was sorry it had to end so soon, and especially the way it did."

Loring smiled at this. "I guess that's what I wanted to hear. But what are we to do about this mess? I admit it, I'm scared."

"I can't say I blame you after what you went through, watching what they did to that girl. You have every reason to back off. I can only repeat what Crimmins said. We all need your help. But remember, Derek, once you have committed yourself, a lot of people are going to be put into action, not only to protect you but to act on all the information you provide."

"I'll go along, if you think I should."

"No, Derek, you'll do no such thing. I'll not be the one to sway you. Not again. If you agree to be the inside man, the decision has to be yours alone. I've carried enough guilt because of you. I can't carry any more. Don't ask me."

"Let's drop it for the time being. Have you people learned anything more about Gwen?"

"Before I tell you, I confess I'm curious. Why did you take up with her in the first place? Isn't that sort of thing out of character for you, if what you told me in Istanbul was the truth?"

"No excuses, other than the fact I was lonely...after seeing you again. I was planning on a wonderful reunion, only to get your message, canceling it. She seemed like an innocent thing and there would have been no further involvement." Loring looked her in the eyes as he said this.

Nadia riveted her gaze on him, her eyes wide in sudden understanding. "Derek, I didn't send any message!"

"Someone did. Obviously they wanted me to be alone so the girl could pick me up. It's clear now that the whole thing was planned to the last detail."

"Never underestimate your enemy. That's lesson number one. Lesson number two is for me...not to keep you waiting."

Loring smiled.

"But seriously, Derek, we came on another bit of information on the Thompson family. It appears that Gwen's great grandfather was Lebanese. Her mother found an old letter tucked into the family Bible. It was from Gwen's grandfather, and mentioned that the family had received a package from Sidon. In the package was a note saying the old man, the great grandfather, was leaving for Cairo to look for his sister. She evidently eloped with an Egyptian stone carver. The date on the letter was August, 1886."

"Did Gwen's mother tell you what the old man's name was?"

"She wasn't too sure of the spelling since her parents cut themselves off from that branch of the family. The name was rarely mentioned at home when the mother was growing up. She said it was 'Saahid', or possibly, 'Shadad'. She wasn't sure."

"That certainly isn't much to go on if we decide to follow through with Gwen's family tree. I still want to know what the killers meant when they said Gwen was killed in the same way her ancestor was. Were you brought up to date about the details of last night?"

"Yes, sorry to say. It must have been horrible. Poor Derek, you really are out of your element, aren't you? What you just said, about wanting to find Gwen's killers. Does it mean you will work with us? Derek, are you sure, really sure?"

"Yes, I'm sure. My only concern is about your safety. Now that I know how deadly these people are, whoever they are, I want to see them destroyed. So how do we begin?"

"First I must read the file Zoser gave you. I have to know the groundwork they prepared. Please fix me a drink while I read it. Why don't you call down for some dinner? I haven't eaten since this morning and I think we're in for a long evening. I'm famished. I eat anything, so order what you like, for both of us."

"Anything else?" he put in sarcastically.

"Just you wait, neophyte. In case some of the hotel staff are doing a bit of spying on the side, I'll put on the old 'let's spend the evening alone' routine. That should convince anyone watching this room that you and I are only engaged in old-fashioned hanky-panky. Now, get me that drink and the file. We have plans to make."

Loring poured Nadia her drink...gin and bitters...then unlocked his briefcase containing the Zoser file. In the meantime, Nadia had taken off her skirt and blouse, tossing them casually over a chair. She was removing her slip when Loring handed her the drink and the folder.

She stood before him in only her bra and panties. She didn't appear to be at all flustered, but her face was a shade redder. Loring stared at her. She was so lovely, so desirable. He swallowed hard to control his feeling of desire. The anger he felt at her deception in Istanbul fell away.

He longed to hold her.

"Derek, get that gleam out of your eye. This is for appearances only and, as much as I appreciate your apparent interest, we do have work to do. Have you a robe I can slip on? And where is that damn file?"

Still shaken by her casualness, he blurted, "It's in your hand, the one not holding the drink."

He went into the bathroom to get his robe which he kept on the back of the door. She slipped it on. The sleeves were about six inches too long so she quickly rolled them up to her elbows before he had a chance to help. She dropped into a chair. The robe parted to her hips revealing smooth and shapely thighs. Loring called room service and then began pacing the floor. Nadia looked up from the file.

"Derek, take off your jacket and tie, unbutton your shirt and pull some of it out from your trousers. Run your fingers through your hair, muss it up a bit. After all, you are in the process of seducing a woman. Get in character. Do I have to do everything?"

"You sound so matter-of-fact. Do you do this sort of thing often? You have it down to a science."

"Only in the line of duty, Derek, and only as a last resort, if there isn't any other way. You might be interested to know that up to now, there has always been another way. Satisfied? Besides, I'm a woman doing only what comes naturally."

Nadia went back to her reading. When she finished the file, she laid it aside and began to think aloud. "If Zoser wants you to research back beyond 1400 BC, something must have stopped them or prevented them from doing it themselves. In your study of architecture and history, can you remember a big event taking place about that time? Think about that, but first, come over here."

Loring walked over to where she was sitting. As he

approached, she left her chair and pulled the bed covers down. She turned and kissed him, first on the lips, then on his cheek and neck. She threw herself on the bed, letting the robe fall where it would. "Now, leave the lipstick where I put it," she said. "When the waiter comes in with our dinner, he'll see what he expects to see, the interruption of a passionate love scene."

Loring was about to answer her when there was a discreet knock on the door.

"Room service, sir."

Loring let in the waiter, who wasted no time setting up the dinner service. He kept glancing at the bed where Nadia was playing her part. Almost too perfect, Loring thought. When the meal was laid out, the wine poured, he signed the check, including a large tip. He guided the grinning waiter to the door, and as he let him out, he said, "We'll just leave the cart for the morning shift. Please don't bother to come back for it." The man gave Loring a knowing wink, and left without saying a word.

"Come here and feed your face, hussy, before I forget you're just putting on an act. And for Christ's sake, cover yourself up! How do you expect me to concentrate on food?"

They forced themselves to engage in small talk while they ate. She asked about his work and about his life in the islands. He told her of his lecture circuit on architectural history and of the research he had done in ancient ruins. She smiled wistfully as he described the sun and the sea, the relaxed way of life in the islands. She shook off the dreamy look in her eyes when he asked, "How about you, Nadia? What has your life been like since Istanbul?"

"Frightfully boring, if you must know. I told you my

parents left me fairly well-off. You must have thought me one of the idle rich. I majored in Middle Eastern languages and on a whim I applied for foreign service with MI 6. That assignment in Istanbul was my first and I really mucked it up."

"Is there a man in your life...someone special?"

"No, there isn't. Life in intelligence doesn't make for any lasting commitments."

"Kind of lonely, isn't it?" Loring saw the hint of a tear in her eye.

"I hope you never find out just how lonely, Derek." One tear flowed down her cheek.

After dinner, they found themselves silent. Loring took Nadia's hand, brought it to his lips and lightly kissed her fingers. She brushed his cheek, pushing back some hair that had fallen over his brow. Almost in a whisper she said, "Derek, you know I'm very fond of you, don't you?"

"I've sensed it. Me too. I guess all the ranting and raving I've done about the way you disappeared was just so much coverup to hide my true feelings."

"I appreciate your concern, my dear."

"If anything should happen to you...well, the danger makes me shudder. I know what bastards these people are. Do you think we can work together under the circumstances?"

"My dear Derek, we have to do whatever the circumstances demand. We've committed ourselves to see this through. Now, I think we'd better get on with our plans. What are you going to say to Zoser tomorrow?"

"I'll ask them to get me the necessary clearances and visas for Egypt. I'm going to take the job. I'm also going to ask that my entire fee be placed in escrow, in cash. If we're successful there might not be a Zoser International to come back to. I'm just greedy enough to want to get paid for putting them out of business."

"Greedy or just spiteful?" Nadia smiled warmly.

"Both, I guess. I'm still worried about you. Do you think Wells will recognize you from Istanbul? That could ruin the whole deal."

She thought for a moment. "I have a plan, Derek, that should take care of that. If they keep watch on you, it'll probably be at the airports, both here and in Cairo. When you tell them you'll take the job make some excuse for not leaving London for a day or two. That'll give me time to go on ahead. I'll meet you in Cairo at the Mena House Hotel. I'll book you a room...no, it'll be better if you have Zoser do it from here, but make sure it's the Mena House. Tell them it's closer to where you'll be doing your work."

"Why the Mena House? I stayed there once when I was in Cairo, but it's not so special."

"MI 6 says it's part of the Zoser holdings. If we stay there we'll be closer to the source."

"Good! We'll just casually meet in Cairo, I'll learn about your ability in languages, and then I'll hire you as my assistant for difficult translations. By the way, can you read the Egyptian hieratic writing? There'll be a lot of it to translate."

"Yes, I'm quite good at it, believe it or not. Don't be surprised when you meet me in Cairo. I'm going to do some quick changes to my appearance, and use another name. I knew a girl at school who got herself killed in a car wreck during our final year. Her name was Carol Ashworth. That should do for an English-sounding name, don't you think?"

"Sounds good to me...ah, Carol. Now the next step is up to Zoser."

The hour was late and a decision had to be made. Nadia walked to the chair where she had discarded her clothes earlier. She stopped and turned toward Loring.

"Derek, perhaps I'd better go back to my flat. We can meet here in the morning."

"I don't think that's a good idea. If our curious waiter tells what he saw here, the staff will think I'm not much of a man if you're seen leaving before morning. I thought the whole idea was to give the impression we're more than casual friends."

"You're right, of course. But it is late, Derek." She faced him as he placed his hand on her waist.

"Nadia, I..." She pulled away slightly, her eyes filled with understanding. The deep violet color became subdued by the mist forming. Loring was honest enough with himself to admit he wanted her. He wanted to hold her, to take her to bed and make love to her. She, however, avoided his eyes, the color rising to her face. Nadia was the one to break the spell.

"Derek, we're both pretty tired. I'm going to crawl into that bed and get some sleep. You take the other bed." Loring couldn't help but feel disappointed.

"Believe me, Derek, it's for the best...for now."

"Alright, young lady, but watch out...there'll come a time when I'm not such a gentleman."

"I'll take my chances. Goodnight, Derek."

As the morning light of the new day flooded their room with bright color, they both lay quietly on their sides looking at one another. Nadia smiled wistfully at Loring, letting him know she felt safe with him being so close, and yet so far away. She spoke softly.

"Some day, soon, Derek. Our time is coming."

Reluctantly, they left the comfort of their beds, showered and dressed. They agreed it would be wiser to have breakfast in the dining room where their business could be attended to without being interrupted by their private thoughts. They kept their voices low, although there were but two others in the dining room.

"Last night, you asked me about some big event that happened around 1400 BC, something that could have made Zoser stop their research. I've just thought of something, but the date is a bit off."

"What event was that?"

"In 1367 BC, Egypt got a new pharaoh. He was Amenhotep and his wife was Nefertiti. You've heard of her. Anyway, Amenhotep was a strange, dreamy man who pushed for a monotheistic religion. He worshipped Aten, the sun disc, and even changed his name to Akhenaten to show his affinity with this god. He abandoned the old ways of the ancient gods, and forced the people and his court to follow the new deity. He built a new city, which today we call El Amarna, and he moved the capital there. He was responsible for a new form of art and culture."

"So?" Nadia was impatient.

"Akhenaten was not too healthy however, and died in 1350 BC. He must have been a lousy administrator to boot, because he lost some of the lands Tutmoses III had won by conquest. He shared the throne with Nefertiti, but when he died, the crown was taken over by Tutankhamun.

While King Tut was only a mediocre ruler, he did demolish the city of El Amarna, erasing all traces of the new religion. He took the capitol back to Memphis and had the memory of Akhenaten vilified. I haven't been to the ruins of El Amarna, but from what I have read, there is not too much to see. It is part of the official ruins of Egypt, about halfway between Luxor and Cairo."

"Derek, what's your point, for heaven's sake?"

"If Zoser's people completed their research as far back

as Tut's time, with Amarna destroyed, records included, they would have to stop because there could be nothing prior to Akhenaten. Everything was lost."

"I see. That makes sense."

Nadia was deep in thought. She brightened at some idea she had, and said, "Suppose it was the other way around. Let's imagine that Zoser has some dark secret that started way back to the time of the Pharaoh Zozer and Imhotep. Zoser could trace it from them up to the time of your heretic pharaoh. When the people destroyed Amarna, also destroying the continuity, Zoser had to create a trumped up lineage of Sadat. Zoser then had a legitimate reason for you to research back to El Amarna. That could be it, couldn't it?"

"What you're implying is that we have a two-pronged job here, working from both ends, meeting at Amarna. Do you have any idea how much work we're letting ourselves in for? Suppose Zoser is really on the up and up, and Wells has his own plans, separate from Zoser? Still, there is only one way to find out, and that's to get started. I say we go with the original assumption, that the trail starts at Amarna, and it might go in either direction."

Nadia wrote something on a business card then handed it to Loring. "Here is my address in town, with my unlisted number. After you talk with Zoser, ring me up first, then come over. Plan to spend the night."

His eyebrows raised slightly. He smiled openly.

"Honestly, Derek, you men are all the same! It's just the smart thing to do, nothing else. In the meantime, I'll clear things with MI 6 and start the ball rolling. Now, I'll leave first. You might as well have another cup of coffee. I never will understand how you can drink so much of that stuff. Until later, Derek." She left him, walking out into the busy London world.

Chapter 4

Heavy clouds of off-gray smoke hovered above the walnut conference table in the center of the Director's Room of Zoser International. Subtle air currents from the ventilation system forced the smoke to eddy around the heavy wood beams which supported the deeply paneled ceiling. The recessed lights were faintly obscured by the wafts of smoke. The four officers of Zoser sat huddled together at one end of the massive table. These four were alone in the room, yet each of them cast wary eyes toward the door, as though they expected to be interrupted at any time. Their faces betrayed a feeling other than anxiety. These men were afraid.

The silence in the room was pierced sporadically by the commonplace...a nervous cough, the soft click of a cigarette lighter, or the sharp tap of a pencil on the table top. The group had come together to assess the danger now facing the Zoser organization. All were aware of how recent events in the city might compromise the goals to which they had committed themselves. The atmosphere in the room, together with the attitudes of these men, gave silent voice to their concern.

It was George Wells who finally spoke, his voice all but a hiss.

"We have to face it, this trouble. Our men had their throats cut early yesterday. Their bodies were found in St. James Park. Loring identified them."

"Can they be traced to us?" Tupps whispered.

"No way, you jerk! Give me some credit. The police found nothing on them that could point to us. They were obviously followed after they left Thompson's flat."

"Loring could have," Claridge ventured.

"Christ, wise up! He didn't leave there until after two in the morning. Besides, Loring doesn't have the guts to do something like that. He went straight to the hotel...we had him followed."

"What do you think happened?" Claridge spoke again.

"This killing has to be a message to us from the damn Menefee. They want to scare us, and it seems to be working. Look at you, you're all scared shitless!" Wells slammed his fist on the table, hard. The others literally jumped from their chairs.

Claridge asked another question. "How does the Menefee know where to strike? We have evidence and reports from Zurich telling us the Menefee never kill. They get in our way, harass us, and make us change our plans, but they don't cut throats."

Wells turned sharply to Claridge. "You idiot! Have you ever thought that the Menefee might just change their tactics? Maybe they're getting impatient and decided the time and circumstances required killing, to prove a point."

"Why did you have the Thompson woman killed in the first place?" Claridge was surprised to discover he could stand up to Wells. "That's what caused the problem, no matter what you say."

"You bastard! Are you questioning my authority?"

"Not at all, George. I would like an honest answer to the question. It seems to me the organization is too close to success to gamble on this setback. Why did you kill her, and in front of Loring, of all people?"

"Mr. Sempher in Zurich ordered her killed. He said it

was an old score, from long ago. I merely embellished the execution by having Loring there. The blame will be pointed at the Menefee...our men were supposed to talk a lot about Zoser interfering with their plans. It was set up that way to show Loring we aren't the bad guys. Does that answer your questions, Claridge?"

"Yes. I'm satisfied."

"Okay. Now, how about the rest of you? Any more questions, or can you think straight enough to have some worthwhile suggestions?"

Tupps cleared his throat, coughing up yellow phlegm and spitting it in his handkerchief. He then added, in a tightly whispered voice, "What about MI 6 or the CIA? We know they suspect something because our people on the inside have tipped us off. Our CIA man, Morgan, said they were backing off, letting MI 6 call the shots. Could MI 6 be the ones responsible?"

"Tupps, you're stupid as well as ugly," Wells retorted, watching the man shrink under his insult. "If it was any of the intelligence agencies, except maybe the KGB, they wouldn't have cut throats. Stabbing or garroting, maybe, but not this way. No, our enemy is from the past, as it has always been. And they are here, in London!"

Claridge timidly ventured a possibility. In spite of the stand he took earlier, Wells still frightened him as he did the others. "Could MI 6 have hired it done, a contract, I think it's called? Some types will do anything for money, and if that was the case, MI 6 would not be connected if they were caught".

"You're a pompous ass, Claridge. You haven't heard a word I said. Now listen, all of you. We've been compromised, and I intend to find out who's responsible. Someone inside is tipping the Menefee. I can't think of any other way that they could be on to our plans so fast. That's another reason why we need that fool, Loring. With his credentials, he can go anywhere, and question people we don't dare approach. If we shove him in the right direction he's bound to discover the local Menefee connection. The search we send him on is just window dressing...it's the Menefee we're after."

The blaring ring of the phone cut off Wells' remarks. MacIvor answered, listened to whoever was on the other end, made a curt reply and hung up the phone, turning to the group.

"We have another problem. The Shepherd woman has disappeared. That was our tail who just called. She shacked up with Loring at the hotel last night and left him this morning, supposedly on her way to work. She never got there. Our man tailed her as far as Oxford Road, then lost her in the traffic. She hasn't turned up at her office. Jameson told our man that Hopkins has been trying all morning to reach her, calling her flat and all the other places she might be. Seems she just dropped out of sight."

Wells spat out the word. "Damn! That's all we need. She knows me from Istanbul, and I want her where I can keep track of her. We must assume she told Loring about me. Don't say it, any of you. She's more valuable to us alive than dead. We need her to keep Loring in line. If it weren't for that, I'd gladly cut her throat myself."

"She'll get in touch with Loring. All we have to do is keep him in sight," MacIvor said.

"Maybe, maybe not. They could have hatched a plan to stay away from each other. In the meantime, I'll have to remove myself from Zoser, for appearance sake. Damn! Claridge, when you talk with Loring, let him know that I have been canned by Zurich. Bad security risk, or something. That should satisfy his stupid sense of morality and increase his confidence in Zoser."

"Will do."

"Dorian, get back to the tail and have him keep look-ing. Have him report back as soon as he has something we can hang on to. Find Shepherd!"

"You got it, George."

"Okay. This is how we play it. Convince Loring to take our deal. Offer him more money if that's what it takes. But keep him away from here until we find Shepherd."

Claridge simply asked, "How do we do that. We have a meeting scheduled."

"Do I have to do all the thinking? Call him, you idiot! If he accepts, tell him to postpone Egypt until he verifies our data at the museums."

"And if he doesn't accept?"

"Sweeten the offer. He'll take the money, believe me. Have him call us the first of the week. We'll be ready then. And Mac, keep looking for Shepherd."

Wells gathered his notes and left the room. The meet-ing was over.

The others left, but MacIvor, nagged by curiosity, lagged behind, standing in the corridor out of sight of Wells' office. Two men waited for Wells. They stood up when Wells entered, both large with heavy, swarthy features which stamped them as non-European. One of them spoke when Wells nodded to him.

"We did it just like you said, Mr. Wells. We had some trouble getting their bodies over to St. James Park. There's a lot of blood in our car but it should dry out in a few days. Do you have another task for us?"

Wells looked at the men with a sense of satisfaction. It was an inspired plan and it was his plan. Kill the oppo-sition, then kill those who did the killing and rig the evidence to point directly to the Menefee. They were the only ones remaining who stood in the way of Zoser's complete control of the Mediterranean. The plan was right out of Genghis Khan. There would indeed be more work for these two.

"Leave now, by the back way, and go to the Ram's Head pub in Soho. There you'll meet Brian Tupps. He's a faggot so proposition him. You Arabs know how. Take him somewhere and execute him in the traditional way. Dump his body in a public place where it'll be found right away. Report back to me when it's done, not before. Now, go."

The two men did not notice MacIvor watch them leave by the back stairs. MacIvor never completely trusted Wells. He was much too bloodthirsty to run a smooth operation. Too many things could get fouled up with his tactics, especially since indiscriminate killing seemed to be his answer to every problem. MacIvor vowed to keep his eye on Wells and to protect his own back as well. He hoped Wells was not aware of him watching the sinister meeting in the office.

Claridge made his call to Loring when he was alone in his office. There was no answer at first. He had to keep trying until he reached Loring. He felt that Wells was right in thinking Loring must know about Wells' part in the Istanbul operation and would undoubtedly refuse to have anything to do with him. But how much more did Shepherd tell him? How much more did she know? Claridge himself didn't know the details of Istanbul, other than the fact that Wells failed to finish what he had started.

Loring had finished his umpteenth cup of coffee about an hour after Nadia left. He was concerned about Wells, worried that somehow he would get to Nadia. He hurried to his room, remembering he had promised he would call Crimmins. It was after nine by this time so Loring figured the policeman would be at his desk. What he didn't expect was the reply he received when he called Crimmins' office.

"Oh, Mr. Loring. The Inspector isn't feeling too well this morning...a bit of a virus, he said. He rang up to say he wouldn't be coming in today, but did mention that should you call, he would contact you later from home. If you want to speak with him, I think that under the circumstances, we can bend the rules a bit and give you his home number."

"Thank you. I think I should wait for his call, but in case we miss each other, perhaps you better give it to me. I do hope he feels better."

Loring wrote down the number. He was uncertain as to what to do. If Crimmins was sick, it would be in bad taste to bother him at home, and still, it was important he talk with him. Loring decided to wait for an hour. If Crimmins didn't reach him by that time, he would phone him.

Just as he settled down to finish his paper, the telephone rang.

"Mr. Loring?" It was the hotel switchboard. "A Miss Carol Ashworth rang up while you were on the phone just now. She said she couldn't wait on the line, but that she would get back to you in fifteen minutes. She also said that you shouldn't call her because her phone was being repaired."

Loring was panic-stricken. Something must have happened to make her call. He started imagining all sorts of possibilities, none pleasant, while he paced up and down the room.

The phone rang. "Derek? Thank heavens I got to you in time. I was followed when I left you, and I think I recognized the man. It was someone associated with Wells in Istanbul."

"Nadia, are you all right?"

"Don't worry, I lost him, but I had to warn you. They probably have someone watching you, too. Get in touch with Inspector Crimmins. He'll spirit you around out of their sight. Now listen carefully. Please don't go near MI 6 or the CIA."

"For God's sake, why?"

"I'm not absolutely sure, but I believe there is a plant in each of them. Stay close to Crimmins...he's as clean as they come."

"Where are you? I have to know!"

"I've taken a room at the Brinkley Hotel in Mayfair. Room five-eight-seven. Pack your bags and take them with you when you see Zoser this afternoon. Take the tube to Sloane Square and walk from there. Put your bags in a locker at the station. When you leave Zoser, come straight here, but in a round about way. I'll be waiting here all day. Be very careful, Derek."

"Nadia, what the hell is going on?" Loring was angry and frustrated.

"I'm not at all certain. I'll know more when you get here."

The phone went dead and Loring found himself shaking inside. There was no question about him calling Crimmins now. He started for the door, thinking it best to call from outside. This whole business had him paranoid, thinking of tapped phones, spies around every corner, armies of shadows waiting for his next move to fall in line, following his every step. Before he reached the door, the phone rang again.

"Loring? Joshua Claridge here. Have you come to a decision on our proposal?"

Now Loring was truly baffled. Why the call from Zoser, when they were scheduled for a meeting later in the day? Play it straight, he reasoned, play it real cool.

"Yes, I have, Josh...may I call you Josh?...I want very much to do the research. I spent considerable time reading the material you gave me. Your people are thorough, I'll say that for them. I should like to start right away."

"My dear fellow, we are delighted." Loring could picture Claridge pushing out his chest over this news. The two-faced bastard, he thought. Claridge continued. "Now there is no need for us to have the meeting this afternoon."

"What about your files?"

"You keep them for now. There is something you should know, however. Mr. Wells is no longer with Zoser. Zurich dismissed him last evening. I don't know the details or the reason for his termination other than it had something to do with his past activities in Istanbul. However, rest assured Zoser International is still interested in having you under contract for its research project."

"I'm glad, Josh."

"This is Wednesday. Drop around to see us the first of next week so we can sign the contract and send you on your way. You will get your expense cheque, too. Mr. Tupps suggests you visit the British Museum to verify some of our findings, if you haven't anything better to do."

"That's fine with me, Josh. I'd like to see some old friends of mine out in Surrey and this should make it perfect. Tell Tupps and MacIvor that I'm happy to be working with you people. It's too bad about Wells, but the project sounds fascinating. I'll call you on Monday to let you know when I'll be in your office. So long, for now."

Brian Tupps hailed a cab and headed for the Ram's Head pub. All this business about killings and spying wore him to a frazzle. He needed some relaxation, and the pub was one place he knew he'd find it. They were his kind of people, so much more civilized and well-mannered than that barbarian, Wells. Lord, how he had come to despise that man!

Several of his friends were already there when he arrived. They greeted him with unbridled enthusiasm as he took a seat at a corner table. The bar-keep approached his table almost at once. He was dressed in flamboyant slacks and a pullover sweater that emphasized the false breasts he seemed to flaunt. His natural hair was hidden by a flaming red wig which accentuated the garish makeup on his eyes and lips.

The publican leaned over the table and whispered in a low, sexy voice, "Brian, darling, there are two fellows over there who have been waiting for you. I never saw them before and they obviously didn't come here to drink. Whatever you do, don't give me the brush-off. We mean too much to each other and I'd be devastated if you threw me over, especially for someone like that. Will I see you later at my place?"

"Of course, my dear. But right now, perhaps I'd better see what they want with me. Never fret, my sweet, you are the only one for me. Nothing can ever change that."

When Loring was through talking to Claridge, he threw himself into a chair. He needed to sort out the jumble of conflicting messages hammering in his brain. Someone was following Nadia, and she was now in hiding. Zoser wanted to delay the project, but why? And what about

Wells? There was no question about it now, he had to reach Crimmins.

This time he made it out the door without the phone ringing. At the cigar counter in the lobby, he took his time in selecting some English cigarettes while watching the busy lobby through the mirror behind the counter. He noticed one woman who was staring at him. She nodded to another woman by the door leading out to Regent Street. He selected a pack of Players, bought a copy of the latest tabloid and sat down in a lobby chair, pretending to read.

The two women were now in conversation, pointing down the street and making a very convincing attempt to act confused as to which direction they should take. They left the hotel, but Loring knew they would be right outside waiting for him. There had to be some way he could throw them off the track. He went out a side door in the lobby onto Jermyn Street which was behind the hotel and away from the main traffic. Down the street, in the middle of the block, he spied a familiar red phone booth. He called Crimmins' home number.

"Oh, Mr. Loring," a pleasant woman's voice answered, her brogue very pronounced, "my Bertie said you might ring up. I was to tell you to meet him in the Egyptian gallery at the British Museum. Bertie also said for you to be careful, as you're being watched. He said he would be there until one o'clock. Does any of this make sense to you?"

"Yes, Mrs. Crimmins, it does. And thank you. Is your husband feeling better? I called his office and they told me he was ill."

"Mr. Loring, I've been married to Bertie for thirty years come this fall, and when he's involved in a difficult case he does make up some awful stories now and then. He isn't sick. Just wanted to do something on his own."

"I'm glad to hear that, Mrs. Crimmins. Thank you again, ma'am. Goodbye."

Loring glanced up and down the street before leaving the booth. The two women were near the front of the hotel, waiting at the bus stop. He hurried back inside and hid himself by the lobby bar, watching the entrance. As he suspected, the women rushed into the lobby and examined the people waiting for the elevators. Their agitation was obvious until they turned and saw Loring standing in plain sight, looking at them. Flustered, they hurried outside and hailed a cab. Loring smiled to himself as he returned to his room. He had to get over to the museum.

Crimmins was waiting on a stone bench alongside a sarcophagus. He appeared deep in thought, but brightened as Loring came up to him.

"Derek. Glad you got my message. Here, sit down. We can talk without being overheard. What do you have to report?"

Loring sat down beside him, not overly happy to spend any length of time on the hard stone. He looked at Crimmins, searching for an indication of what the policeman was up to. There was nothing but the calm and patient mien of a man who knew what he was doing. Loring started to speak, warily at first, but as he got into the details of events which happened since they last spoke, his thoughts became more cohesive. When he concluded his account, mentioning Nadia's words of caution and instructions regarding Crimmins, the policeman replied with emphasis.

"I knew she was a smart woman the minute I laid eyes on her. I believe she is absolutely correct in suspecting a leak in intelligence. It has happened before and will most likely happen again. Now, what are we going to do about you, young man? We can't have you traipsing around London, waiting to get yourself hurt. We have to give that some thought."

"But what are we to do about Nadia?" Loring broke in. "We can't let her shift for herself. I don't relish the thought of leaving her alone."

"Derek, believe me, she won't be alone. I have a plan which the three of us can discuss later. But first, let me fill you in on what the Yard has come up with. First, those two blokes who were unfortunate enough to get their throats slit, were former employees of Zoser. Interpol has placed them in Istanbul four years ago in the company of one George Wells. This makes it look less likely that Zoser killed them. Still, Wells could have had them killed to remove Zoser's connection to them, seeing as what they did to the Thompson girl."

"I lean more toward your second idea, Inspector."

"Quite. Our Mr. Wells is an American, real name is, or was, Wallace Engleson. He used to be with your CIA, but resigned five years ago. He joined Zoser right after leaving the agency."

"That's real interesting."

"Tupps is a homosexual recruited by Wells to front for Zoser. He doesn't have a thing to say about what Zoser is doing. Dorian MacIvor is a blank. We haven't been able to trace his background. To the best of our knowledge, he joined Wells and Tupps in Istanbul after he left Edinburgh."

"And what about Claridge? Anything on him?"

"Claridge is just a nobody with dreams of importance. He came from Chester...did some small-time advertising work for a chain of women's apparel shops. So much for the list of evil characters at Zoser."

"You people at Scotland Yard don't waste much time, do you?" Loring meant the praise that showed in his voice. "By the way, why did you play sick today?"

"The Yard has complete jurisdiction in these murders, so naturally we try to find out all the facts concerning the people involved...the perpetrators as well as the victims. You would be amazed at what we dug up on you. Intelligence agencies notwithstanding, I took a holiday from the office so I could meet with you quietly, and, more importantly, to do a bit of research by myself on that fellow, Imhotep. Didn't find much other than what is generally known and what you told me. But I do have a greater respect for him. Does that answer your questions?"

"Yes, I guess so. What do you make of Zoser's canceling the meeting today and saying that Wells was fired?"

"I don't believe for one minute that Wells was fired, as you put it. His announced dismissal was for your benefit. They undoubtedly deduced Miss Shepherd told you all about him and his role in your Istanbul affair. Zoser was certain you wouldn't have anything to do with them if Wells was visible. As for the meeting, I think they canceled it to gain time and locate Miss Shepherd. We must assume that she's the one in danger, not you."

Loring felt a chill creeping up his spine. He turned to Crimmins and shouted, "My God, Inspector, if you believe that, we've got to do something, and fast!"

Crimmins fell silent, his brow creased in thought. He looked at Loring briefly, then said, "I think she had better disappear. I have a plan. Stay with me a bit longer, then leave. It might be well if you visited your friends in the country...Surrey, isn't it?"

"Yes, Surrey."

"Ring up Miss Shepherd when you leave here. Tell her I shall come to her hotel later this evening. Now, you.

Take the train to Surrey and stay with your friends for awhile."

"I was going to do that later." Loring was anxious to get back to Nadia, to make sure she was safe.

"No, do it now. I want you away from London for a few hours."

"Why?"

"There are things I must do before I see Miss Shepherd. You will only be in the way. Sorry, but I do insist."

"All right, if you put it that way. I'll call Marc and ride down with him. It's the way I always go when I'm in town. I'll come back by train later and meet you at Nadia's hotel."

"Capital idea, my boy. Be careful not to lead anyone to Miss Shepherd."

Loring went to the lobby of the museum where he called Nadia. She answered almost immediately, breathless.

"Derek! Why are you calling so early? You weren't to call me until after the meeting."

Loring explained the change in plans. "I'll see you later, Nadia. Keep the coffee hot."

He returned to his hotel and called Marc Merrick.

"So good to hear from you, Derek. It's been far too long. You'll stay with us, of course?"

"Thanks, Marc. I hope I'm not putting you out."

"Not at all. Veronica will be delighted. In fact, I'll ring her now and let her know you're coming home with me."

Loring felt guilty about using these fine people in his plans. They'd been his friends for a long time. Merrick was intrigued with Loring's work, especially since he and Veronica had restored a sixteenth century farmhouse to its original condition. Loring had helped with the plans and details of the reconstruction. The Merricks were very special. He hoped they wouldn't be affected by all this. However, they did offer a way back to Nadia safely, so he was compelled to go ahead with the plan. The Merricks would understand.

He carefully packed his suitcase, checked the briefcase, then called down to the desk for his bill. Ten minutes later he headed for Picadilly Station to catch the tube to Sloane Square.

The man stood alone outside the subway station. He glanced casually in both directions along Picadilly, not too concerned by the rush of pedestrians pushing their way into the station. He wore a soft felt hat which shaded his watchful eyes from the late afternoon sun, and carried an umbrella hooked over his arm and a gray raincoat slung over his shoulder. He acted as though he expected someone.

A woman approached and stood beside him. She was dressed in an elegant suit with a fur collar. She looked older than the man next to her. She tapped her foot in irritation, obviously waiting for someone. Her frown deepened and she spoke aloud.

"Some people are so bloody insensitive of the feelings of others. Honestly, I should leave and let him wait."

"The tube is so crowded these days," the man muttered without turning his head.

"Shepherd is at the Brinkley. Where is Loring?"

"I watched him catch the Bakerloo train, southbound. No telling where he's headed. Was the woman followed?"

"Yes, but not for long. I'll give her credit...she spotted the man at Oxford Road and lost him in the underground station. I was able to trip him up long enough to keep him off the train."

"We'll watch the hotel. Loring will get there sooner or later."

"I don't like us just babysitting Loring. Why don't the limeys take care of him?"

"The Brits promised him protection. The Home Office has agreed to their plan and we keep him in sight. When he leaves the country, our assignment is over."

"Okay, so we keep watching. But I could use a drink, couldn't you?"

"I don't drink."

"Just thought I'd ask. I'll take over at the Brinkley now. Any other instructions?"

"No. I'll be in touch."

Chapter 5

The village of Pyrgate had lost considerable prominence when the M3 motorway was pushed through to connect London with Southampton. Until then Pyrgate adjoined A3, a well-traveled highway which coursed through southwest Surrey. The village, thirty miles from London, was a hub of rolling hills and dappled green pastures. Because of its near isolation, Pyrgate was slowly withering toward abandonment. The villagers had long ago given up their dreams of eventual resurgence. The twentieth century had all but passed them by.

Marc Merrick turned off High Street in the center of the town. He drove down the narrow country lane which featured stony hedgerows on each side of the rutted pavement and accelerated slightly when the last of the clustered farms were left behind. Priory Farm, which the Merricks had restored, was two miles beyond the village and actually encompassed that part of the shallow valley which marked the beginning of forest land. Merrick usually drove this road by rote, his mind cluttered with a myriad of nagging problems he could not leave behind in London. Today, however, he eagerly pointed out familiar landmarks to Loring in an obvious attempt to steer his mind away from his troubles.

"There it is, Derek, up ahead on the left, the 'Golden Eagle' pub. Remember all the jolly times we've had there? We'll drop in later...Veronica's waiting, and so is Briget."

Loring had considered telling Merrick some trumped-up story about him being followed by a rival researcher who wanted to beg, borrow or steal some of his notes on the runic writings at Newgrange in Ireland. But then, believing Marc deserved better than that ridiculous excuse, he started to tell him the entire story, all the pertinent details. He recounted the project with Zoser, the murders, all the shadowing, his association with Inspector Crimmins, his involvement with MI 6, and about Nadia, especially about her.

Merrick was silent during the telling of it all, giving Loring a chance to relate the story uninterrupted. When the story was finished, Merrick was silent, deep in thought. Merrick rarely gave voice to an opinion without first considering all facets.

"Seems to me you have one hell of a problem. Why can't you ever come over here merely for relaxation and good company? But no, you never do that. You always bring complications along with you. You're a very complicated man, Derek Loring."

"Sorry about that, old man," Loring responded.

"I can see you need help and need it right away. I haven't made up my mind how much of this we should tell Veronica. You know how she worries. Perhaps we better leave her out of our little secret entirely for the time being."

"All right, if you think it best."

"Let me finish, Derek. She's very perceptive...that's part of her charm. She'll know straight away that something is the matter with you...it's written all over your face."

"Am I that transparent?"

"Yes, I'm afraid so. We'll just tell her you're avoiding some unpleasantness connected with your work and leave it at that. From there, we'll play it by ear, as you Americans say. Let's wait till we reach the farm before we decide what choices we have in getting you back to London unseen."

The two friends continued on to the Farm. St. Nicholas Church came into view on the left, a short distance beyond the pub. This Saxon church was built in 1142. It held a special fascination for Loring. Whenever he visited the farm he spent many pleasurable hours in the little chapel, marveling at the random-laid stone work and the other Saxon architectural features which were usually ignored by curious visitors. Loring never tired of the place.

Merrick eased the car through an ancient gate, the entrance into the grounds of Priory Farm. Their arrival was announced loudly by the gleeful yelps and cavorting of Briget, the Merrick's huge, magnificent wolfhound. As soon as he got out of the car, Loring was greeted by the dog who was intent on sniffing for the telltale odors of a friend. Finding them, she reared up and placed her paws on Derek's shoulders. In this stance, she could look at him, nose to nose. Briget's black eyes glistened in the sunlight, her moist tongue only partially obscuring the huge fangs hidden in the cavernous jaws. Heaven help anyone but a friend who invaded her yard.

Veronica Merrick appeared at the door, all aflutter. As always, Loring's spirits soared when Veronica came on the scene. She was an extraordinary woman, rather striking in appearance although totally indifferent of her beauty. She and Marc were about the same age, mid-forties, with similar backgrounds and interests. Loring was aware of the cliche...made for each other...and envied Marc and Veronica the life and love they shared.

"Derek Loring, you old darling," she bubbled, throwing her arms around him, "where have you been keeping yourself?"

"Here and there, Veronica. I keep waiting for you to

dump Marc so we can run away together to some far-away Nirvana. You really should consider it." Loring returned her hug with joy.

"Not much chance of that, old friend. Marc keeps me satisfied in every way, take my word for it."

Veronica Merrick was never at a loss for a lively come-back. "But do come in. Briget, let Derek go! Honestly, that animal would go anywhere with you at the drop of a hat."

"It just goes to show you the power I have over females...females of every kind."

"That's one of your more endearing qualities, Derek...your modesty. I have the kettle on, and I baked some fresh scones, your favorite."

"I smelled the heavenly aroma when we drove through the gate."

"We'll eat later. Right now I want to know all about what you've been doing since you were here last. One would never know anything from your letters. With all that education you have, Derek, don't you know how to write? What girls have you seduced lately? I want to know everything...don't you dare leave anything out, you rascal."

In the restored sixteenth century farmhouse, with its half-timbers and three inglenook fireplaces, Loring felt the same comforting peace he always experienced there as he roamed from room to room. If ever he wished to be anywhere other than Hawaii, this would be it. Here with the Merricks he enjoyed the tranquillity and peace of mind and spirit he so sorely sought. His one regret was the vast distance which kept them apart. They had a knack, a propensity for putting him at ease. They were there when he needed them, like now.

Over tea and scones, the story came out...there was no

attempt to hide it from Veronica, for she would have sensed the truth regardless of how he might hedge.

"We have one very sticky wicket here, old chum," she ventured after Loring and Merrick were finished with the story. "It would appear we must do some fast stepping to get you and your Nadia away from London and safely here at the farm."

Loring interrupted. "I don't think that would be too good an idea. The ones who're after us will certainly trace Marc here. They'll be keeping this place watched. The only reason I came as I did, was to throw them off the track long enough for me to get back to London without them knowing how I do it. Still, I'll be taking a chance on going back on the train from town."

"We'll think of some other way back, Derek."

"I certainly hope so. They work fast. They appear to be everywhere, and they might have a tail posted anywhere along here, including the station."

"Have you noticed anyone following you?"

"That's just the problem. I don't know what to look for. I don't believe they want me hurt. Not yet, at least. It's Nadia I'm concerned about. She's the one in immediate danger."

"Drink your tea, Derek. We'll think of a trick or two."

"I won't take a chance of you two getting in the middle of all this."

Merrick had seemed deep in thought during this exchange. Finally he spoke...with conviction. "Say what you will, but we are involved. Do you think for one moment Veronica and I could stand apart and let you face this alone? You know us better than that, Derek. If Veronica agrees, and I'm sure she does, I say we put our heads together and work out a plan."

"Hear, hear!" Veronica voiced her agreement.

"Quite. Now this is my plan. From what you tell us, we must assume the bad guys are following you. So we'll go down to the pub for a drink. Briget is waiting for her afternoon plate of beer anyway."

"You're putting me on. When did Briget start drinking beer?" Loring laughed.

"Well over a year ago. I'm serious, Derek. To continue with my plan...those who might be following you will stay fairly close, which works to our benefit. If no one is behind you, we still haven't lost a thing."

"How do you figure that, Marc?"

"Because, my impatient friend, after a short time spent in small talk, you will sneak out the back way. You borrow Jack's auto and drive over to Guildford where you take a train back to London."

"Who is this Jack who's so free with his car?"

"Jack? He owns the pub and we consider him a friend. I'm certain he'll furnish his auto if we ask him."

"Think it'll fool my shadows?"

"I do. They won't suspect you going anyplace without us. I believe they will stay close to the pub as long as Veronica and I are there. It should give you at least a two hour head start. By that time you should be safely back in London with the fair Nadia."

"That sounds okay to me. If your friend will trust me with his car, I'll get to Guildford without any trouble. My friend, Crimmins, has given me some rushed instructions on how to avoid being followed once I get back to town. Now all I have to do is put them into practice."

"Leave your luggage here with us."

"Thanks, I will. No sense carting it all over London, especially if I have to beat a hasty retreat. In the meantime, I can buy whatever I need. Yes, that just might work."

Veronica spoke up. "None of us knows much about

this sort of thing, but common sense should tell you, Derek, to melt into the crowd...be inconspicuous."

"How do you suggest I do that?"

"In those horrid clothes you insist on wearing you'll be spotted at once. They advertise the fact you are an American...you might as well carry a sign. I suggest you wear some of Marc's things, including a hat. Proper Englishmen always wear hats. Marc, think you can outfit our friend here?"

"I believe I have just the ticket. I'll fetch down the outfit a bit later. Even his mother couldn't recognize him when we're through with him. Actually, this would be quite jolly if it weren't so serious."

They were more relaxed once the details of the escape were ironed out. To wile away the hours before going down the road to the pub, they reminisced about old times, like how they first met some twelve years before when Derek was wandering over the ruins of Tintagel Castle. The Merricks had gone to Cornwall for their holiday, and were enjoying an afternoon's excursion to the little coastal town to do some sightseeing on their own. That chance meeting grew into the lasting friendship they treasured over the succeeding years.

"Did you ever forgive the English for advertising that pile of rubble as the place of Camelot?" Veronica asked. "I've often wondered who dreamed up that ridiculous claim."

The rest of the afternoon passed pleasantly until it was time to drive down to the pub to begin their charade. The pub was all but deserted when they arrived. The two other customers were sitting at a corner table engaged in a heated political discussion. Briget led the group into the bar, waving her powerful tail in anticipation of her afternoon plate of beer. Jack met them at the door, holding the frothy brew for Briget. Without so much as a glance at the others, she commenced to lap it up with gusto, pausing only once to let out a resounding belch.

Loring and the Merricks sat in a booth toward the rear of the pub and spent a few minutes talking with Jack. He agreed to let Loring use his car, merely on Merrick's word. That part of the plan settled, the three relaxed over a drink. Veronica was adamant at having Nadia come to the farm when the time was right. Loring could think of no quieter place for him and Nadia to get better acquainted. He promised Veronica they would come as soon as it was safe for all concerned.

"Mind you, Derek Loring, see that you do." Veronica smiled. "I'm dying to meet this woman who has you so bonkers."

It was time. Loring left the table, ostensibly on his way to the loo, but instead, he skirted out the rear door to the back of the pub, going directly to Jack's car parked in the lee of the building. Jack had left sun glasses and an old cap for him to use which Loring pulled down over his forehead, taking off the bowler hat Marc had insisted he wear. The car started with a muted roar. He shoved it into gear and edged out onto the road, turning toward Pyrgate and the road to Guildford. Glancing in the rearview mirror, he saw that no one was following him. A sense of relief came over him as he streaked toward Guildford.

Once out of Pyrgate, Loring cut over to A25 using a deeply rutted but serviceable farm road. A few miles after he turned onto the main road, he turned off again and was soon in the outskirts of Guildford. He cautiously drove through the more squalid and rundown section of town, knowing the rail station was just ahead. He pulled into the car park across from the station, locked the car with the cap and glasses on the seat, and walked briskly into the station, the bowler once again in place.

It was the dinner hour. Not many passengers were waiting for the train into London. The next train was due in ten minutes, but he noted the one after that was destined for Victoria Station. Even though his plans were centered around Waterloo, he figured a change to Victoria would trip up any who might be waiting for him at Waterloo.

His train arrived at Victoria Station precisely on schedule. Loring hurried off the train and proceeded to lose himself among the milling throngs of passengers standing at the various ticket counters. He ducked into a bookstore located in the center of the vast station. The shop had glass walls on all sides, allowing him to browse and still watch the main section of the station. He tried to remain inconspicuous, feeling very foolish when he realized he was probably chasing shadows. He could see nothing out of the ordinary. He bought a copy of the Times and raced to the underground entrance to the subway. He boarded the first northbound train, the one which would take him to Oxford Station, the critical stop for Mayfair and the Brinkley Hotel.

"Hello, Derek," Nadia said, opening the door to Loring's knock. "Where the hell did you get those clothes? You look almost native." She started to laugh.

"Hello, yourself. My friends thought I looked too American. Like it?" Loring followed Nadia into the room. Inspector Crimmins has seated near the window. "Sorry I'm late, Inspector. What's happened since this morning?"

"I just now arrived myself so Nadia doesn't know our plan."

"Have you two been talking about me behind my back?" Nadia smiled.

"Not at all, my dear." Crimmins proceeded to explain his plan. "Nadia Shepherd will cease to exist. You then, as Carol Ashworth, will go to Cairo and wait for Derek."

"How do you propose I do that, Inspector?" Nadia asked.

"How well did you know the real Carol Ashworth?"

Nadia thought for a moment. "Carol was in the same classes with me at Bryn Mawr. That's a posh school in Pennsylvania. We double-dated a few times, had some good gab sessions in the dorm instead of studying. She told me she was an orphan, born in Windsor, Ontario. She said she had no living relatives and that she inherited the money for school from an aunt. When she was killed, right before graduation, her classmates were the only ones at her funeral. It was a tragic loss."

"I can well imagine," Crimmins said, "but it happens. Where was she killed, and when?"

"She died in an auto accident on the Pennsylvania turnpike, just outside of Philadelphia. It was in May, 1975. I'll never forget it."

"Most important, Nadia. What did she look like?"

"Well, she was exactly my height...five-foot-five...with reddish hair. It was called auburn in those days. She had a figure that just wouldn't quit. We all were damned envious of her. And she was a pretty girl, unassuming and totally frank."

"You might have just described yourself, Miss Shepherd, aside from the hair. So, it seems that if you do something about that small detail and speak more like a colonial, we can make you Carol Ashworth without any problem. I have friends outside of Scotland Yard...we'll provide you with a new passport, Canadian, in her name."

"But Carol is dead!" Loring interjected.

"Not our 'Carol'. I'll have the records checked for the pertinent data about her birth. Now comes the tricky part. I'll have to pull some strings to get the accident report changed. Our Miss Ashworth didn't die in that accident, but was severely injured and required a long hospital stay with extensive plastic surgery to put her features right. I'll have the FBI do it for us. We'd best stay clear of the CIA, for now."

"Couldn't MI 6 get the new passport and give Nadia a new identity? I understand it's done all the time."

"We can't take the chance with MI 6 or the CIA. If there is a leak in those agencies, Nadia's new identity would get out to Zoser."

"I see. Nadia, you never told me you went to school in the States."

"You never asked. Besides, it wasn't important at the time. Now, Inspector, what else do you suggest we do? Oh, by the way. There was one other thing about Carol I just remembered. She was not all Caucasian...she had some other blood in her past. I believe it was semitic, not Jewish...Arab, I think. Anyway, she had a slight off-white color to her skin, as though she had a permanent sun tan. We used to joke about it, telling her it made her look mysterious."

"That is extremely important," Crimmins added. "You will have to do something about your skin. You are far too fair. We have a preparation over at the Yard, which was developed during the war by the American OSS chaps when they needed a long-lasting disguise. I'll bring some around tomorrow. But I'm afraid you will have to bathe in it. Your skin must be the same color all over...you know what I mean. It's very stable, will last for about three months without fading or rubbing off."

"What about my hair?"

"Get your hair colored at the beauty shop here in the hotel. The exact color isn't too important, what with the way women change their hair tones these days. Almost any color will do, but let's be as authentic as possible, shall we? Don't leave the hotel, either of you. Stay put. And even after you've made the changeover, don't be seen together here in London."

"Anything else, Inspector?" Loring asked.

"One thing more. We'll wait until you are completely made over before we take your picture for your new passport. I'll bring a small camera with me when I come tomorrow. Derek can take the photo after all is ready. Until then, I'm sure the two of you can find something to keep yourselves occupied. Make the most of this time. It will be awhile before you see each other again in Egypt. Now, I must be off. Remember, do not leave here. Have your meals sent up."

"Inspector, wait." Loring stopped him at the door.

"What is it?" Crimmins was obviously in a hurry to leave.

"Nadia, Inspector, as you both can appreciate, this is all new to me. I'm basically a scholar, out of touch with most of the seamier side of life. What I have to know, have to understand, is why me?"

"I was under the impression we had settled all that."

"We discussed it, yes. You both said that the CIA and MI 6 have known, or at least suspected, what Zoser is up to. Why don't they do the job they're trained for, use the money and agents and informers I believe they have to get to Zoser? I'm no good at intrigue, or lying, or killing. Again I ask, why me? I'll screw everything up."

"Derek," Crimmins said patiently, "you have been contacted by Zoser to do a project for them. They evidently hired you because of your reputation as a historian. You are now able to walk in their front door, something no one has been able to do before. You are on the inside, able to see and hear things first hand. Don't you see how valuable you are to us? The intelligence agencies are good, I'll give them that, but as good as they are, they are also paranoid."

"What's that got to do with it?" Loring was edgy.

"They don't trust each other or anyone else. Look at your own country. There is the CIA, the National Security Agency, the State Department, Naval and Army Intelligence, Consular Operations, all doing essentially the same thing but not willing to share their intelligence findings. We British are almost as bad.

"I have no idea where the idea first originated, but MI 6 and the CIA agree you are the best chance any of us has to defeat Zoser. Personally, I don't like the risks involved."

"Why not?"

"You are naive, inexperienced, and a decent individual. These are not the best traits for an agent. However, we have been given assurances that the agencies will give you protection. Miss Shepherd, can you explain it better to his satisfaction?"

"You said it all very well, Inspector. But I want to add this. Neither the CIA nor MI 6 can do the job from the inside like you can, Derek. After the Istanbul fiasco, I was relegated to routine translations and ciphers. I'm no good at covert operations, but I'm damned good at languages and codes. If we get in a jam, I won't be much help to you. I have to believe the agencies will be there to get us out."

"Talk about being no help in a jam, I'm not sure how I'll measure up if push comes to shove. But I gave both of you and the agency, my word. I'm in it to the end, and heaven help us all."

Crimmins put his hand on Loring's shoulder. "I don't

have a doubt in the world about your courage, my boy. You'll do just fine, and Nadia will be more help than she realizes. Now, I have to get back to the Yard."

The inspector left, closing the door silently behind him. Loring stood there, feeling rather foolish over his admission of fear. One doesn't say such things to a woman he cares about.

"Derek, do you want out?" Nadia came to his side. She had a look of concern in her eyes. "Please be honest. I have to know."

"Nadia, this sort of life is what you have been living with the past four or five years. The situation is not the same, but your methods and arguments sound routine. We're getting into very deep water, and I don't want to let you down. That's what bothers me the most...the possibility of failing in your eyes."

"Derek, listen to me. Maybe you'll fail, perhaps I will too. There are no guarantees. That's no reason for us not to try, is it? You said you made a commitment to me, to Crimmins, to the agency. I'd be the last person in the world to hold you to that commitment if I thought you couldn't go through with it."

"I didn't mean..."

"No, hear me out, please. I wouldn't care for you any less...nothing can change how I feel toward you. I'm in this because of choice and unless you choose to do it yourself, don't. Don't let me or anyone else talk you in or out of it. Make your own decision."

"Oh hell, you know perfectly well I'm with you in this. I told you before. All I'm trying to say is that you shouldn't put too much faith in me. Whatever happens, I'll do my best."

"That's all any of us can do, Derek. We just try to do the best we can."

Loring looked at her, at the defiant gleam in those violet eyes, her full lips pursed in a severe slit. He saw a strong, vibrant woman who set almost impossible goals for herself just to meet the challenge. He saw Nadia returning his stare, believing she was weighing his strengths and weaknesses. He wondered how the scales would balance.

"Nadia, what do you really think of me?"

"Well, for one thing, I think enough of you not to try flattery. You respect honesty, so here goes. I think you're too soft for this work. You don't have a thick enough skin to ward off the dangers ahead of us. For that matter, I doubt that I have, either. You're far too honest, as a man, to fight dirty and believe me, dirty fighting will be called for."

"Is that all?"

"No, that's not all. As we've said before, you can't hide your feelings. Your emotions could get in the way. Do you think you could kill someone, steal, cheat, lie and all the other despicable traits we in intelligence have? No, you can't do these things, but neither can I. You see, Derek, I'm out of my depth, too."

"That I can believe. That's one reason I find it hard to accept your being in this business."

"We're talking about you, remember? I believe you have deep convictions and you stick to them. I don't think you would run from danger...you'd rather avoid it. I don't wish to run this into the ground, but your integrity, honesty and intelligence are really what is needed for this problem. With what you have and with what I know, I honestly believe we can do it."

Loring reflected on this straightforward assessment. He finally spoke. "Nadia, I care for you, probably more than you care for me. I don't want anything to happen to you because of me, of what I do or don't do. We were slightly more than friendly in Istanbul and I lost you. Now that you've come back, I don't want to lose you again, especially through my own doing."

Loring looked into her eyes. Tears were starting to form at the corners, threatening to spill over at any moment. Not bothering to wipe them away, Nadia put her hands on his shoulders.

"Derek, it may be just rationalization on my part...hiding the fear that I might not find the right man, but the truth is that since I met you, my ideas have changed."

"Changed? How?"

"I no longer want the lonely life I mapped out for myself. I know we haven't talked about this yet, but I know it as sure as I'm standing here waiting for you to kiss me."

Loring slowly took her in his arms, feeling the warmth of her body as it pressed against his. Their lips touched and his desire for her burst into a searing flame of passion. Her body moved in concert with his own trembling form. Pulling away slightly, she whispered, "Derek, dearest, is this the beginning for us? When we were torn apart in Istanbul I had a lot of time to think of what might have been. I do admit it now, Derek...I could easily fall in love with you."

"Nadia, there's no doubt in my mind. I love you. I have ever since Istanbul. But darling, I want you to be absolutely sure. That's why I'm sleeping on the couch tonight. I suggest you get some sleep too. We have a busy day ahead of us, my love."

When Loring awoke, he found a note pinned to Nadia's pillow. She was off to get her hair dyed. By the time he showered and shaved, Nadia had returned with coffee and scones. She stood in the middle of the room, turning slowly as a dancer might, to give him the full treatment of her transformation. Her hair was now a rich auburn, draping down around her shoulders instead of piled on top of her head as was her usual style. The overall effect was breathtaking. Loring let out a long, low whistle.

"That, my sweet, is some hairdo," he stammered. "Remind me to have you wear it that way always."

"Do you really like it? You don't think it a bit much?"

"I think it looks great! Now, how about some coffee? Oh, by the way. Remind me to buy my own razor. That one of yours won't last long with my beard."

They decided to sit on the floor and eat their scones picnic style. Holding hands and staring in each other's eyes was soon overcome by their nervousness about what lay ahead.

"Let's see what's happening in the rest of the world." Nadia reached up and turned on the radio beside them on the table. Suddenly, their private little Eden was shattered.

"Early this morning the mutilated body of Brian Tupps, President of Zoser International, a worldwide research and consulting firm, with its London office situated near Sloane Square, was discovered in Hyde Park. Scotland Yard has been called in, but no information about this bizarre murder has been released as yet. Tupps left no family or other relatives. More news as it develops. And now for the cricket results at Brighton...."

"One down, three to go," Loring said without thinking. "I wonder where this leaves us."

Just then the telephone rang. Loring raced for the phone, only to stop short. "You better answer it. No one knows I'm here."

Nadia spoke into the phone, her eyes questioning. She brightened a bit, then said, "We'll be here." She turned to Loring. "Crimmins will be here in fifteen minutes."

Before they knew it, Crimmins was at the door.

"You heard? Tupps was killed last night and dumped in Hyde Park by Carriage Drive at the Serpentine. He had the same ghastly paint on his body as the Thompson girl. The same, yet...different."

"What do you mean?" Loring asked after his initial shock.

"The same type of dagger was in his chest, but his throat had been cut from ear to ear. Horrible way to die."

"Any leads, Inspector?" It was Nadia who spoke now.

"I'm afraid not. We're as much in the dark as with the others. First Thompson, all painted up and stabbed. Then the two who killed her, done in, not painted but with their throats cut. And now Tupps, all painted up in some weird ritualistic manner, stabbed and throat cut to boot. It's a pattern, but damned if I know what it means."

Loring faced the sturdy cop and said, "I think it might be a good idea if I called Claridge to express shock over the news. Maybe he'll let something slip, something we can follow up on."

"That might get things moving, Derek," Nadia ventured. "What do you think, Inspector?"

"I say, yes, do it." Crimmins seemed to relax a bit. "I say, Miss Shepherd, or should I say Miss Ashworth, you look positively smashing."

"Thanks. I hope my disguise is going to work."

To Loring's surprise, Claridge, himself, answered the phone. "Sorry, but we're not taking any calls today. Please call back."

"Wait, Josh, don't hang up. This is Loring. I called to express my shock and to offer my deepest sympathy to all of you. Do you know how such a thing could happen?"

"Loring! Damned decent of you to call. No, we don't have a clue as to why it happened. Poor Brian. He had so many friends, but I suppose he must have had at least one enemy, what?"

"I suppose you people want to cancel our agreement now."

"Oh, by no means, Loring. MacIvor and I are more anxious than ever to have you proceed. Zurich has agreed as well."

"I'm glad to hear that, Josh."

"Can I reach you at your friends in Surrey in case of a change in plans?"

"Yes. I'm staying at Priory Farm, outside of Pyrgate. But I have to warn you, I make it a habit when I'm there to go off exploring in the old country churches, so I might not be around when you should call. But I'll return your call."

Loring repeated Merrick's telephone number at the farm and hung up. Now he had to get in touch with Merrick to cover for him in case Claridge went looking for him.

Crimmins understood Zoser's insistence that Loring continue. "I believe they are worried that some mysterious chickens are coming home to roost. Hitting too close to home. Tupps' death doesn't seem to affect what they want you to find, though."

"It certainly seems that way."

Before Crimmins left he gave Nadia the dye for her skin and instructed Derek on how to use the camera he

gave him for Nadia's passport picture. He told Loring to
return to Surrey to await further instructions. "You have
done all you can here for the moment. The rest is up to
Nadia...eh, Carol. I'll have Ron Menefee, my brother-in-
law, stop by for the film. One of us will bring around your
new passport tomorrow."

He instructed Nadia to leave for Cairo without going
back to her flat. "You can buy all you need in Cairo. Derek,
you should be leaving here next week. I'll be in touch. By
the way, you really do look smashing, my dear." With
that, Crimmins turned and left.

Nadia and Loring stood facing the door for a brief
moment, then Nadia said, "We might as well get on with
the transformation. Draw me my bath, will you, dear?"

The tiny splash of green across the street from the
Brinkley Hotel is not officially called Oak Park. The name
doesn't appear on any map of London, but the residents of
Mayfair know it well, and with fondness. In the center of
the park stands a solitary oak tree, gnarled and twisted by
the years. It has withstood fires, riots and wars, not to
mention the feeble attempts of well-meaning city planners
to do away with it. Neighborhood nannies, for the most
part attired in identical mid-calf length dour gray dresses
with long sleeves and starched white dickie collars, watch
over their charges, while the children scamper about mis-
chievously. It is only when harm threatens do these women
leave the shade of the old tree to cajole or reprimand.

One such woman sat on one of the benches under the
oak. Her black-stockinged legs were demurely crossed at
the ankles, her eyes were far from vacant. She was pretending to concentrate on the needle work in her lap while
her eyes kept vigil on the Brinkley Hotel. From her van-

tage point she could see both the front entrance as well as the side delivery door. She appeared not to notice the neatly dressed man who sat on the bench beside her, scanning the front page of the paper he took from his briefcase. After five minutes he turned the page and muttered to himself, as though commenting on the news. The woman, however, strained to catch his words.

"Anything new?"

"We haven't seen hide nor hair of either Loring or Shepherd. Crimmins was there for an hour last night. He came back fifteen minutes ago. He looked upset."

"Did anyone talk with the staff?"

"Yes, Richard scouted them out last evening. No one has seen either of them. Doesn't sound right to me. Either Loring paid for their silence or Richard didn't ask the right questions."

"We have to make sure they're in there. Hopkins wants us on Loring's tail right up to the time he leaves for Cairo. After that, we're off the case."

"Want me to stay here?"

"Yes. Later you might check some of the Room Service staff. See if two meals are always sent up. In the meantime, keep watching for anything unusual. I'll be in touch. By the way, that outfit doesn't do a thing for you."

"You should see what's underneath it."

"If I wasn't married, I'd be tempted."

"Forget it. We don't have the time. Keep the faith."

"I will. See you later."

Chapter 6

George Wells was furious. He stormed from one end of his office to the other, kicking the furniture, tossing empty chairs about and leaving chaos in his wake.

"That miserable son of a bitch is out there, waiting to pick us off one by one! But who is it? And where is he?"

He turned and faced MacIvor.

"Why can't your men find out anything? They're useless! The Shepherd bitch is still on the loose and Loring is sitting around doing nothing, waiting for God knows what. Damn it, I want results!"

"George, they're doing everything they can. It takes time to find someone in London who doesn't want to be found." MacIvor was afraid.

"Then get more men on it. If they don't find her soon, the whole caper goes down the toilet. We need to get Loring down to Egypt to trace the goddamned Menefee, but we need to get Shepherd first. She knows too much about me."

Wells stopped his pacing and sat down at his desk. His voice dropped to a lower pitch, almost deadly.

"When I joined Zoser, Sempher gave me the job of getting rid of the Menefee and I mean to do just that. His private ambitions suffer because of Menefee's interference. Now it seems they're killing again, like they did in the old days."

Claridge returned Wells' stare. He spoke quietly. He, too, was afraid.

"George, what other killings? What interference are you talking about?"

"The American cardinal, Fitzwater. Right after he was made a Vatican delegate, through our help, he was killed. An accident, the papers said. I say rubbish! The Menefee killed him. Zurich knows it and so do I."

Claridge looked aghast. Wells continued. "Our converts in the Vatican are well placed. They plant the seeds of distrust everywhere so that when we kill the Pope one of our people will take over. That's why we needed Fitzwater. His vote would have been crucial."

Claridge and MacIvor were visibly shaken. MacIvor whispered, his disbelief apparent. "What the hell are you talking about? What's this about the Pope?"

"He has to go. It's as simple as that. We have most of the Protestants controlled by our television preachers. We need to swing the Catholics over to our side, too. They're the main stumbling block to our control of Western Christianity. So even you idiots can see that the Pope has to be replaced by one of ours...someone we can trust."

"You can't be serious!" Claridge found his voice.

"Quite serious. When we have control of the Christians, Zoser's 'Operation Amun' will start. That's the way the ancient philosophy of Zozer will be realized. Sempher claims it's his destiny, whatever the hell that means."

"But the Pope? What's Sempher thinking of?"

Wells looked up at the two men before him, his anger still very real. "We don't question, we just do our job." He wiped away the sweat under his chin and glared at MacIvor and Claridge, when suddenly, for no apparent reason, he actually smiled and said, "Josh, old man, I have a job for you. Get hold of Loring. Convince him to come in here, right away. We want to settle his fee and send him on his

way to Egypt. Tell him Zurich has pushed up the time
schedule."

"I'll get on it right away."

"Mac, do what you have to in order to find Shepherd.
I've changed my mind about finding her first. Once in
Egypt, Loring will forget her and be able to concentrate on
our job."

Claridge and MacIvor looked at one another, puzzled.
The phone on Wells' desk interrupted any reply.

"Yes?" Wells barked into the instrument. He didn't
speak for some time, then, "Good work. You'll find we
know how to show our appreciation. Let me know if anything else develops."

The bitterness was gone from Wells' voice when he
hung up the phone. "That was Jameson at MI 6. It seems
our Mr. Loring called there, asking for Shepherd. She
must have given him the number. Jameson got his girl-
friend on the line, pretending to be Shepherd. According
to Jameson, this woman sounds exactly like Shepherd on
the phone. She sweet-talked Loring, telling him she had a
sudden special assignment which would take her out of
London for a few days, and that she would get in touch
with him when she returned. Worked like a charm."

"What does that do for us?"

"Let's assume that information has relieved Loring's
anxiety over Shepherd so he'll get busy on our job. Now,
another change in plans, Mac. Find that bitch and kill her.
Use as many people as you need. We don't need her around
anymore, and good riddance. Get with it. Josh, get Loring
over here. This meeting is over."

Loring strolled into the Midland Bank, hoping he'd
catch Merrick before he left for the day. Everything had

been done. Nadia had transformed her creamy white skin into a sultry tan tone. Her eyes, still a vivid violet color were modified by eyeliner into a very slight Eastern oval. The overall effect was amazing, especially with her new auburn hair. When all was ready, Loring took several pictures of her for the passport of Carol Ashworth. With a heavy heart, he gave her enough money to purchase clothes and supplies that she needed until he met her in Egypt.

"Until Cairo, my love. Take care." He left the hotel.

Merrick was at his desk when Loring arrived. He jumped up, rushed over to Loring and made him sit down while he closed the door. He wore a wide grin.

"Your Nadia just called to tell me you were on your way over here. She sounds absolutely delightful, old chum. She also said the film was picked up right after you left. She's flying out this evening. She also told me to watch out for you."

"I asked her to phone you. And yes, she is delightful. Someday you'll find out for yourself. I stopped by to get a lift back to the farm. When do you plan on leaving?"

"I have some work I must get out, but it won't take me long. Just make yourself comfortable. Do you want something to read?"

"No, Marc, but could I use a phone? There's a couple of calls I want to make."

"Go into the next office. You can have some privacy there."

Loring dialed the number Nadia had given him. He knew it was MI 6. He wanted to find out if they were concerned about her not calling in. A man's voice answered.

"Mr. Jameson here. May I help you?"

"Miss Shepherd, please. Derek Loring calling."

"One moment, sir," came the calm reply. "She should

be around here someplace. Yes, she went to the ladies' room. Do you wish to wait, or will you call back in a few minutes?"

"I'll wait, thank you." Loring gripped the phone until his knuckles turned white. These people are playing with me, he thought. They know she isn't there. Finally, another voice came on the line, a woman's voice.

"Derek, darling, how good of you to call. I was just about to ring you. Bad news, I'm afraid. I must leave town for a few days on special assignment. I'll call you when I get back. Darling, the other night was super. That's what I'll remember while I'm gone."

Loring couldn't believe his ears. He knew it wasn't Nadia, yet it was, in a way. The voice was so like hers. It was uncanny. And her reference to the other night. Nadia would know there was nothing special about that night they stayed together at the Regent. This must be the leak in MI 6 Nadia warned him about. He decided to play along.

"Don't worry, Nadia. I just called to ease my mind. You didn't call when you said you would. Now I understand. I have to leave London myself, for some time. Don't know how long the job will take, but I'll get in touch with you when I get back. I mean that, darling. No more Istanbul. Take care of yourself. Goodbye."

When he hung up, he immediately called Crimmins.

"Inspector? Loring here. I have some information which is important." He related his conversation with Jameson and the girl, and the latest word from Nadia. Crimmins sounded relieved.

"Good. I'll get to Hopkins right away. They'll know what to do about this Jameson. Wish we could jam the leak at the other end, in the CIA. Anyway, Miss Ashworth will be on the evening plane to Cairo. Get used to calling her that. You take very good pictures, Derek. Keep me informed."

That business taken care of, Loring stared out the window, looking down on King's Road. The late afternoon crowds were milling about as usual. In the little park across the way, a group of mimes were performing silent acts from the latest theatrical rage, but the passersby were much too preoccupied to pay any heed. Merrick rushed in, hurriedly.

"Veronica rang up just now. Claridge is looking for you. He called the farm. Veronica said you were out, but that you'd be back. She didn't know when. What are you going to do?"

"I'll just have to play it straight." Loring called the Zoser office. When Claridge answered, Loring said, "Josh? Loring here. I understand you're looking for me. Is it important? I'm here in London, right down the street from your office. I could be there in five minutes, if necessary."

"Yes, Mr. Loring, it's rather urgent. Please come over. We'll be waiting."

Loring walked into the Zoser conference room with Claridge. MacIvor sat at the head of the table, looking uncomfortable. He did all the talking, coming right to the point.

"Dr. Loring, how soon can you leave for Egypt? It is vital you start your work right away."

"Almost any time, Mr. MacIvor. There's no reason to delay. I'm very anxious to get started myself. If we agree to one minor change, I'll be ready to take the evening flight day after tomorrow."

"Splendid. What minor change did you have in mind?"

"It's the matter of my fee, Mr. MacIvor. Or rather, the manner of the fee. I should like the whole fee paid now, to be placed in an escrow account here in London.

Should you agree to that, I see no reason for me to put off going."

"I can see that you have been cheated in the past, Loring. Playing it safe, are you? Very well. We have no objection to that arrangement. Josh," he said, looking at the quiet Claridge, "make out both cheques as promised. Loring can take them with him." Then to Derek, he added, "Glad to have you with the team, Loring."

"Thanks."

"I'm sure you'll deliver. If you need anything in Egypt, call on Achmed Yamani. He's the manager of our Cairo office. He will see you have everything you require. But anything of substance, regarding your primary task, cable us here right away. Your visa and necessary exploration permits will be waiting for you at the airport manager's office in Cairo."

"Good. Then I'll be on my way." Loring was anxious to leave.

"I believe that takes care of everything, for the time being. One more thing, though. Zoser has a permanent suite on reserve at the Mena House. Use it, with our compliments. Have a good and fruitful dig, Loring. We'll be waiting for results."

Loring returned to the bank where Merrick was waiting for him. He handed Merrick the cheque representing his fee.

"Marc, open an escrow account with this, will you? Make it interest bearing...use your own judgement, and take out your usual commission. Have the cheque cleared right away. And make this other one for fifteen thousand dollars into a letter of credit to be honored anywhere. Can do?"

"This will take a little time, but I can do it. Just endorse them. I'll do the rest. Are you coming back to the farm now?"

"Yes, let's go someplace peaceful. London has suddenly become very oppressive."

Merrick had the escrow papers waiting for Loring when he went to the bank the following morning. The letter of credit was ready as well. Loring had come into town with Marc after a very relaxing evening at the farm. For reasons known only to herself, Veronica had hovered about him constantly, watching his every move with worried glances. On the surface she was her usual buoyant self.

He left Merrick's office and went directly to Scotland Yard, hoping to find Crimmins there. He was directed to the inspector's office, a small cubicle on the third floor.

"Derek, my boy. Do come in. Here, take this chair. Just toss the mess on the floor. First off, Carol got away as scheduled. I put her on the plane myself. Didn't recognize her. A beautiful bit of disguise, that. I received word that the Ashworth records have been taken care of. That's one less worry she has."

Loring smiled in appreciation.

"Talked with Hopkins last night. Told him about Jameson. He wasn't at all surprised, and said that Jameson would be neutralized. Anything new from your end?"

Crimmins' habit of talking in facts and short spurts left Loring breathless. He smiled at the inspector and related his meeting with Zoser, and the matter of the money. He said he was to leave for Cairo the next evening.

"I guess that's about it, Inspector. I have your home address. I'll cable you when I find anything you can use."

The inspector looked at him fondly. "That will be fine, Derek. Please do that. One more thing. Can you come over to the house this evening for dinner with the missus and me? My Nora said she would like to meet you. Told her a few things about you, my boy. Of course, if you have other plans with the Merricks, I'll understand."

"I'd be delighted, Inspector. Marc and Veronica will have no objection, I know. I'll catch a later train down to Surrey. What time would be convenient?"

"Why don't you come back here about six? We'll drive home together."

Loring called Merrick with the change in plans for the evening. Marc said he and Veronica would wait for Loring's call from the station.

His next stop was the British Museum to bone up on El Amarna. What he remembered about the ruins was sketchy at best, and he thought there might be some later findings that might help his explorations into the lives of Akhenaten and Nefertiti. He knew the curator of the Egyptian exhibit. He might be of some help.

Foster Gibbs greeted Loring warmly. "Derek Loring! It's been ages. What brings you to London this time?"

The old curator shook Loring's hand with a grip that turned his knuckles white. Gibbs was the typical scholarly type with bushy eyebrows that almost obliterated his piercing blue eyes, and a shock of white hair that always stood on end. Loring was very fond of the old man and called on him every time he was in London.

"Just doing some esoteric research, old friend. I was wondering if you have some unpublished material regarding El Amarna that I might take a peek at."

Gibbs looked at Loring with a twinkle in his eye. "You always know the proper time to come see me. As it happens, we just opened some material last week on that subject. It doesn't look too promising, but you can browse if you like."

The old curator led Loring down into the basement chambers of the vast museum. Various rooms and cubicles were identified both by period and by civilization. In the Egyptian room, Gibbs showed Loring the catalogued material of the Amarna period, boxes of shards, rolls of papyrus, a few sculptures and stone carvings. Loring wished Nadia was with him. Her knowledge of the hieroglyphics was much better than his.

Gibbs left him, chuckling as he said, "Make yourself at home. Don't steal anything and be sure to turn off the light when you leave."

Once he was alone, Loring went about searching through the artifacts, most of which had been recovered from the most recent explorations...ten years ago. There had been no discoveries regarding the El Amarna period unearthed since then. The papyrus scrolls he found were accounts of the actual construction of the new city of Akhenaten — the number of stone cutters employed, the number of laborers, the hordes of artisans and scribes. This was an important find for historians. However, it was not what he was after. He was looking for something else. He wasn't sure what it was, but he'd know it if he found it.

He searched further, uncovering more scrolls and stone pieces. These he set aside, carefully, with only a hurried glance. Finally he came upon one scroll which held promise. It was a crude plan depicting the proposed city. Whether it represented the actual site plan or merely the envisioned concept, he couldn't tell. He understood enough of it to make out the temple to Aten, the sun disc deity of Akhenaten.

He found the dwellings of the priests and scribes on the south side of the temple complex, and up to the north he made out the village of the peasants. The drawing showed a wall, extending from the temple out to the river, about one mile away as he mentally calculated the scale of the entire city. He could find no explanation as to what the wall represented.

He came upon a piece of highly polished granite which measured approximately ten inches square, two inches thick. One edge was jagged, as though it had once been part of a larger stone. On closer examination, he could clearly make out the incised characters carved in the hard stone. The cartouche of royalty was dominant. It was the cartouche of the queen, Nefertiti. The inscription he deciphered told about the queen drawing the plan of the city. Nefertiti herself was the scribe. The stone also mentioned the hand of Akhenaten guiding her work.

Eagerly, Loring dug deeper into the box of findings. He came to another highly polished piece of granite, similar to the first. The granite's jagged edge matched the other piece perfectly. His heart beat faster at this discovery. He continued the translation of the cryptic characters. Was he finally onto something? The inscription concluded the tale presented by the first stone. The pharaoh was entrusting the rule of the city to his queen while he traveled elsewhere to attend to other matters. The story ended there.

Loring was trembling with excitement over this find. Everyone believed that Akhenaten had always remained in the city, ruled for his few remaining years, then died. It was thought his son-in-law, Tutankhamun, took over the throne when the old man died. But this stone now revealed that Nefertiti ruled when the king was gone. It couldn't have been for very long as the data concerning Tut's rule had him taking over the kingdom shortly after Akhenaten died. Loring now had a few doubts about the truth of accepted history.

The truth had to be someplace in Egypt. Was it at Amarna?

He put the things back as he found them and left the basement room, remembering to turn off the lights. He could not find Gibbs to thank him or to bid him goodbye, so Loring wrote him a note, then went back to Scotland Yard to pick up Crimmins. He was looking forward to the coming evening.

The woman arose from the bench under the oak tree. She straightened her nanny dress where it had bunched up around her hips. She smoothed the starched apron, clutched her needle work under her arm and left the park. A man fell into step beside her, matching her determined stride.

"Slow down a bit, can't you? What's the latest?"

"They're both gone."

"Are you sure?"

"Loring left yesterday afternoon and hasn't been back. I showed Shepherd's picture to the staff. They remember her checking in, but no one recalls seeing her since."

"Did you see the room?"

"Richard did. I don't know how he did it and I didn't ask."

"Find anything?"

"Not a single damn thing to show they were ever there."

"They had some help from Scotland Yard. They vanished too neatly for amateurs."

"What do we do now?"

"I'll talk with MI 6. They should have the latest. There is the possibility that Shepherd contacted them with a change in plans. It's all we can do for the time being."

"What about the rest of the evening?"

"How about going to your place? I'd like to get you out of that atrocious outfit."

"I thought you were married."

"No, not really."

"Why did you tell me you were?"

"I always tell my women that, at the beginning. Keeps them off balance."

"That's a hell of a thing to do."

"I know. Do you really care?"

"No, not at all. Come on, it's getting late."

Nora Crimmins was an excellent cook. She served steak and kidney pie, the best Loring had ever eaten. She was beside herself with pride when he helped himself to a second portion of the delicacy.

"Americans don't usually take to kidneys, you know, Mr. Loring. But we like 'em, we do. Don't we, Bertie?"

"Yes, Nora," the inspector agreed, "we surely do."

"When I'm in England, I usually try to have this at least twice a week. It's difficult to find it in Hawaii. You make an excellent pie, Mrs. Crimmins."

"Oh, Mr. Loring, you do go on so. You'll be turning my head with all that blarney. Won't he, though, Bertie?"

"Most certainly, Nora, most certainly. But he does speak the truth, at that."

"Tut, tut. You men will make me blush. Tell me, Mr. Loring, how do you put up with living alone? Bertie, here, tells me you aren't married. Excuse me if I'm a bit nosy...blame it on my own contentment."

"Not at all, Mrs. Crimmins. I've never felt the need to be married, what with my work taking me all over the world. That is, until now. Perhaps Bert has mentioned Nadia...Nadia Shepherd. I have hopes she and I might eventually get to the altar."

"Well, now, I don't know if that's wise. Bertie has mentioned her...not much, mind you...but enough to cause me some worry. In her line of work the danger is always there."

"Now, Nora. Don't bother Derek with your wild notions. He has a difficult job ahead of him and he doesn't need any more to worry about."

"Bert Crimmins, I'm not meddling! But this young man should have a good, comfortable home to come back to. Don't expect me to hold my tongue if the truth is called for. You know me well enough to understand how I feel about a wife being a help to her man."

"Hey, wait a minute," Loring interrupted. "Don't you two get into an argument over my love life. Nadia and I are not that involved. Why not wait and see what happens."

"I'm sorry for Nora, Derek. She does have a will all her own." Crimmins was uncomfortable.

"Yes, Mr. Loring. Please forgive my sharp tongue. Bertie and I want to send you away to Egypt in a good frame of mind."

They were sitting in the parlor enjoying their coffee when Ron Menefee dropped in. Crimmins didn't look overly pleased as he made the introductions.

"Derek, this is Ron Menefee, Nora's step-brother."

Menefee got himself coffee and joined the others. He was an average person, about thirty, who looked out of place in the English family with his rather dark coloring. Crimmins said the man's father was from Malta which probably accounted for his appearance. Menefee didn't join in the conversation but rather he continued to gaze at Loring, as though he was about to say something profound, but thinking better of it.

Loring wondered why this man was showing so much

interest in him. Crimmins had said he was a moody person, read a good deal, and was subject to periods where he would disappear for days at a time. Loring wondered, too, whether Menefee lived with the Crimminses, not that it really mattered.

The inspector had been speaking of the murders without compromising the security of the Yard.

"Ron, here, helps out now and then with some of my leg work. Gives me time for the more trying aspects of my cases. Yes, Ron is a big help."

It all sounded rather patronizing to Loring, and he felt Menefee sensed it as well. To ease the tension, Loring asked the strange young man, "Were you born in Malta, Ron?"

"No, sir. Our family moved there from Egypt when I was quite young. My father, Nora's stepfather, was a Copt. Do you know what that is, Mr. Loring?"

"Yes. The Copts were some of the earliest Christians. They settled primarily in Egypt. I've attended their services in Cairo."

"Our family originally came from El Dab'a, a small fishing village west of what is now Alexandria. It's a very old village, dating from the days of the pharaohs."

"Why did you leave Egypt?"

"We had no future there, so my father moved the family to Malta."

"That's interesting. Perhaps the inspector's told you I am leaving for Egypt tomorrow on business."

Displeasure showed on Menefee's face. "Yes, Bertie has told me." Then Menefee became silent.

"I really must be on my way. Big day tomorrow, and I want to catch the early train back to Surrey. Thank you so much, Mrs. Crimmins, for the superb dinner. It was indeed a pleasure." Loring edged toward the door.

"Wait, Mr. Loring," Menefee spoke up. "I'll drive

you down. There're some things I want to talk to you about your work."

"That's very kind of you, Ron. Are you sure it won't be putting you out?"

"Not at all. Let's be on our way, shall we?"

Menefee drove in silence for quite a while, until he crossed over the Thames to the south side of the river. He turned off onto the motorway, heading southwest. When he finally spoke, his voice was strained and aggressive.

"Why are you working for Zoser? Is it for the money?"

"It's partly for the money. They're paying me very well for the work, but I really don't see where that's any of your business. However, the main reason is that I think the same as your brother-in-law. This Zoser group is mixed up in something I don't like. Also, I have a score to settle with them. The Thompson girl. Does that answer your question?"

"Yes. Thanks for being honest. Tell your friend, Miss Ashworth, she's in danger. The real Carol Ashworth had a dark past. With Miss Shepherd posing as her, that past could catch up with her. It could mean trouble. Tell her to be careful."

"Does Crimmins know all this?"

"No."

"Why are you telling me? Shouldn't you be warning Crimmins?"

"He has no part in my plans. You have. Look for the real truth about Zoser at Amarna. Look for the wall leading to the Nile. It's all there."

"You're being too cryptic, Ron. What am I to find, and what do you have to do with all this?"

"You know some things regarding Akhenaten, but not

the important facts. You know only what others want you to know. In truth, he was a great man, very enlightened for his day. His enemies were from the old ones, the ones who started back in the past, and wanted Egypt to return to that past. Akhenaten stopped them."

"What about you?"

"Me? I'm just one displaced Egyptian who believes that Akhenaten could have changed the course of Egyptian history if he hadn't been killed...by the old ones."

"What do you mean, he was killed by the old ones? Who are the old ones?"

"You'll find out soon enough. I'm positive the truth is written on that wall. You must find it. Zoser is the modern extension of the old ones. It's been almost five thousand years since the time of the pharaoh, and they're still with us."

"You say that Akhenaten was killed? We all thought he died from some disease, a crippling form of arthritis. All his statues show him to be disfigured and misshapen."

"One of the greatest propaganda con jobs of all history. The old ones did it, after they tore down Amarna, his beautiful city. The famous King Tut, renown for ages through the discovery of his rich tomb, was only a puppet of the old ones. Look well, Derek Loring. And be careful of Zoser."

It was Loring's turn to fall silent. Was established history entirely wrong? Had Akhenaten been misjudged for all these centuries? How did Zoser tie in with these 'old ones'?

Who were the 'old ones'? It was obvious he wasn't going to get anything further from Menefee. And what about Nadia...Carol? Could he get to her in time to warn her of some untold danger?

Priory Farm was around the next turn in the road.

Part II
Chapter 7

When Loring walked into Zoser's suite at the Mena House Hotel, he was taken aback with the lavishness of the accommodations. He was prepared for some show of luxury, but what he walked into boggled the mind. He rightly thought an organization such as Zoser International would naturally do all in its power to impress its clients. If what Brian Tupps told him in London was only partially true, their clients represented power and wealth on a world scale. The layout and appointments of the suite gave evidence as to the lengths Zoser extended itself for the comforts of its guests. Royal personages could ask for nothing more.

The array of rooms was not pretentious. The living room commanded center stage and was bracketed by respectably-sized bedrooms on either side. Each bedroom had its own dressing chamber separate from a luxurious bathroom, dominated by a sunken marble tub flush with the floor. A wide terrace stretched across the entire windowed walls of the suite with access from each room. This terrace overlooked the southwestern horizon, and offered an unobstructed vista of the pyramids and the stark desert beyond. On any moonlit night the panorama of legendary splendor would be gloriously spectacular.

As he stood on the terrace, Loring watched the moon

rise over the desert. It cast long and inky shadows over the earth below, shadows which changed their shapes in concert with the moon's drift across the dark sky. He felt himself succumb again to the spell of Egypt. It never failed to engulf him each time he found himself in this land of mystery. How well he understood the legend that predicted the eternal pull of the desert to the visitor with an open mind. He could attest to the charm and attraction of this land of the ancient pharaohs. A picture, a phrase, even a word could ignite in his mind's eye the glow of Egypt's history slumbering in the hot desert sand.

Loring left the tranquillity of the terrace to reenter the reality of his mission. Uppermost in his mind was the matter of secrecy which he attributed to the rigors and intrigues of the past days in London. The murders, the shadowing and the suspicions which had recently become an integral part of his life prompted him to undertake an uncharacteristic chore.

He went from room to room searching for evidence of hidden listening devices. He admitted to a growing paranoia. Nevertheless, he surveyed the place, looking closely into lamps, under tables, behind pictures, all the likely hiding places for microphones. He even examined the potted plants which were scattered around the suite. He had to remind himself that if Zoser was telling the truth about its clientele, it would need to know the goings-on in the suite. Hotel rooms were notorious for secret meetings and clandestine compacts. Zoser would certainly be at least curious. Loring found nothing out of the ordinary in his search. Normal dustballs under the beds, cobwebs in the corners, and sand...a considerable amount of sand ground into the carpets, was all he uncovered. So much for surveillance. Still, he had the uneasy feeling he was not absolutely alone in the room. His thoughts turned to Carol Ashworth...Nadia.

How would she make herself known?

His flight from London to Cairo had been late in arriving. It was nine-thirty in the evening when the plane touched down. Cairo Airport was in worse chaos than usual. The Christian and Muslim students were feuding again, creating unpleasant incidents for tourists and Cairo residents alike. The specter of terrorist attacks was never minimized in this part of the world, and every foreign plane was met by armed men in uniform.

Passengers were literally escorted off the aircraft by the military and into the terminal. Hand luggage was inspected before one entered the terminal building and again when the other baggage was claimed after an unreal length of time. Everywhere one turned, he was met by the serious stares of the soldiers with guns at the ready. Loring took these measures as over-kill, however safe one felt because of them.

Once his luggage was safely in tow, Loring immediately made his way to the office of the airport manager. He had trouble gaining entrance due to the tight security, but after his identity was established and verified he was admitted. His visa and the exploration permits he needed for the project were waiting for him as Zoser had promised. He began to wonder to what limits the influence of Zoser reached. He didn't believe the historical name and the significance of that name had a thing to do with the efficiency it produced. It was one more instance where money will buy anything.

The ride across Cairo to the Mena House was an aging experience, white knuckles included at no extra charge. He gave up, long ago, attempting to explain a Cairo cab ride to the uninitiated. Once, and only once, he tempted the fates by driving a rental car himself. Never again, he pledged to himself.

At last he was deposited at the Mena House with flair and elan, forty minutes after leaving the airport. A stern policeman opened the car door for him, asking for his passport. He checked Loring's identity with what was listed on an official document. Satisfied that Loring was the same passenger who entered the airport taxi, he bowed stiffly and motioned Loring to the hotel entrance.

He was expected. He registered, left his passport at the desk, and was promptly escorted to the Zoser suite. It was then, when he was alone, he conducted the search of the rooms. Afterwards, considering it was still early according to Egyptian standards, he went down to the bar for a quick nightcap. He didn't particularly want company. He just didn't want to be alone.

The mezzanine lounge bar was jammed with tourists, eager and ebullient, each displaying varying degrees of sunburn. The place was much too noisy for his taste but Loring forced himself to endure the clamor for a while. He wanted to get a feel for the place, to recapture its ambiance. He had no intention of becoming an integral part of the merrymaking.

He was fortunate to find a small table off to the side of the lounge where he settled himself. He realized that he didn't really want a drink after all, but occupying the table necessitated that he order. When his drink arrived, a note was discreetly tucked under the napkin. He sipped on the scotch and ordered another before he read the note.

The message instructed him to be at the public phones in the lobby in thirty minutes. It said he was to expect a call. The note was unsigned. Loring scowled at the thought of more intrigue, especially after being in town only two hours. But it occurred to him that this might be Carol's way of getting in touch with him. In any case, he had to find out.

The lobby was deserted at that hour. The tourists were either still in the bar or snugly tucked into bed. One of the phones rang and he hurried to answer it. The voice on the other end was smooth, oily and heavily accented.

"*Masa'il khayr.* Welcome to Cairo, Mr. Loring. We have been expecting you. May Allah smile on your quest. My name is Achmed Yamani. I am calling to inform you that we are at your disposal should you have the need. Do you require anything, anything at all...liquor, hashish, women, boys? Just let your wishes be known. Are your rooms satisfactory?"

"Thank you, yes, Mr. Yamani, everything is just fine. Let me get my bearings first. I might call on you, in a day or so, to provide me with the necessary equipment for my work here. I'll pay for it, of course."

"*Ma'assalama.* Goodnight, Mr. Loring. May Allah watch over you."

"Goodnight to you, sir."

Loring hung up the phone, confused. Why the hell did Yamani contact him in the bar with a note? Either he was there himself, not wanting to be seen as yet, or Loring was still being watched. If he was being watched, Yamani would have been informed. Was that why he sent the note? In any event, Loring now knew where he stood with Zoser. They were not letting him out of their sight.

So much for mutual trust. The idea of listening devices in his suite suddenly became more plausible. He was certain of one thing, however. He and Carol could not use his rooms for anything but proper business discussions relating to her working for him. He went back to his room to plan for the next day. Where was Carol?

The silver moonlight streamed into his room through

the open terrace doors, flooding the entire place almost bright enough to read by, and fingers of light crept across his bed as though animated. Loring was not finding it easy to fall asleep. He tossed about, his ears tuned to the myriad of night sounds which were all around him.

He turned over in his mind all the details of his assignment. He was to prove or disprove a concise lineage back into ancient Egypt. Was this the sum total of what Zoser wanted, or did it have some hidden agenda? The intelligence communities were convinced Zoser was involved with schemes having no relation to the research it retained him for. Scotland Yard wanted proof that Zoser was a killing machine, responsible for cluttering up London with dead bodies, all murdered in a ritualistic pattern. And Nadia...she was connected with those out to prove Zoser was simply evil, killing the opposition for some unknown purpose.

What about himself? What really were his motives in being a part of all this? He saw Gwen Thompson murdered. Was that act enough to set him on this path? It was true that being forced to witness a girl's brutal killing filled him with outrage, but he admitted to himself that it was the subsequent violence centered around Zoser that shaped his decision. Zoser had to be stopped.

Everyone alluded to it but no one came right out to say it. Zoser had to have a purpose. He didn't believe what it told him regarding the research. They could've obtained the information themselves. They needed him for a purpose, had to use him to achieve something else. That was the maddening thought, that elusive goal Zoser was after. He was trained to be analytical. Damn it, man, put that skill to use! He would, as soon as Carol surfaced.

An unfamiliar sound interrupted his thoughts. The night whisperings had the usual comforting sonance as always, but a foreign presence was there. Loring lay still, his eyes straining to pierce the shadows between the splashes of moonlight. His ears tried to isolate the strange sound, separate it from the familiar. He heard it again. A faint click emanated from above his head, high up on the wall. A click, yet not a click. It was more like a noise made by the breaking of a damp twig, soft and, at the same time, sharp.

He got out of bed, avoiding an impulse to turn on the lights. The bright illumination of the moon bathed the room, but areas close to the ceiling were black as pitch. He stepped out onto the terrace, thinking the strange noise might be an insect or nocturnal animal. He could find nothing out of the ordinary with the furniture arrangement on the balcony. He didn't see anything crawling on the pink stucco walls on either side of the sliding terrace doors.

Puzzled, slightly afraid, he went back into the room and turned on the lights. What he saw over his bed, just below the juncture of wall and ceiling, embarrassed him. An air conditioning grille proved to be the night invader. Loring told himself he should have known better, should have reasoned the sound he heard might be purely mechanical. All things should be so simple, he thought, when he went back to bed and finally to sleep.

On the east bank of the Nile, in the posh Garden City district of Cairo, the American Embassy never closed. True, the public was attended to only during posted hours, but in-house affairs recognized no clock. This night was no exception. On the upper floor of the ornate structure, tucked away in a remote section of the north wing, a smallish office was occupied. The office door, unmarked, was closed. The door had a self-closing device which automatically locked when the door was shut. Inside, manning a bank of telephones of different colors, two men sat at a plastic console. One of the men smoked incessantly to the obvious discomfort and annoyance of the other.

"Goddamn it, do you have to smoke all the time?"

"Tough! If you don't like it, ask for a nice transfer. I'd be glad to get rid of you."

"This duty is the pits. What the hell did we ever do to be stuck with each other in this godforsaken hellhole?"

"Beats me. Regardless, we're here and its here we'll stay until told otherwise. Hold on...the green phone is ringing."

The green-colored phone emitted a discordant buzz while the signal light flashed weakly. The man who picked up the phone switched on the recorder to tape the coming classified conversation.

"Yes?"

"Converse?"

"No, this is Caine."

"I see. Has Mr. Clean been around to do his usual good job?"

"Yes, as always. He found two local cockroaches and a Russian scorpion. Nothing else. We're sterile."

"Where was the Russki bug?"

"Stuck to the back leg of my chair...very amateurish. What do you have for us?"

"The Home Office wants to know if you picked up our man."

"Yes. Loring came in at nine-thirty tonight and went directly to the Mena House. We have a man over there to follow if he leaves."

"Good. What about the woman?"

"No sign of her. We've watched all incoming flights for the past two days. The only woman who might even come close arrived two nights ago, from London. She turned out to be a Canadian named Ashworth. Good lookin' broad."

"Did you follow her, find out where she went?"

"Sure did. She's at the Mena House. She went to the Ministry of Industry yesterday to apply for a work permit. Our man there doesn't think she'll get one."

"What about our limey friends?"

"They're all edgy. The Brits have Yamani fairly well staked out. Want us to lend them a hand?"

"Hell no! This is their ballgame. Just stay loose and keep on Loring. These civilians don't play according to our rules so there's no telling what the hell he might do. We can't have him run amok and queer the whole caper."

"Will do. Same time tomorrow?"

"Yeah, I'll contact you. How's Soloman?"

"Still bitchin' He's here now. Want to have some words with him?

"No, not necessary. That's all for now."

The man called Caine hung up the phone, turned off the recorder, then faced the other man at the console.

"That was the Home Office, as you probably know. We just keep our tail on Loring and let the limey bunch handle Yamani. It's the same scenario."

"Just another lousy day in camel land."

Chapter 8

The sun was breaking over the eastern horizon when Loring awoke. Yellow fingers of light played across the ceiling above him. He eased out of bed and went out on the terrace. In the quiet of the dawn he stood facing the desert expectantly. The rising sun tinted the barren landscape with hues of yellow and gold, gradually erasing the dark. The apex of the distant pyramids were wreathed in golden sunlight, the wash of which flowed down the stone as the sun rose higher in the sky. Their western slopes which face the endless desert remained darkened, almost black. The glory of those magnificent structures broke over him in grandeur.

This was the sight he had been waiting for. Every time he gazed at them he imagined the pyramids to be the glorious sentinels of antiquity marching off into the desert to join the gods. The pull of the tombs was exceptionally strong this morning, more so than ever before. Ever since he first looked in awe at these monuments he felt an unexplained affinity toward them. Were the pyramids sending a ghostly warning to him because he was about to delve deeper into this land's history? He dressed quickly. He was compelled to have a closer look at them.

The lobby was empty. He walked away hurriedly, turning onto the main road. The morning air was clear, not yet warm. The pyramids were part of a vastly larger complex sprawled across the Giza plateau. The way to the compound was up the road and across a narrow stretch of sand. The proximity of the necropolis to the modern road caused one to wonder if civilization was encroaching on the past, or if the past was actually embracing the present.

Loring sat on a low stone wall in front of the Pyramid of Cheops, the largest and oldest of the complex. His back was toward the sun which gradually rose above the distant skyline of Cairo. He allowed his gaze to fall on the stone face of the structure, studying it in awe. What stories these scarred and eroded stones could tell. Thousands of years have passed into oblivion since these monuments were anchored to the bedrock of the plateau. Uncounted millions of forgotten visitors have looked upon these masterpieces of architecture, unappreciative of the shear scope of the work.

In his mind he conjured up the voices of the thousands of laborers who toiled for twenty years so their pharaoh might rest in peace for all eternity. He envisioned the devout processions of priests performing the funerary rites for their dead king, themselves pledged to serving the pharaoh for the remainder of their lives.

Loring remembered the layout of the tombs. The inner chambers and passages that he had explored in the past were still fresh in his mind. Did the stone walls warn of the multitudes of invaders who changed the life of Egypt, making off with the smooth marble facades? Is that marble, whatever structures it now adorns, still rife with the souls of the pillaged pharaohs? Loring felt sad, reminded again of the havoc wrought by unthinking humanity.

A boisterous caravan of tour buses invaded the complex. Crowds of tourists, shouting in many languages, broke into the solitude of his reverie. It was time to leave. Loring walked back to the hotel, picking his way through the noisy clusters of the intruders. The emptiness he felt in his stomach came from more than sorrowful reflections. He was hungry.

There was a small dining room at the rear of the U-shaped hotel compound where early-rising guests gathered for breakfast. It was a convenient place for the tour buses to pick up hordes of camera-laden foreigners. Loring noticed, thankfully, that the buses had already departed to get an early start on the sun-baked day. He ordered toast and coffee.

A woman was sitting by the doors leading to the hotel garden. Loring could not help but notice her. She was one of the most striking women he had ever seen. She sensed his stare and turned toward him. He found himself gazing into those deep violet eyes he knew so well. Nadia...Carol Ashworth. She gave him a quick toss of her head, which he read as a warning not to recognize her. He took the warning, and continued with his breakfast.

He ordered more coffee as an excuse to linger near her. He had to see what she was up to, where she went when she left. As he sipped the heavy black coffee, he stole furtive glances at her. She was stunning in her sun dress pulled down off her shoulders, stretched over her full breasts. She wore a wide brimmed hat which concealed most of the mass of auburn hair and shaded her violet eyes.

She arose suddenly, paid her check and left the dining room without looking his way. She had done nothing to indicate she was even aware of his presence much less knowing him. Their meeting had to wait until she felt the time was right. He had to be patient, but it would be difficult. He ached for the nearness of her and the sound of her voice.

Loring leisurely finished his coffee. He wanted to give the impression he had nothing better to do. He casually signed for the check and wandered back to the hotel lobby, going through the garden. Now and then he stopped to admire a particular flower or shrub, glancing about to watch the others in the garden. He quickly entered the hotel.

He was crossing the lobby when the desk clerk hailed him. There was a cablegram. Would he pick it up or did he want it delivered to his suite? Puzzled, he walked over to the desk and signed for the cable, putting it in his pocket. Who would be sending him a cable so soon after his arrival? The only guesses he allowed himself were Crimmins or MacIvor. But MacIvor would have called if he had urgent information. It must be from Crimmins.

The cryptic message read:

> "Midland Bank is following your
> inquiry regarding the availability of
> Priory Farm for purchase. The
> terms do appear to be satisfactory.
> The yard and outbuildings will
> need your attention. Please advise.
> Merrick, Mgr."

The message was from Crimmins. The 'yard' needing attention was an obvious reference to Scotland Yard. There had to be something up, or else why would Crimmins use this round about method of getting in touch?

Loring was cautious enough not to make a call or send a cable from the hotel. During his walk to the pyramids, he had noticed a public phone where the road ended and the desert began. No doubt it was there for tourists to call for mobile transport after the grueling trek around the pyramid enclave. That pay phone was his best bet.

"Derek?" Merrick said. "Thank heavens you got back to me so fast. Crimmins found something important on the Thompson girl. The name you should be looking for is Salome Selim. She left Sidon for Cairo in July, 1886. The man she was to meet there was Amin Salazar. I haven't the foggiest idea how the inspector discovered this, but he said you should have this information. He says it's reliable."

"Thanks, Marc. Anything else I should know?"

"Yes, and it's not pleasant. There was another murder last night...MacIvor. He was killed in the identical manner as Tupps. I don't relish the idea of you taking up with people like that. Please be careful. Do you have anything I should report to Crimmins?"

"There's nothing as yet. I haven't been here that long. I'm being watched, however, and Nadia is here in her disguise, but I haven't made contact. I'm waiting for her to make the first move."

"I'll be sure to pass that on."

"One more thing...ask Crimmins to give me a name down here, someone we can trust, who can act as intermediary and bail me out if I get into any jams. I'll be careful, never fear. Give my love to Veronica."

Loring went back to the hotel after making the call, but instead of going to his rooms, he wandered into the gardens and found a bench in the shade near the swimming pool. It was not yet ten o'clock in the morning but the temperature was almost ninety degrees. A few fools were lounging by the pool, not realizing how treacherous the sun could be without the filtering effect of smog or cloud cover.

Loring gave considerable thought to what Marc told him. First Tupps, then MacIvor. Both killed in the same sadistic, ritualistic manner. Claridge must be running in circles, scared out of his wits, being the only one left in London, if he didn't consider Wells. Who was calling the shots? And how does he go about tracing the Thompson relative? He didn't have any training in this sort of thing. He would have to rely on Carol for this part of the puzzle. Perhaps she had a local MI 6 contact. Speaking of Carol, where in the hell was she?

His attention was suddenly drawn back to the pool. Two elderly women were now the only occupants at poolside. They had their heads together in earnest conversation, nodding in concert. One other woman was in the pool, swimming leisurely back and forth. She stopped suddenly, then threw up her arms and sank below the surface. When she came up, she thrashed wildly about, her arms flaying the water before she sank again. Loring heard the word 'help'. The woman was drowning! The elderly ladies stopped their chatter, their hands clasped over their mouths. Silently, they pointed to the struggling swimmer.

Loring could see there was no lifeguard on duty. He ran to the pool as quickly as he could, kicking off his sandals as he ran and jumped in after the girl. He reached her after a few strong strokes and grabbed her by the chin to get her head out of the water. He eased her to the side of the pool and placed her hands on the ledge. He turned toward her to lift her lithe body further out of the water and noticed the smile on her face.

"Make this look good, Derek. What better way for us to meet than let you save me from drowning? I'm a real damsel in distress."

Carol feigned helplessness, spitting, coughing and generally making a hysterical fuss. Loring pulled her from the pool, placed her down on the apron, and massaged her arms and hands, all the while bending toward her. Her deep violet eyes reflected her sense of accomplishment.

He gave her a sly wink and helped her to her feet. He walked her up and down the tiled apron a few times, then guided her to one of the nearby lounge chairs.

The two ladies came over to ask if she was all right. By this time there were several onlookers watching intently. The contact had been made. Who would now question their being together after so dramatic a meeting? Loring realized he was in love with a very clever woman.

He escorted Carol back to her room, playing out the pretense of being concerned for her condition along with the solicitous hotel staff. Once inside she fell into his waiting arms.

"Darling," she whispered between kisses, "I took a calculated risk you could swim. With my luck, one of the old ladies should have jumped in after me. Tell me, Derek, did you miss me?"

"More than you have any right to know, my darling. I was beside myself in the dining room this morning when you made signs to keep me away. Someone watching you?"

"I haven't noticed anyone in particular, but I feel eyes all over me. I didn't want to take a chance."

"We better make this quick. After all, I'm just being considerate in returning you to your room, not spending the afternoon here. Meet me at the pool bar in an hour. We can talk then. God, it's good to see you."

They occupied a table in the shade at the bar adjacent to the pool. If anyone was watching them, they appeared to be merely new friends having a drink together. They sat apart, very decorous, in spite of their private wishes. Loring told her all that had happened since they were together in London. She was silent until he told her about his strange conversation with Ron Menefee on the drive to Priory Farm.

"I met Menefee when he brought my passport. I thought him a little strange. Have you any idea what he meant by looking for a wall at Amarna?"

"I've been thinking about that. When I was at the museum checking on Zoser's data, I came across a papyrus plan of the city. It did indicate a wall of sorts leading from the temple to the river. I'll do some additional research here in Cairo. I know the curator."

Carol smiled, "My goodness, you've been busy, haven't you?"

"Hell, ma'am, I sure do try. But seriously, Carol, there's more."

Loring told her about the cable he received from Marc and his return phone call along with his theory that with Tupps and MacIvor out of the picture, Wells had to be in charge.

Carol interrupted his account. "Derek, that man who's sitting across the terrace, at the last table. I've noticed him before. He was in the coffee shop this morning. And I've seen him in the hotel lobby."

"I'd best go and see what's on his mind. You stay put."

"Be careful, Derek." Then as Loring got up, she said, "He's leaving, and in a hurry, too. Never mind...let it go for now."

"Okay, but at least we know one who's watching. Are you sure he's not just trying to pick you up? I would, if I was in his place."

"Don't be cute, Derek. This is serious."

"You're right, of course. Now, to continue my list of activities."

When he finished telling her about his talk with Yamani, and his search for microphones in his suite, he asked what she had been doing.

"Not much. Basically I've been trying to get a work

permit." she said. "I'll need one if I'm to help you. The Ministry of Industry wasn't too encouraging when I talked with them yesterday."

"Yamani might be our best bet to get you cleared with the authorities. I'll ask him."

"Thanks." Carol then added, "So, MacIvor went and got himself buggered. You're right when you say Claridge must be wetting his pants. Think he'll bolt?"

"It's hard to say. Someone's net is closing in on Zoser, and they all know it."

"Now," she said, "about the Thompson followup...I might have the answer. I have a friend here with MI 6 who owes me a favor...Peter Bradshaw. He's the good old solid reliable type. A few years ago I warned him about something which probably saved his career. He claims to be in my eternal debt."

"Can you trust him?"

"We'll see. I'll ask him to pull some strings to trace both Selim and Salazar. For the time being, I think it best to tell him I've left the service. That way he can do it as a friend."

"You know best, but be damned careful."

"Trust me, I shall. This Yamani sounds weird, though. Let's keep as far away from him as possible. He probably has a harem of young men for himself. I know the type...Istanbul was full of them."

"How do you know?"

"I was there, remember. It was common knowledge."

"You're suspicious of everyone, aren't you?"

"Damn right I am. I'll come to your suite later today. We'll talk about the job you're offering me as a translator. Go into details about the job, and what you expect me to do so I can have time to look for bugs. That's one useful skill MI 6 taught me."

"Good. I'll feel better with you checking my rooms. I probably missed something."

"Darling, buy me another drink, while I just sit here and look at you."

"All right, but let's not take too long. We've work to do."

"You're a party-pooper, Derek Loring. I'll forget the drink. Let's go."

"See you later in my room. I'm going to check the desk for messages."

Carol came to his suite about four o'clock. He let her in, remarking in a loud, clear voice, "Ah, Miss Ashworth. So good of you to be so prompt."

"Mr. Loring. Yes, I make an effort to be on time. I'm quite interested in what you were saying earlier about the position. Please tell me more about what you'd expect me to do."

She began her search immediately. She looked in all the places he had, but she went about it in a more systematic way. He continued talking about her credentials and about the research he was to do in the Amarna region up the Nile. Carol signaled him to keep it up while she interjected comments from time to time. Her search continued, but she was unable to uncover anything out of the ordinary. Shaking her head, she came back to the center of the room, questions still mirrored in her eyes.

"I think the arrangements will be quite satisfactory, Mr. Loring. The money is more than I expected. If you think I'm up to doing the required work, I'll be more than happy to begin whenever you say."

"Yes, Miss Ashworth, I'm convinced you'll be of great help to me. It must have been fate that sent me to the pool this morning. Why don't we meet for dinner this evening. We can discuss what preparations you'll need to make."

They left the suite together. "That was jolly quick thinking on your part, Derek, getting us out of there."

"Did you find anything?"

"There aren't any bugs that I could find. That doesn't mean they're not there. These people are smart. We'll stay clear of your room when we have to talk. I did notice one thing, however. Over the head of the beds, there are air grilles on the wall. You're the great architect...isn't that an unusual place to put air ducts?"

"Not necessarily, Sherlock. They should be nothing more than exhaust air ducts. I'll check it out when I get back. That would be a great spot to plant a microphone, but there might be a lot of interference from the flow of air. Unless, of course, it is just a dummy duct."

"You will investigate it, won't you?"

"What do you think?"

He left her at the door of her room and returned to his suite. He began to check the air duct. It didn't appear to be out of the ordinary, just the normal return air duct he saw during the night. However, not to assume anything, he decided to explore the inside of the ductwork.

Loring took a small utility tool kit out of his suitcase and chose a tiny screwdriver to unfasten the grilles that covered the duct opening. When he removed the grille over his bed he found a miniature microphone attached to the duct lining. He repeated the search in the living room and the other bedroom and made the same discovery. Only the bathrooms were free of microphones. He left the bugs in place, then refastened the grilles. No point in alerting the eavesdroppers. He felt that Carol would agree.

They had dinner in the main dining room of the hotel. Loring found the Egyptian-modern design of the place to be garish and offensive, but their meal was excellent...and expensive. They played the roles of employer/employee very convincingly, as they laid their plans for the next day. Loring told her about finding the microphones and what he did about them.

"You were right...best we keep them in the dark."

Carol was to make contact with Peter Bradshaw outside his office, since he was their best bet to unravel the missing parts of the Thompson puzzle. Bradshaw could call in his sources without alerting the wrong people. She'd still pretend to be out of MI 6.

Loring had the job of getting them outfitted for their exploration of the Tell El Amarna ruins with the right kind of clothes and tools needed for the hard digging they would be doing.

"So in spite of your warnings, my worry wart, I think it best to get in touch with Yamani for help in gathering the supplies. For me to contact him for the needed things would be the most natural thing to do. He knows who to go to, what to pay and what to expect. We also need that work permit for you."

"You're probably right in that, Derek. Just keep him away from me. The more I think about it, the less I trust him. Just to satisfy my own sense of curiosity, I'm going to get Peter to check the creep out. Who knows, perhaps we can get something on him, something we can use later if he becomes difficult."

"Do it, if you think it wise. Tomorrow, while Yamani gathers up all the equipment we'll need, I'm going to the archives at the Egyptian Museum. I need to do some more research on Amarna, and the mystery of Akhenaten. The data here should be more complete than what I found in

England. Now, have we worked everything out?"

"I think so," Carol said. "I'll get to Peter while you massage creepy Yamani. I might just do a bit of shopping myself for a proper desert wardrobe. Now, let's get out of here and take a walk in that gorgeous moonlight."

The door to Carol's room was barely closed and latched when they fell into each other's arms. Their kisses were wild with abandon, alive with desire and passion. Her ardor was as intense as his. She tilted back her head slightly to look into his eyes. She smiled and softly murmured, "I told you in London that someday I might beg you to make love to me. Darling, I'm begging you now. Take me!"

Loring lifted her gently and carried her to the bed. He lay beside her and kissed her again. Carol pulled his waiting body to her and groaned with happiness as passion flowed over and around them both. Their love for each other consumed them at last.

Finally, they lay still, totally spent. "My God, Derek, is this love or lust?"

"It has to be love, my darling. Lust could never be this wonderful. By the way, did I tell you how much I love you?"

They were quiet then, their breathing calm. Soon the sounds of their slumber mingled with the night whisperings coming off the desert. The moon fled behind a solitary wisp of cloud, bidding them a quiet goodnight.

The green telephone buzzed in the remote office of the American Embassy. The man known as Soloman flicked on the recorder.

"Yes?"

"Is Mr. Clean finished?"

"Yes, we're sterile."

"Caine?"

"No, this is Soloman."

"I see. What about Loring?"

"We still have him covered. He met the Ashworth woman today. Fished her out of the swimming pool. Now they appear very, very chummy. Think she's the one?"

"Could be. I'll check her out from this end. The Brits could have changed personnel. Something might have happened to Shepherd. How're things over there?"

"Not as quiet as I would like. The religious fanatics are stepping up their incidents. It might get sticky."

"What's Mubarak doing?"

"The President is worried. He isn't strong enough yet to face the religious fights. Say what you will, he's no Sadat."

"Nobody said he was. Any squeals from the other Arabs?"

"No, they're staying to themselves, at least we think they're staying home. There's been no indication of anything from that quarter."

"Okay. I'll call tomorrow, same time."

When Soloman hung up the phone and turned off the recorder, there was a quiet knock on the office door. He opened it and a man entered. It was Caine.

"How did it go?" Soloman asked.

"Ashworth fingered me, pointed me out to Loring."

"Guess I'll have to take over now. How'd she spot you?"

"I can't figure it. I was damned careful, too. She's got to be with the Brits. No amateur could have spotted me."

"Well, some good came out of it. We have them both and they're together."

"Did you get the call?"

"Yeah, just before you came in."

"What say we go out and get bombed? I'm fed up."

"Sounds good to me. Where do we go?"

"Someplace wild and noisy. I'll buy."

Chapter 9

When Loring called the Zoser office, Yamani himself answered. Loring quickly got around to the reason for his call.

"I hate like hell to impose on you with such short notice, Mr. Yamani, but there're a lot of things I need in the way of equipment before I go off into the desert. I'm not that familiar with Cairo to do it myself. I thought you might help to get me what I need."

"I shall be only too happy to be of service to you, *effendi*, whether it be a great or small accommodation. I have been instructed to offer you any and every assistance. Now, tell me, my friend, what is it you wish, and how soon do you want it?"

Loring read off the list of equipment he and Carol had prepared, including a hunting rifle and a Land Rover with extra fuel tanks. They planned to pick up their food along the way to augment what they would get in Cairo. Yamani asked a few questions pertaining to types and sizes, then promised everything would be delivered to the hotel later in the day. He tendered a wish for the success of the exploration.

"Keep an accurate tally of these things, Mr. Yamani. I'll pay for them out of my expense account."

"Do not worry yourself over such matters, Mr. Loring. I told you my orders are to get whatever you need. As I said before, I am at your service, no matter how large or small."

"There's one other thing, Yamani. I've hired a woman to do translations for me. She needs an official work permit. Her name's Carol Ashworth, a Canadian citizen."

"It shall be taken care of."

Loring hurried from the hotel and hailed a cab. He went to the Egyptian Museum in Tahrir Square. Dr. Imin Nashtoi, the curator, greeted Loring with genuine warmth and, after the usual polite inquiries about health and family, Loring divulged the reason for his visit. He said he needed to clarify some data and he asked Nashtoi if the museum had any recent information in its archives dealing with Amarna. Nashtoi appeared surprised at Loring's request.

"There was someone else here asking for the same thing about a year ago, as I recall. The man's name was MacIvor. I did not like him...he was too pushy and bossy. I refused to show him anything. Now, you arrive here and ask to see the same material. Do you not think that strange?"

"Perhaps, Doctor."

"And perhaps not. Regardless, I know you, Dr. Loring. You are a dedicated scholar who appreciates culture as well. That is much more than I can say for most of the people who come here. Yes, there are some things you might find of interest to your research. Come with me, please."

He escorted Loring to the basement and the archive section of the museum. He took him to the vaults which housed the more valuable parts of the collection. Pointing to one of the vault chambers, he said, "This is what I think you might be looking for. You read the hieratic text, do you not?"

"To some extent. Not as well as I should like, but enough to get by."

"Then I shall leave you alone to your endeavors. If you discover anything that puzzles you, call me. You may use the phone over there on the wall."

The curator left Loring alone among the shelves and boxes full of artifacts pertaining to El Amarna. He unrolled the scrolls of papyrus attributed to the time period of 1355 BC. Loring found eight scrolls in all, dated from 1354 to 1357 BC. The hieratic writing, a form of shorthand the scribes used to put information down rapidly to be transcribed into formal hieroglyphics later, was difficult for him to read. This was what he needed Carol's expertise for.

Loring continued to delve into the dusty, fragile rolls of papyrus. He uncovered one scroll in particular which gave him hope. It was written in 1355 or 56, its exact date wasn't too clear. The scroll described the departure of the king from Akhetaten, the original name of the city which was translated later in history as Amarna.

The text he read stated that the gods from the old days were rising against Aten, but Aten would defeat those ancient gods with help from a chosen few who had risen from beyond Kemet at the beginning of time. Aten would be able to look back from his final resting place and gaze at the names of these faithful few, recorded for all eternity. The scribe who wrote this signed the scroll boldly. His name was Nephgeton.

Using a pocket notebook he always carried with him, Loring copied the text exactly as it was written. He had to show it to Carol to see if his translation was correct. He then made a second copy on a separate page of the pad as insurance. Finally, he closed up the vault, and returned to the office of Dr. Nashtoi. There were some questions he wanted to pose to the Egyptian.

The elderly scholar indicated a chair for Loring, then

settled back, waiting for him to begin.

"Dr. Nashtoi, what is your honest impression of Pharaoh Akhenaten? What do you think he was like?"

"I have always believed he was an enlightened ruler who came on the stage of history far too soon. Kemet, as Egypt was called in those days, was not ready for him, any more than was the rest of the civilized world." A quixotic smile crossed the old man's face.

"How about Nefertiti?"

"Ah, now, she was something. She was intelligent as well as extremely beautiful. The wives or consorts of the rulers were not noted for their brains in those days. She was an exception, however. You are familiar with the theory that Nefertiti ruled as co-regent with Akhenaten. I believe there may be more than a little truth to that theory. She was a strong woman, able to read and write, which was itself very unusual. It would be a very natural thing for Akhenaten to have her help him."

"Why did Akhenaten have so much trouble with the high priests? How did they gain enough power to interfere with the king? I always thought they were supposed to do the bidding of the pharaoh, since he was considered to be divine."

"Let me answer that by drawing you an analogy. Suppose your president, a staunch Republican, had a solid Democratic Congress. Suppose, also, that the president wanted to alter or eliminate the Social Security Act which Franklin Roosevelt established. Could he do it?"

"Hell no! The Congress would fight him every step of the way and vote down any change the President proposed. The people would scream bloody hell and threaten revolt. Oh, I get the picture. Akhenaten was pushing for a complete change in the religious thinking which had been thousands of years in the making. The high priests were like Congress. They naturally felt threatened and fought against the change. But weren't the people, the common man, shut off from formal religion?"

"In a way, yes. But remember, they had to depend on the pharaoh for their livelihood. What affected him, affected them."

"What do you think really happened to him, to Akhenaten? How did he die?"

"The priests had him assassinated. They told everyone he died from a sickness and even staged a grand state funeral for him. But they buried an empty sarcophagus. I believe they allowed Nefertiti to rule for the sake of appearance, but in the end they killed her. She would have been just as dedicated as Akhenaten was."

"And King Tut?"

"Tutankhamen, her son-in-law, ruled for a short time after they killed Nefertiti. The younger generation of today have an apt term that could be applied to Tut. He was a wimp."

"Were Akhenaten and Nefertiti alone? Weren't there some others who were close enough to the throne to ward off the coup, some who thought as they did?"

"Yes, there was a clique who tried to stop the priests. This group referred to themselves as the Menefee. The old legends of the desert say they originated during the reign of King Menes. They resorted to all manner of tricks and subterfuge to thwart the efforts of the priests.

However, by trumped-up charges, the Menefee were finally outlawed from Amarna and it was shortly after this that Akhenaten was killed. The Menefee disappeared from the pages of our history, and we do not know what happened to them. Most likely they drifted back into the desert from where the legends said they came. In any event, we can find no reference to them after the death of Akhenaten."

"What is the truth about the belief that Nefertiti was put away from the court, made to stay in the Queen's palace for three years?"

"More of the false propaganda seminated by the followers of the priests. Nefertiti remained at Akhenaten's side right up to the end, until he was killed. The priests could not let her live after they killed the pharaoh because she knew too much about what really happened. They allowed her to rule for a brief time, but did not permit any contact with the world beyond Amarna. They could not take a chance of her gaining strong support from their old enemies."

"Doctor, you've no idea how much this information will help me in my research. I've always felt that Akhenaten got a raw deal when his city was destroyed and his name vilified. Now with someone of your reputation to back up my theories, I think I can make progress. Do you mind if I quote you now and then?"

"No, I am happy to be of some service. Please call on me whenever you feel the need. I will always take time for you, Mr. Loring. *Ma'assalama.*"

Carol was in her room when he returned to the hotel. She let him in, saying, "Derek, this is Peter Bradshaw. He just arrived with tidbits of information we might be able to use. I was fixing drinks when you knocked. Want one?"

"Yes, I could use a drink. Glad to meet you, Bradshaw."

Loring wasn't about to like Peter Bradshaw. He was an Oxford man, through and through, even sporting the old school tie. He appeared typically British upper class.

"Let's sit, shall we?" Bradshaw ordered, his words clipped. "When you asked me to look up those old records,

Nadia, regarding people I never heard of, I thought your were around the bend. And what is this Carol Ashworth business? You told me you were well out of the Agency, so why the name change?"

"It's a long story, Peter. I'll tell you about it someday, but for the time being, I'm Carol Ashworth. Let's leave it at that, shall we? Now, what did you find?"

"This is what I found, and I'm not too sure I like it. The Selim woman registered with immigration in July, 1886. She gave her address as some hovel in the old city, in the cemetery. Do you know people actually live in the cemetery, even today? Well, no matter. We have a copy of the recorded marriage certificate dated September, 1886, between Salome Selim and Amin Salazar, stone cutter."

"You're sure of the date?" Loring asked.

"How can one be sure of anything in this bloody country? I'm just telling you what I found."

"Sorry, Bradshaw. Please go on."

"Well, there's nothing in the records for the next few years, but in January, 1907, there was a police report filed. It concerned a murder in a place called El Dab'a, a small fishing village this side of Matruh on the seacoast. It seems our Mr. Salazar was found dead one morning, and his wife and kids nowhere to be found. This wouldn't normally be an item for the Cairo records except for the method of death. Salazar was killed ritualistically."

"Ritualistically killed?"

"I should say so. Throat cut from stem to stern, and a dagger left in his chest. The body was painted in all sorts of weird colors and designs. They never found a trace of the killers or the rest of the family. The file is in limbo as far as the authorities are concerned...not active, but not closed either. Afraid that's all I could muster up, old thing."

"That's a hell of a lot more than we expected to get,

Peter. Thanks loads. How about another drink to get the dust out of your mouth?"

"Thanks, old girl, but no. I have an appointment and I'm late as it is. Perhaps another time. Glad to have met you, Loring. Take care of our girl here. Your work doesn't sound like historical research to me, but to each his own. Ta ta."

"I'm glad he couldn't stay. I want to talk with you alone. Besides, I don't like him," Derek pouted.

"Darling, you're jealous. I like that. It shows you care. Don't concern yourself with Peter. He's gay."

"That's a relief. I like your Peter Bradshaw better."

"I thought that might make a difference. Come over here and kiss me, right now."

Later, Loring told her about his find in the museum archives. He took out his notebook and showed her the copies of the scroll he made. As she studied it, he recounted his discussion with Nashtoi. When he finished, he asked, "What do you make of it?"

"Your translation is pretty accurate. You might not need me after all if you're this good with the hieratic script. Anyway, this scribe, Nephgeton, left us a clue. At least, I think it's a clue. Do you see this little squiggle here? If you copied it exactly, it shows a mark that was a less common abbreviation for the word 'wall' or 'pylon'. The way I would read it would be that Aten could look back toward the wall from his final resting place, and so on."

"I'm sure I copied it right. Both copies are the same, as you can see. I'm usually very careful with this kind of work. This is how I would interpret the legend. Aten was the sun disc, the new deity of Akhenaten. Every night he would rest in the western desert when the sun sets. If Aten looked back, he could see Amarna to the east across the Nile. The 'wall' must mean that there was a wall or pylon in Amarna where the names of the faithful, the Menefee, were recorded. When the sun sets in the west, it shines on that wall. That's the wall we have to find, if there's anything left of it."

"That has to be it. It's the list of the Menefee we're looking for," Carol added.

"By the way, what do you make of that mysterious brother-in-law of Crimmins? His name, Menefee, is unusual for today's Egyptians. Do you think there might be a connection to the old cult? The name, plus the fact he came from that village of El Dab'a, makes it all too coincidental for my money."

"Derek, the name, by itself, may mean nothing. You said Dr. Nashtoi told you this Menefee group was thought to be named for King Menes. It's a common practice, all over the world, to acquire the namesakes of prominent leaders. It doesn't mean they're all related. However, that village of Dab'a has to mean something in this puzzle. I say we check out this place, El Dab'a or whatever, and get on to Amarna when we can. We can't afford to overlook anything. Now, have you finished your shopping?"

"Yep, it's all down stairs, as promised. Yamani was most helpful. He even got you a work permit. How about you? What are you going to wear?"

"Don't you worry about that. I know we aren't going to tea at Balmoral Castle, so do trust my good judgement. When do you plan on leaving?"

"As early as possible, about four-thirty in the morning. We can get to El Dab'a by first light."

"Derek, dear, that's an obscene hour to do anything. But, if you insist, there isn't much point in us going to bed...to sleep, that is."

The morning sun was rising behind them as they passed through the town of El Alamein, the scene of vicious fighting in World War II. Visions of Rommel and Montgomery flashed before their eyes, armadas of ugly tanks spitting death at each other and the screams of the wounded underlying it all. The dirty desert town by the blue Mediterranean still wore the gashes and wounds of the battle fought so many years ago.

Good men on each side gave up so much, sacrificed their blood on the altar of war and really never fully understood why they had to fight and die. Just traveling through that town cast a gloomy shadow on what otherwise had been a delightful ride.

"Makes one stop and think, doesn't it, Carol? This remote town, with nothing at all to recommend it, has been immortalized because of the brutality of man. Now that I've seen it, I wonder why I ever thought it would be romantic to visit such battle sites."

"Don't be so morbid, dear. Your work takes you to places where battles have been fought at one time or another. I don't look upon them as being particularly romantic, but I do understand their significance to man's history. Derek, I'm somewhat surprised at your attitude. What is there about El Alamein that brings out such cynicism?"

"I can't really define it. Maybe it's just because this place got such big press coverage. It was blown way out of proportion. Perhaps if they had newspapers back then, the Greek and Roman battle fields would be just as distasteful to me. Don't mind me...I'm just a bit ashamed of our civilization, that's all."

"How much further to El Dab'a?"

"A couple more miles, if this map is right. Wonder what we'll find there."

"Probably more of the same," Carol muttered.

The village of El Dab'a was indeed as windblown and dirty as all the other coastal villages they passed through. It was stretching a point by calling the place a village. It was nothing but a crude settlement made up of several hovels built haphazardly from mud brick and scattered around in no logical pattern. Dust was everywhere, filling the body pores rapidly as the wind whipped the superfine sand in every direction. All the roads, or dusty trails, emanated from the squalid harbor where a few dhows swung at anchor. They both wondered if the hour was too early for the inhabitants. There was not a soul in sight.

Loring turned the Land Rover toward the harbor, hoping to find some evidence of life nearer the water. He braked at the water's edge and as they got out of the truck, Carol noticed a man squatting on the single dilapidated pier. He was gazing out to sea. They approached the old man and tried to start up a conversation. Carol spoke in Arabic which the old man apparently understood. When she asked where the other people of the town were, he turned toward them and shrugged his bony shoulders, saying sadly,

"All are in their homes, waiting for the desert wind to stop. It will do them no good for the sand finds them wherever they hide. The desert is taking back this place. Soon there will be no Dab'a. What we shall do then, only Allah knows."

The man turned back to the sea, continuing to stare, the sadness in his eyes deepened as the sun rose higher in the sky and the wind whipped the sand and dust about. Derek had Carol ask him if he had lived there long. His answer, forced through lips already caked with grime, was short.

"Yes, all my days have been spent here."

"Why don't you leave...go somewhere else where the wind doesn't take your home?"

"The wind is everywhere. One cannot escape one's destiny."

Taking a chance, Loring asked, "Did the wind take away Amin Salazar, many years ago."

"It was not the wind then. It was something even worse for the people of El Dab'a."

"What was that? Will you tell us?"

"I am old, but I am not a fool. What do you know of the old ones? You speak our language but you are not one of us. There is no advantage to tell you of our past. Some of the braver ones have left here, escaping the wrath of the wind and the old ones, but they are never heard from again."

"Have you heard from Menefee?"

The old man sucked in his breath, turning toward Derek and Carol with a look of absolute terror. They thought he was about to have a seizure, trembling as he was. With a quick furtive glance over his shoulder, he muttered.

"The Menefee are not to be spoken of within the limits of El Dab'a. The old ones have eyes and ears everywhere. Look to yourselves, strangers, for the wrath of the past will descend upon you if you utter the name here. I have lived my years and do not fear death, but the others might send out word about your interference. Leave it alone. Leave this place to the sand and the wind."

"How many people live here in Dab'a?" Carol asked.

"There are but seventy-five people left within these walls. All the others have departed. Soon there will be only the sand and the wind. I was here when the great war was fought. The armies trampled our land into the dust you see and, even though the armies left, the dust remained. And the wind. It is said that we pay the price now for the sins of our fathers' fathers and their fathers before them.

They gave sanctuary to the Menefee in times long past. In truth, we are paying the price. There is no future for us, no matter where we go."

"What is your name, old man? What is it you are called?"

"I am called Mustapha. Everyone knows Mustapha."

Carol and Derek got back into their truck. It was obvious they would get no more information from the old man. When they were leaving the harbor area, they looked back and saw the man again staring out to sea, waiting for...what? As they drove through the town, they could see hostile eyes following their progress, peering at them from behind shuttered slits in the mud walls. No one was in the streets. They were as deserted as when Loring and Carol first entered El Dab'a.

"Derek, how dreadful to be compelled to exist under these conditions. How do they stand it?"

"I don't think they know a different way of life. From what I can see, they've been this way from time immemorial. Take that old man, Mustapha, for example. He's trapped in the ways of the past and he refuses to take whatever steps are necessary to change. I don't think he's content at all. He is just resigned to his fate, as he sees it.

"We learned one thing, though. The Menefee were here some time in the past, and the old ones, whoever they were, traced them and punished the entire village for harboring them. The idea that keeps gnawing at me is that these old ones were the high priests who chased the Menefee out of Amarna. If that's the case, where are they now, the Menefee and the old ones?"

"If the old man is to believed," Carol said, "the old ones are still around, someplace. Did you notice the fear in Mustapha's eyes when he was warning us? I think we better get to Amarna as soon as possible and find the list of the Menefee, then try to discover what happened to them. I think that list is what Zoser wants, regardless of what cock and bull story they fed you. If we find it, are you going to turn it over to them?"

"I don't know, yet. There's still too many unknowns to wrestle with to give you an honest answer. Let's find the list first, before we decide what to do with it."

"We might as well turn this truck around. We aren't going to find anything different on this road."

"I'll go along with that idea. All this desolation gives me the creeps. Let's head for Amarna."

Loring turned the Land Rover around before they got to Fuka. The roofs of the village huts were visible over the rise in the road, but neither of them had an appetite for more wind and sand. One disturbing thought was that they never saw a living soul since they left El Alamein, except for Mustapha. As they approached the outskirts of El Dab'a, the sight that greeted them was vastly different than before. Now there were thirty or more villagers milling about in the street, waving their arms wildly, fists clenched. When the crowd spotted Loring and Carol it surged forward, encircling the truck. Carol grabbed Loring's arm.

"Derek, what the hell are they shouting about? I can't quite make it out. Wait...I can understand some of what they're saying. They're calling us murderers!"

"Murderers?" Loring shouted. "They must be out of their minds. Who're we accused of killing?"

Carol stood up in the truck, motioning for quiet, then shouting, "What do you want from us? We haven't done anything to you. Let us through."

From out of the crowd an aged crone shuffled forward, pointing her bony finger at them. In a voice cracking with anger and fear, she croaked, "You are the ones who brought them back to continue their vengeance. Go back and tell the old ones we have had enough. We are all leaving this miserable village, leaving it to them for their legacy."

Carol hollered back, her own voice steeped in fury at the foolishness displayed by these people.

"We don't know what you're talking about. We're merely driving through your village to gather information for a book. We know nothing of these old ones you speak of, and do not wish to know. They are of no concern to us. Now, get out of the way and let us pass."

Most of the crowd stepped out of the road, but the old woman held her ground. As though possessed, she shouted to Derek and Carol.

"Go, but know you this. Look at what you have done. Observe! Look!" She pointed her bony finger to the side of the road, her entire body shaking with her anger. "Look well, then be gone! May Allah turn His face from you."

The blowing dirt and dust had not quite covered the contorted body of old Mustapha. He lay, half on his back, his face uncovered enough to show his eyes staring into nothingness. Blackish blood mingled with the dust of the road and flies swarmed over the corpse. Mustapha's throat had been cut from ear to ear, and a curved dagger was still quivering in his gaunt chest. Derek pulled Carol down into her seat, gunned the engine of the truck, and roared away toward the east and civilization.

"You what?"

"We lost both of them, Loring and the woman." The man called Caine whispered into the green telephone. "It isn't our fault, God damn it! They had dinner together, went back to her room for a while, then Loring went back to his suite. Our man stayed with him the entire evening. This morning, they were both gone."

"Did either of them check out?"

"No."

"Then maybe they went for some sightseeing and will be back later."

"I don't think so. Loring had a truck full of supplies parked at the hotel. It's gone, as well. They took off for someplace and we don't know where."

"The Chief will have you for breakfast, and me for dessert. You better find them, and fast. How about checking with the limeys?"

"No good. Bradshaw won't talk to us. Can't figure what he is up to. We're stymied for now."

"Get it unstymied, if you know what's good for you. Any leads at all?"

"Just one. The Ashworth broad had some local go to bat for her and she got her work permit approved. Some of the equipment Loring gathered together had to do with camping. I think they went exploring out in the boondocks. That's a very big desert, my friend."

"Don't call me friend. My name is Morgan, and don't you forget it. I'll call back tomorrow and you better have some answers."

The green phone went dead. Caine shrugged his shoulders and left the remote office in the American Embassy, muttering to himself,

"These goddamned amateurs. Get you in trouble every time."

Chapter 10

Loring didn't slow the truck until they were nearly into El Alamein. Behind them, billowing clouds of desert sand and road dust soared upward to coalesce into an opaque curtain blotting out the horror of El Dab'a. His hands were wet with sweat, the moisture tracing rivulets through the dusty grime clinging to his arms. He knew better, but Loring still harbored a dread of their being followed by some part of the demonic crowd at El Dab'a.

From out of the corner of his eye, Loring glanced at Carol. Her face was white with terror in spite of the ochre-colored dust which covered her. He saw the trembling of her hands as she gripped the dashboard, the knuckles as white as her face. Her whole body twitched as she turned to Loring, her eyes pleading for control.

She motioned for him to stop the truck, pointing to the side of the road. Loring sighted a stand of almond trees up ahead, a good place to stop and gather their wits. The past several miles had been a nightmare. He eased the Rover to a stop. They left the dirt-caked truck and strolled in the shade of the solitary trees, a shade which shimmered in cadence with the swaying branches. Carol was holding onto his arm.

"Oh my God, Derek," she cried, "what do you think happened back there? That poor old man...I can still see him lying in the road with the knife in his chest. And those flies, those goddamned flies. Oh, Derek, I think I'm going to be sick."

"Easy, Carol. Take deep breaths...it's over now."

"Is it...really? Isn't this just the beginning of an awful time for us in Egypt?"

"I wish I knew." Loring glanced out to the blue waters of the Mediterranean. He repeated, "Oh, how I wish I knew."

Her trembling abated slightly as he put his arms around her. "It's obvious we were seen talking with Mustapha, Carol. Someone must have thought he told us about what goes on in that place. He warned us it was dangerous, that the old ones have ways of finding out."

"But why blame us? Those eyes we saw watching us when we left could see the old man was alive. We couldn't have killed him."

"Those people don't know what to believe. They've probably lived with fear so long they'd believe anything. I could almost taste that fear and smell that hatred in the air. Evidently someone wanted Mustapha silenced for good."

"Where does that leave us? Oh, Derek, I'm afraid. What if they contact the police, or whoever handles these things? They could claim we actually killed him."

"I don't think they will, even if they dared. They're all too frightened. I believe a few will just leave and the others who stay will cover it up." Loring held her a bit closer.

Carol ventured another thought. "Do you suppose we've stumbled into an up-dated version of the old fight between the high priests and the Menefee? Was Sadat's assassination a part of all this? If so, we might expect more political murders down the line. Damn! I feel so helpless."

"All the cards haven't been dealt yet, Carol. The more we dig into this, the more we should be able to understand. The important thing for us now is to get down to Amarna fast and find the list of the old Menefee...if that's what it actually is. If we find it, and if we turn it over to Zoser, we might get a clearer picture of what is going on. Granted, that's a lot of 'ifs', but I think it's the only thing we can do right now."

"If you say so, oh mighty leader." Carol feigned a weak smile. Then, "Let's get on with it, and the devil take the hindmost."

"I haven't heard that expression since I was a kid. Where'd you dig it up?"

"Well, you finally found me out. I'm really an old-fashioned girl at heart who clings to the old ways. So let that be a warning to you, lover boy. Who knows what I might want from you in the future?"

"Stick with me, sweetheart, and you'll have anything you want. Ready now? Let's be on our way. Amarna, here we come!"

It was just after eight when they turned south to skirt Alexandria. They took the highway on the west side of the Nile because the east bank road turned off to the Gulf of Suez at Beni Suef, some seventy-five miles south of Cairo. There was no east-bank road from there to Amarna. They planned to cross over to the east bank by ferry from the town of Dairut, which was almost directly opposite Tell El Amarna.

They stopped for breakfast in El Aiyat, a small village below Saqqara. Loring didn't think there would be anything resembling a restaurant, but reason told him there had to be some place they could find food. It was an inn, of sorts where they stopped. Much to their pleasant surprise, they were invited to eat with the innkeeper and his family.

The family was a warm, friendly bunch, all stares and giggles. The conversation was carried on in a mixture of

Arabic, French and English with Carol doing most of the talking. Her grasp of the languages was much better than Loring's. The wife insisted they have more of the goat stew, heaping it on their plates, and commenting that the stew was their main diet. The children, two of them, could not take their wide brown eyes away from the camera Loring had slung around his neck. It was easy to see that they wanted him to take their picture. He herded the young-sters outside amidst their whoops of glee, while Carol re-mained at the table with the parents, who were only inter-ested in whether President Carter was coming back to Egypt. It was difficult to tell them Carter was no longer the president, that President Reagan now ran the country. These Egyptians had no idea who Reagan was; Carter would always represent the United States to them.

Carol and Loring promised to stop by again when they returned from their work. Amid low bows and fervent handshakes, they took their leave. The innkeeper would accept nothing in the way of payment for his family's hos-pitality. Instead he thanked Loring and Carol for stopping and seemed to sincerely mean it.

In Dairut they located an open market where they stocked up on non-perishable food, local beer and home-made bread. They now had supplies for a week in the desert and, although they had some bottled water they brought from the Mena House, they purchased more from the market. Water was very precious in the desert, often being the difference between life and death, and no for-eigner could drink the water of the Nile for fear of the dreaded Pharaoh's Revenge.

Their ferry was not scheduled to depart for another two hours. That meant they couldn't expect to be in Amarna until the afternoon, late, but they'd still have enough day-light to make camp before dark. To wile away time, they sat in a dockside cafe drinking local beer and watching the town people going about their business.

"I would give anything for a cup of coffee," Loring muttered in his beer.

He no sooner said that when the cafe waiter eagerly brought him a steaming cup of black coffee, it's aroma drifting around him like a heaven-sent zephyr.

"My friend, you have probably saved my life." Loring took a gulp, almost burning his mouth in the process.

"It's American...Maxwell House. Someone left it here last week. Is it satisfactory, sir?"

"Most satisfactory, *effendi*. The nectar of the gods."

"My love," Carol cajoled, "if you would break yourself of that awful coffee habit you'd probably get along better in foreign lands." She was laughing at him.

"Carol, when all this is over, I'm taking you back to my islands where all you will do from morning till night is make me coffee. What do you think of that?"

She stopped laughing, suddenly becoming serious. With a wistful sigh, she murmured, "Derek, I doubt I'll ever get to see those islands of yours."

"Don't be silly. Of course you will...with me. Now, no more of that morbid talk." Why such a change in Carol's mood?

Tell El Amarna was less than five miles from the river landing, yet the drive north took well over an hour. The road was not a road, but simply a cleared path between the higher sand dunes. Drifting sand had blown across the way, filling the ruts and holes, and no attempt was made to keep the road cleared. It took all of Loring's concentration to keep the Land Rover on course and out of the dunes.

With each mile they drove, the landscape became more desolate, more barren. The heat was heavily oppressive to the point of being almost intolerable. And the sand was never-ending. The only encouraging sight was that of the majestic Nile off to their left, forever flowing north. The sole evidence of their arrival at the abandoned site was a weatherbeaten wood sign which identified the surrounding rubble as 'Tell El Amarna'. The sign hung precariously at the side of the road, half propped against a huge rock, doubling as a perch for the river pelicans.

"My God," Carol croaked, "I knew we were going to be in the wilderness, but this is ridiculous." Her throat was caked with the blowing sand, making her voice sound as though she had a cold. "We've been dropped into the middle of hell. Our only hope for rescue is for Lawrence of Arabia to come riding over yonder sand dune on his trusty camel."

"Pretty grim, isn't it?" Loring was beginning to have second thoughts about their staying in the ruins. "Shall we make camp, or would you rather go back and stay in Dairut?"

"By which sand dune would you prefer, oh mighty sheik? Take your pick. We're here, and here we stay, but good lord, Derek, how are we to survive?"

"You'll get used to it in time. I've been in far worse places. I don't plan on our being here very long. Right now we have to get our tent up...to get out of the heat. We'll be working in the very early mornings at first light, and in the evenings when the breeze comes off the river. We'll rest and sleep in the middle of the day to get our strength back. Those are the ground rules."

Loring scanned the immediate area. "How about setting up camp over there, by that rock outcropping? It'll make a good backdrop for the tent, and be in shade part of the time." He began to unload the Land Rover, the sweat plastering his shirt against his back.

They pitched their tent on the lee side of a craggy rock

ledge where evidence of some earlier excavation by another archaeological party remained strewn about the site in a messy haphazard fashion. Evidently that excavation had come across what it set out to find, or else it discovered all there was to be found, then abandoned the dig. All over the temple site Derek and Carol observed the stakes and grid lines used in the layout of the exploration. Loring lamented the fact that whoever conducted that particular expedition was sloppy and undisciplined, leaving the site in such a state. Could there have been unauthorized investigations tearing up the ruins of Amarna? Zoser, perhaps?

When they had the tent in place and their food stored safely, they laid on blankets spread on the hard sand. They had worked through part of the hottest time of day, and now they were compelled to recover their energies. Carol was apparently feeling the heat much more so than Loring. She was actually limp. Loring tried to raise her spirits.

"Not much like Kensington Park, is it?"

"Derek, this is going to be a real ordeal for me. Let's pray we find whatever we're looking for, soon. As for now, I'm going down to the river and take a bath. I don't give a damn who sees me in my all-together."

"Wait, I'll come with you. We don't go anywhere alone. Another ground rule. I'll take the rifle in case you scare up some crocs. They still roam these parts."

"Oh, that's just peachy! Crocodiles, yet."

The Nile was close to three hundred meters from their campsite, all downhill. Loring remarked at the gradual slope of the land.

"The city had to be on higher ground as protection from the flood tide of the river. Somewhere around here we should be able to uncover the remains of the channel they cut from the river up to the temple."

"Why a channel?"

"Some of the ceremonies held in the temple required the gods to come from the river with their attendants. It's most likely filled in with centuries of sand and we won't be able to find it. We should keep our eyes open for signs though. We might get lucky."

Carol shed her clothes on the bank of the river. She stood for a moment in the descending sun, its light shining on her glistening body which took on the appearance of burnished gold. Loring looked at her and marveled at a woman like Carol being in love with him. She was exquisite.

Casting him a loving glance, she daintily dipped her toes into the flowing brown water. A giggle came from her throat, then with girlish abandon she jumped feet first into the river. She came to the surface, spitting out the dank water, and began to swim. She had to keep circling back upstream as the strong current pulled her north. She was out of breath when she came ashore. Shaking the water from her hair, she said, "Lord, that feels good, but the current's fierce."

She stood on the bank letting the setting sun dry her body. The underside of her full breasts and the inside of her thighs took longer to dry. She dabbed at herself with her discarded shirt and peered at Derek. He tried his best to keep from staring too intently at Carol, but to no avail. She smiled invitingly, then went over to him. Without saying a word, she took his hand and led him up the hill to the tent. Once inside the shelter, she unbuttoned his shirt and rubbed her hands across his chest, murmuring in a low voice, "This could be the best part of the day." Together, they sank down on the blankets, their arms encircling each other.

Later, when the sun was low on the western horizon, they stood in front of the tent holding hands. Loring wore a pair of tattered shorts while Carol had just a thin towel over her shoulders. Darkness was creeping over the east bank. The evening breeze had come up, and the air took on a decided chill. Loring turned to her.

"I'll let you get by with parading around like that just this once. Come tomorrow, we have work to do. You will, I repeat, will dress accordingly. We can't keep our minds on the job if you're running around naked. Besides, this sun is a bitch. It'll burn you to a crisp in nothing flat. We can't have you laying around with sunstroke or third degree burns. I'd have to do all the work."

"Yes, my lord. We will be on our most proper behavior come the morrow. But right now I want to revel in absolute nudity. Passion aside, it makes me feel so alive, so in tune with nature. Derek, look how the sun is casting those long shadows over this awful landscape, right up to the cliffs to the east. Makes it look almost beautiful, and yet, so very sad."

"When you have enough of the view, come inside the tent. I want to show you the layout of the old city."

"Darling, there's one small thing I wish you would do for me before we start digging tomorrow. Make me a proper latrine. I'm no prude, heaven knows, but seeing as how you can just meander up to the nearest sand dune, I can't. It doesn't have to be elaborate, merely something where I won't get sand in the wrong places."

"Yes, my love. Anything else your heart desires?"

"No, not for now."

By the light from the Coleman lantern, Loring sketched out the plan of the city as he remembered it. Their camp was north of the temple location, with the priests' houses and the palace on the south side of the temple. The workers and peasants were housed further north, between the temple and the palace, well beyond the religious area.

Further to the north, about a half mile, was the official residence of the pharaoh and his family. The palace adjacent to the temple was the ceremonial palace where Akhenaten received visitors. The city stretched approximately five miles along the banks of the Nile, a quarter of a mile to the west. On the east, the city extended another half mile from the temple site up to the base of the cliffs. The cliffs served as a natural buffer, offering protection against whatever was east of the city. The whole city was elevated fifty feet above the river level which prevented flooding at the annual inundation.

While Derek was explaining the layout to her, Carol was busy putting together their evening meal, such as it was.

"I could cook you a decent meal if I had the right stuff," she muttered half aloud. "But I guess we'll make do with what we have."

They ate out in the open, under the stars. The moon was illuminating the campsite by now, casting weird shadows that gave it a look of unreality. The reflected light thrown off the river accounted for some very eerie effects. The dark shadows were almost animate. The night creatures began their nocturnal trek to the Nile in their never-ending search for food. Cries, sounding like wounded animals at times, could be heard along with the throaty growls of crocodiles and the bark of the jackals. The persistent hum of insects filled the air. The night, indeed, was not silent, as Loring and Carol spent their first night camped in the heart of an ancient, dead city.

Loring stretched. "We better get some sleep. We start work at daybreak, just like the natives, Carol. Come on, let's hit the hay."

By now the air was quite chilly. They lay side by side on their blankets with a light cover over their still forms. Loring had placed their sleeping bags under the blankets to soften the hard sand. They held hands at first, but the nearness of Carol aroused Derek and he took her in his arms. He whispered to her the things that were on his mind, expressing his love for her. She responded, not completely yielding to his pleas.

Tomorrow, she said, was to be a busy day and they would need all their strength. He had to agree to the logic of this, and satisfied his feelings with an ardent kiss. Before long, the quiet sounds of their sleep merged with the night sounds around them.

It was around four in the morning when Carol had to get up to relieve herself. She took the small trenching tool they had, and left the tent, mumbling to herself.

"Here I go again, getting sand up my bottom. He better get that latrine built today, or else."

As she found her way back to the tent, first light was breaking to the east. The high cliffs kept the camp in darkness, although the reflections on the sand toward the river dispelled most of the shadows. Carol threw back the flap of the tent and stopped abruptly in midstride. In the dim light she saw on the blanket next to Derek, a snake worming its way toward his head. Without hesitating a moment, she struck out with the trenching tool, severing the reptile by the force of her blow. She screamed. Loring jumped off the blanket, and rolled over to one side. He was half asleep, but he saw her standing over him, shovel in her hand, screaming and pointing to the blanket.

"What the hell are you doing with that shovel?"

"Light the lantern, for God's sake. Hurry!"

Loring got the lantern going. "It's a cobra!" he shouted. "Get the hell out of here while I make sure it's dead." He picked up the two ends of the snake, went out to the sand, dug a hole with his foot, and then buried the thing. He came back to the tent to see Carol on the ground, arms laced around herself, sobbing.

"God, how I hate snakes. Just looking at them makes my skin crawl." Loring went to her, holding her in his arms, calming her sobs.

"When I saw that thing crawling toward you, I just struck out at it. Thank goodness I had the shovel."

"It's gone now, dear."

"Why didn't you tell me there would be snakes here? I wouldn't have come."

"I didn't think of it. Snakes normally don't come to where people are. This one must have wanted to get in out of the cold night air. We probably won't see another one the whole time we're here." Carol was calm now, but she kept looking down at the blanket where the snake had been.

"One more, Derek...just one more damned snake and I'll swim back to Cairo. I swear it!"

When it was light enough for him to see what he was doing, Derek constructed a latrine for Carol. He found a natural depression in the wall of the temple and some pieces of wood. He smoothed and shaped the wood, using the abundant sand at hand, and built a seat spread across two stone sides. It was finished in an hour, and when she came to inspect the work, her comment was, "Not bad. Not bad at all."

After a simple breakfast, Derek explained to Carol what signs to look for, signs which might denote the presence of a wall structure below the sand. He was convinced the wall was the key to everything. There were remnants of minor structures remaining above ground, their outlines fairly easy to trace. Loring told Carol that earlier explorations had uncovered the significant buildings, but those were not what they were looking for. They had to find evidence of a wall.

Soon they were working together, side by side, searching for unusual outcroppings in the sand, or sharp rises. After awhile, they exhausted the possibility that a wall was buried anywhere near the temple. If it existed at all, it was probably further south, nearer to the ceremonial palace site.

The burning sun was high in the sky when they finally abandoned their search and retreated to the relative comfort of the tent. Inside, they threw themselves on their blankets. They were hot and sweaty, too exhausted to eat. All they craved was water and sleep.

Later, when they awoke, they made their way to the river. They took turns bathing in the murky water while the other kept watch for danger. While Carol was enjoying her spell in the river, Loring observed a trio of crocodiles on the opposite shore. His concern heightened when he saw one of the ugly brutes slither away from the sandy shallows and glide toward their side. He noticed the trail of the croc as it approached, breaking the surface with the protruding hump over its eyes. The current of the river was swift but the reptile never wavered in its pinpoint accuracy toward Carol. Loring sprung into action.

"Carol, get out of the water...crocodiles!" He aimed the rifle at the eyes of the beast and fired. The shot missed its mark and he fired again. There was a wild thrashing in the water and the other two crocs were alerted. They, too, moved into open water, intent on attacking their wounded companion. The river's course carried the action away from Loring, but violent white-water signaled the outcome. Amidst the thrashing and bellowing of the attackers and the injured, the Nile was churned into chaos. The blood

and flesh of the wounded animal was being devoured rav-
enously by the others. It was over in an instant.

Carol scampered out of the water and ran to where
Loring was watching the gory feast, rifle at the ready.
"Derek, that was far too close! See any more?"

"No, there were just the three...I think. Let's get the
hell away from here, just in case. Don't forget your
clothes."

"I think we're in a no-win situation here, Derek." They
were relaxing in the tent, discussing their progress. "We
won't be able to find anything in this place under all the
sand and ruin. If the wall ever existed, it's gone now. And
add to that, the heat, snakes and crocodiles...it's hopeless."

"Carol, I hope you're wrong. I know that wall is out
there someplace. I feel it. We've only just started. If this
is too much for you, I'll take you back to Cairo and continue the search alone."

"You can't get rid of me that easily, old thing. We
started this together and we'll finish it together...in spite of
the dubious wonders this tourist attraction has to offer."
She smiled warmly.

"That's all I wanted to hear. Let's get on with it, shall
we?"

"Yes, Derek, let's. I'm sorry, but I'm a bit frustrated.
No...I'm a whole lot frustrated. Perhaps I set too much
trust in the clues we had. I'll be good, I promise. Just
keep that rifle handy. Now, what are the options we have?
Be honest."

"First, we should start with a plan. I wish those other
bastards who did all this digging didn't leave the site in
such a God-awful mess. We're looking for a wall, right?
Or a structure like a wall?"

"Yes, if we believe the scroll of Nephgeton."

"Okay. If what he wrote can be taken literally, the wall had to run north and south, facing west. That's the only way the setting sun would shine on it, on the face where the names are supposed to be carved. Such a wall would have to be large, and high enough for the names to be seen from across the river. From a purely structural standpoint, a wall that size would require a tremendous foundation, going down to solid bedrock. The only evidence of rock we can see is that range to the east where the cliffs are. I suggest we start our search there, concentrating on the foot of the cliffs."

"Spoken like a true architect. Mind if I poke some holes in your reasoning? Now, just suppose the wall didn't have to extend above the city to be seen. In that case it wouldn't have to be terribly high or large, and thus should require that much less foundation strength."

"Go on."

"I see a wall, a much lower wall than yours, down on the bank of the river. If my wall paralleled the river, it could easily be seen from the western bank, and the sun would still shine on it. Maybe it was merely a ceremonial wall, highly decorated and the names we're looking for are disguised in the overall design. Does that make sense?"

"It sure as hell does! We'll forget my idea for the time being and concentrate on yours. Where the hell did you develop such a grasp of the obvious? You've been holding out on me. Tomorrow, we start to look down by the river for evidence of rock or stone, manmade."

"Always happy to oblige, my dear."

They talked while they rested. They listed what clues they had. Aside from the scroll of the scribe, they had the words of Nefertiti on the scroll and the drawing she made of the city. The beliefs of Dr. Nashtoi could not be dismissed; he was too reliable an authority on Egyptian history. And what was the truth in the words Ron Menefee spoke on the ride to Priory Farm?

"Perhaps I was wrong in seeing a wall on the scroll of Nefertiti. It might have been the indication of a channel from the river up to the temple. As to the words of Menefee, I don't have any idea, except perhaps he saw the Nefertiti scroll and came to the same conclusion I did."

"Speaking of Menefee, what do you make of the Salazar murder in 1907?"

"I think it's the connection to the Thompson murder. Salazar was Gwen's ancestor, but I don't think the trouble started there in El Dab'a. When we get back, we're going deeper into the history of Salazar. I may be wrong, but I believe this place and Salazar and Gwen Thompson and Zoser International and Ron Menefee are all tied together with some common thread. I'm also inclined to think the assassination of Sadat fits into the same puzzle. We're looking for a common denominator."

"You make a better intelligence operative than I," Carol said with conviction. "I haven't contributed any good, solid logic to this caper. You've done it all. My hat's off to you, Derek."

"You probably say that to all beginners," Derek answered with a grin.

Even though they weren't particularly hungry, they knew they had to eat something. Mostly they had been sipping the water, trying to get moisture back into their systems, but food was essential for their energy. Loring took his turn at the chore and whipped together a simple meal which would sustain them through the night. As before, they ate out in the moonlight, watching the shadows play on the river in the distance. The enervating action of the day caught up with them. They curled up in their blankets and fell asleep.

They were at the Nile eager to begin when the sun first lit up the east bank. The going was rough because the banks of the river had been collecting the refuse of centuries. Paper, bottles, beer cans, plastic of all descriptions were mixed in with the debris of the times, past and present. What rocks they encountered they found to be of recent vintage, with no stone or shaped rock to indicate man's handiwork. Instead, the further they traveled, the more the Nile resembled any other modern cesspool. They went up the river for two miles, then backtracked, in case they missed something. But there was nothing to be seen.

"What a damned fool I am," Loring remarked. "I forgot to consider that the course of the river has changed over the centuries. In 1355 BC, the Nile could have been much closer to the city, or much further away. Why didn't that occur to me before? Damn!"

"Let's orientate ourselves to the temple," Carol replied calmly. "Can you make it out? We might as well walk back toward the temple. Maybe we can find some evidence of a channel further back."

Loring mentally pictured the drawing of Nefertiti he saw in England. The temple was more to the left of where they were standing, further to the north. He approximated the location of the temple by the higher ground south of their camp. Nefertiti's drawing showed either a wall or a channel on the north side of the temple, almost in line with where they pitched their tent.

The sightings complete, they walked back toward their camp, searching about fifty yards on either side of the sight line. About forty yards from the river bank they stumbled on a rock outcropping nearly covered with sand, but enough of it was exposed to show it was not natural. Eagerly, they dug away the sand and found what appeared to be a stone pier. They dug deeper. Four feet down from the top, they found a stone ring on the side of the pier. Derek was excited now.

"This could be a mooring ring for the barges waiting to go up to the temple. Over there, further south, there must have been another pier which marked the entrance to the channel."

They quickly hurried south, scanning the ground for the rock they felt was there. "I don't think the channel could have been more than twenty feet wide," Loring exclaimed. "Let's dig right about here, making a wider circle the deeper we go."

The second pier came into view, about three feet below the surface of the surrounding desert. As with the first pier, four feet below the top, they found a similar stone mooring ring, facing the first ring. Now they could define the entrance and the width of the channel which led to the temple. Loring was elated. As an archaeologist, this meant a major find. He took out his notebook and sketched the piers, indicating the dimensions of the rock and the stone rings.

"Now we know the wall isn't here. It has to be closer to the cliffs. Nefertiti's drawing was accurate in that regard."

"Could the wall be on the north side of the channel, or on the south side?"

"In my opinion, no. Not if it was ceremonial. The channel for the boats of the gods had to be the center attraction. There might have been a low boundary wall for the channel, but then it would be perpendicular to the river and not clearly visible from the other side."

In spite of their find, they were crestfallen as they dragged themselves back to the tent. Now they had to tackle the ominous cliffs. It would be a much hotter task, since they would get the direct blast of the sun overhead without the cooling effect of the river. Nevertheless, they felt a sense of accomplishment in finding the channel. Perhaps it was an omen of a turn in their luck. Tomorrow would tell the tale.

They sat outside their tent, drinking the local beer and watching the sun drop over the desolate ruins of Akhenaten's once beautiful city. Long shadows lay where the higher remnants of buildings rose above the sand. Carol slowly turned her gaze to the east of the main ruins.

"Derek, look...over there...the cliffs. What do you see?"

Loring turned his body to get a better view of the shear cliff walls. At first all he saw were the cliffs, the same as yesterday. Then his heart began to beat wildly. He jumped up and pointed.

"Of course...the cliff...it's the wall!"

Carol yelled. "We found it...we found it!" Loring put an arm around Carol's waist, pointing again at the wall, glistening in the setting sun.

"Look at the way the sun shines on it, as though it were a stage and the sun a spotlight. Tomorrow we start examining that cliff. Oh, Carol, I love you!"

As they stood there, the wall quickly plunged into inky darkness and only the cliff's silhouette remained apparent in the twilight.

They awoke very early the next morning, too early to start their exploration, so they took their time over a simple breakfast Carol threw together. Loring gathered what tools they would need, packed them into a tight bundle while Carol put together a supply of food and water. When the sun broke over the western shore of the river they headed for the eastern cliffs.

The drifted sand made it difficult to walk but their determination made up for the difficulty. They arrived at the base of the stone cliffs when the sun started to shine on the eastern side of the Nile. Loring stowed the supplies off the ground in a crevice of the rock formation.

They each took a separate section of the cliff to examine, their eyes scanning the pitted stone for any sign of it being the ancient wall. The search was in vain. They found nothing but the natural rock, eroded and creased by the ravages of time.

"Have we struck out again?" Carol sighed. "Maybe we were too hopeful last night."

"We're not licked yet, old girl. Let's take a break."

They sat on the sand in the only sliver of shade. Loring knew they were on the right track. They just had to be patient and figure it out. "Carol, in your experience with the old Egyptian ruins and tombs, where did you find most of the hieroglyphics? I mean, were they close to the ground or were they higher up, near the top?"

"Well, we know the writings on the columns in the temple of Karnak are up high, because they were for the eyes of the gods only. At the temples of Edfu and Esna, the carvings are at eye level, for man to read about the exploits of the pharaoh."

"I was thinking...if the words of the scribe were up high, they would need to work from scaffolding. If they were close to the ground, at eye level, the work could have been done from down here."

"I see what you're driving at. So what do we have here?"

"Remember the words of Nephgeton? The names of the faithful would be visible to Aten. Aten was their god, so the names must be higher up, not to be read by the people. Especially since those times were unsettled, the high priests would love to have the names of the few followers of Akhenaten. The list would be a death sentence. I think the names are up there, near the top of the cliff."

"That makes sense, more than anything else. Now, how do we get up there?"

"We climb." Loring walked to his bundle, taking out the rope he'd packed. "Here, tie one end of this around your middle. I'll do the same, then we start climbing, me first." Carol made a face.

"Don't worry, these sandstone cliffs aren't vertical. They slope inward, and are full of hand and foot holds, easy to climb. Just don't look down or step back to admire the view."

"You're funny, Derek...really funny."

"I'll go first. I'll be about twenty feet ahead of you. Just watch me and place your feet where you see me put mine. Hold your body close to the face of the wall. Ready? Here we go."

Carol had tied the rope around her waist while they talked. He checked the knot. He tied his, then said to her as he began his climb, "You do have something to write with, don't you? We can't trust our memories."

"Yes, I have. Give me credit for having some brains, Sir Hillary."

The ascent was fairly easy going in the beginning. Loring found enough places to put his hands and feet so the weight was off his arms and shoulders. Carol followed, using the same holds Loring did. Loring reached the top without finding one single thing that resembled carvings in the stone. He called down to Carol, telling her he was moving to his left. She was to follow, scanning the rock face beneath him. They had gone about fifteen feet when Derek shouted down to her.

"Carol, I found it! My God, I found it!" Loring started

brushing off the portions of the writing nearest him. "Carol, come on up so you can see it. Put your feet where I did. Oh, hurry!"

Carol gritted her teeth and started to climb. Steady, old girl, she said to herself, it wouldn't do to fall now. She gradually made her way up to where Loring was waiting for her. She couldn't believe what she saw. There, as clear as could be, were the characters carved so many years before in the soft sandstone, the characters forming the hieratic script they were seeking.

She found it easy to read. It was a list of names, hopefully those who were faithful to Akhenaten as Nephgeton said. She had a bit of trouble at first trying to write on her note pad, and hang at the same time. After some trial and error, she found she could write by leaning against the wall and double-checking her translation before going on to the next character.

There were thirty names in all, carved in a single row, including that of the scribe, Nephgeton. Carol felt so elated at their accomplishment, she threw her head back and shouted to the sky, hoping that Aten could hear her.

Loring watched her, wishing he could feel as free to show his own excitement. All he could think of though, clinging to the side of the cliff in the burning sun, was to find shade and read Carol's translation. He called over to her. "We're fairly near the top, Carol. Do you want to climb up and get back to camp over the hill, or do you want to climb down?"

"Let's use the wall and climb down. It wasn't as difficult as I thought. But please stay close, just in case."

"Wait. Let me ease over a bit to the north. I want a stronger handhold before you work your way down."

Loring slid his way along the cliff's rugged surface. He had moved to his left about ten feet when he noticed an odd formation breaking the random pattern in the stone.

"Hold on, Carol. I want to check this out." He moved in closer and was surprised to find an entire section of the cliff face loose, as though it might fall. He examined it closer and found he could move one side of the section by leaning against it. The opposite side rotated when he did. It was a pivoted door!

"Carol, come here! There's something you should see."

She moved slowly to where Loring was. "What is it, Derek?"

"I believe we've stumbled on a cave of some sort. Over here. Stand next to me and push when I tell you."

"What the hell are you doing? Push what?"

Carol was standing next to Loring on a narrow ledge looking at an odd break in the stone. "Do I see a door?"

"I think so. Now, lean against this side, next to me. Got it? Okay, now push!"

Together they leaned against the rock and pushed. The stone section groaned as it gradually rotated on the opposite side. It was a door leading into a dark and acrid void. The stone stood half open into the mouth of the cave, the sun in the western sky shining in. Carol and Loring moved cautiously and entered the cavern, not knowing what awaited them. Once inside, Loring pulled at the door stone, swinging it to its full open position. Now the light from outside streamed into the cave, the darkness completely gone. They were not prepared for what they saw.

In the center of the stone floor, near the rear wall, lay a human skeleton partially covered by sand and rock debris. The bones of the body, bones which once formed a hand, were still clutching a thin roll of papyrus.

"Carol, this must be some sort of burial chamber."

"It certainly looks like it. I wonder who it was. That

scroll might tell us something. Wait, I'll get it."

She made her way to the remains and gingerly removed the scroll from the bony grip. In so doing, the bones were dislodged and fell away, spreading around the rest of the hand. Carol shuddered as she moved closer to the door, unrolling the papyrus very carefully. Derek stood beside her in the sunlight as she translated the formal hieroglyphics, still vivid in their line and color.

> "This one betrayed his ancient gods.
> This one is known in the city as
> Nephgeton the scribe. The true
> believers of Amun-Ra leave this one
> to the ages. His dark deeds are known
> to Amun-Ra. Those of his kind will
> be scattered to be mixed with the
> desert sands. Amun-Ra will have no
> gods above him. If else but divine
> eyes are cast upon this heed the signs
> well. Zozer dwells with Amun-Ra. It
> is he who so commands the hand of
> vengeance."

Loring exclaimed, "Carol, this is all that remains of our faithful scribe, Nephgeton. Do you know what this means?"

"Yes. The priests found the names of the Menefee, then they killed Nephgeton and sealed him in this tomb, right next to his list of names. This clinches it. The priest cult from the days of Pharaoh Zozer knew about the Menefee and had them thrown out of Amarna. Just as Nashtoi said. Derek, I'm scared spitless. What are we into?"

"Easy, Carol. Don't panic. Let's reason this thing through. Okay, so the priests had the names of the followers of Akhenaten all along, right from the start. Since we're obviously the first to read this scroll, nobody knows we have it. It's an archaeological gold mine, but we won't share it with the world until we get to the bottom of this. Does that make sense?"

"Yes, you're right. And as long as nobody knows we have it, we should be safe."

"Yes."

"I'll buy that, but, Derek, look around. See anything else?"

"No, nothing but the dead body. You find something?"

"Maybe. Come here, next to the body. When I took the scroll I thought I saw a few scratches under the chest bones. See them?"

"Barely. Give me the brush. Now, you try to shift the body a bit so I can sweep the sand away." As Carol gently moved the brittle bones, Loring lightly brushed at what appeared to be some roughly carved characters in the soft stone floor.

Carol translated the faint script...

"My time is short. It was the last who would be first. Seek..."

"That's it. I think Nephgeton was still alive when they left him in here." Carol's voice showed her excitement. "He must have had enough time before he died to leave a message...only it's a riddle, Derek. It's a goddamned riddle!"

"Riddle or no riddle, we have to get back to the tent

and translate the list. Let's get the hell out of here. I'm getting as jumpy as you."

They took a last look at the scribe's grotesque skeleton, then Loring swung the stone until it was closed, sealing the cave.

Back at the tent, Derek took the pad and wrote what Carol had translated. He listed the names vertically, so they would each stand alone. They looked at the list of names, most of which meant very little to them. However, two names did stand out in Loring's mind. One was Nebmarestut, and the other was Smenkhoremhab. He and Carol considered these two.

Nebmarestut was the son of Nebmare, the pharaoh before Akhenaten. The big question they asked was why the son of the former pharaoh was in the camp of the heretic pharaoh, and a follower of Aten.

"Perhaps he was illegitimate and couldn't inherit the throne," Carol ventured. "This might have been reason enough for the son to fight or rebel against everything his father stood for."

"Let's assume that's the reason, for now. We'll come back to him later. How do we explain Smenkhoremhab? Doesn't the name mean 'a brother of Horemhab'?"

"It sure does. Keep going."

"Well, Horemhab was a great general at the end of Akhenaten's reign. He served King Tut and King Ay after Akhenaten. He eventually ruled the country, started the nineteenth dynasty. Do we have a case of sibling rivalry?"

"Perhaps the brother did feel cheated, with Horemhab getting all the attention and honors. Still, the brother might have been sincere in his beliefs, regardless of his brother. My money's on Horemhab. We'll have to look a hell of a lot deeper into that."

"Right. Now," Loring said, "let's add the family skeleton of Nebmare. You start reading off the names, exactly in the order they were on the cliff. I'll give them each a number here on this list. Who's first?"

Carol recited the names slowly in the order she took them from her notes. When she finished, Loring had his list marked with assigned numbers.

"What's the last name on your list? Who's number thirty?" she asked, holding her breath.

"Semphere. Don't know if it's a man or woman. Do you know?"

"I should say it's the name of a woman. The 'ere' is usually used to denote a female family member. We've proved that it doesn't mean wife or sister. And 'stet' seems to be always used for daughter. But I've seen 'ere' used for both aunt and half-sister, so I guess this could be either one. It means we have an aunt or half-sister of Semph at the end of our list. Now what?"

"Damned if I know. Doctor Nashtoi might have some ideas. I want you to meet him anyhow. Now, are you ready to head for the barn, and civilization?"

"No. Let's spend the rest of the day relaxing, hot as it is." Loring looked at her with surprise. "When we return to Cairo, we'll both be too busy to spend much time with each other. Let's head back in the morning. Just lay back with me now, darling, and make love to me. Again and again."

Chapter 11

Inspector Crimmins sat at the conference table in the Directors Room of Zoser International. George Wells and Joshua Claridge were across from him, each with distinct emotions mirrored in his eyes. Wells' eyes shifted from hate to indifference, then back to hate. Claridge's eyes showed fear and anxiety. Crimmins purposely showed no concern in their attitudes. He was after facts.

Crimmins was frustrated. So far, not one single clue had been found to connect Zoser to the deaths of MacIvor and Tupps. He was angry over the blatant disregard the two Zoser men sitting across from him expressed in the deaths.

Wells answered the questions put to him by Crimmins in his surly way. Claridge couched his replies in evasions and fiction. While Wells was generally unpleasant, Claridge tried to placate.

"Mr. Wells, you said MacIvor left his office at six o'clock, his usual time. Did he mention he might be meeting someone?"

"No, he just left. Didn't even say good-night."

"I saw him take the lift." Claridge seemed to need acceptance. "He didn't appear to have anything unusual on his mind."

"Was MacIvor married?" Crimmins directed his question at Claridge.

"No, there wasn't any woman in his life, that I was aware of."

"Mr. Claridge, what was MacIvor working on, what type of project?"

Claridge looked over at Wells, who remained stoic. He turned back to the inspector, answering with a slight tremor in his voice.

"I don't know all of the details of his project. He was working with an American architectural historian, Derek Loring. They were tracing some old records and buildings which concern a client of ours."

"Care to tell me the name of that client?"

"Sorry, that's privileged information," Wells interrupted. "Look here, Inspector, what more do you want from us? We don't have any idea what MacIvor was involved in. His collaboration with Loring was his project. All our top men work essentially alone. He was probably murdered by some pervert for some unknown reason. Who knows? I don't.. and I don't care. It's up to you to find him. Now, I must ask you to leave now, Inspector. We can offer nothing further."

"I see." Crimmins replied softly, not letting his rising anger show through. "Perhaps you are right, then again, you may not be. I'll leave now, but I'll likely be back. Keep this in mind...until this murderer is apprehended, everyone is suspect. Good day, gentlemen. I'll let myself out."

Crimmins returned to Scotland Yard in a foul mood. He had expected some word from Loring by this time. He needed some shred of evidence to connect Zoser to all these killings, and he hoped Loring could find it. He was sure the killings were all tied together, and should he loosen one knot, he knew the whole bundle would come unraveled.

When he entered his office, Ron Menefee was waiting for him. Menefee was agitated, more so than usual.

"Have you heard anything from Loring?"

"Not yet. He's only been gone a few days. Why do you ask?"

"There was more information I could have given him, but forgot in the rush of his trip. It's something I believe could help in his research. Do you know where he's staying in Cairo? Maybe I could call him." "Don't know." Crimmins wondered at the sudden interest Menefee was showing toward Loring's work. "When he gets in touch with me, if he does, I'll let you know. Now, if there is nothing more, I have some pressing Yard business to attend to." Crimmins had to let Derek know about Menefee's comment. But more important, Loring should know that Wells was still with Zoser. If he would only call!

Menefee stormed out of Crimmins' office, looking more dark and sullen than ever. Damn, he thought, Loring had to have the truth. Everything depended on how he dealt with Zoser. How to get the facts to him? Should he cable Cairo, and have his friends there get to Loring? He realized there was but one sure way to reach him. He had to fly down there and confront him. It was time for Menefee to disappear for a few days.

Derek and Carol decided not to return the Land Rover and the rest of the camping gear when they arrived back at the Mena House. Perhaps they could take time for themselves and go touring one day when their assignment was over. Loring wanted to show her the rebuilt temples of Abu Simbel, and the newly uncovered tombs at Abydos. For now, however, they had much more pressing business concerning their discoveries at Amarna.

Loring suggested it was time to visit Dr. Nashtoi at the museum. If anyone could help decipher the puzzle, it would be Nashtoi. The curator would be interested in their finding the tomb of Nephgeton should they decide to let him in on the secret.

"As far as I'm concerned, Derek, we can let that go until tomorrow. Right now I want a good bath and shower. I have the sands of Amarna in every pore of my body, and my hair took an awful beating from the sun."

"What's wrong with your hair? It looks fine to me."

"That shows how much you know. If I'm to continue to be Carol Ashworth, my hair needs to be touched up. Egyptian weather'll turn me into an old lady yet. Do you think you'll still love me with white hair?"

"You just wait and see."

"Regardless, I'm going back to my room and don't want to be disturbed for two hours. I owe my vanity that much. You could stand a good soaking yourself, dear. When the wind is right, you're positively ripe."

"I guess the honeymoon's over," he replied.

Loring parked the truck in the circular drive by Carol's wing of the hotel. She went to her room while he headed for the main desk to check for messages. Carol had been right about one thing, he did need a bath.

"Yes, Mr. Loring, you do have some calls that came in while you were out in the bush, so to speak. Mr. Kurt Sempher wants you to call him the instant you arrive...no matter what the hour."

"Kurt Sempher? Who's he?"

"He is the chairman of Zoser International, in Zurich. Also, Dr. Nashtoi of the Egyptian Museum would like you to call. And finally, this cablegram came for you yesterday. I believe that is the lot. Did you have a successful excursion?"

"Yes, thank you. The trip was well worth the heat and dirt. I'll take care of these messages from my room."

Loring went to his suite, determined to bathe before doing anything. The messages could wait. He undressed while the tub was filling, then called Carol's room. After three rings she answered.

"Yes?"

"Carol, why do you think Kurt Sempher wants me to call him?"

"Derek! You disturbed my bath for such an asinine question? Who the hell is Sempher?"

"The big cheese of Zoser. In Zurich. He wants me to call, regardless of the time."

"Well, I'm sure I haven't the foggiest. Let's discuss it later. Now, no more interruptions. Is that clear?"

"Perfectly. I'll see you later, grouch."

Loring took a long soak in the hot water. The tensions and aches of the past days were washed away with the Sahara grime. He dressed casually and mixed himself a drink, then turned his attention to the telephone. He called Dr. Nashtoi.

The curator inquired about the explorations at Amarna. He was anxious to learn of Loring's success. Loring said he would see him tomorrow and tell him the whole story. He added that he needed Nashtoi's help in some of the hieratic translations.

"Certainly, Loring, by all means. But not here at the Museum. I prefer to meet you elsewhere. Do you know Saint Barbara's Church, in the Old City? Meet me there at one o'clock, tomorrow."

"I'll be there, Doctor." Loring was surprised at this sudden secrecy on the part of the curator. Everyone was getting jumpy.

The cable was from Claridge. He wanted Loring to call him as soon as possible. He provided a London number, but Loring knew it wasn't Zoser's. Most likely it had to do with MacIvor's death. He thought it would be best to talk with Claridge before calling Zurich.

"Loring? Thank God you got through to me." Claridge was excited and afraid. "Have you heard? MacIvor was murdered, brutally. I got sick when I saw his body. Wells is going off his rocker. He doesn't even speak to me. I wanted to know if you found anything yet, anything that might break Wells out of his foul mood. In case you hadn't heard, Wells has been reinstated by Zurich. No, of course you didn't know...how could you?" Claridge stopped to take a breath.

"No matter," Loring said. "I think I've found the information to close the gap in your puzzle, Claridge. Tell Wells I'm sending it out directly. Will that be all right?"

"I'll leave word for George because I won't be here. I'm taking a few days' holiday to gather my wits." Claridge sighed heavily. "These past several weeks have about done me in. I need the rest, you understand?"

"I'm certain you can use the time off, Josh. Take care of yourself. Goodbye."

So, Loring thought, they had been right, all along. Wells never was fired. Chalk one up for intuition.

Next, Loring called Zurich. He dialed the switchboard for an outside line and placed the call direct. When the call was answered, he asked for Kurt Sempher.

"This is Kurt Sempher." The heavy teutonic accent was very pronounced. "Dr. Loring? Thank you for calling. How is the work progressing? Do you have anything to report?"

"Yes, sir. I do have a report to make. I'll call Mr. Wells in London tomorrow."

"You must give me the information, Dr. Loring. I am responsible."

"Sorry, Mr. Sempher. No disrespect intended, but I

was retained by Mr. Wells. He insisted that any information I gathered be given to him personally."

"Very commendable, Mr. Loring. Not only are you loyal, but ethical as well. I like that. However, I must have the information myself. There is a solution to this dilemma...come to Zurich in two days. I shall call Mr. Wells and have him meet with us here. In that way, you can give him the information as promised, and I shall have it, too. Isn't that the best, all around?"

"Yes sir, that is the best way. I'll call you when I arrive."

"Very well. That will be satisfactory. Goodbye, Dr. Loring."

Derek hung up the phone, more confused than ever. What was this feeling of fear? Sempher's name? It's almost identical with the name of Nephgeton's traitor. Coincidence? Or omen?

Carol and Loring made their way to the Church of Saint Barbara, the Coptic church in Old Cairo, near the cemetery. Dr. Nashtoi was already there when they arrived. Loring introduced him to Carol.

"It is good to meet you, Miss Ashworth. I understand you do translations of the old hieratic."

"Yes," Carol said with pride.

"Good, but it is also rather unusual."

"She's rather an unusual person, Doctor," Loring added. "But why did you want to meet us here, in this out-of-the way place? Your office is more convenient."

"Actually, it was not I who wished it. There is someone here with me who had to see you. He wanted privacy. He is over there, in the side aisle."

Just as all three of them looked in that direction, Ron

Menefee stepped out of the shadows. Loring stared with surprise. Menefee was supposed to be in London.

"Mr. Loring, Miss Ashworth. I had to see you." He extended his hand in greeting. "I not only must warn you, but to beg for your help as well. Doctor Nashtoi knows of what I have to say. He has known for some time. It's time you knew the truth."

"Does Crimmins know you're here in Egypt?" Loring put to him.

"No. I told you in London he has no part in this. But, please hear me out first. Please sit down. I'll answer your questions later. Let me start in the beginning...forty-five hundred years ago."

Everyone was quiet as Menefee told his story. He began with the secret society, the Zozer Brotherhood, and the escape of a pregnant woman who chose to take her chances with the desert rather than remain with the Brotherhood. He told them of the birth of the first Menefee, brought into the world by a group of nomadic tribesmen, and how the family found its way to the coast. They settled in what's now called El Dab'a. The young Menefee was about seven when the Brotherhood found his mother and killed her. The boy and his father were saved from the same fate by being out at sea, fishing. The villagers hid them from the grasp of the vengeance-seeking Brotherhood. The man and boy fled into the desert where they lived a nomadic life, never remaining very long in any one place.

The father raised the boy alone, instilling in him a hatred of the Brotherhood and all that it stood for. Eventually the father died, but not until he exacted from the boy a promise to avenge his mother. Young Menefee, nearly seventeen at the time, gathered together a band of his good desert friends. They formed a blood pact in which they vowed to fight the Brotherhood and to seek retribution. That was the beginning of the Menefee Society.

The Society remained in the shadows of Membre, the ancient name for Memphis. They had to become familiar with the ways of the high priests, most of whom were members of the Brotherhood. In time, the Society became strong enough to start their plans for revenge. The caste of priests was infiltrated by the Menefee, and some of the high priests were killed off. When Menefee finally died, the oldest of the remaining Society became the leader and assumed the name Menefee. Each generation from then on had a strong group, always led by a Menefee.

Hundreds of years elapsed until a new pharaoh came to the throne. He brought with him a new religious philosophy centered around a single godhead, Aten. That king was Akhenaten. The Menefee became his champions and lived openly in the city of Amarna. They saw this to be their one chance to stem the influence of the priests. However, Akhenaten was not a strong king.

Even with the Menefee behind him, his new religious revolution collapsed. He was assassinated by the Brotherhood at the urging of the high priests. With the king dead, the Menefee lost their royal protection. They were outlawed and driven from the city, scattered into the desert.

As Egypt became more powerful and influential in the known world, the Brotherhood retreated into the background. They acted as the secret arm of the high priest caste. Even when Egypt was under the foreign rule of the Kushites, the Hittites, the Assyrians, and finally the Greeks and Romans, the Brotherhood remained active, always in the background. Time and events changed them into a private cult, completely separate from the priests. They became the power behind the throne, never concerned as to what nation ruled Egypt. They furthered their ambitions with assassinations, drugs, blackmail, and treasonous pacts with foreign rulers. Power had become their only god.

Menefee stopped his story and looked at his listeners. All were quiet, waiting. He continued.

"They are still with us...the Brotherhood of Zozer. It puts on the trappings of civilization. You know it as Zoser International. The Brotherhood was responsible for the assassination of Sadat, the attempted assassination of the Pope and others.

"Zoser wants to control the thinking of the western world. They plan a religious revolution among all the strong religions...Christianity, Islam, and Judaism. They will kill off or render helpless any who stand in their way. The one thing we don't know is the reason. We don't know Zoser's ultimate goal."

When Menefee finished his story, the others were silent. For Loring, the legend or story of the Menefee was easy to accept, but the rest, the Zoser group conspiring in political assassinations, was hard to swallow. Yet, Loring did remember Wells and Istanbul.

"Let me ask you a question, Ron," Loring said, finally breaking the silence. "And this comes right out of left field, as we say in America. Do you know of a Amin Salazar who was killed in that village, El Dab'a?"

"He was my grandfather."

"He was what?"

"My grandfather. My grandmother, Salome, had taken my father and his sister over to the next village to visit a sick friend. When she returned to El Dab'a and learned her husband had been killed, she packed up everything and fled to Alexandria with the children. The Brotherhood caught up with her eventually and killed her and the girl. Father escaped and sailed to Malta at night.

Years later he returned to Dab'a where he married a local woman. It was there I was born. I never knew my mother. After she died, father took me back to Malta. As was the first Menefee, I was raised with a strong hatred of the Brotherhood."

"But isn't your name really 'Salazar'?"

"I changed it legally when I went to England. It was when I became of age and assumed the leadership of the Menefee Society."

"And Crimmins doesn't know?"

"No."

"Carol and I were in El Dab'a a few days ago. It's a miserable place. When we were there, we talked with an old man named Mustapha. Later, when we were driving back through, on our way to El Alamein, we found that he had been ritualistically murdered. The people there thought we were responsible. They accused us of being from the old ones, as they called them."

"Mustapha killed?"

"Yes, did you know the old man?"

"I knew him. He was one of us. I tried to get him to leave the town, but he claimed he could do the most good by staying there. The Brotherhood has that village terrified. Little by little the people are leaving. Soon there won't be an El Dab'a. The same holds true for all the other small coastal villages."

Carol broke into the conversation, apparently bothered by something Menefee said. "Then your Society, as you call it, was responsible for the killings in London. The men who murdered Gwen Thompson were killed by your people."

"No, Miss Ashworth, it wasn't us. Wells did it. He had the two Turks killed after they murdered the Thompson woman to further the concept of a vendetta. And MacIvor.

Wells did that himself. He also arranged for the death of Tupps through hired assassins. The man is a psychopath."

"How do you know all this?"

"One of our Society is hidden in Zoser International. He has been for a long time. He reports their plans to us so we can take precautions and interfere with those plans. Our man in there is Joshua Claridge."

Now Carol and Loring really showed shock. How could Claridge be a hidden Menefee? He was right up in the high echelon of Zoser. When he could find the words, Loring said, "I just talked with him. He told me he was taking a vacation for his nerves. He sounded agitated. Do you think Wells has found him out?"

"I'll call my people there to get him out of town...out of England. He must have the evidence Bertie needs to nail Wells for the MacIvor killing. That, by the way, was done by Wells because MacIvor failed to locate you, Miss Ashworth."

"Oh God! We need the intelligence agencies in on this," she said emphatically. "Since Jameson has been neutralized, MI 6 could jump in. This is what Hopkins has been waiting for, the reason he assigned me to this case."

"No, Carol," Loring said. "They have ties with the CIA in this part of the world and until we find the leak in the CIA, we can't afford the risk. We're on our own, for the time being."

Menefee added, quietly, "The CIA leak is a man by the name of Morgan...in Washington. Claridge gave me the name."

"You can't tell Crimmins this without giving away your position. But Carol can. She can say she found this out through some old MI 6 contacts here in Cairo. I'll cable the information to Crimmins and let him handle it. When are you going back, Ron?"

"Tonight. I only came here to talk with you, to give you the whole truth. Now that I have, what's your answer? Are you willing to help stop these people?"

Loring looked at Carol as she returned his stare. Their eyes reflected the concern they felt.

"We can give you information, but we remain in the background. That's the way we work. We help to tie up the package, then turn it over to the authorities."

Loring turned to Menefee, "Ron, I'm not sure how to answer you. Before I do, I have to ask you something. You said you had to warn Carol. What about?"

"We discovered that the real Carol Ashworth had an Arab ancestor. He was one of us. If Zoser checks into Ashworth's background, they will find the connection. They won't hesitate to kill her."

"But I'm not Carol Ashworth!"

"They think you are. You went through a lot of trouble establishing that fact. And if you deny it, they will find you to be Nadia Shepherd who they want out of the way, too. You could lose in either case."

"That settles it...for me, at least." Loring was firm in his reply. "Since Carol...Nadia...is in danger, running away won't solve anything. We have to stop them before they find out the truth about her. Count me in, Ron."

"That's a load off my mind, Derek," Menefee said. "But what about you Carol? Or should I call you Nadia now?"

"Let's keep it Carol for now. I don't have much of a choice. Derek and I are a team. We may be inept, but we're a team, nonetheless. We're also something else, very private and very special. If he wants to do battle with these maniacs, I'm with him. Can't say I like the idea, but I've no other recourse, considering the alternatives."

Menefee shook Carol and Loring's hands.

"You can contact me through Nashtoi. He knows how to reach me. What are your immediate plans?"

"Well, when we left Amarna, Carol and I planned to tell Doctor Nashtoi what we discovered. Other than that, we were going to keep it to ourselves until we knew who we could trust. Now, it seems, we all better know what Carol and I found. Loring looked over at Carol for confirmation. He continued.

"We found the list of Menefee names carved on the eastern cliffs behind Amarna. There were thirty names in all including that of Nephgeton, the scribe. Carol copied and translated the names, and between us, we narrowed them down to two who might be important. Doctor, we think Nebmarestut and Smenkhoremhab are the names Zoser is really after. Are we right?"

"You have done a remarkable thing," said Nashtoi. "Not only have you found the list of names, which no one else outside our Society ever could, but you have isolated the names of the two persons you had to find. Very remarkable."

Loring was beginning to understand what he and Carol had really accomplished. "Smenkhoremhab was the intelligent brother of Horemhab," Nashtoi continued. "He tried to sway Horemhab away from the control of the priests, but the general's ambition for glory made the effort useless. When Horemhab realized how sincere his brother was in the teachings concerning Aten, and how much influence the Menefee had over him, he went out of his head. That is the real reason he had Tut destroy the city.

His sister, Psmake, was like Horemhab, and it was her lineage that leads to Anwar Sadat. When she married her husband, who was in the army under Horemhab, she went back to Memphis. That would be the link you are looking for as far as Zoser is concerned. They want to distort the connection between Horemhab and Smenkhoremhab into a continuous line, up to the present. Zoser wants Menefee blamed for the assassination."

"What about Nebmarestut?"

"He was continuing the work his father had started before he died. Had he lived a while longer, King Nebmare would have accomplished what Akhenaten did. He was killed by the Brotherhood who then put Akhenaten on the throne.

You wondered why the son did not inherit the crown? The priests knew he was too strong, and they would have trouble keeping him under their thumb. Akhenaten, on the other hand, showed a streak of weakness which the priests knew could be used to their advantage. However, Nebmarestut did the honorable thing...he joined with the supporters of Akhenaten, hoping to bring about the conclusion and fulfillment of the work his father started. Interesting, yes?"

When Nashtoi finished his explanation, Carol dropped the other shoe. "Doctor, after we copied that list of names, Derek discovered a cave in the cliff wall, sealed off by an ingenious stone door. Inside, we discovered the remains of Nephgeton who was obviously put in there while he was still alive. In his hand he held a scroll which condemned him as a traitor, and also promised that his companions, obviously the Menefee, would be thrown out of the city and scattered into the desert. We brought the scroll with us. Give it to him, Derek."

The curator virtually grabbed the papyrus and became instantly lost in its reading. He nodded his head, pursed his lips and muttered an oath in Arabic which made Carol blush.

"My apologies, Miss Ashworth. How uncivil of me. I find myself extremely agitated over this blatant arrogance of the old high priests. This document is truly a significant discovery, however evil it depicts my ancestors."

Loring interjected, "We're not finished yet, Doctor. We found a few hieratic scratches under the body of the scribe. He left a clue as to who was responsible for the coup. Show him, Carol."

Nashtoi repeated the riddle from Carol's notebook: "'It was the last who would be first.' Tell me, have you two extraordinary people solved this as well?"

"We think we have. I had Carol repeat the names in the exact order they had been carved. I assigned a number to each on the translated list. The last name was someone called Semphere. Carol believes it is the name of a woman, an aunt or half-sister of Semph." Carol showed him the hieratic and her translation. "Is she right, Doctor?"

"Yes, she is. Allah is good!"

Menefee finally joined the conversation. "Do you people realize the significance of what you have there? Do you know that the head of Zoser International is named Sempher, Kurt Sempher? Now, I ask you, do you suppose there is a connection, however remote?"

"That's what's bothering me...the name. Sempher wants me in Zurich the day after tomorrow. What do I tell him? I did mention that I found what I thought they were looking for."

"I suggest you tell them about finding the names," Menefee countered.

"Tell them one of the names was that of Horemhab's sister, instead of the brother. The translation of the hieratic script denoting brother or sister is difficult, and could easily be confused. The connection between the sister and the Menefee will then be established, much to their delight. If they announce this fact to the world to support their contention that Sadat was murdered by the Menefee, we have more than enough intelligent experts to refute this and put the blame where it belongs. Beyond that, Derek, I can only add to what I said before...be careful and play it as you see it."

"That would be a mistake," Carol said quietly.

"Why?"

"Look at the logic. We know from the scroll that the priests had the names all along...since right after they were carved by the scribe. I didn't have any trouble translating the characters for Smenkhoremhab, even after all this time. Imagine how much crisper and precise the name was when it was first carved. Zoser knows the right name, believe me."

"You're right, Carol," Loring said. "If I tried to pass off the sister for the brother, Zoser would know I was lying. I'd be putting my neck in their noose."

"So, what'll we do now?" Carol put in.

"Nashtoi, is there any record of what happened to the brother, Smenkhoremhab?" Menefee asked.

"It has always been assumed he fled into the desert with the others of the Menefee. Why do you ask?"

"Suppose he didn't disappear into oblivion. Suppose he just went into hiding, waiting for a chance to strike back."

"There are no known facts to back up your supposition. All we know is what happened to the general and Psmake."

Loring saw the merit in Menefee's thinking. "But suppose Carol and I found evidence to show that Smenkhoremhab didn't leave Amarna?"

"But there is no evidence, Mr. Loring."

"You know that, Doctor, and so do we. And we must believe Zoser does, too. But suppose I make them think I found something that they never knew about?"

"Derek, if you tell them that, they have ways to check

THE ZOZER BROTHERHOOD 203

on it, and they'll know you're lying. You'd be in worse trouble when they do."

"Not if my source of evidence is dead."

"What do you mean?"

"Mustapha, in El Dab'a...Zoser killed him. They don't know what he told us."

"Brilliant!" Nashtoi fairly shouted. "How do you propose to do it?"

"Leave that to Carol and me. We'll manufacture some story that leads back to Psmake and ultimately to Sadat. That's the only answer. What do you think, Carol?"

"We'll have to be very careful, Derek. They'll want solid proof. We don't have it."

"I know. We'll make it up. I've some ideas we'll discuss later."

"I hope no one ever asks me for a character reference on you, Derek." Carol hid her anxiety.

The foursome broke up then. Menefee flew back to London, Nashtoi returned to the Museum while Loring and Carol went back to the Mena House. They had a lot of work to do before Loring took off for Zurich. The findings of Amarna had to be collated and written up to resemble a finished report. The true facts had to be skewed just enough to show the false connection leading to Sadat, augmented by the information given them by Mustapha. By the time they finished the report, there wasn't much time for anything but bed.

"Morgan? They're back. Both of them." Caine had a note of triumph and glee in his voice as he cupped the green telephone.

"We know. They went to the ruins of Amarna."

"How the hell do you know?"

"You should understand we have extensive contacts."

"How long have you known?"

"Since right after you bastards lost them. I still say you and Soloman have a lot of explaining to do. I don't know how long I can keep a lid on your foulups."

"Someday, I'm going to meet you, Morgan, and when I do, I'll beat you to a pulp."

Caine was yelling into a dead telephone. Morgan had already hung up.

Chapter 12

The afternoon shadows were creeping across Zurich when Loring arrived at the Glarnishhof Hotel. He had missed an earlier direct flight from Cairo, and had settled for the longer trip through Athens. Consequently, Swissair arrived too late for his meeting with Zoser.

The day started off badly. He and Carol had a slight disagreement about her coming along. She argued that her expertise in the translations of the hieratic inscriptions would give more authenticity to the information in Loring's report. He, on the other hand, didn't want her that close to Zoser. They might get too interested in her background and start to check. If they didn't know about her already, why give them this opportunity? Besides, Wells would be at the meeting and might easily recognize her as Nadia Shepherd.

He thought it would be far better to leave well enough alone. He practically ordered her to stay in Cairo with Dr. Nashtoi. He also reasoned that Menefee might forward some information from London they could use. Carol reluctantly stayed in Cairo.

The taxi, which brought him into the city from the airport, made good time in spite of the afternoon traffic. Even so, it was quite late when he got to the hotel. He had stayed at the Glarnishhof once before when he was in Zurich. It was a superior rated hotel, much too expensive for him under ordinary circumstances, but he decided to use it now since he was on Zoser's expense account.

His room was on the fourth floor with a view of the river and overlooking the old section of town. Loring never particularly liked Zurich. He considered it too commercial to really be a part of the normally clean and orderly Switzerland he was accustomed to. He was prepared this time to ignore the condition of the city. This was not a pleasure trip. He wasn't planning on remaining any longer than was absolutely necessary. He placed a call to Zoser as soon as he was alone, not bothering to unpack.

"Mr. Sempher? This is Loring. I just arrived. What time would be convenient for you to see me tomorrow?"

"Why should we wait until tomorrow, Dr. Loring?" Sempher sounded half asleep. He spoke with a heavy German accent. "Please come over now. Mr. Wells is here with me and we are most anxious to hear your report. We have waited for a long time for a breakthrough in this matter. Shall we say, one hour?"

"That suits me. I'll be there in an hour."

Loring decided to call Carol to say where he could be reached. He also wanted to see if she had forgiven him for leaving her in Cairo. He called the Mena House, but there was no answer from her room. He next called Dr. Nashtoi only to learn he didn't know where she was. He said she hadn't been in contact with him since their meeting at the Coptic church.

"I shall give her the message when she calls. She is most likely out shopping. I should not worry if I were you. When are you to meet with Zoser?"

"In a few minutes. I'll call back later if I don't hear from Carol. In the event she calls me, I'll tell her what the meeting was about, and she can pass it on to you. You should send it on to Menefee." Loring was beginning to worry. Carol promised to stay close to the phone.

Zoser's offices were close enough to the hotel for
Loring to walk rather than fight for a taxi. They were located on the Lowenstrasse, a tree-lined boulevard which
started at the Bahnhof Platz and meandered through the
quieter section of Zurich. Lowenstrasse was one of the
old genteel streets, a one-time posh residential drive.

Most of the multi-storied houses had been refurbished
into office complexes due to the scarcity of commercial
space brought on by Zurich's entry into the world of high
finance. Though they were extensively remodeled, the
buildings still retained their residential flavor. Most of them
featured the original baroque wrought iron gates facing
the street which hid the corporate money beyond. Zoser
International was housed in one of these, number 301.

Loring was ushered into the august presence of Kurt
Sempher by an elderly man who had the mien of a family
retainer. Loring was taken aback by the room as well as
by Sempher. He and Wells were waiting for him in the
parlor, the only term Loring could think of to adequately
describe the room.

Its ceiling was at least twelve feet high, a marvelous
example of the lost art of sculpted plaster, intricately carved
in the rococo fashion of the eighteenth century, and embellished with deep floral patterns. The walls were paneled in solid Brazilian rosewood which had been meticu-
lously oiled, then buffed to a lustrous, shimmering sheen.
Sconce lighting along the walls produced a subdued halo
effect reflected off the deep red luster of the wood. The
carpets were real wool, deep and luxurious, of a mellow
shade of gold, delicately sculptured. The furniture was all
in good taste to compliment the room. It was comfortable,
yet serviceable, inviting confidentiality.

Kurt Sempher did not quite blend into the delightful
room regardless of his elegant manner. He was a large

man of nearly two hundred pounds, of average height with a cautious predator's face, and cruel eyes of transparent brown. His nose was bulbous, lips sensual, and jowls pronounced, drooping over the tight collar of his immaculate white shirt. Loring couldn't determine whether Sempher's baldness was natural or if he shaved his head. It actually glowed in the dim light of the room. Sempher presented a grotesque picture with his thick hands laced over his enormous belly and Loring recognized in him a dangerous adversary not to be taken lightly. Loring would be on guard.

Wells, on the other hand, was definitely out of place, slumped next to Sempher, with his usual unpleasant sneer and demeanor polluting the room.

Neither of them stood when Loring entered the room. The expression on Wells' face showed anger. He merely nodded to Loring, showing his contempt, probably because he had to make the trip to Zurich. Or perhaps his glare was meant to throw Loring off guard over the false story of his dismissal.

A slight smile crossed Sempher's obscene lips. One thin eyebrow raised imperceptibly. Loring had the impression his entrance interrupted a bitter argument between the two. Sempher offered Loring his hand.

"Mr. Loring, right on time. I like that. Let's dispense with all the formalities, shall we, and get right to the heart of the matter? There is whiskey over there on the sideboard if you wish. Please sit down." He motioned to the chair opposite him and Wells.

"Now, what do you have for us?"

Loring felt uncertain as to how to begin. He would have to be extremely careful not to give these two any doubt of his sincerity. He began slowly, carefully.

"The information that Mr. Wells and his partners gave me in London was very precise. I had no trouble at all in verifying it. In Cairo, I went to the Egyptian Museum for all available data I could find on the Amarna period in Egyptian history. Your research account stopped near the year 1400 BC. My findings show that one reason you couldn't get beyond that date was because your people took the wrong turn from Amarna, a very understandable mistake.

In case your history is a bit rusty, El Amarna is the city Akhenaten founded in 1360 BC. He was pushing for a new religion which his people didn't appreciate. When he died, King Tut came to the throne. With him was the great general, Horemhab, who destroyed the city."

Loring looked at the two. They were bored. Tough, he thought. They wouldn't know a good story if it came up and hit them in the face. He continued with his account.

"Horemhab had a sister and brother who were twins. The sister, Psmake, married an army officer and left Amarna to live in Memphis. Her twin, Smenkhoremhab, stayed behind. My research uncovered evidence that Psmake and her husband were members of a secret militant organization who were backing Akhenaten in his attempt to change the state religion.

This organization, called Menefee, was banned by King Tut, but Psmake and her husband continued the work of the Menefee from Memphis with help and information supplied by Smenkhoremhab. They didn't hide the fact, either. Horemhab was furious with his sister and had her expelled from the family after Tut outlawed the organization and banished its members from the city. However, Psmake continued working with the Menefee in Memphis in defiance of her brother.

It was in the lineage of Psmake that I found the connection to a branch of Sadat's family. In fact, the connection comes out in the open in the year 1267 AD. From then on, it was a fairly simple matter to trace the whole family tree. As for Smenkhoremhab, he settled in the village of Dab'a after leaving Amarna. I couldn't find any report of him ever seeing Psmake again."

Sempher was at last leaning forward. At the mention of Menefee, his interest increased. Even Wells was showing some animation.

Sempher interrupted. "Loring, what precisely was this connection between Sadat's family and this...Psmake?"

"When Horemhab expelled her from the family it was very similar to what excommunication is with Catholics. All society shunned her. We can well imagine how she felt at being cut off from all she had enjoyed...social position, wealth, prestige. It is understandable why Psmake and her husband vowed to get even. The loss of her family position plus the scattering of the Menefee and her twin brother were enough to set her off.

"The couple had a son and a daughter who married each other. This was not uncommon in those days among higher castes. The son and daughter had a son. This boy, Smente, was the forerunner of the Nebukwat family. The Nebukwats became assassins who systematically killed anyone connected with Horemhab in an effort to destroy all the general stood for and valued. Although Horemhab escaped their wrath, the Nebukwat did murder his children and his grandchildren. A younger brother, who was out of the city, went into hiding. There is no further record of him.

After this, the Nebukwats went into hiding to escape the vengeance of Horemhab, and they remained secluded for centuries. It was in 1297 AD, in Lebanon, when they came out into the open again. By this time they were back on top, socially, politically and financially. It was then that the Muslim branch of the Sadat family arose in Egypt. They had converted to Islam around 1200 AD. Both families co-existed, continuing a parallel line up to the present. The soldiers who killed Sadat were distantly related to the Nebukwats. They are called Hassim today."

Loring stopped his report, wondering if these two would accept this story. The only important deviation from the truth was in his telling them that it was Psmake who broke with her angry brother, Horemhab. It was actually the other brother, Smenkhoremhab, who was thrown out of the family. The tale of the Nebukwat was pure fantasy.

Wells finally broke his silence. "Loring, what proof, if any, do you have, and where did you get it?"

"I have it all written down here in my report. It started in the Museum archives. I found an old scroll written in hieratic script. It was by a scribe named Nephgeton. The scroll said the names of the faithful to Akhenaten could be found carved on a wall in Amarna. It took some deduction, trial and error, but I eventually found the names on the cliff walls behind the old city.

The list had thirty names, one of which was Smenkhoremhab which means 'the brother of Horemhab'. Once I had that name, and knowing the importance of this Horemhab, the rest was discovered in the written records at the Museum. The list of names is in the report."

"What did you find concerning the brother?" Sempher asked.

"Not much, really. The close relationship between Psmake and Smenkhoremhab is part of the history and legend of El Dab'a. It was told to me by an old man when I visited the village about a week ago."

"Who was the man...do you remember?"

"He called himself Mustapha. He was a withered old man who complained about the wind and sand. I understand he's dead...killed right after I left there. Maybe it's for the best. He appeared to be totally defeated by life."

"Is that all he told you?"

"Well, now that you ask, he did say something that I thought very strange. He said the village was paying for the sins of the fathers." Loring handed Sempher the document.

"Loring," whispered Sempher, looking at the list of names. "You have done a remarkable job of deduction. I congratulate you. Mr. Wells and his London associates did assure me you could do it, if anyone could. Their faith in you has been confirmed. Remarkable."

Now Wells smiled. "Yes, Loring, old Josh said you could deliver. With Mr. Sempher's approval, I want to give you a bonus of twenty-five thousand dollars in addition to your fee for finishing this far ahead of schedule. Do you agree, Mr. Sempher?"

"By all means. He has more than earned it."

Loring was relieved. They apparently believed him. "I appreciate that. Well, I guess I'm free to go back to Hawaii and resume my teaching and research. I'm glad I was able to meet your request."

"Here is your check, Loring." Wells was on his feet guiding Loring to the door. "You can rest assured that if we ever need you again, we'll call. Your reputation for thoroughness is well founded. Yes, you can go home, now. Your job here is finished."

Loring was more than elated as he walked back to the hotel. Wait until Carol and Dr. Nashtoi hear of what happened. He found himself whistling which was something he rarely did. Loring was sure his deal with Zoser was finished at last. He didn't notice the two swarthy men fall in behind him at a distance when he left the office of Zoser.

With Loring gone, Wells faced Sempher. He said rather quietly, "What do you think? Did Loring find the truth?"

Sempher hoisted himself out of the chair, walked to the sideboard and poured himself a drink. He turned to Wells, glaring.

"Let us consider two scenarios. First, Loring found the truth. In that event, we shall commence the religious riots in Egypt over Sadat's murder. By so doing, we will make the Muslims look bad and lose face, which is not exclusively an Oriental trait. Loring's information, if true, provides us with the means because the Hassim connection is Muslim. Loring's reputation erases all doubt. We have it here in black and white."

"But suppose he lied...produced a phony trace?" Wells asked.

"If Loring has given us false information, the pressing question is, why did he do it?"

"Revenge?"

"For what reason? He has no reason to connect us with the Thompson woman."

"You believe that?"

"Of course. You shifted the blame to the Menefee very convincingly, and the Shepherd woman has not contacted him to our knowledge. Yamani told us he has been working alone on our project except for a translator. He has been under our surveillance ever since he arrived in Cairo."

"Then you believe this report."

"Yes. We know for a fact that he did go to the Museum and he did travel to Amarna where he searched out the names on the cliff. He did stop at El Dab'a and speak with that old fool. It all checks out. Yes, I'm inclined to accept the information as being accurate." Sempher paused, trying to read Wells' reaction. "I say we proceed with the next phase of our operation. Besides, he has no reason to deceive us. On the outside chance he is suspicious, it must have been Claridge who warned him...he recommended Loring in the first place."

"Just for the record, I'm the one who recommended Loring for the job. I remembered him from Istanbul. He is dedicated and does methodical research. He's ethical and has the qualifications and credentials we needed for this work. Claridge made the initial contact, but hasn't had any private contact with him to my knowledge. All the calls he made to Loring were made with me in the room. Claridge is too scared of his position to chance anyone knowing about his association with the Menefee."

"But he could have warned Loring without you knowing it."

"If Loring is double-crossing us, it had to be the Shepherd woman who got to him. I say you have Yamani check on all the incoming passengers who arrived two days before Loring, and two days after. That would correspond with the time frame she disappeared in London. And speaking of Claridge, what do I do about him?"

"Kill him when you get back to London. Since we now know he is one of the Menefee, if he remains alive, they will know about our plans. Make it appear that he killed MacIvor. That would be an ironic twist."

"Okay. I'll leave for London tomorrow. Where do we go from here? What's the final payoff and what's my share?"

"Never fear, my dear chap. You have truly been my right arm in this venture. I could not have done it without you. Your share will be forthcoming soon, very soon. How would you like to control all the drug traffic in the Mediterranean area. Think of it. From Damascus to Gibraltar, and from Khartoum to Amsterdam. Once my plans are finalized, all this will be yours. Will that arrangement be satisfactory?"

"That suits me to a just fine. I'll take over whenever you give the word." This was more than Wells expected from the fat German. He continued, "If there's nothing more, I'll head back to the hotel and grab an early flight to London. I'll wait to hear from you."

"Yes, you do that."

Alone in the plush parlor, Kurt Sempher contemplated his next move. If there had been anyone else in the room they could not have possibly known from the expression on the huge man's face what was going on in his mind. The cruel eyes were closed, the fat hands resting peacefully on his stomach. Kurt Sempher was not sleeping, however. His sharp mind was churning over the events of the past couple of hours, not altogether liking them. "That greedy little man," he said aloud.

As far as he was concerned, Wells was nothing more than a grasping, ambitious thug, who valued money above all else. Loyalty and honor meant nothing to him. He would ever be a thorn in Sempher's side until he was brought under final control. What could such a person understand about the exquisite machinations of Kurt Sempher's mind? No one could, with the possible exception of Achmed Yamani. "Yes, I shall take proper care of George Wells when the time is right," he whispered to the room.

Derek Loring was another matter. What did he hope to accomplish with that ridiculous fabrication he just gave them? What did he suspect? Loring must have found something to make him play out this charade. The records

Sempher knew about, including the list of names, gave only superficial facts which hide the real information.

Why did Loring falsify the lineage of Horemhab, giving the sister rather than the brother as the Menefee contact? Could it have been an honest mistake? No, it was doctored for a reason. Loring's type never makes such mistakes. What exactly did old Mustapha tell him? Did the fool die too soon? Perhaps he should have another chat with Loring and that translator he used. Yamani will be able to get the background on her.

Kurt Sempher arose from the chair and retired to his apartment adjoining the office. He had to prepare himself for his return to Egypt and the Brotherhood. The Brotherhood was waiting for his instructions regarding 'Operation Amun' and the final time sequence for the action. In one way, he was anxious to return. His destiny was about to be realized. But on the other hand, his return to Egypt would place him precariously close to his enemies, the Menefee.

The next day the three of them met as planned. Loring was able to catch the late evening plane to Cairo. He had finished his business with Zoser so there was no point in remaining any longer. He called Carol from the airport and asked her to get in touch with Dr. Nashtoi for a meeting at Saint Barbara Church.

Dr. Nashtoi was beside himself with expectation while Carol was her usual sweet, impatient self. She didn't give Loring much time for the formalities. She prodded him for the entire story of his meeting in Zurich. She and Nashtoi would not be put off.

Loring began with his phone call to Sempher and concluded with the false tale of the Horemhab family scandal.

He told them about Sempher's reaction to his story. The old curator jumped at the opportunity to put in his thoughts on whether Zoser believed the lie.

"I believe they gave you every indication of accepting the facts you presented. I do not think they will be in a hurry to do anything foolish with them."

"They want the data for some reason," Loring added, "a reason we know nothing about. We need to ask what their interest is in connecting the Menefee with Anwar Sadat."

"What do you think, Doctor?" Carol asked.

"Everyone knows the assassination was an expression of the general dissatisfaction with the Camp David Accords. We in Egypt have thought all along that Sadat was hasty in agreeing with Begin and President Carter. This agreement did not sit well with the average Egyptian. We have too many ties with the Arab world. Sadat's death did nothing to change that feeling. Most here believe that the Arabs are entitled to their lands in Israel."

"Whatever their motive, it will be obvious soon. I think their plan has been set in motion." Loring stopped to look at his friends for their assurance. "Sempher was very anxious to have me leave. So was Wells. They wanted to continue with the discussion I intruded upon. I'm certain of this.

I think we can assume that their next move will be one to discredit the Menefee. There could be no other logical explanation why they accepted my story so willingly. They didn't care who the good guys were or the bad guys, as long as it was me who dug up the data. They're banking on my credibility to authenticate the lie of Menefee's involvement. Whatever the overall objectives, Menefee has to first be discredited because they stand in their way. They intend to make the Menefee scapegoats for Sadat's murder. If we only knew their ultimate goal."

At last, Carol had her chance to put forth her ideas. "I think whatever they're up to is just the tip of the iceberg." She was worried. "All the assassinations they've been responsible for, or orchestrated, were done with the sole purpose of creating chaos in certain countries."

"What about Gwen Thompson's murder?" Loring asked.

"Her killing was just a blind alley, no way connected with their intentions. It was an act of vengeance because Gwen was a distant relation of the Menefee. We have a two-edged problem here. On one hand, they kill the Menefee wherever they can be found. On the other, they want the Menefee to be blamed for those killings. They have to give the impression that Zoser is lily white. But even with all that, we still don't know their intentions."

"You're probably right there. We should get in touch with Ron immediately. His group is on top of the whole thing. Doctor, can you get word to Menefee to come here, or we shall go on to London?"

"I shall get in touch with him right away and call you at your hotel. This is not the end of things, my friends."

On their way back to the Mena House, Loring said off-handedly, "Now that our work for Zoser is finished, I think I'll go back to calling you Nadia. Would you like that?"

"I like what you like, my love. I do prefer my own name, I'm sort of attached to it. But what makes you think our work with Zoser is over? Do you actually believe they'll leave you alone after they find out about your false information?"

"Like I said before, I don't think they give a damn about what I found, just that it was me who found it. Yes, I think we've seen the last of them."

"What of our promise to Ron to help stop Zoser in what they're doing? We can't very well go back on our word. And what about the deal you made with Scotland Yard, not to mention MI 6, to help find the killers and to gather evidence against Zoser? Derek, we have too many commitments to just walk away, as much as we might want to."

Loring was silent, deep in thought. "You're absolutely right, of course. I guess I was just hoping it would go away like a bad dream."

"We've gone too far for that, darling."

They were lying on the bed relaxing after making love. Nadia had taken a shower and was wearing his terrycloth robe. It didn't cover her completely. "I think my tan is starting to fade. What do you think?" she said with a sexy smirk.

"I really hadn't noticed...too many other things on my mind. But now that you mention it, I believe you're right. In fact, you're a bit white behind both elbows. Better jump back into the tub and I'll paint you all over."

"The hell with that crap. We decided I was Nadia Shepherd again, and I want to be myself. When the hair dye fades out, I'll be a blond again. So there, smarty."

Languishing on the bed, Nadia stroked Derek behind the ear. She whispered to him softly, "Darling, I've decided to quit the service when this is over. From now on, wherever you go, I go. Can't you just see me as the proper little island girl in my sarong serving you your everlasting coffee?"

"Hey, I like that, but our girls don't wear sarongs. All I really want is for you to never leave me again."

"I won't, darling. You can depend on that."

Later, Dr. Nashtoi met them at a restaurant on the Cornisch, the boulevard of the rich and famous. He had obviously made reservations in his name, because when Nadia and Loring arrived they were seated immediately. Nashtoi appeared agitated, as though he had some bad news.

"Mr. Menefee said you two have done your work well. He thinks the story you planted with Zoser will hamper their plans, in spite of what those of us here believe. He found out, since last seeing you, that they plan to kill the Pope and the Archbishop of Canterbury. They plan to eliminate several American bishops with close ties to the Vatican. A few influential members of Protestant sects are marked for assassination as well.

It doesn't stop there. The Patriarch of the Greek and Syrian Churches come next, right after the murder of the Grand Mufti of Baghdad. The assassinations of the Greek, Syrian and Moslem religious leaders will be placed on the doorstep of Gadhafy in Libya. The fanatic Muslims will be blamed for the Christian killings and the Soviets are to take responsibility for the murders of the Pope and the Archbishop. Zoser wants all of the major western religions to witness catastrophic upheavals, to create distrust and dissent throughout the western world. He plans to make the Sadat incident the catalyst for all this."

"That doesn't make sense! What about Claridge?"

"Menefee has not been able to reach him. Claridge seems to have disappeared. The information I just gave you came through the mail to Menefee."

"Did Ron say what he wants us to do with this information?"

"He said for you to stay here for the time being and to keep a low profile."

"We can't just sit here on this information. We have to get to the authorities. Someone has to warn these people."

"Menefee says it will be taken care of. You are to do nothing for now."

"This is unbelievable," exclaimed Nadia. "We know what the Sadat connection is, but why does Zoser want the religious upheaval?"

A gloom fell over the dinner party. When they finished eating, they bid each other a hurried good night. Whatever was to come, Loring and Nadia knew they were to be a part of it.

"Morgan? This is Caine."

"I know. Are we sterile?"

"Yeah, it's okay." Caine hated the man at the other end of the green telephone. Someday, he thought, someday I'll kill that bastard. "Anything for us here in hell?"

"You still have our man in sight?"

"He flew to Zurich yesterday and was back here today. He met with Zoser."

"Any idea what that was all about?"

"Probably to report on what he found in the desert."

"And what was that?"

"How should I know? You have all the answers, Mister Wiseguy. You tell me."

"Don't use that tone with me, Caine. I can still break you, and don't forget it."

"Just you try it. Soloman and I are fed up with your righteous ways. As soon as we put this to bed, I'm away from this hellhole and I'm coming after you. I don't care where you hide, I'll find you."

"My goodness! Aren't we touchy? Cool it. We have work to do. The job comes first. Try to get Loring back to London. He's in our way here."

"And how do you propose I do that? Send him a note?"

"Yes, in a way. Get word to him that Shepherd needs him in London. That should send him packing."

"What about the Ashworth dame?"

"Forget her. Concentrate on Loring."

"I'll see what I can do. Same time tomorrow?"

"Yeah. And I hope you are in a better frame of mind."

THE ZOZER BROTHERHOOD 223

Chapter 13

Bert Crimmins was not a happy man. His investigation into the murders of Gwen Thompson, Brian Tupps,
Dorian MacIvor and the two Turks who killed the Thompson woman, was at a frustrating standstill. There were no
clues, no leads, nothing but suspicions so nebulous he
couldn't act on them. If that wasn't enough, there was the
matter of the intelligence leak in both the CIA and MI 6.
That situation did not lend itself to efficient police work in
his opinion.

He wondered if Hopkins got through to Washington
with the identity of Morgan, the CIA plant. Strange, he
thought, how Nadia was able to get Morgan's identity from
her source in Cairo. That bit of luck was almost too pat.
However she accomplished it, they should be thankful for
a cleaner agency. He had just called Marc Merrick, only
to learn there was no news from Loring. This certainly
was not a good day.

Constable Hughes came into his office to deliver the
daily post. The mail appeared to be the usual—responses
to his inquiries regarding wanted criminals, and inquiries
requesting similar information from Scotland Yard. However, amidst the stack of paper, one large envelope caught
his eye. The return address in the upper corner bore the
name of Zoser International. Hurriedly, he tore it open.

From the envelope Crimmins extracted a letter addressed to him personally. It was from Joshua Claridge.
He named George Wells as the one responsible for the

London killings. He explained that it was Wells who had the Thompson girl killed by the two hired Turks. These two were then killed on orders from Wells.

The letter stated further that Wells arranged for the killing of Brian Tupps, and that MacIvor was stabbed by Wells himself. The killing of MacIvor was done in anger because MacIvor had allowed Nadia Shepherd, an agent of MI 6, to escape Zoser's surveillance and subsequently vanish. All these killings were done in such a manner as to implicate an organization which was an avowed adversary of Zoser. The organization was identified.

Crimmins finished reading the document. He wasn't sure how to interpret the incriminating information. Frowning in uncertainty, he called in his aide.

"Hughes, read this and tell me what you make of it."

The constable took the letter and quickly read it over. He read it a second time. Finished, he faced Crimmins.

"It could be a red herring to purposely throw us off the scent."

"Possibly. Or it might be a ruse to shift the blame from one source to another." Crimmins was still frowning.

"Inspector, this Claridge is taking a bloody risk in writing this. What will happen if Wells finds out about this?"

"You know the answer as well as I do. Wells will kill him without batting an eye. That is, if what Claridge says about Wells is the truth." Crimmins thought for a moment, then said, "We have to assume that Claridge will run. I don't think he will stay to bluff it out."

"I agree, Inspector. Do you want me to put someone on him?"

"Never mind, Hughes. Right now we need to follow up on this information. It's the nearest thing we have to a lead. Let's presume Claridge can take care of himself."

Constable Hughes looked at his superior, a question in his expression. "Sir, I do think we should keep Claridge in tow. We'll need him for corroboration of this evidence if we hope to make a case from it."

"Good thinking, Hughes. Do it."

Hughes left and Crimmins turned his attention back to the envelope. He examined the other documents and papers stuffed inside. There were letters from Wells to people and organizations Crimmins either didn't know, or only knew slightly. He would have Hughes send the names through the computer...no telling what might emerge.

The final piece of paper in the envelope was a memo from Claridge telling the inspector he had talked with Loring in Cairo, and that Loring said he had uncovered the information Zoser needed for its global plan to disrupt Western religious thinking. The memo added that he, Claridge, was leaving London, going into hiding because he feared for his life. He stated he was a member of a secret organization that wanted Zoser destroyed. The memo ended in telling Crimmins there was a safe in Wells' office which contained additional incriminating evidence that tied Wells and Zoser into the London killings.

"Hughes," he shouted to his aide. "Don't bother to find Claridge."

"Sir?"

"He's gone. Left London for parts unknown."

"Very good, Inspector."

All these accusations, although unsubstantiated, agreed with his own suspicions. What could he do with it all? Certainly Wells would deny all of it as being the ravings of a disgruntled employee. He needed actual proof and without confirmation by Claridge the information was useless. Should he go barging into the offices of Zoser, Wells would be on his guard, and the investigation would be ruined.

If he didn't get what was in the safe, if there was anything, Wells most likely would destroy it and Zoser would be home free. Crimmins knew he didn't have legal cause to demand what was in the safe. He felt it imperative to get in touch with Hopkins at MI 6 for help in getting the data. But he would wait one more day for Loring to call. No, he thought, he had to call Loring. This couldn't wait. Merrick knew how to reach him.

Nadia and Loring were leaving their room when the phone rang. It was the desk.

"Sir, a Mr. Merrick in London phoned and wanted you to contact him as soon as possible. He mentioned something about a farm for sale that you were inquiring about."

Loring thanked the man, saying he would place the call later. Nadia wanted to know who it was.

"Marc wants me to call him. I think it would be better if I called from your room."

When the call went through, Marc came on the line. He told Loring that Crimmins was in his office and that he had to speak with him.

"Derek? Where have you been? Why haven't you contacted me?"

"Inspector, I've been busy doing the job I was hired to do.

It's finished now so I'm winding things up here then we're coming back to London. What's up? Why the urgency?"

Crimmins told Loring about the information he received from Claridge. He had to know if Loring came up with facts which might be helpful in his getting to Wells through proper channels. He also made mention of his idea of getting MI 6 involved.

"I met with Wells and the big boss of Zoser in Zurich just yesterday. You and I were right in believing Wells never left Zoser. I gave them a doctored account of what Nadia and I discovered in the old ruins. They seemed to be satisfied. They even presented me with a bonus. I never found a thing which connects any of them with the London killings. If I had, you would have heard from me. About getting MI 6 in the act, why not ask Nadia? She's here with me."

"Inspector? Nadia here. I overheard what Derek said. Why do you think MI 6 should be called in?"

"I believe I would muck up the whole thing if I went after Wells out in the open with nothing but my suspicions. This requires covert action, as you would say. I desperately need some information locked in his safe, but I can't get to it legally. You Intelligence people don't always concern yourselves with legalities. What is your honest opinion?"

"I think you should do whatever has to be done to get into that safe. If that requires the cooperation and special talents of MI 6, so be it. Mr. Hopkins will be honest with you. He'll tell you right off what he will or will not do. I honestly don't think restricting legal ramifications will color his actions."

"That's what I thought. He owes me...us...something for pointing out the leak in his office. I believe I shall get in touch with him. Do you have anything else which might be of interest to me?"

"Nothing other than I'm quitting the service, going back to Hawaii with Derek. He's promised to make an honest woman out of me. How does that strike you?"

"I'm delighted for you both. It's about time that young

man realized how lucky he is to have someone like you, Nadia. We'll celebrate when you get back to London, give you a real sendoff. My best to you both."

After Nadia hung up the phone, she turned to Loring. "Why didn't you tell him about the assassination attempts?"

"He'd want to know where we got the information and that might bring Ron into the picture. Menefee doesn't want Bert involved with that. I think we should let that information come from Ron, in his own time."

Word from Menefee did come. Nashtoi called.

"Mr. Menefee wants you both back in London right away. He said he has information concerning the assassinations that you should know about, and that you, Miss Ashworth, will know what to do with the facts. He has reserved a room for you at the Brinkley Hotel. He claims you both know the reason for this. Something about memories. Does that make sense to you?"

"Yes, Doctor Nashtoi, it does. We'll leave right away, as soon as we can get a flight. Don't know if we'll ever see you again, but we do thank you for all your help, and if we're ever back here, we'll stop to visit. Goodbye, and thanks again."

British Airways Flight 14 took off on schedule. Loring and Nadia settled back into their seats to get comfortable for the long ride home. Nadia held Derek's hand tightly. She let it go only to fasten her seatbelt. She had the look of a happy woman.

Thirty minutes after takeoff the plane commenced a shallow turn to the west. None of the passengers seemed to notice the change in direction until a gruff voice came over the intercom.

"All passengers will remain in their seats. We have taken control of the aircraft. We have commanded the pilot to follow our instructions. No one will be injured provided the pilot does as he is told. It will serve no purpose to create a disturbance, so you will please remain seated."

From where he was sitting Loring could see the man at the phone. He was unkempt in appearance, dressed in filthy military fatigues and his accent placed him from somewhere in the Near East even though he was speaking clear, proper English. He used words that didn't come from a tourist's dictionary.

"Where do you think he's from?" Loring asked Nadia.

"Some Arab country. The inflections he's using give it away. I wonder what they're after. Do you think this is another senseless hijacking to get some terrorist out of jail?"

"I guess we'll just have to wait and see. It might get a bit hairy, though. The British keep saying they won't deal with terrorists, and I've always agreed with that policy. It looks like we'll get the chance to see how firm they really are." Loring took Nadia's hand. It felt better to do that.

Completing its turn, the plane began a long descent toward the North African coastline. Off in the distance, Loring could make out the skyline of Alexandria, but the plane was headed west of that city.

The brown, mottled shoreline was broken by scattered villages, some of which he and Nadia had recently driven through. The green hills rose in the south, close to the seacoast, and beyond was the endless desert stretching to infinity. On his left, Loring made out the large indentation of a gulf. The only sizable gulf on that part of the coast was the Gulf of Sidra, off the Libyan shore. In realizing the implications, he voiced his concern to Nadia.

"Unless I miss my guess, we're headed for a landing in Libya. Gadhafy doesn't give terrorists any trouble. Most likely, he sent them. I suspect we're going into Benghazi, the only place this side of Tripoli big enough to handle a plane like this. Just keep calm. The British will handle this."

"Don't kid me, Derek. You're just as frightened as I am. One can never tell what these radical lunatics will do. If nothing else, they usually do the unexpected."

The pilot made a long straight-in approach and landed the 747 in a swirling sandstorm. Any good pilot would be cautious about landing a plane full of paying passengers in marginal weather conditions, but their pilot didn't have too much to say in the matter with a gun in his back.

The blowing sand stopped as the plane was taxiing to the tarmac apron at the edge of the field. When the plane braked to a stop, it was immediately surrounded by several grim soldiers armed with automatic weapons. The escape chute in the first class section was released and the hijackers came forward. There were three of them brandishing guns and knives. They came up to where Loring and Nadia were sitting. The one with the gruff voice spoke.

"Out, both of you. Slide down the chute.

We shall be right behind you. The soldiers will shoot if you make a false move."

"What the hell is this all about? We're private citizens and under the protection of Great Britain. I'm an American, and she's Canadian. You can't do this."

"We know very well who you are, Mr. Loring. And Miss Shepherd. Just leave the plane and these other people can be on their way. You two are all we want, this time. Go! Leave the plane."

Nadia and Loring looked at each other fearfully. His first thought was that Zoser was behind this, somehow wanting them alive. And how did they know Nadia was Nadia Shepherd? Refusing to comply with orders would be futile on their part and might endanger the other passengers. All they could do was bluff it out and obey.

The three hijackers were not overly courteous or gentle in pushing them to the escape hatch. They left everything behind as they slid down the chute, burning themselves in the process. When they reached the ground, the terrorists slid down and the group was escorted to a waiting car displaying Libyan army markings. As the car sped away toward the east, Loring and Nadia saw the plane taxi and takeoff. Nadia sat very close to Derek, holding his arm in a tight grip.

"Where do you think they are taking us?" she whispered.

"I haven't the slightest clue, Nadia. But I'm worried. These guys look dangerous to me. This must have been planned for some time...it's going too smoothly to suit me. Somehow they found out we were taking this plane and set the takeover in motion. Every step is well rehearsed. Just be yourself, and don't show them fear. That's what these sons of bitches thrive on...fear."

The car raced along the dusty road, clouds of sand and debris blowing up in their wake. After about an hour, the car pulled onto an airstrip outside the town of Tobruk, one more battle-scarred remnant of war. The terrorists motioned them out of the car and herded them to a small single-engine plane parked on the runway, its engine idling. The army personnel waved to them as they climbed aboard the plane, got back into their vehicle and drove off.

The small plane, now loaded with the five passengers, turned into the wind, engines at full throttle, and took off. Once it was airborne, it banked to the east toward the Libyan-Egyptian desert region. The pilot hedge-hopped a few feet above the desert floor apparently as a ploy to avoid the Egyptian radar.

For the better part of an hour, the hapless passengers fought off waves of nausea. The flight came to a stop when the plane circled a lone airstrip in the desert. It landed smoothly and rolled to the end of the strip. When they all climbed out of the cramped cabin the desert heat engulfed them with arms of fire. It was a small but welcome comfort that the pilot had to wait, probably for orders, which allowed the passengers to seek the shade cast by the wings of the plane. Nadia and Loring were dripping wet from the heat, their clothes no longer offering any protection.

Moments later, from the deep, featureless desert to the south, the sound of a helicopter broke the silence. None of the terrorists had spoken a single word since they boarded the plane. The chopper hovered over the them, banked slightly and settled down to the sand, blowing storms of cutting sand in every direction.

Loring and Nadia knew the procedure by this time and made their way to the chopper, followed by the three kidnappers. With a groaning shudder because of the added weight, the helicopter rose from the sand into the clear, cloudless sky, and headed south. By his reckoning, Loring felt they were hundreds of miles from the nearest civilization.

The chopper came to rest in the desert wasteland. There was nothing to be seen except sand and more sand in every direction. No landmarks, nothing. The sound of a motor searched them out, and into that hot, empty world came a four-wheeled vehicle with over-sized tires to navigate in the sand. Two of the terrorists remained behind with the helicopter while Nadia and Derek were taken aboard the truck, the third kidnapper mounting guard.

They turned to the east, driving recklessly in the shifting sand, over a rise in the ground which defined a large hollow, arid depression. Past this depression, the truck came to a stop beside a green oasis.

Their guard ordered them from the truck, remaining three paces behind them with gun at the ready. He prodded them forward to the far side of the oasis. They came to a cleft in the rock outcropping which bordered the oasis. They were pushed through the opening in the rock into shadow and darkness and then prodded ahead until they came into a dimly lit passageway, hewn from the parent stone. They were urged forward, passing wall-hung torches used for illumination from time to time.

The rock floor of the passageway was uneven and strewn with rubble making it difficult to walk. They entered another passage, at right angles to the entry corridor. It led to a wide opening in the tunnel, creating a fairly large room. There they were stopped and made to sit on a low stone bench hugging the far wall of the rock room. Loring and Nadia held hands, tightly. It seemed they were about to discover their fate.

Distant sounds came from one of the other passages intersecting the room, at first no more than a monotonal hum, but as it came nearer, they recognized it to be a chant, a kind of monastic chant very similar to those heard around abbeys. The chant broke all around them, cascading over the stark, unyielding rock walls of the chamber.

From out of the gloom, beyond the light, a procession of robed figures entered. The hooded figures, still chanting, milled about the room, placing their torches in empty wall brackets. Soon the chamber was ablaze with the yellow light cast from the burning torches. When the chant reached a crescendo, it suddenly stopped, cut off by some unheard signal.

From a passageway on the opposite side, came the

sound of more voices, not in a chant, but in discourse. The voices belonged to men who appeared, naked except for brief starched loincloths, each carrying a torch in one hand and a gold-tipped spear in the other. Nadia and Loring understood some of what they were saying. They were giving orders in archaic Egyptian for all to step side for the approach of the ruler. Hearing these old commands, Loring and Nadia stared at one another, not believing what they were hearing, and yet, with the surroundings in which they found themselves, it was not at all unexpected. Even so, they both shrank back against the rock wall, shuddering in terror.

Loring couldn't believe the sight before him. Out from the midst of the group strode the evil, ugly, grotesque figure of Kurt Sempher. He was regaled in all the trappings of the ancient rulers of Egypt, complete with the double red and white crown of kingship. He had gone as far as to wear the false beard of office attached to his several chins with a gold chain looped over his head and under the crown. The chains of jewelry he sported around his neck were draped over a linen waistcoat.

In one hand he held a gold scepter and in the other he carried the tasseled whisk of the pharaoh's office, casting it over the bowed heads of those who were on their knees in adoration and supplication. Sempher turned to Loring and Nadia, hate flashing from the his piercing eyes. He spoke aloud for all to hear.

"The spirit of Mighty Zozer has returned as promised. I am here before you, you of the Brotherhood, to say that the past days of this land's glory are returning with me. I am Sempher the First, Pharaoh! My enemies, who are also your enemies, have tried to stop my return. They have tried to prevent the resurrection of glorious Kemet, the Black Land.

The tides of history have brought us to this day. Our enemies might well have tried to hold back the waves of the sea. These two foreigners before you are among those who would deny us the glory which is rightfully ours. They shall be dealt with in the prescribed manner as written by the scribes of bygone days. We return to that time. Therefore, their punishment shall be as it is written. Others beyond this place have attempted to stop the fulfillment of our destiny, and they, too, have been eliminated according to the old writings. Bring these two along where they will be restrained until the moon is in its proper phase for their execution."

Loring and Nadia were thrown into a rock dungeon carved from the solid stone of the caverns. The massive door was solid bronze with no other opening in the room. The only light was provided by a single torch set in a wall bracket. The air that ventilated the cell came from a wide crack under the door. There was no way out of their prison. Loring wasn't prepared for this. Their situation had an aura of finality about it. He took Nadia into his arms, holding her tightly.

"Looks like we bought the farm, Nadia. Just when we found each other, too. I'm sorry about all this. Maybe, if I hadn't agreed to Ron's plea for help so readily, you could have found some other way without me putting us in this mess. This is all my fault, damn it!"

"Oh, my darling." Nadia hugged him close. "It is not your fault!"

"I can't believe this is happening in the twentieth century, right in the middle of a civilized country. How could Sempher get so much control that he could bring this about? Is he all that rich and powerful?"

"He's insane," Nadia said, emphatically. "He actually believes he's the reincarnation of the pharaoh."

"From all I've read, the code of justice in the old days was pretty bloodthirsty. The pharaoh had the first and last word."

Nadia looked deep into his eyes, tears on the verge of flowing. "Derek, my love, no matter what happens, do not, I repeat, do not believe you're responsible for this situation. I came to you, and worked with you, with my eyes wide open. I knew the danger, even though I tried to ignore it. Perhaps I thought our love would carry us over any and all obstacles. Remember this, darling...my only regret is that we can't go back to your lovely islands. Hold me close until it's time to go."

They were in each other's arms when the guards came for them. Motioned out of their cell, they followed the stoic men along the dim passage they'd traveled earlier. They were led into a large room with stone floors instead of the packed sand and rubble. The walls were festooned in draperies emblazoned with the art work which rightfully belonged in the tombs of the ancient kings. Ensconced on a gold-encrusted throne, was Sempher. He was still dressed in the regal attire as before and still as ugly and grotesque. He resembled a child playing at make-believe, only Sempher was not playing.

He waved at them haughtily with the whisk, motioning for them to be seated on the bench to his left, well below his line of sight.

"I imagine you both are wondering why I am condescending to this audience with you. The truth of the matter is I found you two to be worthy adversaries and that, in mutual respect for a defeated enemy, I felt I owed you an answer as to why you are here."

Loring squeezed Nadia's hand and continued to stare at the grotesque sight before him.

"You are fools, Derek Loring and Nadia Shepherd.

Did you really think you had me believing that cock and bull story you told me in Zurich? Never! I had you followed from the time you left my office, just waiting for the right time to get you both here. I dared not let you escape back to England.

You see, Loring, the entire escapade you were on was so much camouflage. We've had the data we needed for our plans for some time. You were hired to give credence to that data. Those names you found? We had them all the time. The Brotherhood discovered them as soon as they were carved on the wall by Nephgeton.

And you, Miss Shepherd...you were coming much too close to leading the entire intelligence community to us. Oh, yes, I imagine you are wondering how we found out who you really were. Your eyes, Miss Shepherd, the color of your eyes gave you away. We had your description from your file in MI 6. I cannot understand why you didn't wear colored contact lenses for a complete disguise. No matter, you both will die regardless." Sempher put his head back as far as he could push the rolls of fat on the back of his neck, and laughed uncontrollably.

Loring put his arm around Nadia now. If there were just some way he could save her from this fate. Too many of Sempher's disciples lining the walls of the room for him and Nadia to make a dash for it. He began to shiver.

Sempher finally got control of himself. "For your edification, the Brotherhood was a disorganized bunch of rabble when I found them, but they suited my purposes perfectly. The Brotherhood has been part of the legends of this land from earliest times, back to the reign of Pharaoh Zozer. This is where it all started, in these caves carved from the rock of Egypt.

I gave the Brotherhood a new purpose in life, promising to return them to their former status, feared by all.

Money can be used in so many different ways. It has provided me with what I need most in life...power. I have my army now, an army willing to die for me, and thousands more waiting to be called to join this elite group. We kill to justify the end, regardless of what you heard from the Menefee.

The Menefees have been our enemies since the beginning. They have done their work well, too well. They hamper us at every turn, but now that my plans are in place, they won't be in the way any longer. The Brotherhood doesn't care who rules this land as long as they get what they want. I have promised them that, showed them how to get it. I am the pharaoh of Egypt...it is my destiny!" Sempher shouted this last statement loud enough to have it reverberate around the stone walls.

"In a few weeks, my 'Operation Amun' starts. The self-appointed religious leaders throughout the world will try to stand in my way, try to prevent me from taking over this land under godly kingship. They shall not succeed. There will be riots and assassinations of religious leaders all over the Western world. I shall be a god here in the new Egypt. All who oppose me will be wiped from the face of the earth. You two fought me. Therefore, you will be put to death in the prescribed way, according to the writings of the past."

Sempher motioned to two of his aides to take Loring and Nadia away. "Oh, by the way, Dr. Loring and Miss Shepherd, you might as well enjoy yourselves for the brief time you have left. You can screw yourselves into oblivion for all I care. Or you can pray to your gods. It doesn't matter, for you are to die the day after tomorrow."

Back in their cell, Nadia and Loring sank to the floor, clinging to each other as never before. They couldn't believe the enormity of the worldwide upheaval that would come with the implementation of 'Operation Amun'. The people around the world wouldn't let it happen. Someone would stop Sempher. For the sake of all mankind, someone had to.

The prisoners were brought food, simple and well cooked. They weren't hungry, having resigned themselves to the inevitable. Each made peace in his own way, silently. To each other, they reaffirmed their love, not in the physical sense, but with the words and looks of lovers. They were sadly content just being together. As the hours went by they knew their fate was sealed. What glimmer of hope they once shared no longer existed.

The green telephone rang. It was the man called Caine who picked it up.

"It's clear here."

"This is Masters, your new control."

"What happened to Morgan?"

"He swallowed his .38. Seems he was playing for the other team."

"I knew there was a reason I hated that bastard."

"You know about the plane?"

"Yeah. It's all over this place. Mubarak is making noises about turning the army loose to find them. We'll be lucky if he gives us one platoon. What's the order from Home Base?"

"We're sending a team over to search from the west. You and Soloman are to join the British people and work your way to Matruh. If Gadhafy is behind this, a lot of people want his ass in a sling."

"What about Canada? The woman was Canadian."

"No. She was really Shepherd in disguise. She had everyone fooled, so don't feel too bad you didn't know."

"Damn! I give those two a lot of credit. They played it real cool."

"No matter. We have to find them for political reasons you don't know about. As people, they're expendable, but we need the information they have. Is that clear?"

"Yeah, very clear. You coming over here?"

"No, not at this time. Keep us informed. I'll call tomorrow for the latest on the search. Let the Brits call the shots from your end."

"Okay. Caine out."

Chapter 14

The evening newscast came over the BBC at 10 PM.

> "British Airways Flight 14 was
> hijacked by three armed men shortly
> after the aircraft left Cairo. The aircraft
> was forced to land in Benghazi. Two
> passengers were removed from the plane
> and were taken away in Libyan army
> vehicles. The aircraft was then allowed
> to take off and continue its flight to
> London. The kidnapped passengers
> were later identified by their passports
> left with their belongings on the plane.
> The were a Miss Carol Ashworth,
> Canadian citizen, and a Mr. Derek Loring,
> American. The hijackers gave no reason
> for the abduction. None of the other
> passengers or members of the crew
> were harmed."

"Those sons of bitches got 'em!" screamed Bert
Crimmins to his wife, Nora. "I knew it was too soon to
celebrate. Derek is just a babe in the woods when it comes
to undercover work. He isn't equipped to mentally or physically handle this type of danger. Nadia isn't much better

at it even though she's had some experience. They both are certainly in for it now."

This outburst caused Nora to wince with alarm. It wasn't at all like Bertie to get so excited and upset. She made an effort to calm him down, not realizing he wasn't really listening to her.

"Dear, perhaps things will work out in the end. What earthly reason could they possibly have to detain that nice Mr. Loring? He's just an architect, a scholar. Really, Bertie, it makes no sense at all. Now that Shepherd woman, she's a different story. Her being a spy and all, makes her a prime target. We must keep faith in that everything will be set to rights."

"Nora, shut up, please! You don't know what you're talking about. I'm trying to think, to find an answer to the problem."

Nora Crimmins was stunned at this outburst. Bertie never talked to her like that. Thoroughly shaken, Nora retreated to the quiet of their bedroom.

Crimmins was pacing the floor, clenching and unclenching his fists. His mind in a turmoil, terrible visions ran through his head...visions of Loring being tortured then staked out in the desert. He saw ants and scorpions, biting and stinging, swarming over his naked body. And Nadia, dear, lovely Nadia, forced to submit to the rape and degradation and filth of those verminous men. The defilement of Nadia was more than he could bear. Bert Crimmins began to cry bitter tears.

After a while, he stopped his crisscrossing the parlor, wiped his eyes and opened the bedroom door. Nora was sitting by the window looking out at the London twilight. She, too, was crying.

"Dreadfully sorry, old girl. I shouldn't snap at you. But I feel so responsible, so helpless."

"I know, luv, I know...but we daren't give up hope. I believe I'll pray awhile."

"Quite. It just might help them."

Back in the parlor, Crimmins reached for the phone. He dialed a private number, a number known to but a very few. After four rings,

"Yes?"

"Hopkins? Crimmins here. You heard? What are you doing about it? Those people are in very serious trouble. We have to do something."

"Hold on there, Bert. Take it easy. These things take time. We can't do a thing until we have some idea of where they are."

"Geof, what exactly do we know?"

"We know the plane landed in Libya. According to the pilot, Loring and Shepherd were forced into a car at gun point and driven away. The pilot watched for as long as he could, and he swears the car headed back east, toward Egypt. That lunatic, Gadhafy, naturally denies any part of it. He claims it didn't happen, that it's just an imperialistic ruse to get agents into his country. We can't expect any cooperation from that quarter."

"What are your people doing in the meantime?"

"I called Cairo. Our man down there, Peter Bradshaw, is acquainted with Loring and knows Shepherd from awhile back. He did a bit of leg work for them. He's been in touch with President Mubarak, who promises his full support."

"Have you spoken with the CIA?"

"Yes, I have. Washington is up in arms, making all sorts of threats and accusations. They're sending a team of men out to give Bradshaw a hand. This could turn out to be a real shoot-out. By the way, Washington sends its thanks on the Morgan matter. Turns out Morgan killed himself. I think you'd better get some sleep. I'll ring you in the morning."

A tired and angry Crimmins went back to his pacing. He could hear Nora crying in the other room. She was leaving him alone with his visual nightmares. Hopkins' words of encouragement did nothing to dispel the knot of fear in his chest. His trepidation drove him to the cupboard where he took out a bottle of scotch. Drinking at home was one thing Bert Crimmins rarely did, but this situation was becoming worse by the minute. He needed to calm his fears, if only for a moment.

Even in this singular act of indulgence, he was a failure. After his second drink, Ron Menefee burst into the room.

"Have you heard, Bertie? Yes, of course, you know all about it. What are we to do?" Menefee was quite out of breath. He stood in the middle of the room, undecided if to pace or throw himself into a chair.

Crimmins unbridled his rancor and frustration. He fairly snarled at his brother-in-law.

"What do you mean...'what are we going to do?' You have no part in this mess. Take my advice and stay the bloody hell out of it. You'll only get yourself maudlin, like me. This entire muck-up is my doing. I talked Derek and Nadia into helping me."

"You couldn't have anticipated this, Bertie."

"I should have. My God, I sent them off to Egypt, ill-prepared and unprotected. I actually put Nadia on the plane! Damnation and hell's fire! Do you know that I promised Derek he would be guarded day and night? Just shows you how far I've slipped. If they ever get out of this mess, I'll make it up to them, believe me. Care for a drink, Ron?"

"Bertie, be quiet. I have to talk with you. There is something I should have told you long ago. Derek wondered why I didn't tell you. Bertie, I'm not what you think me to be. Actually, I'm the person responsible for sending Derek and Nadia into danger. They did it for me and my group."

"You what? I think you had better make yourself clear, Ron Menefee, right now."

Menefee told Crimmins his story, the whole story about the legendary Menefee society, the Zozer Brotherhood, and how he came to know about the killings and the coming religious assassinations. He told Bert how he convinced Loring and Nadia to help rid the world of the Brotherhood. Their plan was to publish the facts, to get the outside world interested enough to make a public outcry and demand retribution. There was to be no killing.

He told Crimmins about 'Operation Amun'. Menefee then confessed that he called them back to London, made them take that plane. When he finished the story, he turned back to Crimmins. Tears filled his eyes. His grief could not be hidden.

"So you see, Bertie, I am responsible for whatever trouble they're in. God, I would give anything to undo it all. Derek and Nadia understood there would be some danger, but when they discovered the reason why Gwen Thompson was killed, they actually wanted to help. I was related to Gwen...did you know that? She was a distant cousin."

Crimmins couldn't speak for some time. He started to pour another drink but stopped, the glass halfway to his lips. His eyes glared with contempt.

"You sniveling, self-righteous bastard! Right here, under my own roof. How the hell could you, of all people, be involved in such monstrous things? Didn't you have enough faith in me, trust me enough to confide in me. We might have worked together, or at least tried. But no, you had to do it all by yourself, ride your goddamned white horse into battle and get two special people I care about very much into so dangerous a spot they'll never get out. Right now, Ron, I almost hate you. I want you to leave my house now and go back to your precious society."

Menefee looked sadly at Crimmins. This was what he wanted to avoid, this anger and condemnation from his own family. That's why he couldn't tell Bert about it before. He loved his gruff brother-in-law, looked up to him almost as a father figure. Bert was his hero. With sagging shoulders he walked toward the door. His hand on the knob, he turned and faced Bert.

"I'll be by in the morning to get my things. I'll say goodbye to Nora then. I'm very sorry about this, Bertie...I truly am. God, I feel awful."

"Wait up, Ron. Don't go." Crimmins hurried over to the door to face Menefee. Bert's eyes were filling by now. He grabbed Ron and clung to the younger man. "We can't make any decisions tonight. We're both too upset. Perhaps we're each to blame. Stay here, Ron, stay with Nora and me. We can sort this out in the morning. You only did what you thought you had to do. I can understand that. I do it all the time. We'll make our plans then. Now, come and sit down...let's talk. Maybe the pain will go away for a little while."

In the morning, Crimmins and Ron showed up early at Geoffrey Hopkins' office. The news was no more encouraging that it had been the night before. Neither Washington nor Whitehall was any further ahead in learning which terrorist splinter group masterminded the abduction. There had been no demands announced, no harangues about Arab rights from any quarter. There was no trace whatsoever of the kidnapped pair. It was as though they dropped into a hole, out of sight from the entire world.

Hopkins was on the line to Cairo talking to Peter Bradshaw when Crimmins and Menefee rushed into the office. After a few added instructions to the Cairo man, Hopkins hung up the phone and turned his attention to his visitors.

"Bradshaw has been keeping Achmed Yamani under constant surveillance since the plane was hijacked. He's convinced Yamani is part of a radical group who might be responsible. This Yamani runs the Cairo office of Zoser International, the outfit who retained Loring in the first place. According to Bradshaw, Yamani has an unsavory past and maintains a vicious band of thugs to do his bidding. It isn't too clear what work Yamani does for Zoser, but the connection is there, and Bradshaw thinks it's his best lead so far."

Crimmins was listening intently to this, as was Menefee. Ron had said he was certain the Brotherhood kidnapped Derek and Nadia. Crimmins wasn't all that positive, but now that this Bradshaw uncovered something to connect Zoser to Cairo, he began to suspect that Ron might be right after all. He asked Hopkins, "What was the exact nature of the work Bradshaw did for Loring, Geof? Do you know?"

"Strange you should ask that. He was able to trace some people Loring and Shepherd wanted to find. Peter was able to trace these people back to some remote village on the sea, where the trail ended. One of the people he traced, Amin Salazar, had been murdered in 1907. From what Bradshaw told me, that murder was almost identical to those we've had here in London recently, those ritualistic killings. Loring was extremely happy over what Peter found, but he didn't say why."

"Mr. Hopkins," Menefee said, "Amin Salazar was my grandfather, and was related to Gwen Thompson, the girl who was so sadistically murdered in front of Loring. Derek wanted to know what was in the girl's background that might have triggered her death. Bradshaw must have provided the clue...the murder of Salazar."

"What's your interest in all this, Menefee? I know what Bert's is. Why are you so interested?"

Crimmins saved Ron from having to answer. "Geof, Ron is a friend of Loring and was interested in his research. Ron is Egyptian, you know, and has roots which go deep into that country's history. Loring got quite a bit of background information from Ron on the time of the pharaohs."

"I see. Well, anyway, this is what is being done. The CIA is sending an undercover search team into Libya through Algeria. That particular border isn't nearly as well guarded as that of Chad or Egypt. I understand the members of this team are experts who hope to trace the soldiers who helped in the abduction. MI 6, has a team concentrating in and around Cairo, Alexandria and Matruh. We're using every trick in our cupboard to get a line on where the car stopped.

The CIA chaps will work east from Tripoli to Tobruk. Someone must have seen the car. Mubarak is sending us some of his people to go along, to help with questioning the locals. Other than that, we'll just have to wait. We can depend on Bradshaw. Since he worked with Shepherd a while back, he has a certain fondness for her. If anyone can find a trace, he's the man."

Crimmins and Menefee left Hopkins and headed for Scotland Yard. Crimmins wanted to read the computer printout on the names Zoser had in its files. It wasn't the thing he really wanted to do, but it was his job. What he actually wanted to do was to find Loring and Nadia, but had to leave their kidnapping to the intelligence agencies.

Ron Menefee, however, was not restricted by rules and regulations. He was on the afternoon flight to Cairo.

Loring and Nadia had no way of knowing when daylight arrived. He still had his watch...when they were captured the kidnappers didn't search them or remove any of their belongings. The passage of time, however, had no point of reference in the dungeon. One part of the day was the same as any other. Their finite world was always in the same degree of semi-darkness, dispelled here and there by the smoking torch bracketed to the stone wall of their cell.

Nadia stirred in his arms. She gradually came awake after a fitful sleep. They were lying on a heap of dirty rags which were all that was between them and the stone floor.

"What time is it, Derek?" she asked, muffling a yawn.

"According to my watch, it's six o'clock...morning, I think. That means we've been here over twenty-four hours. Scared?"

"You have to ask? I'm petrified, but they won't see it, those maniacs." Hearing Nadia talk about that made Loring's heart ache. His beautiful Nadia couldn't die. He couldn't believe this was happening. "Derek, if we have the choice, let's go out together. I can't possibly watch you die. It's the least they can do."

"My God, Nadia, I can't stand to have you talk like this."

"Oh, my darling...my dear, darling Derek, I'll keep saying it to the end...I love you with all my being."

Loring had to get hold of himself. If only there was some way he could save Nadia. "However I die, your name will be on my lips and in my heart." He reached over and brushed a tear from her eye.

"I had so hoped I would see your islands one day."

"Darling, you would have liked them."

"I'm sure they're everything I ever dreamed of, Derek. Remember, back in Dairut? I had a premonition then I would never get to Hawaii. Strange, but that day seems so very far away now, and yet, I can still see the waiter bringing you that cup of American coffee. You were so happy. Goddamn it, Derek! Why does it have to end this way?"

Loring didn't answer. He held her closer in his arms. She was weeping softly and clinging to him. In spite of the horror of the time and place, Nadia was trying to stay as cheerful as she could. It wasn't easy for either of them.

The guards came then and led them down the long passageway. They heard chanting up ahead. Before long they caught a glimpse of hooded figures shuffling in a procession toward the light in the distance. They were brought into a large room cut from the same rock as the rest of the caves.

They had not seen this room before. In the center of the area a huge stone altar rose three feet above the floor level. The altar was deeply incised with hieroglyphics which Loring and Nadia recognized to be the blessings of Zozer, Pharaoh of the Third Dynasty. The royal cartouche was emblazoned on the side of the altar, commanding attention. Across the room, on the far side of the stone slab, the hooded figures stood as though transfixed. They gazed at the altar while their chant continued.

Sempher stood apart from the rest of this group. He was wearing the single white crown of ancient Egypt and had only a brief loincloth around his immense waist. His chest was bare except for the gold medallions set in turquoise draped around his neck and over his shoulders. He raised his arms, casting a regal stare at the chanters. Silence fell and filled the room.

"The hour has arrived for the vengeance of Zozer to fall on these two defilers. It was written by the scribes that an unsullied maid be sacrificed on this altar of atonement with the blade of Amun. This woman is not a maid, and surely not unsullied. She is a whore who copulated under the watchful eye of Amun. Her punishment must be by the knife, though different than that prescribed for the act of holy atonement. The man must bear witness to her execution, for he is morally responsible for the actions of the whore. After she has tasted the blade of atonement, he will be taken out into the desert, there to perish slowly under the all-seeing eyes of Amun. Make them ready."

"Sempher, wait!" Loring cried. "Let us die together, for God's sake. Wake up...this is now, today, the twentieth century. Surely you can do that much for fellow human beings."

"Do not dare to compare your miserable selves with the blessed Brotherhood, the chosen of the divine Zozer. We are not fellow human beings. You presume too much. It must be done as it is written...with no exceptions. Now, make them ready."

Hooded figures came forward and seized them both. Nadia tried to fight them off, but she was no match for the stronger men. Loring was pinned to the stone bench by his burly guards who forced him to watch the movements around the altar. The men stripped Nadia of her clothes and threw her on the altar, eaglespread. They tied her arms and legs to the stone rings embedded in the stone.

She laid there naked and helpless, but asking for no mercy. She was weeping quietly. Her eyes sought out Loring who was filled to the point of nausea with anger and frustration at not being able to do anything but watch the girl he loved. He knew what was to come. He had seen it all before with the murder of Gwen Thompson.

"Dear God," he whispered, "spare her any pain."

The thought of what was about to happen to Nadia was too much for Loring. He yelled out, "Sempher, you son of a bitch! I'll find you someday and kill you. I'll cut out your heart and feed it to the jackals. Your god, Anubis, will never find it. The desert won't get me."

Sempher ignored this outburst of Loring's. His gaze was riveted on the stone altar. Nadia's naked body, so beautiful and unblemished, was being painted in the grotesque designs Loring had seen on Gwen. She was lying quite still now, resigned to her fate. The blue paint covered her breasts and flowed down her smooth torso to meld with the red paint on her genitals. She, too, knew about Gwen, knew about the sacrifice these maniacs demanded. A sad smile crossed her lips and she turned to Loring, murmuring, "I love you, Derek Loring. Close your eyes when the time comes. Good bye, my love."

Sempher came up to Nadia, looking into her tear-stained face. "You are indeed fortunate that Mr. Wells is not here. He would have raped you in front of all these men, and taken great pleasure from the act. Something of an animal is Mr. Wells, but he serves me as I want."

With pure hatred pouring out of her violet eyes, Nadia spit full in his face, a twisted smile of contempt on her lips. In a surge of fury, Sempher branished the curved dagger aloft. It glittered in the flickering torch light. With one swift motion, he ripped the blade across her throat, severing the jugular, and continued the thrust downward, planting the blade into her breast.

Blood spurted from her body, deepening in color as it flowed out beyond her still figure. It dripped over the edges of the slab where it merged with the cartouche of the ancient Zozer. Her beautiful violet eyes were closed forever.

Loring's struggle against the steel grasp of his guards

had intensified when he watched the dagger plunge into Nadia's body. His rage welled up from the depths of his soul, giving him the strength to pull free of his captors. As he lunged toward the altar, a blow to his head sent him reeling to the stone floor and into oblivion.

The sun was low in the western sky when he regained consciousness. His feeble bonds were easy to undo and, after removing the filthy blindfold, he pulled himself up to survey the vast emptiness in which he found himself. Nothing interrupted the sameness of the desert horizon. The sand hills and valleys were the only features of this hell. The cloudless sky formed a backdrop for the desert which only emphasized his own desolation.

His willpower pushed his anger to just below the surface, but the pervasive loneliness he felt over the loss of Nadia all but detached him from the here and now. This loneliness gradually became merged with an urgency for survival. Only through his survival could he exact vengeance for Nadia.

Loring was not ignorant of the peril he faced. His past explorations into remote desert sites triggered for him what reflexes he needed for survival. He was aware that panic would destroy whatever chance he might have. His actions had to be carefully planned for him to increase the odds for his survival.

His immediate concern was water. He knew he could live longer without food than he could without water. He must locate a source of water within three days. He would travel at night when the cooler desert air minimized the loss of precious body fluid and during the day he would stay as immobile as possible in whatever shelter he could find.

He sat down in the sand with his back to the setting sun and took stock of his resources. He'd been lucky in his choice of traveling clothes. Through habit, he wore the comfortable bush jacket he used when on the dig with Nadia. The jacket had pouches and pockets everywhere, handy places for small artifacts he might discover or for notes to himself.

He examined the jacket. In a slit pocket in the sleeve he found a small penknife and a waterproof vial of matches. The knife was slightly rusty and the vial held four dry matches. In one breast pocket he found a candy bar, partially eaten. He searched his pockets again, but they were empty. The sun was now poised on the horizon for its final plunge into the sand sea. It would be dark soon. Loring started to walk away from the setting sun, toward the east and the Nile.

With the first false light breaking in the east which signaled the rising of Amun, Loring spied a craggy outcrop of virgin rock. The sharp jutting stone promised some protection from the sun. Before he selected this as a haven for the day, he explored the area around the rocks. He discovered a patch of green in the lee of the rock that had the appearance of lichen. He was not a botanist, but Loring knew lichen meant a water source was close by.

He tossed aside some of the adjacent rocks and began to dig deep into the sand. About a foot and a half down, the sand became slightly moist and less shifting...it was clinging to his hands. He continued to dig, slowly moving the sand away from the hole he created.

When the sun was up, Loring looked at his watch. It was six-thirty. Only a few more feet, please God. He had a depression dug into the sand large enough to conceal and protect his entire body. The moist sand would give him some relief from the sun beating down from above and he could continue to dig one handful at a time. A meager trickle of muddy water began to seep up from below. He plunged his face into the liquid, slowly sucking it in through clenched teeth. He gradually felt life flowing through his body. He stayed in the hole and drifted off to sleep.

Loring slept for most of the day. At four in the afternoon, when the blazing sun began its descent, a few desert creatures congregated on the edge of his water hole, crawling over him to reach the water.

He remained still. As unsavory as the idea was, he decided to catch and eat whatever he could, even if he must eat it raw. His luck held and soon he was skinning and gutting a rat-like creature. He ate it, but not quite raw. He had saved the rope and rags used to bind him in the caverns and from these he made a smoldering fire. The flame was weak but hot enough to take the rawness from the meat. He captured another rat and repeated his culinary feat just as the small fire went out.

Loring lay in the shelter of his depression, absorbing as much of the moisture as he could before continuing his trek to the east. The sun was still too hot for him to start walking. As he lay there, he watched the lazy circling of a lone vulture overhead in the cloudless sky. "I'm not ready to die, you miserable scavenger," Loring cried aloud. "Come around tomorrow."

This outburst magnified the ache in his head behind his left ear. He touched the painful area. His fingers outlined a lump in the mastoid region which felt sticky. His hand was tinged with blood when he pulled it away and looked at it.

The ache brought with it fragmented recollections of the past. He remembered trying to reach Nadia as Sempher's knife was arcing toward her throat. He had the sensation of being hit from behind, then mindful of falling into pitch darkness. He then remembered a hard sandy surface, swaying and bumping without end and he couldn't see or use his hands. These visions came and went in his mind's eye until he recalled laying immobile in the desert sand the day before.

His mind finally told him what had happened... Sempher's men had bound him and transported him out into the desert while he was unconscious. He was destined to die as it had been written by forgotten scribes. "Not if I can help it," he voiced to himself. It was time to leave the comfort of his hole and meet the desert for another night.

At dawn on the following day, Loring was virtually in the middle of nowhere. He cast a fevered glance around. The world that now stretched ahead defied the imagination. Sand filled his view in all directions, with no break in the landscape to indicate rock, tree or dune. It was absolutely flat and featureless.

Just as Loring resigned himself to spending the day burrowed in the sand again with no protection from the burning sun, he thought he saw movement in the distance. It had to be a mirage, he told himself, produced by thirst and weariness. But whatever he saw was moving and it appeared to be moving toward him. It was no mirage! He waved his arms, even shouted although he knew he couldn't be heard. A lone Arab, astride a dusty, gaunt camel, approached Loring, slowly.

The Arab was called Ishmael. He had been wandering the ancient caravan routes seeking remnants of his tribe. He had traveled these sand dunes and valleys for five years.

"I am afraid my people are in the arms of Allah," he muttered. "All these years I have searched but have come across nothing to show they might have passed this way. I do not lose hope of finding them as Allah will provide the clue when He is ready. Until then, I shall wander."

Loring and Ishmael were resting in the hot shade cast by the reclining camel and the skimpy tent the Arab erected. The kindly Arab insisted Loring share his water and food before relating the circumstances of his being alone in the middle of the desert.

"Tell me, Ishmael, how far is it to the Nile? How long will it take me to get there?"

"*Effendi*, it is three days' journey by healthy camel. This miserable beast here might take you there in five days. But I do not go that way. I am committed to travel out beyond the dunes in my search. All I can do is give you this small gourd of water. Food I cannot spare. May Allah forgive me."

"I understand, Ishmael. Don't trouble yourself over this. You have saved me this day, and the water will see me through three more days. Perhaps I'll find another source of water where I'm going. When the sun goes down, I'll continue my journey to the Nile."

"I believe you shall find the river. You have such a large hate seething in your soul, it will sustain you even without the water. Be cautious, *effendi*, ere your hate drive you beyond your limits. May Allah protect you."

Loring left when the sun went down. He didn't look back once he started but he'd always remember the look of sorrow on the face of the withered Arab, a look that betrayed a grieving soul. Loring dreaded the long night of walking that lay before him. He was bone tired. His hate for Sempher and the Brotherhood never diminished but was strengthened with each plodding stride. He had vowed to even the score for Nadia. As long as he had life left in his body, he would continue to seek out his adversary. Like Ishmael, he had to stay with the search.

He walked in the moonlight and rested in the heat of the sun for three more days. His water was gone, he had no food, and he felt the hand of death. If he could not find water or food soon he would perish and his vow to avenge Nadia would go unanswered. Finally, the blackout periods he was experiencing were lasting longer and his strength was gone. He could not go on. In the shade of an outcrop of rock, he curled up and slipped into a blessed oblivion. His last thought was that of his beloved Nadia.

He never knew when he was found. Or how. The chopper spotted his prone, curled body in the lee of the rock. He was quickly brought aboard and taken to Cairo. When he could think clearly again and was able to take nourishment, he was told the details of his rescue. Ron Menefee and Peter Bradshaw had found him. Ron thought the Brotherhood might be using the old caves west of El Fayoum. The ancient myths told of such caves being the stronghold of the Brotherhood. Loring was fifty miles west of the Nile when they found him. He could not have made it alone.

Ron asked him about Nadia. The pain came back, stronger than ever. His words were short and to the point.

"The same as Gwen Thompson."

Loring fell silent then, retreating into himself. Piece by piece, his experience threw up a wall of hate, behind which he hid. Try as they did, Menefee and Bradshaw were unable to find out anything more about that horrible episode. Loring was silently making his own plans. His and Nadia's.

The green telephone in the American Embassy rang. Caine answered, turning on the recorder.

"Caine here."

"This is Masters. I understand they found Loring. How is he?"

"Not good. That poor man went through hell. No one can get a damn word out of him. He just sits in the hospital, staring into the god-awful desert."

"What about the woman?"

"Dead. From what I could learn from Bradshaw, those maniacs of Zoser made a ritual of her execution. She was first stripped, then tied to a stone altar. They painted her body before cutting her throat."

"Good lord! What about Loring?"

"The perverts made him watch it all, then they dumped him far out in the desert. He was supposed to die out there, but he fooled them. Don't know how he did it, but he lasted at least five days."

"Did the Brits get anything more from him?"

"Not that we know of. Loring's clammed up tight. Poor guy. He was more dead than alive. They had some shrink working on him, but still he says nothing. I never thought I'd feel sorry for a civilian, but Loring sure gets my sympathy."

"Tough. Like I said...he was expendable. Care for a change in scenery?"

"You don't have to ask me twice. Where to?"

"We're expecting a touch of trouble from further east. How would you like Damascus?"

"What! That's worse than here. What did I ever do to deserve such preferential treatment?"

"You do good work. Take Soloman along with you."

"No! I'd rather go alone. Soloman and I don't get along very well."

"Okay, if it'll make you happy. We'll put Soloman in that tourist destination Mecca...Beirut."

"Better him than me. I'll call you from Syria."

"You do that. I don't expect you'll be there very long."

"Why's that?"

"Assad might be coming over to our side. He's fed up with Gadhafy. He claims the Libyan is screwin' up his military."

"I wouldn't trust him...under any circumstances."

"We don't, never fear. Call me from Damascus."

Caine hung up the phone and turned off the recorder. He left the office, muttering to himself, "I wouldn't want to be in Zoser's shoes...they're number one on Loring's hit list. Hope he finds the bastards. That Shepherd chick was a good-looker."

Part III
Chapter 15

"Marc, how is he today?" Inspector Crimmins was chewing on his mustache, dreading the answer he knew would be coming from Merrick.

"About the same, Inspector. Neither Veronica nor I can get through to him. During the day, he wanders aimlessly in the fields or just sits around staring into space. After dinner, he goes up to his room and we sometimes hear him sobbing during the night.

"Sorry to hear that," Crimmins replied.

"Quite. Our dog, Briget, is the only one Derek has anything to do with. He responds to her attention. She follows him everywhere like a shadow, even sleeps at the foot of his bed. It's uncanny to see that dog watch his every move...she never takes her eyes off him. I'm convinced that animals have a sense for people's inner feelings."

"I've heard of things like that."

"I sometimes think the reason Derek tolerates the dog is because Briget can't ask questions. Regardless, Veronica and I have decided to let him alone, give him all our love and understanding and not rush things. He'll never forget Nadia...we can't expect him to...but it hurts to see the torment in his eyes. Do you think he should see a psychiatrist?"

"No, I don't think it would do any good. They tried that in Egypt. Derek has to find his own way back. He's strong, he'll come out of it when he's ready. Do you mind if I come out to see him this weekend?"

"By all means, do. Plan to stay for dinner."

"Thank you, I shall. We'll talk again, Marc. I know you and Mrs. Merrick are doing all you can for Derek. We must be thankful he doesn't have to go through this alone. I'll see you on Sunday. Goodbye."

It had been two weeks since Loring had been found in the desert, a broken and disturbed man. His friends at Priory Farm hoped the solitude of the country would hasten his recovery. Their care and concern over Loring's condition prompted a physical improvement in him, but his mental state was as remote as when he arrived at the farm.

When he finished the call, Crimmins was undecided as to what he should do next. The multiple London murders were solved, thanks to the evidence supplied by Claridge and the capture of George Wells. What few details that remained before going to trial could be handled by his staff. He admitted to himself that his dedication to his job had suffered in the past weeks, ever since Menefee called him from Cairo with the grisly facts of Nadia's death and Loring's ordeal in the desert.

He was consumed with guilt over Nadia and Derek which, he felt, diminished his efficiency. He was concerned not only about the hate Loring was feeling, but also about the possibility Derek might do something foolish in an attempt to unleash his urge for revenge.

There was a marked change in Menefee as well. He was no longer a solemn loner, but engaged Crimmins in shoptalk every chance he had. It appeared he was driven by some inner compulsion to assuage the guilt he felt for what happened to his friends.

Since he had confided to Crimmins about the Menefee society, he was much more open with his thoughts. He strived to be actively involved with the destruction of Zoser and took unnecessary risks. It was Menefee who combed the back streets and alleys of Soho until he finally found where Wells was hiding out. Scotland Yard made the actual arrest, but it was Menefee's persistence in following the oblique leads furnished by the unsavory characters he befriended that led to Wells' capture. Wells was awaiting his trial, and the evidence they found in the offices of Zoser International was damning enough. Loring's testimony might not be needed.

There was no trace of Joshua Claridge. It was as though he simply walked off the face of the earth. The Yard was covering all areas of the country in its efforts to find him before Claridge fell into the grasp of Zoser agents still at large.

Crimmins' constable rushed into the office. Hughes' face was flushed and he was sweating profusely. He didn't stand on his usual formality, but breathlessly blurted out the news.

"George Wells has escaped!"

"Escaped? How!" Crimmins turned livid.

"He was being transferred when his guards were overpowered by three armed men. When last seen, Wells and the thugs were headed toward Blackfriars Bridge, driving a Vauxhall saloon. A description of the car and its number has been sent out on all frequencies. What are your orders, Inspector?"

"Oh, for Christ's sake! Can't we do anything right these days? Why was Wells being transferred? To where?" Crimmins leaped out of his chair, slamming his fist on the desk.

"His barrister was having him scheduled for a sanity hearing at St. Giles Hospital," Hughes replied, quaking.

"I want that barrister in here, right now! In the meantime, search our files for all the data we have on him. This has the definite stench of a plot."

The cowed constable left Crimmins' office, grateful at being left with a whole skin. He rarely saw the inspector so upset. Constable Hughes, knowing what was expected of him, sent two officers out to escort Wells' barrister, Reginald Sutton, back to the Yard. Hughes then went to the file room and punched in a computer request for all background data on him. While waiting for the printout, he thought it might be worth something to get whatever Interpol had in its data bank.

Scotland Yard's printout revealed no incriminating facts on Sutton, nothing out of the ordinary. He lived alone in a flat in Knightsbridge, was a member of Old Colony Club near St. James Park. He drove a new model Bentley, license number BC-18-03, and he belonged to a good, restricted golf club. He was a contributing patron of the Royal Philharmonic, and was a registered Tory. From all this data, Sutton appeared to be an upstanding citizen and a pillar of the community.

The Interpol inquiry returned surprising information in another vein. Sutton had no criminal record in Europe, but Interpol reported the fact that Sutton had been arrested in New York, in 1976, with his brother, Ralph. The brother was suspected of having Cosa Nostra connections in Boston. The arrest charge was drug dealing, but all charges were dropped at the request of the CIA.

The agent in charge of the American investigation was Wallace Engleson, assisted by Agent James Morgan. Reginald Sutton had been in the United States for a seminar conducted by Zoser International through its American branch office in New York. Interpol had nothing further in its records.

Constable Hughes rushed back to Crimmins' office with his findings. Crimmins scanned the Yard printout without much enthusiasm, then picked up the Interpol report.

"I'll see to it you get a promotion for this, Constable! This clinches it. There was, or is, a conspiracy afoot. You remain here in my office and when Sutton shows up, detain him. I don't much care how you do it, but keep him here until I get back. And don't let him near a telephone unless you're listening. I don't want him warning Wells."

"You can depend on me, Inspector," Hughes answered.

Crimmins drove himself over to MI 6. He had to see Geoffrey Hopkins with this latest information. An agitated Crimmins was ushered into Hopkins' office.

"It looks to me," Crimmins said, "that Zoser has some questionable and undesirable bedfellows. It would explain how Wells was able to do such a good recruiting job for the murderers they've hired." He was certain that Zoser and the Mafia were in various enterprises together. Hopkins, on the other hand, took a more conservative view.

"It might well be just a coincidence, Bert. Yet there is the matter of dropping the drug charges against Sutton at the request of Engleson...or should we say Wells? I better touch bases with the chaps over at CIA. The Americans are usually quite vindictive with drug arrests. I suggest you question Sutton only on the details of today's incident and let him go. No advantage in us showing our hand just yet."

"We don't have enough to hold him, anyway. I just wanted you in on this."

Sutton was waiting impatiently when Crimmins returned to Scotland Yard.

"Sorry to have kept you waiting, Mr. Sutton. There are a few details you might help me with concerning the abduction of your client. What more can you tell us about the transfer of Wells and his subsequent abrupt departure?"

"Inspector, I thought it best if my client was tested on the state of his mental capabilities." Sutton was too much at ease, in Crimmins' opinion. The barrister continued.

"The indictment charges are pretty gruesome, and if you have the evidence you claim to have, I plan to show that Mr. Wells must have had limited mental capabilities. I obtained a court order for the test. Everything was done all properly legal, I assure you."

"Oh, I don't doubt it. What happened, exactly?"

"On the way to St. Giles, we were accosted by three armed men who forced my car into the curb. They then took my client and drove off with him. I do hope you will be able to find Mr. Wells unharmed. Those men appeared dangerous to me. There's no way to predict what they might do to Mr. Wells."

"We'll find him, Mr. Sutton. Thank you for your time."

When Sutton left, Crimmins told Hughes to keep him under surveillance. He didn't believe Sutton would attempt doing anything more since his part of the plot was finished for the time being. But the wily policeman was taking nothing for granted with this collection of killers. Sutton had to lead him to the next piece of the puzzle. Crimmins was counting on it...his instincts were getting sharper.

Loring whistled for Briget, who came bounding up to him. He loved that dog, grateful for the soothing effect she had on him. Loring scratched both her ears and stroked her wet muzzle.

"Care to take a stroll, old girl?" The dog leaped to the gate, her tail wagging in ever-increasing arcs of delighted anticipation. Loring called into the house, "I'm taking Briget out for a walk, Veronica...down by the church. We won't be gone long."

Veronica watched them from the kitchen window. Together, man and dog made their way down the winding road toward St. Nicholas Church, the old twelfth century chapel. The church was perched atop a small knoll at the bend of the dirt road. A traditional churchyard surrounded it on three sides, the graves of which dated back to the seventeenth century. Huge beech and maple trees shaded the small chapel, making the interior cool and quiet.

Loring was spending more and more time at the church, sitting in the subdued light, thinking and remembering. Somehow, these periods put him at a tranquil peace. Veronica watched until they were out of sight. She brushed a tear from her eye, then turned back to continue with her baking.

Loring entered the dim nave, telling Briget to go off to hunt for a squirrel or gopher. The dog obediently galloped into the fields behind the church. He noticed how she stopped every few bounds to look back to make sure he was going inside. The church was the one place the dog couldn't follow him. Loring knew Briget would be waiting when he came out.

Loring lowered himself into one of the ancient pews, scarred with the devoted use of centuries. He was alone with his thoughts. He looked up at the small stone altar, radiant with the light of many colors streaming through the stained glass, and remembered another stone altar buried deep in the Egyptian desert, one that had been lighted only by smoking torches. He spoke, almost as in prayer, mindful of the ache in his breast.

"Nadia, I know you can hear me. What am I to do? I miss you so much. People are kind, but they can never understand how I suffer without you. I'll keep you close to me, always."

His thoughts understandably turned to Sempher and that awful day. The hatred rose up within him like a powerful blow grinding at the pit of his stomach. Sempher and the rest had to be caught and the full measure of retribution exacted. He had been planning his revenge and how it could be had.

Loring felt they all had to die—all those connected with Zoser—but something deep within him rebelled at the act of killing. He remembered how he screamed his threat to kill Sempher when he was forced to watch the sacrifice of his beloved Nadia. Now, however, in the circle of his friends and in the quiet peace of St. Nicholas, he knew he could not kill. Nevertheless, Sempher and his evil Brotherhood had to be destroyed. They couldn't continue to exist and create the chaos they planned for the world. He had to stop them, somehow.

Loring couldn't be sure if it was pure inspiration, or coincidence, or Divine intervention, but suddenly the plan he needed for the destruction of Sempher came to him.

He remembered the boast Sempher made during their ordeal in Egypt. Sempher inferred that while other men need money, position or women to make life worth living, he, the new Pharaoh of all Egypt, needed only power. Loring realized then that the one thing which would destroy Sempher was the total removal of his power. To achieve that, Derek thought, Sempher would have to be made to look foolish in the eyes of the world and the Brotherhood. After all, who would place trust and faith in the hands of a fool? He'd be laughed off his throne.

Loring smiled. He was at last ready to reenter the world and eager to implement this scheme with the help of his friends and get on with his life. He was certain that wherever Nadia was, she would be smiling, her violet eyes ablaze with delight. Yes, Nadia would approve.

Loring left the church then. As he closed the door, he noticed that Briget was not waiting for him in her usual place. She must have found some good hunting, he thought. He whistled for the dog, knowing she would be at his side as soon as she heard his call. He walked down to the road, back toward the farm. He felt good, the first time in weeks. A hot cup of coffee with Veronica would be just the thing to cap off the day.

On the road, he saw a car pulled off on the verge. As he approached, a man got out of the car and sidled up to him.

"Well, Loring, we meet again. I thought you would show up here, sooner or later, so I waited." George Wells had a .45 leveled at his chest. "I wanted to make sure you'd be taken care of in the good old Yankee way...a slug right in the guts. No ceremony this time. Sempher really blew it, but I'll correct that little oversight right now."

"How did you get out?" Loring asked, still not believing Wells was actually standing there. "You were in Newgate."

"A couple of friends arranged for a break. When we got clear of the fuzz, I left them to come and get you. You bastard, you caused me nothin' but trouble from the first day I saw you. Say your prayers."

"You won't get away with it, you know. Scotland Yard will know it was you," Loring said, a taste of bile in his mouth.

"They'll have to catch me first. Enough talk..." Wells lowered the gun slightly, aimed it at Loring's stomach. He held his breath, preparing to squeeze the trigger, the evil in his eyes drilling into Loring.

From around the far side of the car a beige mass slammed into him, propelling him to the ground. Briget had Wells' hand and lower arm in her huge mouth, biting down hard. With very little effort, she could sever the arm right below the elbow. Wells screamed and swore but Briget didn't pay attention to his cries. The dog weighed close to sixteen stone, all bone and muscle. She had the gunman on the ground with both her front feet firmly planted on his chest. Every time he moved, the dog would turn her head slightly, and bite deeper into the flesh and bone of Wells' arm.

Loring retrieved the gun that had dropped to the road by the swiftness of Briget's attack. He called to the animal.

"Briget! Stay! Let him up."

The dog moved off of Wells' chest and relaxed the hold on his arm, but didn't let go completely. "You miserable son of a bitch...get up and walk to the farm. You make one sudden move and I'll let the animal finish the job. Now, move!"

Loring, Wells and Briget made their way back to the farm. Wells was staggering, partly from the loss of blood and partly out of fear. Briget kept his arm in her mouth, dragging him toward the gate. Blood was seeping out from between her jaws and clenched teeth, running down onto her massive chest. Loring made Wells sit on the ground in the yard, and called out to Veronica.

"Veronica, call Inspector Crimmins! Tell him to get out here right away. Briget and I have captured Wells. Tell him we want Wells away from here as soon as possible, before he bleeds to death. Tell him to use a helicopter."

Veronica Merrick almost ran to Loring to kiss him. He was back with them, at last. But the urgency in his voice prompted her to do just as he asked. The call went through at once.

"Crimmins said he would be here in twenty minutes. How long do you want Briget chewing on him, Derek?"

"Briget, let go!" The dog obediently released her hold, sat back on her haunches, but continued to glare at Wells, fangs bared. Veronica took her a bowl of water which she lapped up, never taking her fiery eyes away from Wells. Loring kept the gun leveled at his head. Wells whimpered only once.

"How about a bandage for my arm? That goddamned dog bit it almost in half."

"The bleeding has almost stopped. You'll live until they string you up. It wouldn't take much for me to let my friend work on your other arm. Just shut your face and hope I don't shoot after all."

The chopper arrived and set down in the field behind the farm beyond the beech trees. Crimmins got out with another policeman and came over to where Briget and Loring had Wells completely subdued. Veronica hovered nearby, handing Loring his third cup of coffee.

"Good show, Derek! How in the world did you do this? What happened to that arm of his...you attack it with an axe?"

"The dog did it, all by herself, Inspector. She takes very good care of me. So do Marc and Veronica. I'm afraid I've been pretty much of a bore lately. But I think I can join the human race again. When can we talk?"

"Marc invited me to dinner on Sunday. Is that soon enough?" Crimmins flashed one of his rare smiles.

"Can't wait to tell you my plans. See you on Sunday. Give my best to Mrs. Crimmins."

"Count on it. Nora's been frantic about you. She'll be ever so pleased. Until Sunday, then. Cheerio."

Crimmins took the gun from Loring and led Wells to the chopper. With a casual wave to Loring and Veronica, the team took off, heading back to London.

They both watched the helicopter hover for a short while until it scurried away over the trees. It was lost to view before the rotor noise died away. Veronica took hold of Loring's hand, squeezed it with affection, and asked in a low voice, "Are you all right now, Derek? Have you come back to us?"

Loring looked into the distance, over the rise of the trees, and saw the clouds building up over the hills beyond. He turned to Veronica.

"Yes, my dear, I'm back from that hell I'll always remember. Now that I know what I have to do to make things right, my mind's more at peace. I'll always remember Nadia, no matter what happens or where I might be. She was so vital, so much a part of me. It's a shame you never had the chance to meet her. She was very much like you in a lot of respects."

"I'm sure I would have loved her, too."

"You would have, I know. I swore I'd get even for the suffering and pain Zoser inflicted on us. What was troubling me was thinking that killing was the only way I could avenge Nadia. It was the classic case of being damned if I did and damned if I didn't. But just now, in the church, it occurred to me how I could get my revenge without killing. I have to deprive Zoser of what it wants most...power. When Crimmins comes over, we'll all discuss the details of my plan. I'll need a lot of help to do what has to be done."

"You know you can depend on Marc and me," Veronica answered, with another squeeze of his hand. "How about some more coffee?"

The police chopper was crossing the river when Crimmins turned his head and looked at Wells who was sitting beside him in the rear of the aircraft. Crimmins had been thinking ever since they took off from the farm. George Wells was the cause of most of his problems and had made a fool out of him to boot. Reginald Sutton, Wells' high-priced barrister, helped engineer his escape so he could continue his evil plans. And Nadia, poor Nadia, a beautiful and talented woman sacrificed on an obscene altar like some animal, bloodied and defiled.

He thought of Derek Loring, crushed and all but defeated by what Wells and his organization were doing, and of Ron Menefee, his wife's stepbrother, who changed from a peacemaker to an avid seeker of vengeance. He thought of Gwen Thompson, Ron's cousin, so brutally murdered, and he thought of himself, his career with Scotland Yard turned into a mockery because of Wells. Finally he thought of the gun in his pocket, the gun which was meant to kill again.

Crimmins saw the river below, and suddenly knew what he was going to do, what he had to do. He took the gun out of his pocket and looked at it for some time. He released the safety, and turned once again to Wells.

"You are a miserable son of a bitch, George Wells. You think you are getting away again, don't you? You think you are immune from the law." Crimmins was fingering the gun lying in his lap.

"I'll escape the gallows, you dumb cop. I've done it before and I'll do it again. I'll plead insanity and be out in a few years. I have friends in very high places who'll go to bat for me. So back off, you lousy flatfoot." Wells turned back to the window, looking down at the murky river below.

Crimmins brought the gun up slowly and deliberately pulled the trigger. The top of Wells' head splattered all over the chopper's window, his brains dribbling down the side. Under his breath, Crimmins muttered, "That's for Nadia, you bastard. One down, one more to go." Then he shouted aloud to the pilot, "He tried to take the gun away...he must have thought he could get it away from me! Let's get this thing down on the ground so we can get a doctor, but I believe it's too late for this chap."

Crimmins looked at Wells. It bothered him to see the slumped body, bloody with vacant eyes staring at nothing. He would have preferred to see the look of fear in Wells' eyes before he pulled the trigger. But then he thought about Nadia Shepherd, so like a daughter, seeing her in the remote desert, stretched out on a stone slab with her lovely throat cut.

Bert Crimmins wasn't bothered any more.

Chapter 16

The news of Wells' death at the hands of the police exploded on the front pages of all the tabloids of London. Charges of police brutality and the killing of innocent people could be heard from one end of the city to the other. Hyde Park rabble-rousers congregated in clusters, intent on being the prophets of legal collapse. This all transpired within a few hours from the time Crimmins notified his superiors of the incident.

Delegations of irate citizens besieged the lofty offices of the Chief Inspector of Scotland Yard with threats of civil disobedience. The Lord Mayor of London fended off all questioning before retiring to his manor house in Kent. It was rumored that the House of Commons would place the issue of police authority on its next agenda. The situation was rapidly deteriorating and the everyday constable on the streets had to endure some heated threats.

It wasn't until the end of a very long and trying day that Reginald Sutton, Esq. stormed into Chief Inspector Donally's office, his face livid with anger and indignity.

"My client, George Wells, was deliberately executed by one of your men, Chief Inspector." Sutton used his most menacing tone. "I demand that the facts be brought out into the open in a public forum. The facts surely will show that Inspector Herbert Crimmins has been harassing both me and my client. George Wells was not killed accidentally. The truth of the incident will show that Herbert

Crimmins murdered him. What do you propose to do about it?"

"Mr. Sutton, please use restraint."   Chief Inspector Donally had been bombarded with questions and recriminations ever since Crimmins landed with the dead prisoner just before lunch. He was tired and he was getting angry now. He turned once more to the irate barrister.

"I know very well the brash implications you are making and I assure you there will be a proper investigation, all in the proper time and according to regulations. For your information, I have already called together an official Board of Inquiry to look into the matter. Because so many of you bleeding-hearts have decided to take this unfortunate incident as a personal affront, I have called for the Inquiry to commence tomorrow."

"But tomorrow is Saturday, Chief Inspector."

"I realize that, Mr. Sutton. However, we feel this to be quite necessary."

"Will this Inquiry be public?"

"No, it will not. This is still police business, and the investigation will be conducted strictly according to the established rules in regard to such matters. You may be called in as a witness, so make yourself available for the entire day. I'm sorry if this interferes with your golf game. Good day, sir. You know the way out."

When Sutton was gone, Donally called Crimmins' office. Constable Hughes answered.

"Inspector Crimmins' office. Hughes here."

"Hughes, Chief Inspector Donally. Where is Inspector Crimmins?"

"I believe he's at home, sir. He left about an hour ago...fairly tuckered out, if I may say so, Chief Inspector."

"Quite understandable, I should say. See here, Hughes, have you been following Reginald Sutton?"

"That I have, sir...under Inspector Crimmins' orders."

"Has Sutton been doing anything suspicious...anything I should know about?"

"Well, Chief Inspector, since you brought it up, there was one thing I believed to be...er, unusual."

"And what was that?"

"Inspector Crimmins ordered me to keep Sutton under surveillance since right after Wells made his escape. We had two other men watching him, besides myself, that is. He did absolutely nothing out of the ordinary."

"Come, come, Hughes. I haven't all night."

"I was in the Royal Crown pub on High Street. We followed Sutton there...about the time Inspector Crimmins was flying Wells back from Surrey. When the telly announced the accident and how Wells was killed, Sutton became rather loud and boisterous...happy, like. He bought rounds for the whole crowd. I considered this as unusual, sir. I mentioned it in my report to the Inspector."

"Well done, Hughes, well done! Has the Inspector read the report?"

"I hardly think so, sir. He's been frightfully busy since the accident."

"Good show, Hughes! I'll certainly tell Crimmins of your diligence."

"Yes, sir. Thank you, sir." Hughes breathed easier.

Donally hung up the phone, frowning. What games was Sutton playing? And, for that matter, what games was Crimmins playing? He felt he had not been given the whole story. He picked up the phone again.

"Hopkins? Chief Inspector Donally here. What the bloody hell is going on?"

The Board of Inquiry found the death of George Wells

accidental, brought about through his own rash actions. The Board further found that Inspector Crimmins had acted in an exemplary manner in preventing Wells from endangering the lives of the pilot and Constable Briggs, all at the risk of his own life.

Most of the facts concerning Wells and the Zoser organization came to light during the investigation, including the circumstances regarding the past association of Sutton and the Cosa Nostra. However, at the insistence of MI 6, the involvement of Derek Loring and Nadia Shepherd was not mentioned. An official commendation from Chief Inspector Donally would be inserted into Crimmins' personnel file. The entire proceeding took but two hours. Reginald Sutton was not called, nor was he missed.

After the hearing, Crimmins returned to his office. The usual clutter in the room was a fact he could relate to, something that illustrated his career with Scotland Yard. He sat at his desk, turned toward the window. The Saturday traffic was milling about below on Victoria Street. Traffic was heavy, but not the usual surge normally evident at this time of day during the customary workweek.

The thick glass of the office fenestration prevented the noise of the street below from intruding into his thoughts. He felt no elation over his being exonerated by the Inquiry. He knew he was guilty as sin, guilty of murder. Had he been charged with complicity, he might have pointed out the extenuating circumstances surrounding his involvement with Wells. The remorse and guilt he felt over Nadia and Loring's troubles, coupled with the machinations of Zoser International, did obviously account for a temporary loss of his professional perspective. This is what a shrewd barrister would argue and make a strong court case out of it.

He thought back over the years he had been with the

Yard. They had been good years, some even happy. Taken all together, his tenure with the department had been a good and satisfying career. He was proud to be a part of the system. Until now. Now, he had actually betrayed everything he believed in, everything he had worked so hard to achieve. His one act of personal vendetta had destroyed all that went before. The cup of tea, left on his desk by an obliging clerk, had turned cold, untouched and unnoticed.

Crimmins turned from the window. He knew what he had to do. Shoving the papers aside, he took a sheet of official stationery from the top drawer of his desk. He laid it out on the bare scratched surface of the desk, smoothed it with care, and stared at the blank paper. The words were all jumbled in his head, words that had to be put down in the proper sequence to not only satisfy regulations, but to assure the Yard's not being painted with the same brush he was using to paint himself.

Crimmins took out his pen, and with a weary shake of his head, he suppressed a throaty sob as he wrote his letter of resignation.

Sunday supper at Priory Farm was a strained affair. Besides the Merricks and Loring, the supper guests included Crimmins and Ron Menefee who had been invited at Loring's request. Both Marc and Veronica acted the perfect hosts, but their efforts appeared over-cautious.

With false gaiety, they steered the talk away from matters best not discussed— the death of George Wells and its aftermath. Instead, the conversation was centered on medieval architecture in England, a subject that Loring loved and could discuss at length. His discussion became more banal and commonplace as the day wore on. No one was paying much attention to him and Loring was tired of the subject. Finally, over coffee, Loring took the bull by the horns and brought up what was foremost on their minds. The matter had to be talked about between friends, out in the open.

"Inspector," Loring began, "why did you really submit your resignation? Surely it wasn't because of the accident. You're too committed to your profession to allow that single incident to influence your decision."

A hush filled the room.

"Derek, there are some things a good policeman can never get used to." Crimmins was finding it difficult to give voice to his feelings. "When that gun went off and I saw Wells slumped over me, I admit I had a sudden feeling of elation. After all, he was partially responsible for Nadia's death. And consider what his damnable organization put you through."

"But why do you feel guilty? You should be glad," Merrick said.

"I was, at first, Marc. Then later, when the full impact of the deed hit me, I experienced a terrible loathing for what I had done. Regardless of the fact that he deserved to die, our judicial system should have been the instrument to bring it about. He certainly would have been convicted, whether or not he would have served his sentence is debatable."

"What are you driving at?" Loring asked.

"Your American legal system evolved from the English, as you well know. I must say, however, that your judiciary has too many loopholes and ways for criminals to avoid their just punishment. And, sorry to admit, many of those legal ploys are finding their way into our courts here. That barrister of Wells, Reginald Sutton, is a shrewd and clever man with very important connections here and abroad. I really believe he might have gotten Wells off."

"That became your reason to chuck it, to resign?"

"No, that was not the reason I resigned. I quit because I feel defeated. In the twenty-five years I have been with the Yard, this is the first time I have ever been connected with an act of violence. I do not like it...I despise it, in fact. I am too old and I think I have too many principles to resort to violence. If keeping the law is a choice of kill or being killed, I want no part of it. Does that give you your answer?"

Crimmins watched the expressions on the faces of this circle of friends. Watching faces for unspoken thoughts was his stock-in-trade. The Merricks displayed relief and understanding...he expected as much. Loring was a question mark. Derek's eyes had a look about them...was it pity or empathy? Ron was avoiding his eyes, gazing instead at the rolling hills beyond Priory Farm.

Menefee had been silent throughout his brother-in-law's disclosure. When Crimmins finished, Menefee spoke up.

"That's a lot of crap, Bertie, and you know it! You didn't resign over principle. You quit because you had the responsibility to bring Wells in and you mucked it. He got away from you, so to speak. You packed it in, not because the system failed you, but rather because you failed the system. Isn't that the truth of it?"

Crimmins was taken aback, shaken.

"No, Ron. You are way off the mark there. Perhaps I did not make myself quite clear. Say what you will, it is still a matter of principle. Someday you will understand."

Loring reached over and touched the older man on the arm. He looked into his eyes and saw the pain there. Those troubled eyes told him that Crimmins was carrying around a load of guilt far beyond the compromise of any principle. He also realized it would do no good to continue in this vein. They would get no other explanation from Bert Crimmins that day. Loring said, quietly, "Bert, I'm satisfied you had a valid reason for doing what you did."

The heaviness in the room was lifted. "Well, now," Crimmins said, "what are those plans you were so excited about, Derek?"

Relieved, Loring explained his idea.

"My plan is to make Sempher and his entire operation look foolish and stupid in the eyes of the civilized world. I intend to write an article about this scheme of his, and slant it enough so everyone who reads it will conclude that he's as mad as a hatter...a madman attempting to take over the government of Egypt."

"What will this accomplish, Derek?" Veronica asked.

"The idea of a twentieth century man believing himself the reincarnation of a long-dead Third Dynasty Pharaoh is insane enough by itself. I'll embellish it enough to show how ridiculous it really is. Some of you know I've been published. I'm going to use these contacts to get the article before the public. The papers will surely pick it up and make sport of the whole thing. A story like this makes good newspaper copy."

"Won't Sempher just laugh it off?"

"Sempher will have to spend his time and effort in explaining to the world why he believes he has a right to the throne of Egypt. He'll discover the entire world is laughing at him. Ron's group is well versed in the doings of the Brotherhood. They'll put the word out in the proper places which should make the plan even more unbelievable. We don't have much time. Their 'Operation Amun' is due to began any time now."

"What do you need?" Menefee responded.

"We need to know how widespread Zoser is, who the top people are, and the ones who call the shots. We know they're spread all over the world. They must have a central headquarters which directs its movements. We must get to it and find the files with the names of those in power. Once we have those names, we can surely get the authorities to act. Right now all we have is our own knowledge and suspicions but no proof."

"That's going to take time. Do we have it?"

"If we get the names to those who can act it'll delay or disrupt "Operation Amun' long enough for my plan to take effect. Some of us had better concentrate on Sempher. We need to know all about him, his background and the source of his wealth. Bert, can you use your contacts with the police or intelligence people to get us more information on him?"

Crimmins answered with his usual tone. "I shall make some inquiries through Interpol and with Hopkins at MI 6. They should get us whatever is on record. It would be much easier if we had a contact closer to Sempher or to Zoser itself. I doubt we are going to get what we need from the records. We should have information regarding his private life...where he was born, the truth about his parents, any girlfriends he might have had."

"I can give you some of that data, right now." Ron offered. "We make it our business to know all about our enemies."

"Well?" Crimmins asked.

"Well," Menefee began, " Sempher was born in Salzburg fifty years ago. His family lived three miles from the Residenz Palace. His parents, of average means, ran a small import-export business. His father had roots in Upper Silesia and Sempher's mother came from Cyprus. She claimed to have royal blood in her veins but no one believed it. He was raised on her stories of regal ancestors stemming from the Near East."

"That's a start," Loring said.

"There's more. When Sempher finished at the Gymnasium, he entered the University of Vienna where he majored in economics and minored in archaeology. He took over the family business when his father died and built it into a vast international combine, dealing in commodities, metals and oil. His money came from Middle East oil...he was a paid advisor to OPEC.

"He founded Zoser International about ten years ago. On the surface, Zoser is a research foundation, but the Menefees discovered that it was a quasi-political front with ties all over the world, but concentrating its influence in the Middle East. The exact nature of its business has never been fully explained nor can we get a handle on it. Claridge could shed some light on that if we can find him...if he's still alive, that is."

Loring waited until Menefee was finished before he turned to Marc.

"Can you find out anything about the finances of Zoser, Marc? I don't want you to put your position at the bank in jeopardy, but it'll help a lot if we knew where he gets all his money, or more to the point, how and where he spends it. Can you do it?"

"Yes," Merrick said, "I can place a few calls and check into some records. I won't promise a complete picture but we should get more than we have now. Why do you need all this information?"

"I've an idea that if we know where he's spending large wads of money, we'll get a better picture of who's sending him the stuff he needs to get his power base established. Now, Ron, do you think you can find out more about Sempher's maternal background? I think those stories his mother told him might have been the stimuli which prompted his claim to fame."

"Yes, I'll get what I can."

Loring was feeling better than he had for days. Having a plan of action was just what he needed.

"Now I want to say this to all of you. This could get dangerous and I don't want the Merricks here getting hurt, anymore than I want you, Bert, or you, Ron, to be in trouble. Whenever any of you feels this is getting too hot or too close to home, please say so and then bow out. I'll understand. I'll do this alone if I have to because I can't have any of you getting hurt. This is my fight. Is that understood?"

Veronica had been quiet all this time but now she spoke up.

"Derek, we're your friends. You've gone through hell and have lost someone very dear to you. We can't bring Nadia back...no one can...but we can see a way of compensating you for your loss. Don't speak to us about danger. We know perfectly what type of danger lies out there. All of us feel that this madman and his organization must be destroyed. We're all in this together."

"Amen, to that, Mrs. Merrick," whispered Bert Crimmins.

"Yes, you've said it for us all," Menefee concurred.

Loring looked at the group, each nodding in agreement. He was so fortunate to have friends like these. After a short pause, he replied, "You've taken a load off my mind. Thank you, one and all."

Just then the phone rang. Veronica rushed to answer it. She returned after a few brief words.

"Ron, it's for you. It's Joshua Claridge. He has to speak with you. Mrs. Crimmins gave him this number."

Everyone was stunned. The emergence of Claridge on the scene, just when he was most needed, was almost too good to be true. Now some of the fog and mystery surrounding Zoser might be explained.

Menefee raced to the phone. When he returned to the group, he said, "Claridge is in Rhodes. He's certain he's lost the bloodhounds from Zoser. He wants me to meet him in Lucerne. Sempher has a chalet there. Josh is positive the list of names we need is there. He was in the place once with Wells when they were planning 'Amun'. I'm to meet him on Tuesday. If all goes well, I should be back in London by Thursday evening. Can we meet here again on Friday?"

Everyone agreed enthusiastically. Crimmins was to use the time checking more on Sempher's background, while Marc tended to the financial picture. Loring was planning to use his time in working out the overall details of their plan. Each move had to be orchestrated and fine-tuned so any margin of error would be minimized. The overpowering fear confronting them was that Zoser would make its move before they were ready. As it was, it be would very close.

Geoffrey Hopkins dialed a familiar number. After two sharp rings, a voice in a thick brogue said, "Yes?"

"Nora, Geof Hopkins here. Is Bert there?"

"No, he isn't, Mr. Hopkins."

"Can I reach him?"

"Well, Bertie is with the Merricks, out in Surrey. 'E's bin gone all afternoon."

"I see. Just a social call, eh?"

"I don't rightly know. Bertie didn't say."

"Quite. Tell Bert to ring me tomorrow, will you?"

"Yes, sir, I surely will. Ta ta."

Hopkins hung up the phone, a deep frown creasing his face. He was suspicious. Was Crimmins merely being solicitous of Loring, or was there something else? If the visit was social, why wasn't Nora included? The Zoser affair was finished with the death of Wells. Crimmins was not the social type so there had to be an important reason for him to be in Surrey. What were those people up to?

Hopkins called his office at MI 6.

"Hopkins here. Who do we have available for a touch of surveillance?"

"Williams and Broadhearst, sir."

"Very well. Send Williams to cover Bert Crimmins. I want to know where he goes, who he talks with, everything. Put Broadhearst out in Surrey at a place called Priory Farm. Tell him to watch Derek Loring."

"Loring, sir? The same Derek Loring who had that bit of trouble in Egypt?"

"The very same. Don't ask questions."

"Yes, sir. I'll get right on it."

Hopkins paced the threadbare carpet in the living room of his flat. He suddenly didn't like himself very much. After all the years he and Bert Crimmins knew each other, he now had to be forced to put surveillance on him. It was just too much. And yet, he had a job to do and if Crimmins decided to take matters into his own hands, the onus fell on him. Too bad, he thought. Crimmins was a hell of a good policeman, but he did take the easy way out in resigning. He should have bluffed it out.

"I hope you stay clean, Bert," he spoke aloud.

Chapter 17

The merchants opened their shops early for business Monday morning in the Khan el-Khalili bazaar. Hoards of tourists were being funneled into the maze of shops full of handicrafts by commission-seeking guides and would soon engulf the area. Most tourists in Egypt did their sightseeing early so as to avoid the hottest part of the day. The temperature could be over one hundred degrees before noon which was much hotter than the majority of visitors were accustomed to. Cairo embraced over sixteen million people, all of whom eagerly had their sights set on the possibility of sharing in the tourist revenue.

The district of the Khalili bazaar was a mecca for every description of poverty-stricken Cairo resident. Each of the wretched souls had the hope of a better life if the tourists continued to pour into the city. The unwritten city ordinance that governed the actions of merchants and beggars alike assured a relatively painless extraction of the visitors' wealth. In this, Cairo was no better or worse than any other cosmopolitan city.

El-Azhar Street fronted the shopping compound on the south and a myriad of grimy pink or off-white mosques dotted Muizzlidini-Ilah Street on the north. It was here the trouble started.

In the sun-baked, dusty courtyard of El-Aqmar Mosque a disagreement erupted between a Sunni student from the nearby University of El-Azhar and a Shiite beggar. Each attempted to wash his feet at the same water tap at the same time before entering the mosque. The student shoved the beggar aside and was pushed in return. The minor skirmish soon escalated into serious wrestling in the dirt of the courtyard.

The mass of milling onlookers egged on each of the combatants according to his bias. A short, curved dagger suddenly appeared in the dirty hand of the beggar. In fury, the man lunged and the Sunni student dropped to the ground, drenched in a pool of his own blood. The dagger quivered in the student's chest as the beggar turned heel and disappeared into the crowd.

The disorderly mass of onlookers separated into two mobs of screaming antagonists, siding with either the killer or the Sunni victim. With loud shouting and fist-waving, the throngs met in a violent battle between the two Muslim sects.

The courtyard of the mosque became too restricted for the crowd when worshippers from inside the mosque joined in the fray. The melee was further gorged by the angry people who squeezed into the quadrangle from adjoining streets. The struggle between the sects soon got out of hand. A torch was put to the mosque which was quickly engulfed in acrid smoke and flames.

Before long, the specter of the burning edifice became a catalyst for the warring factions, inciting further hostilities. The fighting spilled out into the streets where wholesale mob warfare developed. The imam, the religious leader within the El-Aqmar Mosque, was killed by the mob and his bleeding body was thrown into the holy well in the center of the courtyard. All of the other mosques along Ilah Street were similarly desecrated and the imams and teachers killed.

Word reached the shopkeepers within the bazaar. Stalls and shops were closed, boarded up quickly after the tourists were herded out. The fighting entered the bazaar proper and the merchants found themselves caught up in the battle. It became one shopkeeper against his neighbor, depending on whether the wood carver or rug merchant were Sunni or Shiite.

The blood-letting continued unabated. The tourists who were trapped within the confines of the bazaar cowered behind walls or other forms of protection. The peculiar thing was that not a single tourist was harmed in any way other than being roughly pushed aside to allow a Sunni to cut the throat of a Shiite, or vice versa.

When the police riot squad arrived, the fighting was out of control. The police surged into the mass of screaming and bloodied humanity, their truncheons flaying right and left, but to no avail. Cadres of police formed wedges behind which scores of terrified tourists were rushed away from the battle zone.

It became apparent that the police only added to the slaughter as Sunni police turned on their Shiite comrades. The mass of combatants swelled to numbers beyond belief. The few Christian policemen at the scene were powerless to stem the tide and they wisely sought shelter and safety among the tourists who were fleeing in all directions.

Only after the riot spread down El-Azhar Street and approached the Ezbekiya Gardens did the military units intervene and stop the slaughter.

An uneasy truce descended over the district. The dead and wounded were attended to, but the burning mosques were left to the flames. The casualty count was staggering: six hundred thirty Sunni Moslems dead and eight hundred forty-five hurt or wounded; seven hundred twenty-six Shiite killed with twelve hundred wounded.

The most horrible statistic was in the number of religious leaders killed. Every single imam within the district, thirty-eight, was violently murdered. They had not been merely stabbed or burned, they were each stabbed first then their throats were cut, and the bodies desecrated. The brutality of each sect toward their revered religious leaders was beyond comprehension.

Later, when the riot in Cairo was at its height, similar uprisings broke out in Alexandria, Port Said and Matruh. All were the same...Sunni against Shiite. The numbers of killed and wounded on each side ran into the hundreds, and every religious leader was ceremoniously butchered. The Islamic population of Egypt had gone mad.

The bastions of Islam outside Egypt had their turns. Beirut, the perpetual no-man's land, found itself engaged in new terrible fighting. This war was between the Sunni and Shiite sects with splinter groups joining one or the other. The previously embattled Christians were left alone to sit on the sidelines with no one to fight. They stood by watching brother kill brother, and each killed the imam.

Sidon and Tripoli, cities accustomed to civil war, became new sites of battle later in the day. The count of dead and mutilated bodies compared with the earlier tolls. Syria, Iran, Jordan and Iraq came next. The imam leadership had some advance warning and fled, leaving their mosques to the flames of strife. Khomeini retreated to Qom with his Shiite advisors, heavily guarded by his bodyguard compliment.

President Assad of Syria declared martial law, as did King Hussein of Jordan. Armies patrolled the streets and alleyways of all the major cities where the warring broke out. The majority of the people barricaded themselves in their homes, none wanting to add to the slaughter. Enough malcontents, however, roamed the Muslim districts, seeking out the enemy and begging for a fight.

By sundown on Monday, thirty-seven thousand Sunni had been killed or wounded along with forty-six thousand Shiites. In all, sixteen hundred imam were murdered; only four hundred remained throughout the Near East, and those few were in hiding in remote areas or were protected by armed guards. The carnage reached deep into the bowels of the entire Islamic world.

The war between the Christians started Tuesday. In Cairo, St. Barbara's Coptic Church was bombed. Forty-seven people were killed or maimed. The priest had been mutilated sadistically when he was later found. It was not known who was responsible for the bombing, but the act itself was enough to set off the fighting, especially in view of the blood bath of Monday.

Bands of Christian Copts paraded the streets searching for Christians of other faiths, primarily Roman Catholics. When contact was made, the fighting and killing swelled in block after block until the whole of Cairo was caught up in the carnage. El-Moallaqah, the 'Suspended Church', built atop an old Roman fort, was not spared. The light from its fire cast an eerie glow which danced on the waters of the Nile, one short block away to the west.

As with the situation on Monday, the police were no help in stemming the tide of battle. Moslem officers stood by while the Christian police joined in the fighting. It was the army who finally succeeded in stopping the riots, if only for a short time. They had to shoot quite a few in doing so.

Alexandria did not escape its baptism of fire. The holy revolt was similar to the Moslem upheaval of the preceding day. The devastation of the Mosque of Abul Abbas stood as a grim reminder of religion turned inside out, its embers still smoldering from the inferno which engulfed it on Monday.

But it was beyond the mosque where the brunt of Christian hate was most prevalent. Mobs of people, male and female, young and old, herded over to Saad Zaghloul Square with their collective hatred turned against other followers of Christ. The ensuing melee was short-lived. The army patrols were still in the area because of the Muslim riots so they didn't have far to travel to quell the trouble. This fact, together with the relatively small numbers of Christians who lived in Alexandria, kept the casualties low.

The bloodiest and fiercest fighting took place in Rome and Istanbul. The Roman Catholics slaughtered the Orthodox in both cities, but retaliation on the part of the Greek and Armenian Orthodoxies evened the score.

All manner of rumor placed responsibility for the carnage on either the Catholics or the Orthodox, depending on which sect had the advantage. The word of the Christian riots in Alexandria and Beirut had reached the northern Mediterranean ports which triggered the Italian skirmishes. It was only a matter of time before the riots spread into the provinces and then across the water to Athens and Istanbul.

Thousands of militants were involved in the actual uprisings, regardless of the cause. Local police were ineffective...the military intervened and brought about the cease fire and an uneasy truce. The heads of state quickly met, as did church leaders. The meetings proved useless in that without a known cause, no solution could be found. The one fact that did surface was horrible. All priests, monks, nuns, patriarchs, ministers and bishops who were in or near the trouble spots were killed.

Tuesday's toll was as staggering to the Christian world as Monday's was to Islam. Of all Christian sects in Cairo, six thousand were killed, fourteen hundred in Alexandria, four hundred in Matruh, two hundred-thirty in Port Said.

Around the Mediterranean basin, Rome counted twelve thousand killed, and Beirut had forty-eight hundred. Naples, Istanbul and Athens together had thirty-one thousand six hundred dead and wounded. The total number of religious leaders killed was two thousand and ten, including three bishops and one cardinal. The religious world surrounding the Mediterranean came to a standstill.

"It's started," Loring remarked, as the BBC reports continued throughout the day. "'Operation Amun' has started. Now we have a terrifying example as to what lengths Zoser will go to achieve its aims. And this is only the beginning, I'm afraid."

Loring was sitting with Marc and Crimmins in Merrick's office at the bank. The television had spot coverage of the fighting in the Khalili bazaar district in Cairo. Menefee had just left for Heathrow to catch a flight to Lucerne for his meeting with Claridge. The three friends lingered in Marc's office to clear up some last minute details when the news broke about the uprisings. They sat riveted to the set, none speaking for fear of missing some crucial point or observation. When the live coverage was preempted for local news, Crimmins stood up and began pacing the floor.

"This is worse than any of us ever imagined," he said. "How was Zoser able to pull this off? Do either of you appreciate the enormity of the planning and preparation that must have gone into all this? Consider the manpower alone Zoser needed to start the riots. Those fights didn't just happen on the spur of the moment. Imagine the propaganda and seeds of discontent that were planted all over the world. That strategy alone required an enormous leadtime.

Mark my words, more battles are going to be waged before we see the end of it all. Northern Europe, Britain and even America can expect their fair share of blood. The one fact we can be sure of is that Zoser is far more powerful and organized than any of us believed was possible."

"Bert," Marc broke in, "stop pacing and sit down. We have to figure out how this will effect our plan."

"Marc's right, Bert," Loring interjected. "Let's review what we know. Zoser has to have a secret master file of the top people it depends on worldwide. Ron and Claridge will find it, if we're lucky. With that list we'll be able to get the authorities up off their collective butts and shut Zoser down...again, if we're lucky. If not, we'll have to find another way to get Sempher. Bert, what did you come up with on Sempher's background? And Marc, what about his financial picture?"

Merrick answered first. "I placed a coded computer request to all major banking circles, here in Europe and in the States. Zoser's assets are three and a half billion pounds...roughly five billion dollars. It's subsidiaries are in chemicals, oil, real estate, drugs...you name it, they're into it. That kind of money buys a lot of power. Even though Zoser doesn't trade on the major stock exchanges, all of its subsidiaries do.

Sempher must be extremely wealthy in his own right. When he founded Zoser, his personal fortune was seven hundred million pounds that we know of. We haven't been able to trace any of it since he set up Zoser."

"Damn, it sounds like Sempher is either a financial whiz or a high roller," Loring replied. "With that kind of money he could have anything he wanted. Then why this charade of being the reincarnation of Pharaoh Zozer? He could buy the power he needed to turn him on. It would be interesting to know how he got his money in the first place and where it is now. Marc, do you think he used it all to set up Zoser?"

"We can't find any evidence to bear that out. From what the printout shows, Zoser was capitalized for ten million pounds...one hundred million Swiss francs...ten years ago. The corporate records show that the original investors each put up one million pounds, including Sempher. That means that Sempher ventured less than a quarter of one percent of his own money. Interestingly enough, of the original ten investors, Sempher is the only one remaining. All of the others were bought out by Sempher within the first five years. Sempher owns all of the stock today. Zoser is totally his."

Crimmins then asked, "Marc, who were the other nine investors, and where are they now? Knowing that might give us a clue as to how we proceed."

"I anticipated that. I have the list of investors right here, but I can't find their present whereabouts. Perhaps you can."

Merrick handed the sheet of paper to Crimmins. He stood next to Loring so they could read the names together.

1. Anton Graff, Stuttgart
2. Clyde S. Montgomery, London
3. Anthony Genovese, New York
4. Frank Bommarito, Detroit
5. Lewis Tiganelli, Los Angeles
6. Sidney Garth, London
7. Heinrich von Pfalz, Berlin
8. Mohammid Idris, Benghazi
9. Achmed Yamani, Cairo
10. Kurt Sempher, Vienna

Marc waited until his friends studied the list of names, then added, "Derek, from what you said, this fellow Yamani is still connected with Sempher. Do either of you recognize any of the other names?"

Loring saw a pattern as he scanned the list. "Numbers Three, Four and Five are, or were, godfathers of powerful Cosa Nostra families. I believe Genovese is dead, murdered. I don't know about the others. What about you, Bert? See anyone you recognize?"

"Yes, I do. Montgomery was a major crime figure in London for several years. He controlled the gambling casinos and prostitution. He was found floating in the Thames about five years ago, his throat cut. Sidney Garth was a diamond importer, the biggest and richest in all of Great Britain. He dropped out of sight five years ago and has not been seen nor heard of since. The Diamond Exchange has sealed his business affairs and the entire matter is hush-hush to keep the price of diamonds stable."

"I know from the banking files," Merrick said, "that Graff is connected with the munitions branch of the Krupt empire, and that von Pfalz is a retired general. He was on the German General Staff until Hitler replaced him with von Rundstedt. He deals in surplus armaments shipped to him from Russia."

"As I see it, Sempher got these characters to set up his organization and provided them with a legitimate front." It was Crimmins who spoke now. "The Cosa Nostra got its drug connection in return for assassins Zoser might need. The Germans got a legal outlet for arms and munitions, either funneled through Zoser or for Zoser's own use. Yamani is still with Sempher, doing his dirty work, but this name, Idris, has me stumped. What do you think, Derek?"

"I'll bet anything we'll find that Bommarito and

Tiganelli are dead, killed right after Sempher bought them out five years ago. It might be enlightening to discover the condition of Graff's and von Pfalz's health."

Crimmins picked up the phone, dialed, then said, "Constable Hughes? Crimmins here. Do me a favor, will you? Take down these names and run them through Interpol. Ring me here at this number. I appreciate it, Hughes. Please keep this to yourself."

To the others Crimmins added, "While we wait for Hughes to call, let me fill you in on what I uncovered on Sempher's background. His father was from Silesia and his paternal ancestors were all from northern Germany. His mother was Lebanese, but lived in Cyprus most of her life. I traced her ancestry from Lebanon to Syria to Libya. The earliest date I could come up with was 1650.

The family was living in Libya then using the name 'Shadoum'. If we had more time I might be able to trace the family back further. One other thing...in 1650 the Shadoum family was part of the entourage of Amir Idris, a puppet potentate set up by the Turks who ruled Libya then. This could very well be the basis of those legends of royalty that Sempher was raised on."

Loring asked, excitedly, "That name on the list of Zoser investors...Mohammed Idris. You think there's a connection to the long-gone potentate?"

"It is not very likely. Idris is a rather common name in both Turkey and in Libya. It is an interesting thought, nevertheless. Ah, the phone."

Crimmins leaped up to answer it, even though the phone was on Marc's desk.

"Hughes? Yes, Crimmins here. What was that? Are you sure? No possibility of there being a mistake? Well, thank you. I owe you for this favor." Crimmins was excited.

"Derek, you were right on the button. Interpol says

that Genovese was killed on June 5, 1980. Tiganelli and Bommarito were both killed, gangland style, on June 6, 1980. Clyde Montgomery was discovered on June 10, 1980 and Garth disappeared on June 7, the same year. And here is the clincher. Graff died just last month in a questionable auto accident outside of Zurich, and von Pfalz is confined to his home with complications from a stroke he had last month."

"I'll be damned!" Loring exclaimed.

"Quite. We have now accounted for all of the original investors except this fellow Idris. If he is alive and well, he must be in Sempher's camp, along with Yamani. It appears as though Sempher has eliminated all incriminating ties with the past and has left no one alive who could resurrect that past. We have no single shred of evidence to show that Sempher had the others killed but I would wager anything it is the truth."

"Bert, isn't this enough to give to MI 6 to get them to move on Zoser?"

"I shall get it to Hopkins, Derek, but do not get your hopes up too high. Intelligence works in very strange ways."

Marc's phone rang again. He answered this time. After a few seconds he hung up and actually shouted to the others.

"That was Hughes again. He said to tell you that he dug deeper in the list of aliases filed with the Home Secretary. Mohammed Idris was one of the names used by Moammar Gadhafy several years ago, before he took over Libya in 1969. We know where he is and what he's been doing."

"Now, we have the missing connection," Crimmins said excitedly. "I will get over to Hopkins, straightaway. The CIA and KGB, too. I shall ring each of you when I know his plan of action. Keep your fingers crossed." Crimmins fairly ran out the door.

On Tuesday, when the accounts of the Christian uprisings were aired on radio and television, the concern of all London was aroused. The newspapers were vivid in their stories, vastly different from their normal sterile reporting. In its editorial, the Times urged the U.N. to get involved. The paper claimed the riots proved there was a general breakdown in Western society which could lead to a full scale war.

The television pictures from Rome and Istanbul depicted the senseless slaughter of Christians and the correspondents in those cities were hardput to maintain their composure. The sights and screams these professionals witnessed triggered horror and helplessness in them which hadn't occurred since the exposure of the death camps of Dachau and Buchenwald. The cameras panned scenes of wreckage in both material things and in human life.

As soul-wracking as the Muslim riots of the previous day had been, Tuesday's fighting hit closer to home for the Londoners. England was, after all, a Christian country and although the break with Rome happened over five hundred years ago, Britain wept for the Romans and Orthodox combatants.

News accounts poured in regarding the situations in other Western capitals. Washington, New York, Chicago, and Los Angeles had their National Guard units alerted for possible trouble. The Moslem riots stunned those cities, but with the predicted Christian uprisings, they responded universally. Bonn, Berlin, Paris, Vienna, all called up their armed forces to counteract any attempt to riot within their jurisdictions.

Loring was at Priory Farm with the Merricks, finding it difficult to be merely waiting for Menefee's report from Lucerne. The television set was blaring out grisly details of the riots, showing frocked priests killed on the spot, and terrified nuns running for safety, their habits billowing up around their hips. Those women who were not quick enough or wise enough to flee, could be seen writhing on the stone surface of St. Peter's Square, their black garb shredded or ripped from their bodies, exposing naked breasts and bloodied thighs.

It was almost as though the rioters were waiting for the cameras to focus on them so they could outdo each other in brutality. One of the news cameras stopped its panning and zeroed in on a particularly gruesome spectacle. A young nun was thrashing about on the stone pavement, held down by two rioters.

The woman was stark naked except for the starched headgear pulled down over her eyes. Her body contorted in spasms with her futile effort to escape. A third man had severed the penis and scrotum of a butchered monk and tried to force the bloody mass into the void between her legs. After several unsuccessful jabs, he pushed it into her mouth. Resisting fiercely, she vomited out the obscenity and continued to scream. The man then slowly cut off her breasts, prolonging her torment, then plunged the knife into her chest, again and again. All movement stopped. The three left her lying in her pooling blood. They ran off into the street looking for more victims.

St. Peter's Square was a shambles with hundreds of milling and scratching people clawing at the doors of the cathedral, trampling hundreds more in their insane frenzy to destroy. Bernini's magnificent arcade was unrecognizable because of the blood dripping from the marble columns, the bodies of the dead or wounded draped at rest around the column plinths. Having to watch all that historic beauty and culture being smashed brought tears to Loring's eyes. Yet, he could not turn away.

The telecast switched to Istanbul where the events were the same with only the scenery different. Loring was mesmerized by the battle as the camera zoomed in on an isolated skirmish taking place in front of the Blue Mosque, the Sultanahmet. One elderly Orthodox priest was surrounded by six burly attackers. Each was armed with a curved knife, slashing and stabbing at the old man. It was at the height of the fight, just as a blade was pushed into the throat of the priest, that Loring let out a loud cry. He jumped to his feet, excitedly pointing to the screen.

"That bastard, the one who just killed the priest. I recognize him! He was one of Wells' men who kidnapped me in Istanbul four years ago. He was a Moslem then, or at least he pretended to be. This should be enough evidence even for the cautious Mr. Hopkins. What channel is this...three? They must have a tape of the telecast. I'll call Crimmins and have him get to Hopkins."

Bert Crimmins was at home watching the same telecast. "Nora watched for a while, but gave up and went to bed. She is there now, crying. Why did you call?"

"The scene from Istanbul. I recognized the one who killed the old priest. He was one of Wells' men. Doesn't that prove Zoser is behind all this? What more does MI 6 need before they act, for God's sake?"

"Derek, listen. What you saw was a man you once knew. He might have worked for Wells then but you have no reason to believe he still does. He was most likely just a hired gun, as he is now. There is no concrete evidence to tie this to Zoser even though you and I know they are behind it. Let's wait for Ron's call."

Loring returned to Marc and Veronica in the parlor.

They had turned off the set. Veronica was sitting very erect in her chair, her pretty face ashen. The concern for the men in her life showed in her expression.

She murmured, barely audible, "Do you think the Jews are next?"

"Yes, I believe they're slated for similar riots. It's obvious Zoser needs all religions around the Mediterranean rendered impotent. The Jews are considered a strong force in the area. Zoser can't have that." Loring was pacing the floor, stopping now and then to rub Briget's muzzle. She followed his every move with her large brown eyes. He continued.

"My whole scheme of making Sempher the laughing stock of the world is unworkable now. He has the best of us for the time being. The only hope we have now is the list that Ron went after. Lord, I hope he finds it."

Merrick was somber. "This makes one believe in the final battle, Armageddon, doesn't it?"

The telephone rang. Veronica rushed to answer. In a few moments she returned, her face white with worry.

"That was Claridge calling from Zurich. He'll land at Heathrow about five AM. He said to tell you he has the information you wanted, or at least most of it. He didn't mention Ron. Do you suppose something has happened to him?"

Chapter 18

The light puffs of fog which had been blowing in from Lake Lucerne became thicker. A steady drizzle replaced the fog as Menefee passed through the village of Dietshiburg, four kilometers north of Lucerne. He slowed the car to merge with a procession of loaded lorries. He was keeping pace with the trucks, more to stay inconspicuous than to call attention to himself by passing them. With the rain beating a steady staccato against the windshield, the glare from oncoming headlights danced across the glass and burned into his eyes.

It was with a sigh of relief that Menefee drove into the environs of Lucerne. Daylight was replacing the wet darkness when he left the main road to take the Lake drive to the southern edge of the city. He had promised Claridge he would be at the Ruckli Hotel as near to six o'clock as possible. The luminous dial of his dashboard clock showed he had fifteen minutes to spare.

Menefee's flight from London landed at Zurich's Kloten Airport at approximately four in the morning. There were but ten passengers deplaning at that hour which made his wait for passport clearance understandably brief. The Immigration official merely compared him with his photo and checked his name against the government list of undesirables who were barred from entering the country. He had no luggage to claim as he planned to be on a plane back to London the following day.

He rented a small sedan and began the drive south. Once he passed through to the south of Zurich, Menefee had the road to himself. He was certain that Claridge exercised every bit as much caution as he in getting to the meeting site, especially since he still had the bloodhounds of Zoser on his trail.

It was 6:05 when he pulled into the car park of the Ruckli Hotel. The feeble light of morning was peeking through the patches of rain as he left the car and rushed into the hotel coffee shop. Claridge was at the counter staring into a forgotten cup of coffee. He was worn and haggard-looking with a stubble of white beard in patches on his face. He looked up when Menefee sat down beside him. A look of relief crossed his face.

"Ron, am I ever glad to see you!"

"Likewise, old friend. You look terrible, I might add."

"I suppose I do, but under the circumstances, I'm just happy enough to be alive." Claridge's face broke into a wry smile.

"How were you able to get away?" Menefee asked.

"I'll tell you all about that later. Right now, I think we'd better get on with our mission. Let's take your car. You drive and I'll talk. Or do you want some coffee or tea first?"

"No, I'm fine. Let's be on our way."

Back on the road, Menefee headed south. Claridge said Sempher's chalet was on the lake near the resort village of Hergiswil.

"It's about fifteen kilometers beyond Lucerne," he said. "Now, what's been happening since I last saw you?"

"A hell of a lot, and mostly bad. The one good thing is that Wells is dead and buried."

"Thank the Lord! How did it happen?"

Menefee related the events of the past month, from the hijacking of Loring's flight and the subsequent killing of Nadia Shepherd to the ordeal Loring survived in the desert. He told Claridge about Loring's slow recovery at Priory Farm and the plan he developed for the destruction of Zoser.

"Loring's plan has some good possibilities but I don't think it'll work. That's one of the reasons we're here...to get the information he needs to get the intelligence agencies in on the case."

"What are the other reasons why we're here?"

"What? What do you mean?"

"You just said that getting some information for Loring was one of the reasons we're here. What are the other reasons?"

"Hell, Josh, that was a figure of speech."

"Was it, Ron...really?"

"Yes. No...hell, I don't know. But now that you mention it, maybe I do have another motive, subconsciously. I think we might find something...anything...that will point out a chink in Sempher's armor."

"I see. What type of thing should we be looking for?"

"Oh, I don't know. Letters, photos, anything that we could use against him. Hell, you know what I mean."

"It's a thought. Let's wait and see. Now, what about Wells? How did he die?"

"The information you sent Bert was good enough to find and arrest the creep. Unfortunately, he escaped and went after Loring. Loring had the opportunity and certainly the motive, but he couldn't bring himself to kill Wells. When Bert was taking Wells back to London, the damn fool tried to take the gun away from Bert only to get his head blown off for his effort. End of story."

"So he was killed by accident?"

"That's what the Board of Inquiry found. So far, no one's questioning the verdict. But let's get back to you, Josh. How did you get away?"

"After I called Loring in Cairo, I put together that packet of facts on Zoser and mailed it to your brother-in-law straightaway. I threw my things together and left London in a hurry. I took the night train to Paris where I holed up for three days. I flew to Madrid and doubled back to Oslo before I made my way down to Athens. I did that leg of the journey by train, second and third class."

"But why Athens, Josh? We all know that Greece is a hotbed of Zoser agents. You took one hell of a chance there, sitting on their doorstep."

"I took a calculated risk, Ron. I figured Zoser would be looking for me anywhere but right under their noses. It worked for awhile, too. But after a week, I noticed too many curious stares in my direction and decided it was time for me to move on. I was staying in the Plaka, in a part-time hotel and full-time whorehouse with the distinctive name of Astarte. I befriended one of the girls who had a customer with a boat. With her persuasion, this Armenian fisherman took me to Crete where I was able to catch a private plane to Rhodes. I stayed in Lindos until I called you."

"Then you lost the bloodhounds?" Menefee asked his friend.

"As far as I could tell, yes. I didn't see anyone who gave me a second glance. Naturally, I kept away from the public places. I rented a room with a fig farmer and his wife."

"Josh," Menefee asked, "wasn't there some way you could have warned Loring how close Zoser was to him?"

"Not while I was in London. Wells was keeping a fairly active weather-eye on me. He knew I was aware of what he did to Tupps and MacIvor and was just waiting for his chance to get rid of me, too. Then after I ran, I didn't know where to reach him. I know it sounds feeble, but I'm truly sorry for what happened. If I see him, I'll tell him so. Think Loring will believe me?"

"It's difficult to say. He had a horrible time in the desert and, coupled with the murder of Nadia, he went rather bonkers. There's no telling how he'll react to you. I did let him know, before I recruited both of them to our cause, that you were one of us. That may carry some weight. That's all I can say. We'll just wait and see."

Claridge pointed to the road ahead. "That's it, Ron. On your left, that break in the trees. It's the road leading to the chalet. Pull in and we'll leave the car. The house is about half a kilometer toward the lake."

Menefee eased the car off the road onto the rutted path through the trees. He drove less than fifty yards into the dense foliage where he parked, the car completely hidden from the highway. They left the car and trudged ahead on foot. It was then Menefee noticed the small duffel bag Claridge was carrying.

"What's in the bag, Josh, a change of underwear?"

"No, smarty. Merely some essential tools for our mission. You don't think we'll be greeted with open arms, do you? Unless I miss my guess, we'll have to break our way in and find some way to avoid Sempher's security."

"What security?"

"Who knows? Whatever Sempher felt was necessary to protect this place from the uninvited...dogs, alarms, armed guards, trapdoors, and other diverse bells and whistles."

"You've been here before, Josh. What did you see then?"

"The one time I was here with Wells, I saw armed

patrols around the perimeter, each with a vicious attack dog along for company. I didn't notice any security inside, but that doesn't mean there wasn't any. We'll just take things slow and easy."

The heavy stand of trees parted and they saw the chalet up ahead in a wide expanse of well-tended landscaping. They noticed, too, the high chain link fence which surrounded the house on each side and across the front. Claridge commented that the side fences went down to the water and extended at least fifty feet into the lake.

"Unless we find a break in the fence, which is highly unlikely, we'll have to get in from the lake approach."

"Do you have a boat in that bag of yours?" Menefee was serious. "I can't swim a stroke."

"If it comes to that, we might get lucky and find a boat. There are several resort places up and down the shore here. One of them must have a boat of sorts we could use."

They cautiously approached the fence on the right side. From all appearances it was intact with not a hint of a break or flaw in the woven steel. The vertical fence was eight feet high and had coils of barbed wire fastened to the top. Scaling the fence was out of the question.

Claridge opened his duffel bag and took out a pair of high-powered binoculars. He scanned the entire front of the estate, looking for any telltale signs of the security system he felt was in force. He saw no rotating TV cameras, no open wires from the fence to the house which could be the evidence of electronic or mechanical alarms. All of the windows of the chalet which faced the main gate were heavily draped. No sign of movement or device interrupted the tranquil setting of the house.

"I don't like this," Claridge said. "There should be someone about. Sempher is too careful to allow this break in his security. There is nothing around that I can see with these glasses, not even a sign of the dogs."

"Maybe he's closed the place up for a time. If that's the case, it could work to our advantage." Menefee wanted to get on with the job. "We'll have to take our chances with the gate."

"Right. But watch your footing. Assume we're not alone here."

They edged up to the gate, a massive two-leaf wrought iron barrier. It was locked and had no visible latch or grab bar.

"It's an electric lock, actuated from the house. We'll try to short it out. This could be tricky. Keep your eyes peeled while I work on it."

Claridge examined the housing of the lock. It was about six inches square, an inch and a half thick and entirely of stainless steel welded internally to prevent tampering. The locking mechanism could not be taken apart, but Claridge knew there had to be a source of power fed into the device. He examined the spindles of the gate itself. Two of the wrought iron bars appeared to have been cut away for the insertion of the lock.

He saw the threads of the bars extending a meager millimeter below the lock housing showing that they were screwed into the lock but not drawn up completely tight. He figured the power source to the lock came from the house, underground, through the hollow stile of the gate leaf bottom and then up the iron tubing to the steel housing. He turned to Menefee, saying, "I think I found the way in, Ron. Look into the bag and get me the pipe wrench. It's the biggest thing in there."

"What made you think about bringing along a pipe wrench? Planning on doing a bit of plumbing on the side?" Menefee handed Claridge the heavy wrench.

"I figured we might be forced to twist off a combination lock on Sempher's safe. I find a pipe wrench pretty good for that sort of thing."

Claridge tightened the wrench on the iron shaft near the threaded connection. He levered it counterclockwise and soon had the bar separated from the housing, but the action tightened the bar deeper into the bottom stile. He had Menefee pull on the bar to keep it from working back into the lock housing while he undid it from the stile. When the bar was free there was enough slack in the electrical line to expose about four inches of it.

"Now all I do is break into this line and interrupt the current. That should open the gate."

"Couldn't we just cut the wire?"

"No. That would keep the gate locked with no way of opening it. We need to actuate the power"

The gate opened noiselessly when Claridge crossed the electric line. They didn't hear an alarm but they couldn't be sure the sound didn't just alert the inside of the house. They proceeded to the chalet carefully, watching for signs of discovery. They were not challenged as they went to the front door. Claridge easily picked the lock and they were inside.

A circuit of the house convinced them they were alone. Claridge said that Sempher's study was on the second floor to the left of the grand staircase leading up from the formal lobby. They crept up the stairs, still waiting for some indication they had been discovered. When they reached the upper floor, they cautiously entered the plush study and began their search.

Menefee found charts and maps on the desk. One of the charts depicted the lineage of Sempher, going back to the Third Dynasty in Egypt. He couldn't be sure of the truth in what the chart depicted. It would require Loring's expertise to authenticate it. For protection, he wrapped the chart in a piece of newspaper he found on the floor. In the meantime, Claridge was examining the vast array of books lining the walls of the room. He called out to his friend.

"Ron, come here. I think I found the file room."

He pulled out a book from the shelf and twisted a lever. A section of the bookcase opened out and they looked into a dark alcove behind. Claridge found a light switch and when they had some light they rifled through the files. Menefee shouted with excitement.

"Here it is! The whole manual of Operation Amun. And it's in several different languages. This is what we came for. Let's get the hell out of here."

"Wait a minute, Ron," Claridge said. "As long as we're here, let's see what else is laying around...that extra ace in the hole."

Claridge continued looking through the files while Menefee went back to the desk. He searched the drawers on each side without finding anything of interest. In the center drawer, however, he came across a file folder containing a complete dossier on Loring. It encompassed Loring's professional and private life, all the way back to his childhood. Menefee didn't waste the time in reading it thoroughly, but determined it was important enough to take along. Loring would certainly be interested in it.

Claridge came out of the file room. "Nothing else in there. Let's go."

They didn't bother to hide the results of the break-in. They gathered up their findings and left the study in a hurry, intent on getting as far away as possible before they were discovered. They stopped abruptly at the top of the stairs. There, waiting for them at the bottom, was a burly sentry, a snarling Doberman at his side waiting for a signal to attack. The man was armed with an automatic weapon which he had pointed at them. No one spoke. The only sound was the throaty growl of the dog. In what seemed to Menefee to be an eternity, the guard motioned them down the stairs and into the lobby.

"Put down what you have in your hands and sit on the floor. Others will be here soon and then we will take care of you. Hans, stand fast!" The man walked to the door, then turned to them. "You would be wise to remain still or the dog will tear you apart. He is very well trained."

When the guard left the house, Menefee quietly asked the obvious. "Do you think he's really going for more guards?"

"Most likely," Claridge replied. "He certainly puts enough trust in that beast to leave us alone. I don't think we have much time before he comes back. I have an idea." He thought for a minute, then said to Menefee. "These attack dogs usually are trained to respond to sudden movements. I wonder what would happen if we both moved at the same time. Who would he attack first?"

They looked at the dog. His black lips were curled back to show his lethal teeth bared for an anticipated lunge. His tongue ran over the teeth, saliva dripping on the marble tile floor of the lobby. His order was to stand guard and he did what he was trained for...to stand quietly, waiting for sudden moves which would signal him to attack his prey.

In a soft voice, Claridge continued, "If we both move in different directions, at the same time, the poor dog might be confused and not know which of us to go after. The one who is free will get to those heavy drapes next to the door. Pull them down and we'll cover the dog, tangle him in the heavy brocade long enough for us to get out. What do you think?"

"I'm game. I'll do most anything to keep from sitting

here with those bloodshot eyes staring at us. He looks mean and ugly. You give the signal, Josh, and I'll jump to my left while you go right. Good luck."

Claridge softly counted to three. "Ready? Go!"

Both men moved quickly, intent on getting to the drapes which covered the windows on either side of the front door. Menefee was the younger of the two and more agile. He made the rush for the drapes first and pulled them from the wall. In one quick motion, he reeled around. The dog was thrashing and clawing at the twisting body of Claridge, trying to gain the advantage and reach his throat.

Menefee's lunge hurled the dog off of Claridge's body long enough for him to wrap the cloth around the animal. Claridge broke free of the dog's fangs, bleeding from the neck and shoulders, but still able to assist in immobilizing the brute. They wound the drape fabric around and around the dog until he could do nothing but howl and bite at the cloth.

"Josh, are you all right?"

"A bit the worse for wear, but there's nothing broken or damaged beyond repair. You all right?"

"Oh, I'm fine. Let's get out while the getting's good. That other brute'll be back soon and I for one don't wish to be around when he does."

They had just gathered the documents up off the floor when the guard reappeared, his weapon slung under his arm. Before he could collect himself, Menefee and Claridge were upon him, trying to keep his hands away from the gun. It was during the struggle that the gun was discharged, sending a hail of bullets into an electric panel box on the stairwell wall. The shots short-circuited the panel which erupted in a blossom of smoke and sparks.

Claridge had a moment when his hands were free and

he struck the guard over the head with his duffel bag, the same bag that held the large pipe wrench. The guard dropped like a stone. Claridge yelled to Menefee to get the documents and the two of them beat a hasty retreat out the door and into the safety of the thick foliage beyond the gate. Neither of them noticed the wisp of smoke seeping through the lobby and out the open door.

On their way back to Lucerne, they took stock of the situation. Menefee made sure the maps and charts were protected and that the Operation Amun manual was safe. He asked Claridge about the wounds on his neck and body.

"You better have those dog bites looked at, Josh. There's no saying what infections you could get. I don't think that animal was too careful about his dental hygiene."

"They're not too serious. I'll have them treated as soon as we get back."

Suddenly, Menefee turned serious. "Josh, if anything happens to me, I left word in London that you should take over the leadership of the society."

"Nothing's going to happen, Ron. We're practically home free with these documents. When Loring gets them to the right people it should spell the end of Zoser."

Five miles south of Lucerne a huge lorry, loaded with lake gravel, swung out onto the highway from a hidden side road. It smashed into their car broadside, pinning Menefee between the crumpled metal of the door and the dashboard. It might have been the shattered glass that severed an artery. Whatever the cause, Menefee was killed by the crash, bleeding to death while unconscious.

Claridge, who had been driving, was knocked out by the impact. When he came to, he had several bad bruises and a fractured right arm. Despite that, he got Menefee out of the car. The lorry driver was sitting at the side of the road in a state of shock. He remembered nothing of the accident and was weeping inconsolably when taken away by ambulance.

At the hospital in Lucerne Claridge had his bruises attended to and his arm set. The staff gave him a tetanus shot to ward off potential infection. He told the hospital administrator he had business elsewhere which could not be delayed and that he would have the British Legation arrange for the disposition of Menefee's body.

It was while he was waiting in the terminal at Kloten Airport that Menefee's death finally hit him.

Chapter 19

The caverns of the Brotherhood were comparatively cool in relation to the torrid heat of the surrounding desert. The air that filtered through the passages and chambers was cooled by the porous rock while taking on a greater degree of humidity. Those of the Brotherhood who resided in the vast subterranean network were comfortable enough although often bored. They went about their assigned tasks purposefully, albeit in silence, unless the work required conversation.

The five thousand year old organization was again functioning as smoothly as it had done before the centuries of internal decay decimated its ranks. The neglect and the lack of forceful leadership in the past were efficiently corrected by Kurt Sempher when he instilled new life and resolve into the motley Brotherhood. He made his purpose their purpose, his discipline theirs. The reformed members exuded an unholy pride and zeal in performing the regimented tasks that Sempher deemed essential to his goal.

It took two years of hard, dedicated work by Sempher to whip the disjointed band of assassins into an army of mindless followers. He infused inspiration through distorted propaganda, and employed the harsh realities of reward and punishment to achieve his aims. Those unfortunate few who failed to carry out an assignment successfully were executed. Rewards of money, drugs or women awaited those who did not fail.

Sempher spared neither money nor technology to shape his emerging empire. The Brotherhood lacked nothing which would further its effectiveness. He insisted the newly installed communication system be manned twenty-four hours a day. The equipment was state of the art, world class.

Whatever occurred in the world outside of the caves was immediately relayed to the Brotherhood. Microwave transmitters scattered in isolated areas beamed the latest information to the caverns. Sempher had the influence and money to invade the transmissions from orbiting satellites which had to be the crowning manipulation of his power. When word of the Mediterranean basin religious upheavals reached the Brotherhood, there arose a swelling pride of authorship among the brethren.

Kurt Sempher was regally attired in the costly robes of office with the red and white crown of ancient Egypt resting imperiously on his head. He sat with practiced dignity upon his throne, by itself an object of beauty. The throne was carved from ebon wood and overlaid with gold leaf encrusted with precious gems.

Sempher was holding a royal audience. His bloodshot eyes darted nervously around the room. He searched the faces of the handful of attendants fawning before him for any tell-tale sign of mockery or condescension. His gaze swung back and forth to each man, never dwelling for long on any face. When he was satisfied with the complete dominance he enjoyed over these simple minions, he raised a regal arm and pointed the royal scepter at the man on his right.

"Yamani, my brother, is it true that all the reports are favorable? Our plans are proceeding on my exact schedule, are they not?"

"Yea, my lord. We have concluded all our tasks as

you commanded and we have achieved the results you so
wisely predicted. Cairo and Alexandria are in turmoil and
no one leaves his home in Port Said. The government, that
foul and false usurper of your rightful authority, has imposed strict controls over the land to maintain some semblance of order. However, the people are restless and suspicious of everyone."

"What say you of the lands beyond Kemet?" The scepter pointed again.

"Oh mighty Pharaoh, Beirut, Tripoli, Damascus,
Sidon, Teheran, Baghdad, all report similar conditions of
unrest. Across the wide sea, Athens, Istanbul, Rome and
Marseilles are helpless, trapped in chaos by their own fears.
It shall be but a matter of days until we hear of disruptive
uprisings in other parts of Europe and America. Our brothers are even now preparing to strike when your royal signal is given."

"Excellent, Yamani, excellent! It is ordained that our
Egypt will return to the all-powerful arms of Ra after being so long in the clutches of false gods. I am the enlightened ruler of these lands who shall lead Kemet to
the highest of heights. Ours shall be glory and power
greater than that of Ramses once the false gods are struck
down.

My people will demand my power to give them renewed strength and purpose. I shall raise them up from
the onerous pit of despair where they now cower under the
heel of the usurper. Very soon now, the hour will be auspi-
cious for my leap toward immortality."

"Pray, oh Pharaoh, can you reveal to us what lies ahead,
and what strategy you shall employ to bring this about?"

Those in the room gathered closer to the throne to hear
the very breath of their chosen leader. With one voice they
praised their new ruler, Pharaoh Sempher. But he, with a

haughty wave of the royal whisk, dismissed his court, not yet revealing his inner thoughts.

To his audience he commanded, "Begone, my Brothers, leave me. The time is not yet upon us. You shall know when the proper signs show us the way. Brother Yamani, stay awhile. I would have your counsel."

The royal court backed away from his august presence. Each raised the hiding hood about his head as he passed from the chamber. Alone, the two remaining figures faced each other, their eyes locked. Sempher finally broke the silence, his voice and tone nearly normal. Gone was the archaic speech.

"Achmed, go back to Cairo and start the next phase. It's time to have your men commence the unrest between the Christians and Moslems. Each religion is fearful of its own kind which illustrates the success of the past riots. It should not be difficult to resurrect the age-old hatreds they have toward one another.

Instruct our people in Alexandria and Port Said to do the same. But I caution you, do not go beyond the boundaries of Egypt. The riots in the other countries were instigated merely to sow utter confusion and mistrust. Now we'll show them a real holy war and make them quake with fear. They'll tremble while waiting their turn in the crucible of hate."

"It shall be as you say, *effendi*."

"Delay the signal to America and Europe in the north. We might not require their riots after all. It depends on how thorough you do our work in Egypt."

"Very well, but I'll put them on alert, regardless."

"I must leave for a while to go north and consolidate the Brotherhood. London is too dangerous now, thanks to the barbarism of Wells. I'll be staying in Amsterdam to direct our northern strategy, but

I'll keep you informed of any important developments which might effect the work here."

"What about the Jews? What are your plans for them?"

"Leave the Jews alone. They'll stay in line. They know they'll be totally eradicated from this part of the world if the Christians and Moslems band together in a single push against them. It's better to keep them quiet with fear than to goad them to resist. We've seen how they fight. Leave them alone, for now. We might have need for them later."

Yamani stepped back, obviously disappointed. Sempher knew of Yamani's hatred of the Jews. He expected Yamani to object to his instructions. Wisely, however, he changed the subject.

"Mr. Sempher, do you think it's safe to go north at this time? We know that Loring survived the desert and is now in league with the Menefee, seeking revenge for the execution of the Shepherd woman. He has the resources of the Menefee to draw on."

"Yamani, old friend, I'm well aware of what Loring is capable of. I studied him closely in Zurich. He has never come up against a dedicated adversary before. He hasn't a clue as to how to find me or even where he might start his search."

"But he's proved his resourcefulness. Consider his desert survival."

"The desert and nature do not think. I do. I shall gather some trusted friends in the north and they will hunt Loring down for me. And I promise you, Achmed, this time there'll be no escape for him, or for the Menefee either. Now I must go. Return to Cairo and further our cause, *effendi*."

After Yamani left the caverns for Cairo, Sempher locked himself in his private chambers, the decor of which befitted his status as a pharaoh of Egypt. The suite was as complete a replica of ancient royal quarters as his imagination and money could provide. It was here, in these plush and ornate rooms, that Sempher experienced the full impact of his role. He spent as much time as he could in these royal chambers, strutting around and around with regal bearing absorbing the atmosphere which shrieked of pomp and glory. The walls were alive with drawings and frescoes done in the old Egyptian style, all depicting his personal role in the resurgence of Egyptian royalty.

He had gone so far as to characterize himself as a semigod conversing with Osirus and Isis, proving to those ancient gods the greatness of his deeds and the goodness of his acts. All would be weighed against the feather of judgement as in the days of the former pharaohs. There was a flaw in these drawings, however; the flaw was not in the pictures themselves, but rather in their being placed on the walls at eye level instead of being up high, near the ceiling. Sempher rationalized this to himself by saying the walls were not high enough to put the pictures up where they would be subject to divine inspection. Deep down, though, Sempher reveled in his own glory, and spent uncounted hours before the paintings savoring what he saw.

The floor of the suite was paved with polished marble. This was a departure from authenticity demanded by his own vanity. He did not appreciate the significance of the ancients using hand-hewn sandstone or granite in that they had neither the materials nor the expertise to produce polished marble. That was to be a Roman contribution to architecture many centuries after the Sahara sands drifted over the tombs of the pharaohs.

Sempher cared not for such matters. To him, marble signified royalty, so his quarters reflected his preference. This was carried even into his bath. The enormous tub was all of polished marble. Perhaps it was for the best he felt the way he did about the smooth stone. Hewn granite would have been hard on his twentieth century skin.

Sempher threw himself down on a cushioned couch and began his mental preparations for going back into the outside world. A part of him rebelled against these necessary trips to his other life, that life of business and money-grabbing. He eagerly longed for the imminent upheaval which would place him in his rightful destiny...the throne of a new Egypt.

However unsavory, he realized these trips to the centers of commerce were vital to his plans. His iron will prevented him from premature actions which might jeopardize his goals. He had worked and planned for too many years to prepare himself for the glory of kingship. The stories his mother told him of the might and power of her ancestors awoke in him the dream. From that dream came the obsession and the drive to recapture those days. It was ordained.

His mother had taught him well. She painted vivid word pictures for him, pictures of the pomp and power wielded by the ruling Turks. It made not a whit of difference to the impressionable youth that the Turks were subjugating a conquered people and forcing them to bend to the Turkish will by whatever ruthless methods worked at the time. No, the politics of the Turks mattered not. It was the power that said it all. Power was that essential element he clearly understood. Absolute power became his beacon. The rest was just so much ornamentation.

The tales his mother told him when he was a child had sent the blood rushing and pounding through his veins. He pressed her for more and more details. What was life like before the Turks and what great deeds had the family accomplished? In these things, however, her memory was vague. She had but dim recollections of the stories her own grandmother told her, only bits and pieces of information regarding the Shadoum clan.

Whenever her tales became disjointed or lacked actual continuity, he suspected she was keeping some vital fact from him, a fact which might somehow detract from the splendor the family enjoyed under the Turks. It was at these times he vowed that the day would eventually come when he would have the time, the connections and the money to uncover the untold truth of the Shadoums. That day did come, twelve years ago. Thinking back on that occasion, he recalled his meeting with the forceful Libyan leader, Moammar Gadhafy, at the hotel in Benghazi.

He was in Libya to negotiate the sale of arms to the Libyan army. There was friction between Libya and Egypt over a disputed border settlement. He had previously sold arms to Egypt at a handsome profit and saw no reason not to do the same with Libya. Gadhafy struck him as being a fanatic, somewhat unstable, and a dangerous man who had his sights on bigger things than the control of Libya. The negotiations required very little of his time...he would deliver the arms Gadhafy wanted at the price Sempher wanted. The sale was concluded.

There was time to wile away before Sempher had to leave and the two engaged in desultory conversation, passing time in a way foreign to Gadhafy's nature. Sempher casually mentioned his personal connection to Libya through the Shadoum family line. Gadhafy said he had a great respect for Amir Idris and those members of his court. He recalled the Shadoum clan came into prominence because of favors rendered to the Turks. There was only a passing reference as to where they came from...Egypt. Perhaps, Gadhafy had said, if Sempher wanted to know more he might find the answers in Istanbul.

That was the spark, the motivation he needed to start him on his quest. His search would change his life forever. As soon as he returned to Vienna, he forced himself to devote the necessary effort to conclude a few important business matters before he rushed to Istanbul.

His perusal of the old recorded chronicles there produced nothing further than what he already knew. An addenda to these records, however, made veiled references to internal scandals connected with various puppet regimes in some of the conquered countries. Libya was one of those countries mentioned. It was recorded that its puppet, Idris, was publicly absolved of political murder through the timely intercession of one Mustapha El-Shadoum, a merchant of Alexandria.

El-Shadoum claimed under oath that Amir Idris was not involved in the crime with which he was charged, and that he, El-Shadoum, produced irrefutable evidence to support his testimony. The year was 1647.

Mustapha El-Shadoum. He, then, was the link. Sempher remembered how he raced from Istanbul to Alexandria to pick up the trail. One so prominent as this Egyptian merchant who saved the ruler of Libya should have many references to the testimony in the archives of Alexandria.

His pursuit of the matter was blocked in ways he could not control—government officials would not open the files to him. Sempher was not one to be defeated by mere mortals though. His money and influence had opened many obscure doors in Egypt in the past and this proved to be no exception. His dealings in arms and drugs put him in contact with a multitude of characters, honest and otherwise. It was through the intercession of one such contact that the files of the Department of Antiquities were made available to him and he was permitted to scour through the records.

To an ordinary man untrained for such scholarly research, the task might have been insurmountable. But Sempher, wrapped in his obsession, was no ordinary man. Even so, the search produced nothing of value. This setback did not dissuade him. On the contrary, it only served to increase his determination. He was able to twist enough arms and call in enough favors to be put on the path which led to the isolated Census Office. There he found the elusive merchant, El-Shadoum. Upon further intensive investigation, he found El-Shadoum had an import-export business, which he established in 1640, and that El-Shadoum immigrated to Egypt from Judea.

It was documented that El-Shadoum was a Jew whose name was Moshe Ben-Shafor. He changed his name to El-Shadoum when he converted to Islam. That was not important. Sempher was not dismayed to find his roots planted in the barren soil of Israel. Any real or imagined stigma of such knowledge made no difference in his political and social circles. The one fact he did not know and the one he had to have, was the name of the woman Shadoum married in Alexandria. That was the key to open the distant past.

Sempher's thoughts were interrupted by the arrival of his helicopter. His trip to Europe could not be delayed, and his private plane was waiting at Matruh. He changed into his western clothes, and collected papers and charts which he stuffed into a battered briefcase. He cast a final look around his suite then left the caverns. He told himself he would have ample time during the flight to savor the heady recollections of the search for his heritage.

For the time being, however, he had to content himself with the business at hand which took his full concentration. Plans had to be finalized in his mind before he landed in Amsterdam. Once there, all his energies would be needed to whip the northern network of Zoser into shape. That goddamned Wells certainly screwed up the north with his misplaced sense of power.

The chopper settled down on the hard sand apron next to the Lear jet. The plane was festooned with the crest Sempher designed, an emblem showing two intertwined cobras coiled around the red and white crown of unified Egypt. With only a brief nod to the waiting pilot, Sempher boarded the plane. It took off immediately once he was settled in the plush cabin.

When the departure formalities had been complied with, Sempher allowed himself the luxury of relaxing to dream of his future. The plans had come together in his head. He would first have his northern agents locate Derek Loring. They would report Loring's whereabouts to him in Amsterdam, at which time he could turn his paid assassins loose. He understood they would want a bonus for the job if it was done with dispatch and with the positive proof of Loring's death. It didn't matter—business was business after all, and this was an important business decision.

His second priority was to gather a cadre of dedicated men, dispatch them to London and reestablish that vital link in his chain of influence. Perhaps some of the old group still remained, those who could be relied on to make the British cell operative again. A name change would be necessary, as Zoser International could not be visible in London after the trouble Wells created. Damn him to hell!

The noiseless travel and the soft swaying of the jet lulled Sempher into a fitful sleep. He tossed about with disturbing dreams which seemed all too real—a vision of his empire crumbling in the desert sands. He jerked up, fully awake, and made himself relax as he realized where he was and that such dreams were for the superstitious. It was then he returned to his recollections of his quest.

In his mind he traveled back to Alexandria where he searched for traces of Shadoum's wife. The existing records were sketchy and contained long periods where no history was recorded. He recalled the frustration which engulfed him and the spark of genius that sent him to the synagogue. Shadoum was a Jew when he came to Egypt.

Knowing the Jewish fetish for truth and records, he had a hunch that some trace of Ben-Shafor would be uncovered in the temple's archives. Temple Beth Ezra had documents which listed the congregations for every year, back to early 1365 when the synagogue was first established. It was his money and influence again that paved the way. He was shown records that listed a Moshe Ben-Shafor transferring into Beth Ezra from Jerusalem in 1639. His marriage to Miriam Haboth, a Jewess from Matruh, was indeed consecrated in 1640.

What followed was relatively simple. In Matruh he found remnants of the Haboth family, although they were reluctant to talk about the scandalous affair of Miriam. It took money and some cajoling, but Sempher became privy to the family history. They told him she left the faith in 1640 to embrace Islam with her husband. The Haboth clan belonged to the true tribe of Levi and the family traced its roots back to the days of the Jewish captivity under Ramses II.

In the royal court, a high priest of the ancient cult of Zozer took as his wife one of the daughters of the Rabbi Haboth. Everything came together then. He, Kurt Sempher, could claim direct lineage back to the Pharaoh Zozer! This amazing knowledge directed his role in life. All that was required to achieve his destiny was a mechanism to clear away all obstacles. Zoser International was that machine.

His plane landed in the early evening at Schipol Airport without incident. He had a suite of rooms reserved at the Delphi Hotel where he started the chain of events to execute his plans. He placed calls to London, Berlin and Paris, contacting the most devoted aides in each of those Zoser cells. He arranged a meeting for the following evening.

The men he spoke with were his to command. They would be in Amsterdam by early afternoon. He did not divulge the nature of the meeting, but by the tenor in his voice the men understood the importance of the session. When that matter was taken care of, he called one other person...Reginald Sutton, Knightsbridge, London. It was time to take care of Derek Loring.

Hopkins picked up his phone reluctantly. He didn't relish the thought of answering asinine questions from his superior, Hugh Clemmons. He was preoccupied with the reports he had just received from operatives Williams and the other one, Broadhearst. Those men had Loring and Crimmins under surveillance and Hopkins was obsessed with knowing what they were up to.

"Hopkins here," he answered curtly.

"Mr. Hopkins, Peter Bradshaw is calling from Cairo," the switchboard girl announced. "Do you wish me to put the call through?"

"Yes, by all means! Hello, Bradshaw? Hopkins here."

"Mr. Hopkins, I have a bit of news. Can we talk?"

"Wait, I'll put us on scrambler. There. Go ahead, Peter."

"Yamani's active these days. The riots are his doing."

"The hell you say?"

"We've not enough proof to feed Mubarak. You know

I have someone planted in his harem. She claims to have heard him giving orders over the phone to start the trouble with the Moslems in Cairo and Alexandria."

"What about the Christians?"

"She doesn't know about those riots, but I'll wager my last pound he's behind them."

"The riots appear to have stopped. Any guesses as to why?" Hopkins was sweating now.

"My guess is that the Jews are next. The entire Jewish community is staying behind closed doors."

"Very well, Peter, I'll pass that on. Good work, and keep your many eyes peeled."

"Certainly. By the way, how's Loring?"

"I understand he's recovering slowly. Only time will tell."

"I'd appreciate it if you keep me informed on him. I rather liked him, in spite of how everything turned out."

"I'll do that, Bradshaw. We'll talk again."

Hopkins hung up the phone. His hands were wet and there was a knot in his stomach. The news from Cairo was not good, not good at all. The religious riots had alerted all the intelligence agencies, but everyone of them were keeping their findings to themselves. "Damn," he said aloud, "what we need is a packet of trust and understanding. There's too much secrecy among us."

He forgot the reports of Williams and Broadhearst. The big picture didn't include the comings and goings of a semi-deranged historian, a former policeman or an overly cautious banker. The big picture required the coordination of professionals, professionals like him and Peter Bradshaw.

He called Hugh Clemmons. It was time to apprise his superior of what was going on.

Chapter 20

Heathrow Airport was a bedlam. Thousands of travelers were milling in or about the vast complex, either scur-
rying to departure gates or jamming into long lines for baggage claim after immigration control. A substantial mix
of greeters and well-wishers added to the chaos which grew
or subsided with each flight announced.

The separate terminal buildings which handled particular routes throughout the world probably worked well
on paper, but the vagaries of modern travel did not keep
pace. Heathrow was in concert with most international
airports in that 'out-of-service' signs on its facilities added
to the confusion and short tempers of everyone. There
had to be a reserved space in Heaven for the unflappable
British terminal staff. Theirs was a sorry lot in airport
life.

Loring and Merrick were waiting with Crimmins for
the flight from Zurich, uncertain as to what to expect.
Loring didn't tell Crimmins that Claridge was arriving
alone. He didn't want to worry him, or more to the point,
he didn't know the whole story himself. Menefee may
have had business elsewhere and sent Claridge on ahead
with the information they needed so desperately. But
Loring had a premonition that something had happened to
Menefee for Claridge to be traveling alone. They would
know soon enough.

The three of them were waiting at the arrival gates in
Terminal Three. It was 4:45 AM. The Zurich flight was

scheduled to land at 4:55. Loring tried hard to hide his feelings by mentioning his mundane observations...the crowds of people in the terminal at such an ungodly hour made him uncomfortable. He watched Marc who was unusually quiet. Loring sensed that Merrick really didn't relish the next few minutes. His expression told Loring that he, too, feared the worse. Marc avoided Loring's gaze, intent on staying close to Bert.

Crimmins, stoic and non-committal, stood ramrod stiff, his eyes on the digital clock suspended from the ceiling. "They should be here at any minute now," he said.

The public address system blared the announcement. "Swissair Flight 455 from Zurich is now arriving at Gate 38. Baggage may be claimed at carrousel 12 on the lower level."

"That's it...Gate 38, over there," Loring said.

At 5:06 the passengers began to stream through the doors. Claridge spotted the trio before they saw him. He hesitated, trying to delay the actual news of Menefee's death. Knowing he should not put it off, he steeled himself for the ordeal ahead. The documents and other information he carried with him were too vital to allow him the luxury of personal feelings. He acknowledges Menefee's friends who hurried toward him as he came into view. Loring and Merrick both winced when they saw the cast on Claridge's arm.

"Josh, it's good to see you again. We were worried until Ron got your call from Rhodes. Speaking of Ron," Loring said, "where is he? And what happened to your arm?"

Claridge watched the three, searching their faces and seeing the apprehension in their eyes. He hesitated for a moment.

"Let's try to find a quiet spot away from all this

babble." The four of them found seats in an out of the way corner of the waiting area.

"Well?" Loring said.

"Well," Claridge began, "I'm sorry to have to tell you this, but Ron isn't coming. He's dead."

"Ron dead?" Crimmins was the first to react, his face ashen.

Then Loring started his questioning. He pressed Claridge for the facts, even down to the most minute detail. Claridge told them what had happened from the time he met Menefee in Lucerne until the accident. He left out nothing. At the end of his story, he turned to Loring.

"Ron wanted you to have these documents, Derek. He said you would know how to authenticate them, and know what to do with them."

He handed the charts and maps to Loring, then gave him the organization chart of Zoser International and the report on 'Operation Amun'. He held back the dossier Ron found. Loring looked at one of the maps, the one which showed the desert area west of Cairo. A spot was circled which he believed was the underground headquarters of Sempher where he and Nadia were held captive. He pointed this out to the others. The chart of the lineage Sempher held to be his own interested the four of them, too, but there would be time later to study it. Right now they all had more important things to do. Loring touched Crimmins' arm gently.

"Bert, we're truly sorry over this loss. Nora will be heartbroken. Is there anything we can do?"

Crimmins stared ahead, saying nothing. Finally he looked up. "What? Sorry, Derek, I wasn't listening."

"Never mind, my friend. We'll talk later."

"No, Derek. We must get on with it."

Claridge watched as Loring smiled weakly, "Please

don't think me callous or unfeeling, but we do have work to do. Ron is dead because he stuck his neck out for this stuff. The least we can do is get it into the hands of the proper people. It's up to us to see it through."

"You're right, of course."

"We have to turn the Zoser organization over to the CIA and MI 6. You must get us in to see Hopkins so we can tell him the whole story. He damn-well better see the urgency in alerting the other agencies to the importance of catching these men listed here. What do you say?"

A saddened Bert Crimmins spoke up. "Right. I'll ring up Hopkins straightaway. He'll see us today...I'll insist. But I really must talk to Nora, to tell her about Ron. You three wait here. I'll find a phone."

"Bert, wait." Loring touched his friend's arm, facing him.

"If Hopkins can see us, make it early enough for him to start working on this today, but late enough to give you some time with your wife. You do owe her that much. A couple of hours one way or another can't be that crucial."

"Exactly," Marc added, speaking up for the first time. "She doesn't deserve hearing the dreadful news over the phone. We can wait for you someplace nearby."

Crimmins was visibly moved by all this. "Thanks awfully, my friends. I do appreciate it."

Claridge didn't say anything. He watched the reactions of these men and heard what they were saying. There was more he could tell them but he remained quiet, letting them do the talking. Let them take the bull by the horns, he thought...I have my own plans. He quickened when Loring turned to him.

"What's that under your arm, Josh. Something we should know about?"

"I was going to give it to you later. It's a little me-

mento Ron found in Sempher's desk." He passed the file to Loring.

"I'll be damned," he remarked when he realized what it was. "No wonder Zoser knew so much about me."

"What is it, Derek?" Merrick asked.

"My complete life history, all the way back to my boyhood. Sempher did a thorough job on me."

"Wonder what's taking Bert so long," Merrick said. "He's taking all this quite well. I imagine he's pretty broken up inside. Derek, what can I do? I have to do something."

"If Bert can get us in to see Hopkins, I think you should come with us. I never wanted you so deeply involved, but since you are, you damn-well should have a say in what we do. Don't you agree, Josh?"

"Yes, I do. Merrick, I only know about you from what Ron told me. He liked both you and your wife. That's good enough for me."

"But what if Bert is unable to get through to Hopkins?" Merrick appeared desperate to be part of the intrigue.

"In that case, provided it's all right with you, we'll pick up Bert and Nora and go back to the farm. I think Nora needs company now. Even though our mission is to destroy Zoser, we can't lose sight of everything else. Bert needs friends now."

Crimmins returned, a stern look on his face. He threw himself into a chair.

"Hopkins will see us at his flat in Mayfair in a couple of hours. He asked me to bring all of you with me. I told him what we had here, the proof he was asking for. Claridge, do you think it wise for you to tag along? I mean, you are part of the Menefee, and that group is frowned on in some circles."

"I wasn't going with you in any case," Claridge

made the statement without any preamble. "Ron told me in Lucerne that I was to take over the Menefee if anything happened to him. I have to contact the group and make our own plans. I assure you, we're working for the same thing. I'll keep in touch so you'll know how to reach me if the need arises. Derek, I'll ring you at Priory Farm sometime tomorrow. I might have some news and I'll need to know what actions MI 6 is coming up with." He left quickly, swallowed up in the crowd.

After he talked with Crimmins, Geoffrey Hopkins raced over to the Director's office. He knocked briefly, then went in. The Director of MI 6, Sir Hugh Clemmons, was middle-aged, an Englishman of the old school. His pale blue eyes and florid complexion, coupled with a quick smile and firm handshake, often threw his adversaries off guard. It was rumored throughout the agency that he had a photographic memory especially for names, faces and events. True or not, Hugh Clemmons was never at a loss for important or relevant data concerning the entire gamut of the MI 6 operation. He nodded to Hopkins and indicated a chair.

"Hopkins, what brings you up here this time of day? More bad news from Cairo?" Clemmons leaned back in his swivel chair, lighting a cigar as an excuse to keep his hands busy. He smiled at his deputy.

"Something has broken in the Zoser case, Sir Hugh, but from a different quarter. I just talked with Bert Crimmins. He was with Scotland Yard until recently, working on those ritual killings. Well, it seems his friend, Derek Loring, has uncovered the proof of Zoser's complicity in these religious riots. They're coming in to see me later to have us alert all friendly agencies and put a plug into Zoser's plans."

Clemmons turned his blue eyes to Hopkins, no longer smiling. He dropped his cigar into an ashtray, then spoke in a soft voice which disguised his anger.

"So, Loring finally has the proof you sent him after. You were the one who enlisted his help to find what Zoser was up to. You assigned one of our agents to assist him, and then promised him our protection.

Now consider what happened next. He and our agent are abducted, she is murdered, and Loring barely escapes death in the desert. Where was the protection you promised? And don't tell me our people in Egypt didn't know enough about what we were doing. And why was the CIA kept out of it? After all, Loring is an American and he should have been their responsibility. We knew all along how vicious Kurt Sempher can be. I should like to hear you explain all this."

"Sir Hugh, I will not insult your intelligence with excuses. I have none. I made a judgement call and it simply backfired. What Zoser wanted Loring for sounded like simple basic research on Sadat's background. None of us had the faintest notion what the research was to be used for, and we still don't. We don't have a clue."

"What need was Shepherd in this?"

"I sent Shepherd along to give him a hand with some of the old translations. She was good in that sort of thing. She was to keep us informed, but she didn't. We don't know why. If fault is to be accessed, it has to be with my not clarifying her role completely before she left. She and Loring did find the leak in our office and in the CIA. I wanted to keep us in a low profile until we had something more substantial to go on."

"And the CIA?"

"They had Loring under surveillance every time he left Hawaii after the Istanbul incident. They believed Zoser would eventually get to him. I've talked with them since Loring returned from Egypt. They admit they lost contact with him just before he boarded that ill-fated flight which was hijacked. It was a complete breakdown in fundamental procedures on all sides."

"I see." Clemmons was visibly irritated, but he apparently had no intention to verbally assault Hopkins. He said, "See here, get all you can from Loring and ring me as soon as he leaves. We shall make a capital effort to correct ourselves if the data is what he claims. What time are you meeting him?"

"Right after noon, in my flat. I thought it might be more conducive for him to talk away from the formality of my office."

"Good. Let me know straightaway."

Hopkins returned to his own office very much aware his career was in the balance. He realized he better not blow it this time. He was determined to wipe away this blot on his record. He began to weigh the possibilities he had, but without knowing the information Loring possessed, all his strategies didn't amount to much. He gave up and left the office. It was better to sulk at home where he could at least have a drink.

It was almost one o'clock when the three arrived in Mayfair. Derek and Marc delayed picking up Bert until the last possible moment. Crimmins was not nearly so crestfallen when he joined his friends.

Hopkins met them at the door of his flat after the first ring of the bell. He was a wisp of a man whose thin gray hair fell over his brow. He had dark brown penetrating eyes which held their target until he broke contact. The clothes he had on were rumpled. He evidently had been lying down fully dressed. Crimmins instinctively recognized his friend as being disturbed, and the odor of brandy on his breath confirmed the belief.

"Care for a drink...any of you?" he asked.

"No. We have to talk."

"I see. Bert, sorry to hear about that nasty business with Wells. Must have been quite a shock. Is that why you resigned?" Hopkins had a habit of being very direct. The short curt phrasing of his speech mimicked that of Crimmins.

"That's one of the reasons, Geof. The other is not for publication. But enough of that. When I called I said we had more information on Zoser International, something you must act on. Perhaps Loring, here, is the logical one to brief you."

Hopkins turned his attention to Loring. "When I agreed to work with you, none of us knew what my research entailed. Kurt Sempher admitted it was only a means to an end. That came out while Nadia and I were being held in his desert cave. Neither Nadia nor I could take it seriously when he boasted about being destined to rule Egypt."

"Can't say I blame you. It does sound preposterous."

"Believe me, he thinks and acts like a real pharaoh."

"Go on, Loring. Please."

"This ambition of his can only be attained if the whole political and religious structure of Egypt is destroyed and the government of Mubarak overturned."

"I can understand his reasoning for disrupting Egypt's politics, but why tamper with religion?" Hopkins sipped his brandy.

"That's the insidious logic behind all this. He knows

that politics, governments and all formal institutions change constantly. The only real things people...the majority of people...can relate to, or cling to, are language and religion. They form the backbone of all cultures. By attacking religion, Semipher is shaking the very foundation of peoples lives."

"That's diabolical! How can he do it?"

"He's already started it. The entire plan, Operation Amun, is detailed here." Loring tossed the manual over to Hopkins. While Hopkins glanced at it, Loring continued.

"The riots you've witnessed on television are only the first phase. He's succeeded in turning Christian against Christian and Moslem against Moslem. We suspect the Jews will be next. The second chapter will turn Christian against Moslem and both against the Jew. It will be a holy war such as the world has never seen."

"Good lord! He can do all this?" Hopkins ignored his half-empty glass of brandy.

"Yes, sir, he can. And now we know the reason why. He is blackmailing the civilized world into leaving him alone. Should the U.N. or any sovereign power interfere with his takeover of Egypt, he'll start the riots all over again. Armies can't deal with the internal chaos and we've seen how powerless the police are. He actually has the Mediterranean by the throat. His only ambition is to rule Egypt, but he's using the cultural upheaval of the world to keep his grip on that country."

"Why Egypt? There's nothing there but sand."

"Semipher is an egomaniac. He believes his true roots go all the way back to the Pharaoh Zozer in 2600 BC. He's obsessed with the ancient pomp and glory, and the power enjoyed by the rulers of antiquity. To us, it doesn't make any sense, but it does to him. He plans to recreate the Egypt of old. To do that, he needs to be left alone."

"Then this Zoser International is only a front?"

"Yes, the face he shows to the world. Actually Sempher has resurrected an ancient army of assassins...The Zozer Brotherhood...to do his dirty work. It's worldwide. Here's the entire organizational chart with key leaders of cells in all major cities. When he gives the signal, all hell is going to break loose. The States, Europe and the Middle East are all targets for disaster."

Hopkins turned a bleak face toward Crimmins. "Bert, is this true?"

"You better believe it, Geof. People have died to get you this, people who were close to me and to Derek and Marc. We've done all we can. The rest is up to the civilized countries. There's no time to lose." The look in Crimmins' eyes was frightening Hopkins.

"Loring, I'm inclined to accept your story, but there might be some hesitation elsewhere. After all, you have to admit this entire scenario sounds bizarre. A modern man who has wealth beyond our own pitiful dreams, actually believes himself to be a real-life pharaoh of Egypt? He really must be insane. That's the response I'll get from all the other agencies. Leave these documents with me. I'll read them very carefully after you've gone and do some checking on my own. I'll be in touch with you, tomorrow for sure."

"Don't wait too long, Mr. Hopkins."

As soon as the door closed, Hopkins rushed to the phone and called Hugh Clemmons. He was certain of his ground now. This information was all he needed, but after his earlier foul-up, he wanted to share the responsibility with a higher authority. When Clemmons answered, Hopkins related what Loring told him. The Director's reply was short and to the point.

"Better get in here as fast as you can. We have work to do."

The bright light of the explosion startled Hopkins as he hung up the phone. When the noise of the blast reached the flat, the windows of the apartment reverberated and cracked. Hopkins jumped to the door and raced out of the flat toward the crowd gathering near the inferno at the end of the block. Several cars were involved, blazing in a chain reaction from the first blast. He saw bodies stretched out on the pavement but he already knew who they were.

Merrick was lying half in the street and half on the curb, bleeding from a gash on his forehead. He wasn't lucid, mumbling, "The man was trying to steal my car. It just blew up."

Loring was unconscious, sprawled in the gutter and bleeding from cuts and scrapes. His clothes were torn from his body, lying in shreds around him. He was breathing evenly, however, in spite of the trauma. Crimmins was face down in the street, his right arm at an unnatural angle. He was covered with blood from the gashes on his body. He, too, was unconscious.

An ambulance roared up to the scene. The three were the only ones injured by the blast. Hopkins directed the medics to deliver them to the emergency center at St. Swithins Hospital. He said he would call Dr. Evans there and have him provide immediate treatment.

"Not necessary for you to call, sir. We have constant communication with every hospital in this area. We can call for you."

"Just so, but I must to talk with Dr. Evans in any case. These men are friends of mine and I want to make sure Evans sees them right away."

Back in his flat, Hopkins called Evans and explained the situation. It was a matter of national security, he said. He didn't want them to see or talk with any outsider. They were to be kept isolated. The emergency suite was to be made to appear as though it was the scene of a major blood-bath. He said he would be there soon and explain. Hopkins then called Clemmons and gave him an update on the explosion. He told his superior how he was handling the case and that he would be in Clemmons' office later when he had the three men safely out of harms' way.

Merrick's head wound was sutured and bandaged and, other than having a severe headache, he was fine. Crimmins' cuts and gashes were treated and his dislocated shoulder was set in place. He ached all over and his trussed shoulder was giving him pain, but he was not critical. Loring regained his senses after a while. He had a slight concussion, but it posed no threat provided he took things easy. All of them looked worse than their injuries indicated.

The attending physician, Dr. Evans, knew Crimmins, but was unaware of his resignation from Scotland Yard. This, plus what MI 6 told him by phone, assured them of prompt and private treatment. They were immediately placed into a small emergency treatment suite, attended to with but a minimum of medical personnel. Crimmins asked that a message be sent to Geoffrey Hopkins, telling him about the explosion. Evans told them Hopkins arranged for their care and that they were to remain where they were until he arrived.

Alone in their suite, Crimmins addressed the others. "This was a deliberate attempt to kill us, or at least one of us. I hardly think you were the intended victim, Marc. I believe it was Derek they were after. This had to be the work of Sempher. Someone followed us from the airport and planted the bomb while we were up in Hopkins' flat."

"But why, Bert?" Merrick asked.

"Sempher knows that Derek was taken out of the desert alive. He also knows Derek might be able to find his way back for revenge. He told Nadia and Derek what Zoser's plans are. Besides I do not think he wants to kill me for killing Wells. I probably did him a favor."

Merrick was visibly shaken. "I've never had such an unsettling experience in my life. I'm a banker, but it seems with every hour I'm getting further away from banking. I think you're right though, Bert. They must be after Derek."

Loring had to agree. "But there's two others who know I came out of the desert...Peter Bradshaw in Cairo and Ron. Sempher can't know that Ron is dead. We better get word to Bradshaw to be on his guard."

"Bradshaw can take care of himself, Derek. After all, your ordeal was in all the papers."

"What do you have in mind, Bert?"

Before Crimmins could answer, Hopkins burst into the room. When he was assured they were all right, he became very businesslike. He had a plan.

"You three are dead, killed by a car bomb planted by persons unknown. I'll give out that information so Sempher can think his trap worked. I'll have the chaps here get you to a safe place for the time being, but we have to give you a good funeral. All for show. Merrick, how do I get in touch with your wife? She will, of course, know the truth, but she must act the part of a grieving widow. And Nora, too, Bert. If I had any doubts before about the truth of your story, they're gone now. Stay here until the morgue people pick you up. I'll get in touch with your wives."

"Do it before the story gets out, please."

"Of course. One other thing. As soon as I leave here, I'm going straight to the agency and send out a coded cipher to the CIA. We don't have enough to detain the Zoser agents for long, but at least we can put them out of commission for a spell. I'll contact the other European agencies as soon as I can, and send a special note to Valenkov of the KGB. He and I had some dealings in the past. He knows I wouldn't ask for his help unless it was urgent. He can speed up the work to be done in the Eastern Bloc countries. Zoser has people in Poland and Czechoslovakia as well as in Moscow."

"What do you want us to do in the meantime?"

"Nothing. I'm sending you to a safe flat in Chelsea. Stay there until after your funerals. I'll arrange for everything. And Merrick, don't worry about your position at the bank. MI 6 has an understanding with the directors. When all this is over, you will back at your desk as though nothing happened. Loring, do you have someone back home who should be told or who must be comforted?"

"No, Hopkins, there's no one who really cares, one way or another, except for my friends here. But thanks for asking."

Hopkins left them at the hospital. Regardless of what he told these men, he had no intention of telling their wives the truth. There was too much at stake to gamble on the rash actions of amateurs. He rushed to MI 6 headquarters to talk with Hugh Clemmons.

Marc paced the floor, obviously worried about Veronica. He was not at all sure she could take all this without breaking. Loring tried to calm his friend, reminding Marc that Veronica was a strong woman who believed in what they were doing. He was certain that she would be just fine. Nora Crimmins was another story. Loring didn't know her very well, certainly not well enough to guess how she would react to the double tragedy of Menefee's death and Bert's injury. But Crimmins assured them that Nora had vast reserves of inner fortitude. She would do fine.

"Now that the various governments are in on the truth, our work is half done." Loring said. "But once the funerals are over, I'm going back to Egypt. Sempher is still on the loose."

"I'm going with you, Derek," Bert answered. "Nora will understand. I hope you both can appreciate why I must go. Sempher represents all that has almost ruined my life. I have to see him destroyed to regain my self-respect. Derek, if you won't take me with you, I'll go by myself. I think that since we started this together, we bloody-well should be together at the end."

"Of course, Bert. I'd be lost without you. But Marc, you stay here. I won't have you in any more danger, if not for your sake, then for Veronica's. For all you've done, I'm grateful, believe me. I'm sure Veronica will agree with me."

It was obvious that Merrick was disappointed. Facing Loring, he stood a few inches taller as he said, "No dice, Derek. I'm tagging along, too. You haven't been able to get along without me yet. What makes you think you can do it alone?"

"We'll see about that. Maybe Veronica can talk some sense into you."

"I've thought about this, Derek. I know I can convince Veronica to agree. I know her better than you do."

The attendants from the morgue arrived and silently prepared them for their exit from the hospital. Each were placed in a body bag and transported by gurney to a waiting ambulance. Doctors, nurses and other staff dispassionately watched them go. All were convinced they were dead. Only Dr. Evans and his meager staff knew the truth, and they were pledged to silence under threat of prosecution. Hopkins saw to that.

After the ambulance left with its cargo, a well-dressed man took the doctor aside and queried him on the details of the dead patients. He mentioned he was the solicitor who was representing the insurance company which issued the policy on one of the damaged cars. He said he needed the identity of the deceased, and had to know the exact number of any other casualties.

Dr. Evans said he was busy, and that all inquiries of that nature must be directed to the police. He did, however, let drop the information that there had been four men involved with the car. Unfortunately, the one behind the wheel was torn apart by the blast and it was impossible to determine his identity. The other three who were brought to the hospital had been too close to the car when it exploded. They only lived a short while.

When the man left, Evans immediately called Hopkins. He gave him the details of the conversation and described the alleged solicitor with enough detail for Hopkins to venture a guess as to his real identity. Hopkins told the doctor to stick with the story if asked, but should avoid discussing the accident with anyone.

"So, Reginald Sutton is back in the cricket match," he voiced to himself. "I wonder who he's working for now."

Chapter 21

The persistent ringing of the telephone interrupted the meeting at the Delphi Hotel. In addition to Kurt Sempher, three other men were in the room. They were seated in the softly-lit living room of the suite listening intently to Sempher explain the final strategy of Operation Amun. Each of the men had a role to play, a role which could permit no digression. Sempher stressed the importance of a unified compliance in 'Amun's' execution if it was to succeed. Sempher reached across to the side table and picked up the phone.

"Yes?"

"Mr. Sempher, please. Reginald Sutton here, calling from London."

"This is Kurt Sempher. Proceed, Mr. Sutton. What do you have to report?"

"Results that were better than we anticipated, Mr. Sempher. The bomb killed all three of them...Loring, Merrick and that insufferable Inspector Crimmins. He was the one who killed Wells."

"I know who he is. Excellent! You are positive Loring is dead?"

"Yes sir, I'm positive. There couldn't have been any other conclusion."

"How did you verify it?"

"I was at the hospital when they were taken to the morgue. I saw the bodies myself and I questioned the at-tending physician about the casualties. I claimed I was representing the insurance carrier of one of the burned-out vehicles."

"What did this doctor tell you?"

"He said one man was dead on arrival and the other two only lived a few minutes after being admitted. He said nothing could be done for them. He also mentioned a fourth man who was blown apart by the explosion."

"Who was the fourth man?"

"From what the doctor said, he was trying to steal Merrick's car. The bomb went off when he started the engine...the bomb was rigged to the ignition."

"Then Loring was not in the car when it exploded?"

"No. The three of them were next to the car...trying to stop the theft. They took the full impact of the bomb."

"I see. Did you believe what the doctor told you?"

"Yes, to a point, but as an added check, I obtained copies of the notarized death certificates. They had been signed by the doctor I spoke with."

"What will be done with the bodies?"

"There's going to be a public funeral. The arrangements have already been announced. The burial is scheduled for tomorrow morning. I'll be at the services to make doubly certain of our success. I trust this is satisfactory?"

"Yes, indeed, Mr. Sutton. You have done your work well. But one thing still bothers me. Did you actually view the bodies?"

"Well, yes and no. When they left the hospital the bodies were sealed in plastic coverings...body bags, they are called. There was no sure way I could see the actual bodies. However, after speaking with the doctor, I sneaked into the emergency suite where they'd been treated. I got in before anyone had a chance to clean up the mess. What I saw in there was enough to convince me that whoever had been treated in that room never left it alive."

"You made certain it was Loring and the others who were treated in the suite?"

"Yes. The personal effects of all three of them were in a cupboard. I examined wallets, jewelry and such which identified them to be Loring, Merrick and Crimmins. The clothes they had been wearing were heaped in a corner. They were bloodied and had obviously been cut from their bodies. There was part of a coat that had Loring's name sewn in. I saw shoes, socks, underwear, everything in the pile. I even had the fortitude to look into a refuse container, one marked for incineration. I saw ripped flesh and broken bones with other body parts. Yes, Mr. Sempher, they're dead. They shouldn't make any more trouble for you."

"You have convinced me, Mr. Sutton. Well done. You shall be hearing from me." Sempher replaced the phone, his eyes gleaming with delight. He turned back to the three with him and continued to outline his plans with a heightened enthusiasm.

"Mr. Schuman, is Berlin ready for the signal?"

"*Ja*, Herr Sempher, ready and waiting. We just need your signal. My people are all in place with their orders well rehearsed. Nothing is in writing, as you directed."

"*Gut*, Herr Schuman. Now, Mr. Dumont. Is Paris prepared as well?"

"*Oui*. We are ready."

"What about London, Mr. Smythe? I admit I have some misgivings about London since our operations there were compromised by internal stupidity. How were you able to salvage anything in such a short time?"

Wilfred Smythe returned Sempher's gaze, a slight smile crossing his lips, as though he thought Sempher's question superfluous.

"It wasn't difficult. In spite of his other faults, Wells

was one hell of an able administrator. He had our London cell organized in military fashion. Capable bodies would automatically fill the ranks of casualties. When our top echelon was destroyed, I was there to take over. Our people, the very good ones, now answer to me, as I answer to you. You could say, it's business as usual."

"That is good to hear. I'll admit, I was somewhat apprehensive." Sempher looked at the group and paused for dramatic effect.

"I have cabled Warsaw, Moscow and Prague. They, too, are ready."

"When will we receive the word," Smythe asked.

"When I leave here I shall stop at Zurich for one day before proceeding on to Egypt. While I'm there, I will contact our people in the States to inform them of our progress and to put them on alert status. Mr. Yamani has Operation Amun well under control throughout the Mid-East and the Mediterranean.

The next riots between Christian and non-Christian sects will commence shortly, but this phase of the plan is to be executed only in Egypt. This will be the last catastrophe Mubarak's government can weather. His cabinet and the army are distinctly divided along religious lines. Everyone is suspicious of his fellow man. The climate is ripe for revolt."

"But when are we to act?" Dumont pressed the issue. "My people are becoming anxious."

Sempher ignored the interruption.

"The reports I have received from you and the others throughout Europe tell me that all governments will do anything to prevent further holy wars. They are all in the dark as to why the riots started in the first place. They will be warned to stay away from Egypt, regardless of any pleas from Mubarak, else their country will be plunged into immediate and far-reaching chaos.

Even though our plans regarding the Pope didn't materialize, the Vatican is busy mending its own fences. The Vatican will be no problem. Likewise, the Anglicans and all other pompous and self-righteous sects are worried. Our riots have them all looking to their own defenses, wondering where they went wrong."

Sempher reached for his half-empty glass of vodka before he continued. "I will inform the Brotherhood in America that if our Egyptian operation causes the liberals over there to give any thought to interfering, Gadhafy will send his eager assassination squads over there to keep them occupied. I have the Colonel's assurance that he will assist us in our cause. Once we have achieved our goals, we will take care of Moammar Gadhafy. I do not want that maniac breathing down my neck."

"And us, here in Europe?"

"With America and Europe neutralized, and all of Islam disrupted, we shall be victorious. Go back to your groups and remain in the shadows. Do nothing yet to come under surveillance. Should I need your assistance, I will contact you. This meeting is now over."

Each of the three men gathered his things and quietly left the suite.

Smythe was irritated with Sempher's ego. When the three of them reached the hotel lobby, he suggested they have a drink to toast the success of Operation Amun.

The hotel bar was practically deserted. With drinks ordered, Hans Schuman began to review his position.

"When I was just a small boy my father often told me how great a man Hitler was. He was doing so much for the country by putting people to work and not letting Germany remain a third class country. Everybody listened, and look what happened. My father was killed at Stalingrad and my dear mother was never the same again. And I lived in the rubble of Berlin." Hans Schuman was feeling sorry for himself, and the alcohol was making him morbid.

"Now Germany is on top again, and living is at least tolerable. So, *meine Freunde*, tell me why am I allowing myself to be led into disaster by another self-styled savior who tells us what we want to hear?" Schuman's heavy teutonic accent was becoming less pronounced in proportion to what he consumed.

"*Mon ami*, we follow Sempher because he pays well." Jean Dumont had no illusions. "He gives the orders, charts the course and we do the rest...for money. There are no elusive principles involved, as far as I'm concerned. How do you feel about it, Smythe?"

The Englishman had remained aloof from this soul-searching. Now that he was being pressed for an opinion, he had enough to drink to be nasty and caustic in his reply.

"You jerks give me a pain. Each of us knows there's no right or wrong in this lousy world. We do what we have to in order to survive...in a manner we've come to enjoy. If it feels good, it's right. If it wasn't us, Sempher could get a dozen other creeps to do what we do. Do either of you guys actually care if he takes over goddamned Egypt, or any other place for that matter? Hell no! We're just little cogs in a big wheel Sempher turns with his money. All we are is manpower, nothing else. But I'll admit, I like the thrills connected with the job. So stop this bellyaching and let's have another drink."

"Smythe, you are a pig," the Frenchman said. "I think you like this work only because you English raped Egypt until they threw you out. This is your way to get even. It would be interesting to hear what you would say if Sempher had his sights on Algeria or Chad. That would be a different story then, wouldn't it?"

"Frenchie, they're all the same to me. Wogs, all of them. We all had our turns exploiting the Africans, and you know it. What about it, Schuman?"

"German colonies were stolen from us in 1918. That's all I need to know. The rest is politics."

Smythe nodded to the others. "Hey, guys, we don't need this bickering. It won't change anything. What say we just do our jobs, take the money and run?"

"Well said, *mon ami*."

"*Jawohl, Freunde.*"

"By the way," Dumont changed the subject. "Who is this 'Loring' Sempher is so obsessed with?"

"A smart Yank who outfoxed him," Smythe answered with a wide grin. "Loring survived a particularly nasty death sentence from Sempher. He swore he'd get even with the old man. I met Loring when he first came to London. Zoser wanted him for a job in Egypt. He did it...far too well. Sempher had to get rid of him but failed. Sempher won't give up until he's sure Loring's dead."

"From what we all heard on the phone, Loring is dead."

"Don't bet on it. I certainly don't intend to. Like I said, Loring is smart."

Forty minutes and three drinks later, the three men left the hotel and separated, each going his own way. Dumont was rushing back to own shabby hotel near the Amstel. He brought his mistress with him from Paris and the night was still young. Hans Schuman had no plans aside from drinking up to the time he had to leave for Berlin. Smythe planned to spend a few hours in the red-light district before flying back to London. He convinced himself he was due the relaxation.

The streets of Amsterdam were crowded with both locals and tourists. Smythe was not aware of the two men who were behind him as he crossed over the Keizergracht Canal. Smythe felt the gun pressed into his side as his arms were grabbed and held firm.

"Come along quietly, Smythe, or you won't get across the next canal."

"Who the bloody hell are you? I don't know you. Let me go, or I'll create such a fuss the police'll be here in seconds."

"We are the police, Smythe. Come along."

The men dragged the Englishman over to a car which had been following close behind. The doors slammed shut and the car surged forward across the canal, turning left at the corner to connect with the airport road. Within fifteen minutes the car pulled up to a Royal Air Force cabin jet and the three men boarded the plane. Smythe was in handcuffs and leg irons as the plane rushed to takeoff for the short flight across the Channel to England.

Both Schuman and Dumont were similarly apprehended and were likewise unceremoniously flown out of Amsterdam. Dumont deplaned in Paris and Schuman in Berlin. None of them...Smythe, Schuman or Dumont...had any outside contact after they left the Delphi Hotel. Once they were returned to their home cities, they were each held incommunicado.

Sergi Ivanovitch Valenkov reread the plain language intercept from Geoffrey Hopkins. The message was clear enough. Valenkov's assistance was needed to detain a handful of men in Moscow, Warsaw and Prague. What was not clear to Valenkov was Hopkins' purpose in sending it. The call for help said it was urgent for European stability. Could this be a trap, a trumped-up subterfuge to make him a scapegoat for an incident? Valenkov had had some dealing with Hopkins and always found him to be a man of his word. Yet, Sergi Ivanovitch was troubled. He wanted confirmation from another source.

He picked up the phone and dialed a series of numbers. Noticing the time, he calculated it to be 6:00 PM in Washington, D.C. Perhaps the man had already left for the day, but after four unnerving rings, someone answered.

"Amos Stone here."

"This is Valenkov. Can we talk? Safely?"

"Yes, this line is clean. What can I do for you?"

The Russian had been in the business for a long time and was never comfortable talking over the telephone. He always made it a habit to have information transmitted by third or fourth parties, keeping himself well out of contact. What he was about to do went against all his years of field training. It was dangerous, but he had to know. Amos Stone was a top advisor to the CIA, and was respected by both sides. Stone never compromised a contact.

"I received a plain language message from MI 6."

"Our own came in code." Stone was pointed and brief. He knew what Valenkov wanted but was going to hear him say it.

"Do you believe the information is accurate?"

"Valenkov, let me say that we over here are rounding up all the names Hopkins sent us. We know how he got the names and from whom. We believe it. I suggest you do the same. This is one instance when we have to work together for all our sakes. You really don't have any other choice.

I tell you what...I'll send you all the information we have on this thing and you can verify it yourself. I'll give it to your ambassador in the morning. But I advise you not to wait for the document before you move on those men in Moscow, Warsaw and Prague. Do I make myself clear?"

"Yes, Stone. Perfectly. I will go along with you on this. As a point of interest, do you know the names he sent me?"

"I believe so. Pietor Piontowski in Warsaw, Vasili Brochofsky in Moscow and Andro Dieterslav in Prague. Do they agree with your list?"

"Yes, Stone. Thank you for your honesty. Good night, sir."

By four o'clock, local time, Zoser International was leaderless in Warsaw, Moscow and in Prague. Pietor Piontowski was gunned down while running from the police. He was killed in mid-afternoon traffic on one of Warsaw's main thoroughfares. Vasili Brochofsky wolfed down a bowl of thin soup in an isolated cell in Lubyanka prison. It would be quite a while before he felt strong enough to eat solid food. Andro Dieterslav's wife returned home from her afternoon shopping to find her husband hanging from a second floor rafter. The police listed it as a suicide and closed the file on Dieterslav.

Under Hopkins' able and dedicated direction, the funeral charade was being played to a diverse congregation. He reasoned that since Loring, Merrick and Crimmins had officially been killed in the same act of violence, they should have their final earthly departure done as a group. Veronica Merrick understood the significance and agreed with Hopkins. Nora Crimmins, with Veronica at her side, had nothing to say. She had completely withdrawn into herself, showing absolute indifference to the performance around her.

Hopkins had visited each woman in an official capacity, giving the tragic details of the bombing. He had been accompanied by an aide, for both show and protocol when he expressed his sorrow over the deaths of their loved ones. As planned, he withheld the truth, believing that their public display of genuine grief would convince Zoser's watchdogs they had succeeded in doing away with Loring and Crimmins.

Hopkins was certain Marc Merrick was included only by chance. In assuming the direction of the funerals, he explained to the women that the sad condition of the bodies was such that closed coffins was the best arrangement. He said he was only thinking of their welfare by not having a public display. His sincerity spilled over so he actually believed his explanation.

Veronica decided that both Marc and Derek should be cremated after the service, and she planned to bury the ashes in the garden at Priory Farm. Since they were together at the moment of death, it seemed only fitting for them to be buried side by side. Privately, however, she acknowledged that by doing this, she could watch over the only two men she ever loved, and be able to keep them with her.

Nora, on the other hand, had no opinion, one way or another. Her life was shattered. First was the death of her beloved Ron, then Bert was taken from her. She had no idea what life would be like without Bert since he was the center of her universe. She could not imagine a future without Bert. It was Veronica who took control.

"Mrs. Crimmins...Nora, if I may...our three men were fast friends who died fighting a terrible evil the best way they knew. My Marc, and certainly Derek, were not violent men. In the short time I knew your husband I came to realize he was essentially nonviolent as well. Why don't you move out to Priory Farm with me? We'll put Bert alongside Marc and Derek. Perhaps in that way we can do for them in death what they were prevented from doing while alive...being together. There's plenty of room at the farm. I think you and I need each other desperately right now. Please come home with me."

Nora brightened a bit at this expression of Veronica's friendship and solace. For the first time since she heard of Bert's death, the tears came. She threw herself into the other woman's arms and wept. She felt as though her heart would break. Veronica, too, finally succumbed to her own feelings of sorrow and loneliness. Soon, they detached themselves and went into the chapel for the service.

Hopkins gave the eulogy for Crimmins. He recalled the dedication of the softspoken policeman, and the number of times his help was invaluable to the agency. The speaker who followed Hopkins was the Superintendent of Scotland Yard. He said his association with Crimmins was on the professional level, yet he found in the man a warm comrade who never admitted defeat. Crimmins' recent resignation from the service was not mentioned. Constable Hughes, always the willing and patient aide, placed a wreath on Crimmins' coffin and made no attempt to hide his deep-felt grief.

Sir Randal Nottingham, a senior officer of the bank, spoke of the fine mind and brilliant financial acumen of Marc Merrick. Merrick, he said, would have become a director of the bank one day had his life not been so callously snuffed out. He promised Veronica that the fiends responsible would be brought to justice, and that no stone would be left unturned toward that effort. Veronica could only nod in affirmation at his words. They really didn't sink in or mollify her sorrow.

When it became obvious that no one there had any words for Derek, Veronica stood up to speak. She didn't go to the lectern, but remained at her place in the chapel pew. In a voice choked with grief and emotion, she started slowly, not sure how long she could continue.

"Derek Loring was an outsider to all of us here, with the exception of Mrs. Crimmins and myself. To me, and to her, he was a friend who sought the help of our husbands in combating a monstrous evil. Now that these three friends are stilled in their efforts, it is with a pleading heart I beg that their work be continued by those of you who can do so. You know who you are. Don't let their efforts be wasted.

"Derek became our friend many years ago and he brought a certain joy to our lives, Marc's and mine. He was a learned man, rich in the things that counted most today...compassion for his fellow man, honesty and integrity. He was a scholar, interested in the past to shed light on the present and hope for the future. I loved him as a dear friend and companion, and...", she had to sit down, unable to continue. The memories were too painful. Her wan face was wet with her tears, her knuckles white from clinging to the back of the pew.

She and Nora stood beside the three caskets, touching each with a light and loving caress. Tearfully, they turned and left the chapel accompanied by Hopkins. The rest filed out into a chill drizzle which dampened all of London, more so the spirits of those in attendance.

The last to leave was Reginald Sutton. He arrived late and took a place in the rear of the chapel. He remained behind long enough to make certain that the caskets were being transported to the crematorium where he had a paid informer who would report the actual burning. When he finally left, he was unaware that his movements were being observed by MI 6.

Hopkins escorted Veronica and Nora to a dark Bentley limousine and dismissed the driver, putting himself behind the wheel. If the women had any thoughts about this unusual act, they didn't let on. Neither were yet prepared for the real world. Hopkins drove out Oxford Road toward Chelsea. Instead of continuing, he pulled the car into Harrod's carpark, turned off the engine and faced the two women.

"Mrs. Crimmins, Mrs. Merrick, what I am about to tell you will be extremely difficult for me. I expect you both to loathe me after you hear the story, and I can't say I blame you in the least. What was done was absolutely necessary. Please believe that. There couldn't be any other way to insure their safety.

"To continue. The bomb that exploded was meant to kill Loring. We are convinced of that. He was responsible for uncovering a plot of worldwide consequences. Your Marc and Bert were unintentional victims. We had to stall for time and prevent any further attempts on Loring's life. He is the key to the entire scheme."

Veronica's gasp was torn from her from deep down. "You are telling me...us...that Derek was not killed? That he is not dead?"

"Mrs. Merrick, no one was killed by the bomb, except for the unfortunate lad who was attempting to make away with your husband's car. Your men are in hiding, safe, although a bit bruised and scratched. I'm taking you there now. You might have to get some new clothes to them, however, since the ones they were wearing at the time of the blast were left at the hospital as evidence of the extent of their damages."

Veronica exploded. "You horrible sons of bitches! What right did you have to put Nora here and me through this awful nightmare? Have you people no sense of decency? Nora's on the verge of collapse, and I'll never be the same. God damn you to hell!"

"Your anger is understandable," Hopkins whispered. "But the only way to save them all from further danger was to convince those responsible for wanting Loring out of the way that he was dead. Your husbands are now in as much danger. Believe me, we had to make sure the deaths appeared to be genuine. You women had to publicly show your grief and loss. We couldn't take the chance you could carry it off as a fake. And for your information, those responsible for the bomb were in the chapel, observing your reactions. We know who they are and to whom they report."

Nora Crimmins finally broke the heavy silence in the car after Hopkins' revelation. "Mr. Hopkins, I can't understand the full significance of what you 'ave just told us. The only thing that gets through to me is my Bertie is alive and waiting for me. You 'ave put me and Mrs. Merrick through a terrible ordeal. Veronica more so because of her attachment to Mr. Loring.

Until just this moment, life for me was over, in spite of Veronica's promises. Should I be grateful that you 'ave pulled me back into life, or am I justified in hating you and all you stand for? Nevertheless, now that Bert is again a part of me, I won't be needing this. Here, take it." She handed Hopkins a yellow capsule. Cyanide. "I was going to take it when I got home. Regardless of what Veronica said, I could never go on without my Bert. He's too much a part of me. I suppose I should just be grateful he's alive."

"Mrs. Crimmins, I'm dreadfully sorry."

"Sorry!" Veronica sneered. "All you secret types are the same. You play games with peoples' lives and think nothing of it. Look what you let happen to Nadia Shepherd. Poor Derek will never get over that little oversight. One part of me, a very small part, can understand why you do the things you do. But deep down I abhor all you stand for. Now, take us to our men."

"Certainly. You're not really being fair, you know."

With only a weary shrug of his shoulders, Hopkins started the car and headed for Chelsea. The flat was at the end of a cul-de-sac with a view of all incoming traffic. The Bentley edged to the curb, its motor a gentle purr. Hopkins turned to the women, the hurt still reflected in his eyes.

"I'll come back for you in an hour. The flat is on the top floor. Tell them what you just told me and listen to what they have to say. You might be very surprised."

Veronica and Nora left the car wordlessly. They walked cautiously to the entry for fear someone would be watching, and because of the unknown. They had no idea what faced them. The street level door opened to their ring, and they rushed to the men they loved.

Marc and Veronica embraced, all arms and tears and laughter. They kept looking into each others' eyes through the wetness, then went back to a close embrace. Nora and Bert were much more sedate in their greeting. At first. Nora started it, after a short restrained squeeze of his hands. She threw herself into his arms, her tear-streaked face burying itself into his chest, and she physically clung to Bert to keep herself from sinking to the floor. Her moans were not of passion but rather those of relief. She could not let him go in spite of Bert's obvious embarrassment over

this show of love. He became more at ease when he
realized that these people were his friends.

Derek stood apart, a knowing smile on his face, rel-
ishing the relief all of them showed. No one knew he was
in the room. His smile faded and he turned to the window,
looking out over the seedier parts of London. He was remembering Nadia. Out from the corner of her eye, Veronica
noticed Derek's preoccupation. She disengaged herself
from Marc's arms, went over to the window with Derek
and pulled him toward her with a warm embrace. She
kissed him fervently, tears again staining her beautiful face.

"Derek, my dear one, don't hurt yourself needlessly.
She would understand. You're here with friends who remember Nadia for what she was and how she died. She
loved you to the end. At least you have that knowledge.
Cherish it."

The group found a semblance of order after a while.
Drinks in hand, they sat around the roaring fire, lit to dispel the gloom and dampness of the day. Question upon
question was asked by the women. Why? How? What
was the reason, the danger? Where do they all fit in this?
Why doesn't the agency take over? And finally, when will
it all end?

Derek said it all. "Greed, ego, power, and Nadia.
Sempher has the first three, and he killed Nadia. I can't
turn away from that. I have to go after him and make certain he's stopped for the good of mankind. He's unleashed
an evil none of us could possibly imagine.

The intelligence agencies and the police of every country are governed by rules, rules that take time to implement. We simply can't afford the luxury of time. Sempher's
schedule has been pushed forward. With the information
Ron found in Sempher's chalet, all agencies throughout
Europe and America are now in the process of picking up

the leaders of Zoser cells. Even the KGB is cooperating in the Soviet bloc countries. But Sempher is being left alone. His organization outside of Egypt is leaderless. He doesn't know this yet, but when he finds out, he'll go berserk and do something foolish. That's when we can nail him."

"You said 'we'. Who's we?"

"When I leave here I'm returning to Egypt. Some close friends of mine have decided to go with me. Our sole purpose is to bring about the end of Kurt Sempher. We'll do it by legal means, but if there's no alternative, I'll kill him with my bare hands."

"You couldn't kill anyone...you said so."

"That was before. This is now."

Marc looked directly at Veronica, his eyes alive with love for her and with determination to have his own way in this matter.

"I'm going along with Derek. He says he won't have me unless I have your blessing."

"My blessing? Fat chance of that." Veronica was not smiling as she nearly shouted this.

"Wait, hear me out before you object. I've always done things for us alone. My actions were always those which we thought were only important to us. The farm, my career at the bank, and all the other things. In these past few months, working on the sidelines with Derek and Bert, I've come to realize there're more important things in life. I owe so much, we owe so much, for our way of life that sooner or later we must pay the price if we expect to keep it safe.

Nothing in this life is free. From what Derek has uncovered, I can see now that our way of life is in extreme danger, and I must, with clear conscience, do whatever has to be done to lessen the danger. What Derek is doing is part of all that, and I want...no, I must, be an integral part of his work. This doesn't mean I love you less, or that I don't value your judgement, but it's because I do love you that I must do this. Can you understand?"

"Marc, when I came up to this flat, I was angry at the whole system that might have killed you. For what? I couldn't understand how the intrigue you men are involved in, or your deaths, could make any difference in the overall picture. Hopkins told us...Nora and me...to listen to you. Now I understand why. I see now that the outcome isn't really the issue."

"No, it certainly isn't."

"The bare truth is you have to make the effort, no matter what may come of it. Yes, my dearest, I understand and I reluctantly give you my blessing. Derek, take good care of my champion here. And Marc, look out for Derek. Recent events have proved to me that life without either of you would be unbearable."

Veronica went to Marc, kissed him lightly on the cheek and whispered, "Come back safely, my dear."

Bert Crimmins had listened to all this with keen attention. He looked over at his wife whose eyes never left him while the others were speaking. She sensed what was on his mind and knew what he was about to say. She steeled herself with the realization she could not prevent her husband from joining in the hunt, and sadly understood why she could not even try.

"You all know why I am joining Marc and Derek. They have about said it all, giving very valid reasons for the fight. But I do have a personal motive in apprehending this fiend. He compromised my principles and that is something I can't, or won't, condone. Wells' killing was no accident."

"What are you talking about, Bert?" Loring asked,

"I deliberately murdered him. I knew he was responsible for Nadia's death and he was trying to destroy you in the bargain, Derek. I allowed my personal feelings to interfere with my better judgement. When this is over, I intend to make a clean breast of the entire matter and take whatever punishment the courts decide. I could not go on living such a lie."

He turned to his wife. "Nora, you suspected the truth from the beginning. My resignation from the Yard was a ploy to allow me freedom of action without the restricting rules. If I get through this with a whole skin, I'll make it good, somehow. So you see, I have to go along with Marc and Derek."

The others could not believe their ears. This man, this epitome of propriety, could not have done what he said. There had to be another reason, but try as they might, Bert was adamant in his story. He lapsed into silence, staring into the fire, thankful for getting his burden out in the open at last. He held Nora's hand, and she looked at him in a new light. She smiled, and her love and pride washed over them all.

Chapter 22

The public funeral held for the victims of the Mayfair car bombing coincided with another event far from London and the secluded flat in Chelsea. The central characters of this event gathered at the train station in Chur in eastern Switzerland. They arrived by plane, by car and by train from both near and distant places. They kept to themselves, staying well removed from the noisy groups of tourists who were eagerly awaiting the cogwheel train which was to take them up to Arosa, a well-known ski resort high in the Alps.

There were no serious skiers among the tourists as this was the off-season. The visitors were all bent on challenging the slopes with cameras and binoculars instead of skis. The somber band of men, twelve in number, were indistinguishable from the happy tourists except for their noticeable lack of enthusiasm. None of this group was laughing as they boarded the rickety train for the short ride up to the mile-high peaks.

If these men were acquainted with one another, they didn't betray any such recognition to their fellow travelers. Each kept his own council, indifferent to the spectacular view enjoyed by the other passengers.

The late afternoon sun was dipping behind towering peaks when the train shuddered to a stop at the Arosa platform. Three black limousines from the Arosa Chalet waited beside the gaily colored station. Groups of station onlookers strained for a glimpse of the privileged twelve who climbed into the plush automobiles. Anonymity was a vital factor of the hurried preparations undertaken in the planning of this unprecedented event.

Later that evening the group came together in the executive suite of the inn. Twelve comfortable chairs circled an oval table, itself bare except for the writing materials at each place. One of the men, who placed himself at the table's head, introduced the gathering to each other. These twelve were clerics who represented all the major Christian denominations, the Islamic sects and Judaism.

The fear and turmoil created by the recent religious riots around the Mediterranean basin prompted this group to meet in this remote site. Theirs was a mission of the utmost importance and urgency, a mission called together by one of the world leaders...His Holiness, Pope John Paul.

The assembly included emissaries from the Archbishop of Canterbury, the World Council of Churches, the Germanic Synod of Lutherans, the Patriarch of Istanbul, the Imam of Medina and Rabbi Aaron Gosloff of Jerusalem. The prelate of the Vatican, Bishop Guido Baldamero, called the meeting to order. None of those assembled had brought their religious garb to the session and now sat relaxed in casual attire. The soft whispers ceased as Bishop Baldamero rapped the table for attention.

"*Kalispera, tou adelee mou.*" My brothers, for the sake of understanding and fellowship, let us conduct these proceedings in Greek. It is the language in which we are all fluent. It will give us a common bond."

"Yes, but speak slowly, *parakkalo*, Bishop. My Greek is weak from lack of practice," voiced Rabbi Gosloff.

"But of course, Rabbi. As you are all aware, the riots we have experienced have created havoc within our individual communities...except for our Jewish brethren. We believe it will be but a matter of time before they, too, will be as one with us in this most terrible of catastrophes."

"You speak true, Bishop," whispered Gosloff. "Remember you well of our history, of the centuries of torture we Jews have endured. This will be nothing new for us. I recall the hot flames of the Holocaust. I survived the death camp of Auchwitz. There has not been a day since my deliverance that I have not given thanks. We Jews have always been targets for genocide."

Baldamero answered in a rasp. "Rabbi, this is not the same. Regardless of race or creed, all are targets. What we are faced with now is far more insidious and threatening. Please hear me out.

"His Holiness and the Archbishop of Canterbury have come into possession of irrefutable evidence which proves these riots are being fomented by a group of extremists who plan to topple the government of Egypt. These madmen want all the civilized countries to stand idly by while Egypt falls. The riots are meant to show how impotent governments become when the cultural roots of the people are destroyed. The recent riots were but a sample of what may come next."

"Bishop, what can we do? We have no voice in politics in our countries." This came from the Imam Al Haaram.

"Imam, that is why we are here. His Holiness, Pope John Paul, requested us to meet together so that we might work and formulate a unified approach to the menace we are all facing. All of us, and those for whom we speak, are the children of one God, be He called Christ, Jehovah or Allah. None of us can remain still and watch our brothers in God wasted in this unholy, satanic holocaust. It is our duty to strike back."

Rabbi Gosloff spoke to the group. "His Holiness is wise beyond his years, but what good can we do? We are but a band of simple clerics. Are we expected to do what our more powerful governments cannot? We Jews will certainly do what we can, but this is an old story to us. I'm sore afraid this may be beyond our talents."

"Rabbi," Al Haaram said softly, "this is not the same menace we all have experienced. We Muslims have seen many conflicts in our history, but those wars were not within our own ranks. Did you see the Sunni and Shiite blood spilled in Cairo, in Damascus, in Baghdad? Or the Catholic killing the Copt and the Orthodox? The Vatican speaks true. We must find a solution. We cannot return to our flocks without one."

The Reverend John Haslip spoke up. "I have come from the Archbishop of Canterbury. He and the Pope right now are targets for assassination. The Archbishop has been in daily communication with the Pope and he wants me to say to this group that neither he nor John Paul intend to shrink from this task. The authorities have been alerted and proper steps have been initiated to protect these holy men. We are not to concern ourselves with that issue. Ours is to find a means to stop these riots."

Reverend Bergholtz of the German Synod spoke in heated response. "Brothers in God, whatever differences we here might have in the dogmas of our faiths, those differences do not warrant the wholesale slaughter of adherents of any faith. We have all witnessed the bloodshed of our Islamic brothers and the terrible clashes between the Catholics and the Orthodoxy. This horror cannot continue. We must find a way to help our civil governments meet this menace without being compelled to worry about the internal revolutions of religious dissent. That is why we are here."

The solemn group lapsed into a long silence. Each man turned his own thoughts into himself, looking into his heart and mind, seeking desperately for a thread of enlightenment well within the tenets of his faith. If that thread existed, perhaps a common denominator might be found or manufactured. The impact of having an all-encompassing bond between the dogmas would be far greater than the irrational hatred spewed from mindless rabble-rousers. Every so often one of the clerics would turn to his neighbor as though he was about to speak, then he would continue his silence.

Finally, the Patriarch of Istanbul had an opinion. "My friends, we are all deep in thought. This is very good, as it should be. We need fervent soul-searching on all our parts. I suggest we retire for two hours. Let us use that time to reflect on the importance of our work, and free our minds to examine all issues in private. We know what has to be done. Let us reconvene here in two hours with the results of our mental and spiritual labors."

Each of those dedicated men retired to his own room to deliberate the problem where he might give voice to thoughts, concerns and possible solutions aloud or in the silence of his own heart and mind. Each of them were aware of the awesome burden their denominations placed on their shoulders, but none would turn away. They were not optimistic of their chances of finding a solution but no one could ever point to them and say they did not try. Two hours seemed a pitifully short time while the faith of millions hung in the balance.

"Brothers," the Anglican priest spoke as they met again, "in spite of our consciences, if we must fabricate a made-up, compelling reason against further bloodshed, we must consider it. Tell me, Rabbi, what is the most unconscionable thing a Jew could be faced with? And you, Imam. What does a true Moslem fear the most? We know the

Catholic fears the threat of excommunication above all else. We Protestants abhor the thought of dying without the grace of Christ."

"I see where you are going with this line of reasoning," Rabbi Gosloff muttered. "We Jews are a stiff-necked people who try to live up to the faith of our fathers. We fear many things, but the thought of not being able to partake of the ceremonies in the temple is something the orthodox fear. It closely corresponds to the Catholic excommunication. Not all Jews, however, fear this sanction for wrongful deeds, as it is rarely imposed. Generally, each Jew has his own personal fears, differing from individual to individual. Some fear dying without having a proper kaddish said for them, others fear being buried in unhallowed ground. There is no one pervasive fear that you describe."

Imam Al Haaram joined the discussion. "We Muslims fear an afterlife, an eternity, without the blessings of Allah bestowed on us as our faith promises."

From these statements of religious belief, a plan of action emerged. It started slowly at first, but with each added dictum explained, the plan took on the desired form and substance of a plausible solution. The group would return to their seats of religious power and issue whatever edicts, epistles and proclamations were necessary to stop the killing and bloodshed.

The message would be clear. If Jew fought against Jew, and spilled Jewish blood, he would be denied the sanctuary of the temple, have no hallowed burial and there would be no kaddish chanted for him. If Protestant killed Protestant, the grace of Christ would be denied him. Warring Catholics would be faced with automatic excommunication, while Moslems who fought would not see the face of Allah.

"But what sanctions could be imposed should Islam go to war against Christian, or Jew against Gentile?" These words were voiced by the prelate from Rome. "Old Islamic teachings held that a true believer was assured a place with Allah by the killing of an infidel or non-believer. Christians have killed Jews, almost with impunity, for almost 2000 years. Our World Council of Churches fights among its own members. And we Catholics are not without blame, considering the awful Spanish Inquisition and the misplaced fervor of the Jesuits. How are we to cope with these age-old antagonisms?"

"We must expand the message to our faithful to include the stated punishment for a religious killing against anyone. We priests, rabbis, ministers and imam must carry this to our flocks. It is our only salvation." The Imam of Medina was credited with the working solution thus formulated.

The Vatican prelate concluded the conclave. "My brethren, we have an awesome responsibility to our common God to see to it we are successful in this undertaking. Let us now return to our own and take up the sword of retribution against our mutual foe."

Bishop Baldamero was not yet finished. He solemnly added, "Brothers, we should have a benediction. I shall begin with these words, *'In nomine Patris, et Filii et Spiritus sancti, Amen.*"

"*Laa ilaaha illa ilaah*!" Imam Al Haaram said..

"Jesus Christ be with you and keep you," Reverend Julius Bergholtz added.

"*Shema Yisroel: Adonai elohenu, Adonai echod.* Hear, O Israel: the Lord our God, the Lord is one." With these words, Rabbi Gosloff pronounced the final blessing.

The conclave was over. The outcome, unknown.

Two hundred kilometers west, Kurt Sempher turned

his Mercedes off the road into the drive of his retreat a short distance from Lucerne. What he saw dumbfounded him. He could not believe his eyes. Ahead, in the gloom of the trees, the headlights of his car illuminated a scene of waste and total desolation. He saw nothing of his chalet but charred timbers and ashes. How could this have happened? His astonishment gave way to fear, then to anger. He was afraid for his personal files and the documents of Zoser, and angry over the apparent breakdown in security. It was with a leaden heart that he stopped the car. He grabbed a torch from the glove compartment and cautiously approached the ruins.

The ashes were cold. The fire which destroyed his cozy retreat was not recent. The beam of the flashlight played over the corpse of his chalet, but Sempher had need of clear daylight to assess the damage. He would return. His fury remained with him on the drive to Zurich, back to his suite at Zoser headquarters.

When he arrived there, he placed calls to London, to Paris and to Berlin. There was no answer from Smythe or from the others. With a feeling of dread, he called Brochofsky in Moscow. Whoever answered that call would give no information other than Brochofsky was being detained by the authorities. Stunned at the news, he hung up the phone quickly and sank deeper into his chair as though to hide from the world.

His imagination started to play tricks on him. Was there an evil conspiracy against him, against all his goals? Panic set in. He huddled in his chair, his dark thoughts hurling aimlessly through his troubled brain. After a while, he sought solace from a bottle of brandy, something he very rarely did. The alcohol had the desired effect. He fell into a tormented sleep with visions of defeat swimming across his mind's eye.

It was daylight when he awoke. The panic which engulfed him earlier in the darkness returned, but in the bright light of day, he calmed the fears by action. He dressed hurriedly, drove the fifty miles to Lucerne and down to the ruined site.

He combed the ashes searching for remnants of his belongings, but he found nothing to indicate the cause of the fire. He could not determine if there had been a break-in. He turned over clumps of hardened ash and debris only to find evidence that others had done so before. Most likely, the firemen in their investigation. The upper floor had collapsed in the blaze and the charred remains of his books and papers from his study showed how fierce and all-consuming the fire had been.

His questions remained unanswered. Looking over the tortured remains if his chalet, he knew that whatever answers there were they would not be found in the ruins.

Sempher drove back into Lucerne and asked the police for information regarding the fire. Did they know when and how it had started? The police did confirm that when the ashes cooled, they discovered the charred remains of a man and a dog. From what they knew about the situation at the chalet, they surmised the bodies were those of a security guard and a watchdog. They could offer no hint as to the cause of the fire or why the guard died.

Autopsies of the remains showed both man and dog were overcome by smoke before the flames consumed them. They had a theory that the guard tripped and fell down the stairs, rendering him unconscious. The dutiful dog tried to pull the man out of the house but the fire was too fast. There was no evidence of foul play. Were there other visitors in the neighborhood? No, sir. In fact, they said, that entire area was deserted this time of year. All the residents in the vicinity were still away, not yet having moved in for the season. The police patrols saw only an occasional car on the roads, or people headed south to Interlochen.

There had been, however, a tragic accident just south of Lucerne, they said. One man was killed by a lorry which turned onto the highway without warning. Unfortunate. As a matter of coincidence, the accident occurred on the same night the fire was noticed by a passing motorist. It was reported, but, alas, nothing could be done. Who was the man killed in the accident? That we do not know. The other man in the car was not seriously hurt. He said he could not stay here to attend to the disposition of the body because of pressing business elsewhere. His body was shipped back to England by the British legation. A tragic accident, sir. The lorry driver still cannot recall the events of that night.

Sempher left the inept police and went to the hospital. Perhaps he could find some answers there. The administrator checked the records, only to find that the deceased was not named in the files, and his final disposition was attended to by the British legation. The other man? Again, no name was on record. He paid for the emergency treatment he received. He paid in cash...British pounds sterling.

Sempher left, convinced that the fire and the accident were connected in some way. He could not let it go. He had to have the answers. There might be a way, if he could get to the records of the airlines for that approximate date.

He rushed back to Zurich and contacted people he knew who would furnish him the information for a price. He had used them before and they were always well paid for their service. When his call was returned, their lack of information was most disconcerting. They were unable to find any suspicious passenger unaccounted for. One man,

Raoul Salazar, passed through immigration and as yet there have been no reports as to his whereabouts. This was not unusual, they claimed, as several of the resort inns are somewhat lax in sending the authorities the names of all their guests. His passport? It was British.

Sempher had to assume his security had been breached...he would be a fool not to. He was convinced that someone had the files on 'Operation Amun'. There was no time for further delay. The information contained in those files had to be kept out of the hands of others or the entire operation was in danger of failure. Surprise had been his main weapon and now even that element was gone. He must set the final phase into motion.

He placed a hurried transatlantic call to Brian Hogarth in Washington. Hogarth was his coordinator for the entire American organization. After a slight delay, Hogarth was on the line.

"Mr. Sempher? Thank God you called! All hell is breaking loose over here. The CIA and the FBI have made a clean sweep of the country, from east to west. They have picked up all our people except our Denver cell. I'm on my way there now to salvage what I can. How did this happen? You were the only one with all the names. Where's the list?"

"I don't have it!" Sempher shouted. "My chalet was burned to the ground and everything was destroyed. But what you tell me means that the fire was deliberately set to cover up the theft of the files.

Don't panic, Hogarth. Stay calm and use your head. I'll be in touch with you through Denver. Go underground there and wait for my call. Do not attempt anything heroic or stupid. I'm going back to Egypt now and commence the final attack on Mubarak's government. Remember, stay calm and don't draw attention to yourself. I shall need you for my later plans. You'll hear from me."

Sempher slammed the phone down and glared out the street window. His thoughts were confused, although he had overcome his own panic. He made preparations for his return to Egypt.

"Very good, Hogarth," the tall, blond agent said as the call was ended. "You played your part very convincingly. We will remember your cooperation. Did you get it all down, Joe?"

The other agent smiled and answered. "Yup. All on tape."

"Fine. Now lets get this bastard down to McLean for a thorough debriefing. Don't forget to bring the tape."

Chapter 23

It was pitch dark over Matruh but the promise of a new dawn was sending dim streaks of light into the heavens beyond Cairo, far to the east. The sleek jet, bearing the entwined cobra emblem, touched down on the remote desert airstrip just south of the coastal village.

Livid with anger and agonizing frustration over the compromise of his secrets, Kurt Sempher alighted from the plane and sulked toward the waiting helicopter. The solitary flight from Zurich afforded him the time needed to cement his resolve to forge ahead with his plans. He had to keep to the schedule regardless of the high probability his security had been breached. Indications were pointing to the conclusion that this was the case, but his plans had been too long in preparation for him to abandon his dream now. He refused to consider any alternate course of action. Egypt was to be his as he had ordained.

He did, however, consider a deviation from his original scheme. There was a lull which settled over the countries of the Mediterranean. The riots indeed threw them into a state of panic but, until the next phase of his plan took shape, he viewed those lands' inactivity as the calm before the storm.

The outside world was wary of further riots and reason told him they were preparing countermeasures to thwart the work of his Brotherhood. What was needed was a diversion to throw his enemies off-balance. His mind turned to Moammar Gadhafy as being the logical instrument to bring all those lands back into line. He had to throw them off guard long enough for 'Operation Amun' to take its full effect. His obsession with Derek Loring and the attempts to kill him threw his program too far off schedule. The European kettle had cooled, and what was needed now was someone to fan the fire, rekindle the flames of fear.

Gadhafy was the logical man. He was eager and willing to jump into the fray, to do anything to pull Mubarak's tail. The Libyan would certainly create trouble for Sempher in the future, but he was needed now. Bridges were made to be crossed in the future.

It was breaking light when he entered the caverns. The Brotherhood was in attendance when he stormed into the stone passageways. He was welcomed by Achmed Yamani, who stood apart from the others.

"The gods are indeed generous, oh Mighty Pharaoh. You have returned to your rightful place in time to witness the fulfillment of your destiny."

"Yes, faithful Achmed." Sempher was not in the mood for pleasantries, but a certain fawning by these minions was necessary. He understood this. They, in turn, expected it.

Sempher turned aside to his henchman. "Brother Achmed, please accompany me to the throne room. The rest of the Brethren will wait here for my further wishes."

Sempher and Yamani retired back into the maze to the throne room, an extra wide enclosure Sempher finished off for his pageantry. He motioned Yamani to sit while he placed himself on his gold-encrusted throne. Several minutes of silence passed, then he addressed his aide.

"I have a premonition, old friend. I feel that I will not live to see my dream come true. There have been signs."

Sempher raised his hand to stop the expected protest from Yamani. He continued. "It is my wish to be entombed in the ancient manner, to be done in the prescribed way. I have prepared my final resting place at Saqqara, at the far end of the funerary temple of my ancestor, Zozer. The old one, Zumab, knows of the place. Please see to it when the time comes."

"But Mr. Sempher, surely you are mistaken," Yamani said softly. There was a tone in his voice that Sempher appeared to miss. "You look well enough."

"Wait, *effendi*. It is my wish that you take my place, both as leader of the Brotherhood and as Regent. When my son, as yet unborn, is ready to rule, you will step aside. The girl, your daughter, is she well?"

"She is well, oh Mighty One. Is it your wish to see her?" Yamani asked.

"No, it is not necessary. I leave her in your care. I trust she will be taken care of until she delivers. Keep her here with my son until he is ready to rule, then she shall be killed in the way it is written. Do you have problems with this?"

"None, your Highness. She is but a tool for your perpetual life. Her life is unimportant, insignificant."

"Good. Now, how are our plans progressing? Are our people ready for the final riots?"

"They are ready. We expect to start in a matter of days or perhaps sooner."

"Don't rush. Stay with the schedule we established."

Sempher now felt the need of council from this Egyptian. "Yamani, we need a diversion for the outside world. I want Gadhafy to prepare and execute an incident which should turn immediate attention away from us. It will throw the others into turmoil and give us the opportunity to strike our final blow against Mubarak. What do you think?"

"I do not trust Gadhafy to stick to any plan he himself does not propose. He is an opportunist who will do anything to further his own ambitions. When you rule this land of Kemet, you will be forced to deal with him as an enemy. He wants to rule all the Arab states. Please be careful in any dealings with him."

"I agree with all you say, but my plan is quite subtle. Listen well. We need two good men who can fly military jet aircraft. It makes no difference as to their nationality. You will have them carry authentic Egyptian identifications. Send these men to Malta at once to be ready to fly the planes I have hidden there. Change the markings now on the planes before they fly from Malta. They carry the Russian emblems. Change them to Libyan."

"It shall be done."

"In early morning, the day after tomorrow, these men are to fly from Malta. They are to cross the Libyan frontier and then turn toward Egypt. If they are sighted near Benghazi, the Libyans will identify them as their own planes. Once they are over Egyptian airspace, they will destroy all civilian aircraft they encounter. Mubarak's foreign radar will surely pick them up and identify them as unfriendly. Egypt will proceed to intercept and destroy our planes."

"The pilots will be killed."

"No matter. Gadhafy will be blamed for a stupid attempt to cause further confusion in Egypt by using Egyptian pilots for his planes. Indeed, Mubarak's vaunted military will be sorely criticized for having defectors in its ranks. When this occurs, we shall be ready to make our move on Cairo. All the people will be behind us."

"Genius, Oh Mighty Lord. With Gadhafy pushed on the defensive, he is bound to undertake a terror crusade which will immobilize Mubarak, as well as Europe."

"Exactly. Now go make your preparations. Have the riots start on schedule. Get those pilots over to Malta right

away. Remember, old friend, if anything happens to me,
you are charged with carrying out these plans as though I
was here, and you take over the movement."

"It shall be done."

Yamani left the room, leaving Sempher alone, brood-
ing.

Alone with his dreams, Sempher should have been
elated that the successful conclusion of his odyssey was at
hand, but the pains in his chest were starting again. These
were more severe than the others had been. They first struck
him when he glimpsed the destruction of his chalet and
again when he learned of the detention of his American
followers.

Now they were back—sharp pains that burned through
his huge body doubling him over. His brow was covered
with sweat, his breath labored. Perhaps the distress would
lessen if he laid down. He stumbled his way to the low
couch at the far end of the throne room. He gasped for
each breath, the pain searing into his chest. With the spasms
of pain came fear, then nausea...he vomited down his chest.
He made an effort to reach the door to the outer reaches of
the entry, but collapsed on the marble floor before he got
there. He managed to call up enough strength to crawl out
the door. He didn't want to die alone.

The Brotherhood rushed to his side when they saw
their leader in agony. He pulled at the ministering arms
around him and whispered to those close enough to hear.
He told them they were to follow Yamani after he was dead,
and that he expected them to carry his dream to fulfillment.

His last feeble breaths were coming in painful wheezes,
but he willed himself to hear them promise they would

honor his burial wishes. They were to have the woman witness the ceremony. She had to relate the details to his son in later years. His final wracking shudder echoed off the stone walls of the cavern, then all was still. Kurt Sempher was dead. The pharoah was no more.

Word of Sempher's death was relayed to Yamani in Cairo. He explained to the Brethren why he could not return for the burial ceremony. He had to organize the final religious riots as ordered by their dead leader. He instructed the group to follow the directions he had given them, and to honor the last words of Pharaoh Sempher. The time of his return would depend on the degree of success of the final phase of 'Amun'.

Those of the Brotherhood remaining in the caverns were on their own and their duty was clear. Sempher was carried to the widened passage and placed on the altar in the center of the room. One of the faithful was sent to get the woman so she might witness the burial rites. Others disappeared into various sections of the complex. When they reappeared in the altar room, each carried implements and preparations needed for the ceremony. They gathered around the stone slab, solemn in their devotion to Sempher, and awaited the woman. A few commenced a low chant for the dead.

When the pregnant woman arrived, she was directed to stand at the foot of the body. They proceeded to disrobe the cadaver and demanded that she watch the ritual. They first washed the torso with precious water mixed with special oils, then dried it with sacred linen strips. The girl watched with vacant eyes as the men went about their work.

Zumab, the oldest of the Brotherhood, took up a curved dirk and held it aloft for all the brethren to see. The low chant increased in volume. He deftly cut the body in several locations. Others placed gourds around the altar to collect the blood which seeped out through the body wounds. Had the dead man's heart been beating, the process would have been quicker...the blood would have gushed. As it was, they had to elevate Sempher's lower body to position the feet higher than the head and use gravity to send the blood to the head. A deep incision made on each side of the throat facilitated the evacuation process. The body was rotated several times to assure complete voidance of blood. The woman's eyes were now less vacant as her attention was riveted on the body.

When Zumab was at last satisfied that the blood was completely separated from the body, he instructed the others to wash and dry the dead leader once more. When this was finished, he nodded to the chanters. They increased the volume and tempo of the chant as Zumab turned back to the corpse.

He used the dirk to cut deep into the chest, opening the body from the neck down to the abdomen. He plunged his hands into the cavity under the rib cage. He removed the heart first, using the knife to cut away the restraining muscle and tissue surrounding it. He placed the organ in a canopic jar carved from pure white alabaster, the cover of which was sculptured in the figure of a scarab. According to the ancients, they believed the heart was the seat of mans' intelligence and that Anubis, the god of death, would seek the heart. The scarab would point the way. Such was it written.

The lungs were removed from the body cavity as were the intestines, stomach and liver. All was done with care and reverence while the Brotherhood chanted the ancient chants and benedictions in keeping with the prescribed ceremony.

Each body part was placed in its own individual canopic jar with each having a distinctive cover. A baboon likeness was used for the lungs, a falcon for the intestines, a jackal for the stomach and a human head adorned the cover of the jar containing the liver. The jars, except that of the heart, were carved from translucent pink alabaster.

The woman was becoming ill, probably because of her pregnancy as well as seeing a human body cut up like a carcass of mutton. But she did not turn away from this ritual which was a part of her culture.

The final excision was that of the brain. Tradition held that the brain was useless and in the old days there was no attempt made to salvage it. Nevertheless, it had to be removed from the body for the same reason the other parts were removed...all were subject to decay. Nothing could be left within the corpse to desecrate the remains.

Zumab took a long, thin hooked instrument, and inserted it up the nasal passages. The hook was turned several times before the brain was drawn out through the nose, bit by bit, and discarded with the other non-salvageable tissue. It was at this sight that the woman fainted. They let her lie where she fell.

Special salts were next forced into the open cavity, well packed and kneaded into all areas of the open corpse. The ancients used common alkali salts mixed with other exotic preparations, including myrrh. But in his foresight, Sempher had other compounds made with modern technology. These served the same purpose of completely drying out the body tissue in a fraction of the time required with the ancient formula.

Zumab inspected the embalming and was satisfied the work was in accordance with tradition. The Brethren left the altar to allow the remains to dry. The actual prepara-

tion of the body for its burial would be done on the following day. Zumab appointed a younger man to stay with the
body throughout the night in deference to the status of their
departed pharaoh. As for the woman, she was taken back
to her quarters where she vomited.

At noon of the next day, the Brotherhood gathered at
the altar accompanied by the girl. Zumab inspected the
corpse and saw it was sufficiently dry. The skin had the
feel and texture of leather, indicating complete absence of
moisture. With the body fat dried from the remains, the
dead Sempher was but a fraction of his live self. The skin
hung in folds about his frame. Zumab directed the others
to anoint the body with fragrant oils after all salt residue
was removed.

The last act was to wrap the oiled cadaver in twenty
layers of linen strips, approximately four inches in width
and long enough to be wound around the body to encase it
completely. Each layer was oiled with the anointing preparation but which was now mixed with gum from the inner
bark of palms. The arms were wrapped separately from
the trunk and crossed over the chest just as the final layer
of linen was applied. The encased arms were thus locked
in position with the torso and the entire mummy was given
the last roll of pure white linen.

The embalmed body was placed in a cedar sarcophagus with the lid pegged down with cedar dowels. An outer
sarcophagus was made ready to receive the cedar coffin.
This casket was constructed of pewter embellished with
gold leaf. The top was ornamented with a death-head likeness of Sempher which had been fashioned in the old Egyptian style. The ritual was finished in silence. All that remained was the actual entombment at Saqqara.

The funeral procession started at nightfall. During the past centuries, the Brotherhood lengthened the main passage which originally emptied far short of Lake Qaroun. This exit now was but a few miles from the water. The Brethren left the caverns by this route in their frequent excursions into civilization, joining an abandoned rock and gravel road which hugged the east bank of the lake. Once on this road they could travel to the towns and villages dotting the delta region as normal travelers. The actual opening in the passage was cleverly disguised, such that it was undetectable from ground level, and most certainly from above. The dried river bed leading to the lake had long since been abandoned. Even the rare rainfall in the region avoided the gully.

The Brotherhood transported the mummy of Sempher along this route. The splendid gold-encrusted sarcophagus was loaded on a flatbed lorry and covered from curious view by miscellaneous baggage. The lorry then joined the train of vehicles which carried the attending Brotherhood and the woman.

The dark cover of night assured an unobserved trip as the drivers used the stars and moonlight as their means of navigation. When the caravan turned to the east toward Memphis after passing north of the lake, a few headlights were turned on to prevent an unexpected accident. The ride was long and arduous because of the care given its cargo.

The procession entered the village of Memphis in two hours. This had once been a splendid city, the capital of a united Kemet. As the seat of the Third Dynasty, Memphis had witnessed untold royal ceremonies, had enjoyed wealth beyond measure. Its fall into obscurity began when the star of the city of Thebes arose further south. Over the centuries, Memphis experienced several brief resurgences, but never regained its former glory.

It was now a squalid, dusty village inhabited by goats, cattle and a modicum of miserable *fellahin*. These farmers continued to work the soil in the ancient way but were losing the battle with the desert. The day would come when all visible traces of Memphis would be swallowed by the encroaching sand.

The village was dark and quiet when the procession passed through, the engines of its vehicles silenced to a muted growl. Neither goat, cow nor resident was about to watch the solemn parade roll over the few miserable streets of the town. On the far edge of the village, which faced the Nile and Cairo beyond, the trucks turned north toward the necropolis of Saqqara.

This road was paved to facilitate the busloads of tourists who came this way so the journey was ending on a smooth note. Palm trees lined the east side of the road, the side which benefited from the annual flood of the river before the High Dam at Aswan was built. The west side of the road was blurred in the vastness of the desert. No tree, bush or blade of grass broke the unyielding expanse of sand.

Saqqara was in two parts. The northern section of the necropolis was dedicated to several pharaohs, whose monuments were scattered over the area. The southern section was entirely dominated by the Stepped Pyramid of Zozer and his funerary temples. A few ruined burial sites of lesser kings were between the temple complex and the tombs further north. All the stone structures were designed and built by Imhotep and were ravaged by age and the elements. Still, their grandeur could not be denied.

The Pyramid no longer had six sharp-edged sloping mastabas piled one upon the other, each one smaller than the one below. Time had rounded the sharp lines to present a modern monument retaining only a fraction of its original shape. To the casual observer, the Pyramid was a ruined heap of rubble, but a discerning glance would reveal the magnitude and the glory of what was once the greatest building achievement of man.

The trucks passed beyond the funerary temples and then stopped in the shadows. The Brotherhood carried the heavy sarcophagus along the strewn rubble of the north side. They stopped before an ancient pyramid of the Fifth Dynasty which was now only a pile of stone. Certain of these stones were rolled aside to reveal a passageway which sloped downward to a vault hidden beneath the old pyramid ruin.

When lamps were lit, their light cast dancing shadows on the tomb of Pharaoh Sempher. His tomb was an authentic reconstruction of that of Ramses VI in the Valley of the Kings across from Thebes. The walls were decorated in the traditional way which depicted Sempher, as pharaoh, explaining his many good deeds to Osiris before his heart was weighed against the light feather of goodness.

The tomb's stone ceiling was emblazoned with the stars of a night sky and the painted figure of the goddess Nut swallowing the sun. The creation of this tomb had required the skilled labor of many hands over a long period of time. Sempher's preparations for eternity had not been done on the spur of the moment.

The men tried to suppress their awe and wonder. The old one, Zumab, started the ancient chant which was soon joined by the others. The sarcophagus was placed in the center of the tomb. Acrid fumes and smoke given off by the oil lamps filled the chamber, yet no man expressed discomfort, so intense was their devotion. The woman was there with the men, her attention fixed on the death head atop the pewter coffin. The prayers of Zumab were directed to the pantheon of ancient gods, pleading for a quick and easy passage of Sempher's *ka* into the afterlife. All this was in keeping with the ancient rites.

The prayers were finished. It was then that Zumab drew out from beneath his robe a curved dagger similar to the one used in the mummification ceremony. He passed the dirk to another, a younger man standing beside him, then walked up to the sarcophagus. There he removed his robe. Clad in only a starched linen loincloth, he raised his withered arms in supplication to the ceiling as though to embrace the goddess Nut. His eyes were ablaze with fervor and expectation of what was to follow. The companion next to him struck firm and true.

Zumab slumped over the sarcophagus, his blood pouring out of his cut throat and oozing over the gold ornamentation of the coffin. This final and absolute show of loyalty and devotion to his pharaoh was true to old tradition. The Brotherhood understood. Only the girl exhibited horror at this act, but then, she was but a woman.

They left the tomb, leaving Zumab where he had fallen. It would be an evil omen to move or even touch the body. The lamps were extinguished and the entrance sealed over. The Brotherhood was quick in hiding or removing all traces of its presence before driving off to return to the desert caverns. Dawn was approaching. They hurried the journey to be safely hidden before Amun broached the eastern sky.

Peter Bradshaw answered his phone. The caller was his agent, Salah.

"Mr. Bradshaw, Yamani is back at the house."

"Has he spoken to anyone outside, as far as you know?"

"Yes, he placed several calls. He used a language I do not understand, so I couldn't tell what was said."

"You're certain it wasn't Arabic?"

"Yes. I know Arabic well. It sounded a little like the Turkish I heard in Cypress. I'm not sure. Sorry."

"Never mind, Salah. Keep listening and report back to me. It's quite important we know Yamani's every contact."

"I'll call you tomorrow, Mr. Bradshaw. Perhaps I'll have something then."

When Bradshaw finished the conversation, he stood at the window, looking down the broad Cornishe. He was troubled with the way Yamani was acting. The reports he got from his other agents claimed the Arab was much too happy since he returned to the city. His usual frown was replaced by a toothy smile.

"He's up to something," Bradshaw said aloud.

Chapter 24

The Cairo Airport was quiet when Loring, Merrick and Crimmins arrived. The stillness in the air hung thickly, like an ominous cloud, ready to burst. Dozens of armed men surrounded the British plane when it taxied to a stop, and dozens more inside the terminal stood guard. Everyone looked calm, but the pervasive tension could be cut with a knife. The armed soldiers unceremoniously urged the uneasy British passengers into the terminal building, eager to see them passed on to the next link in the chain of security. All new arrivals of other nationalities were similarly shunted about the terminal. The Egyptians wanted to distance themselves from all foreigners. A specter of doom had invaded the airport and the look of fear was in every glance of the locals.

Peter Bradshaw was at the gate to intercept them and he facilitated their passport inspection. The officials paid scant attention to the men. Their baggage, however, was subjected to extraordinary scrutiny in a search for weapons. This examination chewed up the better part of an hour.

Outside at last, Bradshaw felt safe enough to state his position. "Hopkins cabled me the details and ordered me to do what I can for you. It appears we'll be working on this together." Then, almost as an afterthought, he said, "I say, Loring, dreadfully sorry about Nadia. When I saw you last, you didn't grasp my deep feelings in the matter." Bradshaw was driving them into downtown Cairo.

"Peter, I never had the chance to let you know how much I appreciated your help. I guess I was in pretty bad shape at the time. There's a lot more you should know if we expect you to help us," Loring remarked.

They told Bradshaw all that had happened since the day he pulled Loring out of the desert. Menefee was dead. Wells was dead and the plans of Zoser were in the hands of the intelligence agencies. They finally knew what to look for. Another series of riots would signal the final phase of 'Operation Amun'.

"Have there been any more disturbances here since the Christian riots?"

"No, Derek, things have been fairly quiet," Bradshaw answered. "Mubarak's government is putting on a show of stability and he vows to treat all rioters with armed force. He can't possibly survive another series of riots. He knows that and looks for outside intervention from the West."

"What are the Arabs doing," Merrick asked.

"The Arab countries are waiting, keeping pretty much to themselves. Dashed if I know why. What are your plans and how can I help?"

"Bradshaw, we're here to put an end to Sempher, once and for all." Crimmins said. "Zoser will be finished when he is out of the way. Each of us has a personal reason for wanting this. All civilized countries want Zoser stopped. Sempher's agents have all been rounded up in the States and in Europe. Sempher is cornered here in Egypt, alone."

"That much I know from Hopkins. I need to know what you three plan on doing."

"The three of us aim to draw him out by various feints or provocations so you chaps at MI 6 can take him. Believe me, Bradshaw, if you people hesitate to take him, one or all of us here will kill Sempher without a second thought. Is that clear?"

"Perfectly. What are your plans?" Bradshaw didn't like what he was hearing.

Loring answered. "We must keep an eye on Achmed Yamani here in Cairo. He's Sempher's second in command, the one who puts the various wheels in motion. The final phase is about to start, and we have to stay one step ahead of it. It'll be a holy war between the Christians and the Moslems. Monitor his phone and his movements, Peter. Let us know everything he does, everyone he sees."

"For your info, old man, I'm already on it. I have an agent planted in his harem."

"Great! We also need a pilot to fly us over the region in the desert where we believe Zoser's headquarters are. It's somewhere around El-Fayoum and Lake Qaroun."

"That's close to where Menefee and I found you."

"Right. These areas are pinpointed on a map we found in Sempher's place in Lucerne. Our NASA people have infrared pictures taken during our space flights over North Africa which show underground river beds in this region. I'm sure the caverns are near those river beds. The water would have created a natural depression in the soft rock substrata and might have carved out a system of caves."

"A pilot and helicopter should be no problem," Bradshaw replied.

"Fine. Another thing...the locals must conduct constant radar sweeps across the airspace between El-Fayoum and Matruh, and even further west into Libya. We'd like to know how much air traffic uses that remote area. Can you get all this done right away? Time is important."

"I can't imagine any problem from our end. The locals might get a bit sticky, though. Mubarak sees goblins under every rock. Meet our man in the morning at the helipad next to the Pyramids. He'll have you airborne at first light. Are you staying at the Mena House again?"

"Yes we are. When word gets back to Sempher that the three of us didn't die in that bomb blast, he'll panic. He's apt to do something foolish. We'll see you later in the morning, Peter, with a full report. And thanks again for all your help and concern. You watch yourself, too."

"Oh, I shall, never fear."

"You can let us out here on the Cornishe. We'll take a cab to the hotel."

"I can just as well take you to the hotel."

"No, it's not necessary, Peter. Right here'll be fine."

"Righto, Derek. Please be careful. Inspector Crimmins, keep these civilians in tow. Until tomorrow, then, cheerio."

When they left Bradshaw, Loring told the others he wanted to call on Dr. Nashtoi at the museum. It was a short walk and, as they went up to Nashtoi's office, Loring sadly remembered that Nadia had been with him the last time he saw the curator.

"Mr. Loring, how sad I am about all that has happened since we last met. Egypt owes you so much. Come in. There is someone here you need to see."

Joshua Claridge rose from his chair as they walked into Nashtoi's office. They shook hands all around. Then Claridge proceeded to give them an update on his situation.

"The Menefee has neutralized Zoser's army in Europe and the States. Thanks to the cooperation of the intelligence agencies, the top dogs have been put out of commission, which leaves the head without a carcass. Our work was easy. You'd be surprised at how effective blackmail can be. We took a chapter out of Zoser's book and it worked. What news do you three have?"

"We've been wondering where you went after you left us at Heathrow. You know about the bomb." This was a statement from Loring rather than a question.

"Yes, I heard about it from one of the Menefee. Zoser must have followed you from the airport. Are you all right, no permanent damages?"

"Other than my dislocated shoulder which is healing all too slowly, we are fine." Crimmins was looking at Claridge in a strange fashion. He continued, "But the news is not all bad. Derek here can fill you in."

"We've a calculated guess as to where the headquarters are. We're planning to draw Sempher out into the open and let MI 6 take him. We start tomorrow." Loring had noticed the uncertainty in Crimmins' greeting to Claridge, but he dismissed it as unimportant. Bert was a policeman, after all.

"Good, and none too soon. We had a man inside, in Sempher's circle, and he just got out. He reported that something big is about to happen."

"Then your man knows where the caverns are located. Are they in the El-Fayoum region?" Loring was excited.

"Yes, next to the oasis the locals call Messneh, but the way in is heavily guarded. It'll require a heavy armed attack to penetrate the caves."

"That might be arranged," Merrick said, smiling.

"This is something none of you will believe," Claridge went on. "Our man told us a weird story concerning Sempher. It seems our nemesis is planning a dynasty. He impregnated a young girl some time ago in a sacred ceremony. She's Achmed Yamani's daughter. The ritual was performed on an altar in front of the entire group. This girl was first painted up in a grotesque manner before she was forced to excite and straddle Sempher. He just laid on his back, letting the girl do all the work. Really weird.

Our man said it was a ritual out of the old times when the high priest felt he needed to provide an heir to replace him when he died. Yamani offered his young daughter...name's Nara...to Sempher. He obviously believed he would have complete control once Sempher was out of the picture. They're all insane."

"I know this Nara Yamani," Dr. Nashtoi said. "She came here often to read of the old days of Egyptian glory. She is eager to learn all she can of her heritage. She is a secret Copt Christian. If her father ever found this out, he would kill her with his bare hands. Yamani is a devious devil, totally irreligious and the perfect tool for Zoser. He will be more dangerous than Sempher himself."

Claridge spoke up. "Our man said the girl is now seven months along and confined to the caverns. He said once the baby is born and raised, it has to cut the throat of its mother. Not a very happy prospect."

"How perfectly awful," whispered Merrick. "And yet, so sad."

"If it is at all possible, you must try to save this girl from these demons. She is a good girl, and destined for finer things. Please try to get her out." Nashtoi was disturbed.

"Doctor, we can't promise anything," Loring said, "but if we can, we'll do our best to rescue her."

They left after this, going across the bridge to the west side of the Nile and on to the Mena House. Claridge did not go with them. He said he had business elsewhere. Loring knew it would be pointless to question Claridge—he worked by other methods. Crimmins made no comment but his brow was creased with worry.

The normally stoic desk clerk at the hotel showed

shock and concern when Loring registered. The Egyptian fluttered and actually blushed as he looked at their passports. His hand was shaking nervously.

"Dr. Loring. We are most grateful to see you again. You were very fortunate to have been found in the desert. The Sahara can be very dangerous. Will you and your friends be staying long?"

"No longer than our business here will require. Our key, please."

When the elevator doors closed, Merrick almost shouted, "He fairly flew to the phone when we left the desk. Sempher has to know by now that we're here. What do we do in the meantime?" The lift stopped at their floor.

"We do nothing till morning. But remember, these rooms have hidden microphones so don't discuss our plans. Let's keep them guessing. Do you agree, Bert?"

"Yes, definitely. Our silence will make them edgy, just the way we want them. But right now, Derek, we have to talk privately. I have something stuck in my craw and I need your thoughts on this. You, too, Marc."

"I thought there was something bothering you," Loring said. "There's a lounge in the lobby at each floor. We can talk there without being overheard."

When they were settled in the lounge, Loring said, "Okay Bert. Out with it. You have something on your mind. What is it?"

"Yes," Marc added. "You have been terribly quiet ever since we were at the museum."

"Well," Bert started, "you both will think me mad as a hatter. The truth is, I don't trust Claridge. I can't say what it is, but there's something strange about the whole setup."

"Oh come now, Bert. Surely you are imagining all this. Josh was a friend of Ron's and stepped into his shoes when Ron was killed. We're all after the same thing."

Merrick was getting heated in his defense of Claridge.

"I have to get this out in the open then you can show me where I'm wrong."

"Go ahead, Bert."

"First, Claridge worked for Zoser International. Ron told us he was actually a member of Menefee, in there to inform on Wells and the rest. I ask myself, was his cover so fragile that he couldn't take a chance to let Ron know how much danger you, Derek, and Nadia were in? He passed along less important information."

"He was in a touchy situation, Bert."

"I know that, Derek, but there's more. He was the one who found the documents on Zoser's organization. By his own admission, Ron merely recovered the lineage chart and the maps. Josh had been at the chalet before and must have been privy to the schedule of 'Operation Amun'. Again, I ask myself...why did he keep it to himself? Why didn't he let Menefee know about the riots ahead of time?"

"Wells was keeping a close watch on him."

"And yet, he sent me all that damning evidence before he skipped. He could have warned us about the riots then. And another thing...where did he disappear to when he left us at the airport? He knew where we were going, and why. How simple it would have been for him to let Sutton know, and let that shrewd bastard take it from there."

"I think you're way off base there, Bert," Merrick said, hotly.

"Perhaps, but why does he show up in Cairo at this time? What was the business elsewhere he found so pressing he couldn't stay with us and work to catch Sempher?"

"Coincidence?"

"I don't buy that. I tell myself there are things I don't know about how the Menefee works and all these facts could be explained in a logical way. But the policeman in me makes me suspicious. He could have been a loyal member of the Menefee, at first. Perhaps when he was with Sempher and Wells in Lucerne, he saw the scope of what Zoser was really after. He could have then changed his allegiance back to Zoser, wanting a part of the action.

That would explain why he kept the schedule of Amun and the riots to himself. He wanted them to happen. That would explain why he led Sutton to the three of us, knowing Sempher wanted you killed, Derek. He's now in Cairo because he has to be in on the final act. Now, tell me, am I overly paranoid?"

Loring and Merrick were speechless. They heard the words, listened to the reasoning, but their minds rejected the implications. Josh Claridge, the new leader of the Menefee, a fraud? Did he spy on them, turn them over to Zoser's killers, let Nadia go to her death without so much as a warning? No, the idea was too monstrous, too diabolical. The arguments presented by Crimmins must have a more innocent explanation.

Merrick spoke first. "Bert, let me offer a separate set of logical reasons for his actions. First, he was a loyal Menefee who felt that the ultimate destruction of Zoser was more important than the lives of individuals, regardless of who they were."

"That would take a fanatical loyalty. I don't think Claridge was that committed."

"Let me finish. Josh knew Sempher kept the documents at his chalet because he had been there with Wells. Even so, there is nothing to show he was ever taken into Sempher's confidence about the details of 'Amun'. He couldn't tell us, or anyone, about things he didn't know."

"That might be true enough." Crimmins was still frowning.

"When we left the airport, some of Zoser's people

could have followed us to your place, Bert. They could have waited until we went on to Hopkins' flat. They could have planted the bomb in the few minutes we were with Hopkins. Josh could very well have gone back to the Menefee after he left us, knowing nothing about Sempher's plans for our execution."

"I don't agree with that. If Zoser was following you and Derek, why wait around for me? It was Derek they wanted. They could have murdered him easily while I was with Nora."

"Then how about this? Just suppose Zoser really did plan to kill all three of us. We only have Hopkins' word that it was just Derek they were after. But suppose it wasn't? Josh is here in Cairo for the same reason we are. He knows about the capture of Zoser's top agents. He told us the Menefee neutralized the lesser army. Where else would he be but here to get in on the final kill? Is this reasoning logical enough to calm your suspicions? What do you think, Derek?"

Loring was tempted to side with Merrick. He liked Josh Claridge and trusted him. However, Bert's suspicions were logical and possible.

"I honestly believe you're both right, or both wrong. Maybe a little of each. Marc, I'm inclined to go along with your reasoning, possibly because I'm too trusting by nature. On the other hand, Bert, you're a professional who's well trained in factual analysis and careful not to make rash decisions. That's why I can't dismiss your logic. You have been right on the mark up to now."

"So where do we stand on this?"

"I say we accept the possibility both situations are possible and act accordingly. We stay away from Claridge and watch our backsides. When this is all over, and Josh proves to be what Marc thinks, we can always apologize.

If he turns out to be what Bert thinks, a traitor, we can deal with it at that time. Agreed?"

"Sounds satisfactory to me," Marc answered. "I know I'm right about him."

"I'll go along with that." Crimmins did not sound totally convinced. "Let's have Bradshaw send us some backup, someone we can trust, to watch these delicate asses of ours."

"Bert, you never used to talk like that," Merrick said.

"I've no longer a need for pompous officialese," he grinned.

"Then it's settled. I'll call Bradshaw from our room and ask him to send some men." Loring was not happy about the doubts cast on Claridge, but felt it best to be on the alert.

Achmed Yamani paced the floor of his room. This room, a part of the second floor suite he maintained in a decrepit building in the Old City, was where he conducted the various business enterprises which made him a wealthy man. He took over this old structure several years before and converted the interior into a sumptuous dwelling, complete with separate women's quarters on the ground floor.

The Old City was that district of Cairo where the lowest and poorest inhabitants of the capital eked out a bare existence. Yamani kept the exterior of the building in a noticeable state of disrepair to thwart thieves who would steal everything he owned if they thought such riches where inside. The building was just the same type of run-down hovel as all the others in the area.

In his pacing, Yamani was both elated on one hand and impatient on the other. His spirits soared when he received word that Sempher was dead. He could now take over the rule of the Brotherhood and hasten the downfall of President Mubarak.

He had promised Sempher he would rule until the child was old enough to take command. He planned to keep that promise as long as it served his purposes. The unborn child of his daughter would be his claim to the throne of a reorganized and restructured Egypt. His own plans were beginning to come together now that he was in complete control.

His impatience, however, dimmed the impact of his new position. He had to wait before he started the final riots. The entire operation was timed to the minute and he could not alter the schedule. Too many men and directions had been sent out. He had to wait.

He had received information from the Mena House that Loring was back, and not dead as reported. That infidel must lead a charmed life, he thought. Sempher would have quaked at the news, but Sempher was dead, and he, Yamani, knew how to handle the problem of Loring. After all, what could the simple American do? Loring would be no problem at all. And once the riots started he would send men to seek out and destroy Loring, to be one more victim of the riots.

He stopped pacing long enough to send for one of his men, the one who would instigate the initial riot in Tahrir Square. He wanted to make a last minute check of the man's preparations. This man, Abdullah El-Zed, was a devious and tricky bastard, but could be relied on if the rewards were great enough.

After the word to El-Zed was dispatched, he resumed his pacing. He needed some diversion to soothe his nerves. He called down below to the women's section for Salah. She was the firm and supple Nubian wench he bought from the trading Bedouin caravan last year. She knew how to please him. The black girl came to him freshly perfumed and oiled, her skin glistening in the light streaming through the shuttered window. Yamani led the woman to the low couch and pulled her down with him, his mind now on matters other than politics.

A slight knock at the door sounded, bringing about a pause in the activity on the couch. This would be El-Zed. The wench could wait. "Enter," Yamani called out.

El-Zed was one of those small, dirty Arabs found in every Mid Eastern city, bent with poverty but having the knowing skills to survive his lot in life. El-Zed never allowed his small dark eyes to stay long on any one sight. However, when he entered Yamani's room and saw Salah, his gaze became fixed on the beautiful black girl, naked and sprawled around the body of Yamani. Yamani's large dirty hands were pawing and exploring the secret crevices of the woman's voluptuous body. Her tapered legs were entwined about Yamani's gross waist, straining against his hairy back, her face expressionless. Traces of blood seeped from the nipple of one contoured breast.

"You sent for me?"

"Yes, Abdullah." Yamani disengaged himself from the girl and faced his minion. "Are your men all in place? Do they know what they are to do? Nothing must go wrong. There is too much at stake."

"Never fear, Yamani. You are paying me to do your work and you shall get what you pay for. The men are all ready. We commence tomorrow, at noon. The first riot will start in Tahrir Square, then in the El-Khalili bazaar. Finally, we do our work at the Kalawun Mosque. I will have men stationed at all spots, ready when the signal is given. Are you pleased?"

Yamani looked at the coarse Arab. He had a deep-seated abhorrence toward this dreg of the Cairo gutter.

Ordinarily, he would have nothing to do with the man, but now he needed what special talents El-Zed possessed. Later, when the work was done, he planned to gladly slit El-Zed's filthy throat. Yamani swallowed his hatred, then replied.

"You have always been reliable. When this is work is finished tomorrow, I shall give you a reward far beyond your dreams. Besides the money, I will include this black beauty here as a bonus." His sweaty hand pointed to the low couch where Salah reclined, immobile. He knew El-Zed desired the whore. At his last words, Salah's black eyes moved quickly from Yamani over to the grinning El-Zed then back to Yamani. Was it fear, or hatred, that each saw in those dark eyes?

"I await your signal. *Ma'assalama*, Yamani."

When the Arab left, Yamani turned to the Nubian, an evil smile on his face.

"That pig will not live to see the day I would give him anything, much less a prize like you. I won't need you any further. I wish to be alone. You may return to your place."

The girl dressed quickly and left Yamani engrossed with his plans.

Downstairs, in the women's quarters, the black woman threw on her street clothes, veiled her face and left the house by the back way. She made her way to El Barrant Road where she placed a phone call.

"Mr. Bradshaw, this is Salah. It is scheduled to start tomorrow. Where do you wish to meet me?"

The chopper had them at fifteen hundred feet above El-Fayoum by first light. The vast expanse of sand and rock outcroppings below stretched a hundred miles west from the Nile. The desert appeared to be a sea of dunes, rolling and heaving as a violent ocean without the breaking crests. Not a cloud or blemish broke the subtle shadings of the morning sky.

The helicopter made an ever-widening circle, keeping El-Fayoum as its center. Nothing moved on the desert below, nothing that could be seen with the eye, but Loring knew they were being watched from the crevices in the ochre rocks tumbling over the sandscape. He also knew the watchers would remain hidden from sight.

"This isn't going to get us anyplace. We can't see any path or trail to the caverns. Everything down there looks the same. They know we're here and they're bound to stay out of sight." Merrick was getting bored and upset.

"Remember, Marc, we want them to know where we are. Our presence will interfere with the time schedule Sempher has to maintain. He's unbalanced to the point that he will make a mistake in his haste. That's what this exercise is all about," Crimmins said.

"Wait!" Loring shouted over the engine noise. "That oasis off to our left looks vaguely familiar. When Nadia and I were taken to the caves, we stopped at an oasis and walked to the cavern entrance from there. See it? That rock cliff just east of the oasis...that's it! I'm positive."

The pilot hollered to them, excitedly. "We've got company. My radar shows two planes coming up fast from the west."

All eyes turned to the vast desert wasteland stretching to the west. Two specks in the distance grew larger as they watched, almost filling the sky above the chopper when they streaked by. Two MIG 19's with Libyan markings screamed overhead, only to circle back and come at the helicopter from opposite directions. The chopper pilot was damn good. He evaded the first pass, the trail of tracer bullets wide of the mark.

"The sons of bitches have help from that maniac, Gadhafy! Loring, get on the radio and report our position. This is an act of war! I'm going to be busy for a while keeping these bastards from blowing us up. Hang on, here they come again!"

The pilot maneuvered the helicopter up and around dizzily to prevent either of the enemy planes from getting a fix on them.

"We can't keep this up for long. Those MIG's have gun sights that are radar-controlled. They'll lock in on us if those bastards are any good. By all rights, we should be done for by now. Our only hope is that friendly planes will get here in time."

The Libyans came at them again. And again they missed the dancing and cavorting chopper. The tracers were closer this time. They would zero in on the next run. Then, from out of the sun rising in the east, two Egyptian F14's streaked by the hapless helicopter to engage the Libyan planes. It was a short chase and after one pass the fight was over. Both enemy planes went down in the western desert several miles from El-Fayoum. The two F 14's wobbled their wings at the chopper in a sign of greeting and cooperation before they disappeared as quickly as they had approached.

"That, my friends, was too close for my taste." Merrick was flushed with excitement.

A crooked smile crossed the pilot's face. "We might as well take a look at our enemy." He flew to where the MIG's crashed, hovered a minute, then settled onto the sand.

The four men left the chopper, walking to the first crashed plane where they extricated the dead pilot and dragged him nearer to the second plane. They retrieved its pilot and examined what was left of the men. There was no fire, but they kept a sharp eye for telltale smoke which could be the start of a blaze.

Each pilot possessed a wallet containing money, pictures and an official-looking Egyptian identification card complete with photo. Why were Libyan planes being flown by Egyptians this close to Cairo? The Egyptians had American radar surveillance planes all over the desert sky tracking Libyan movements. They certainly would have been spotted sooner or later. The pilot ventured a guess.

"These men were never meant to live after shooting us down. Their identities are too pat. They could have been sacrificed by Sempher, using borrowed or stolen Libyan planes to give the impression that some Egyptians are turncoats and with Gadhafy. Sempher knows about the surveillance planes and wanted us dead, but letting Gadhafy get blamed for it. World opinion would not need much convincing that Gadhafy would try something like this.

"Another possibility is that Gadhafy actually did send the planes and had the pilots conveniently holding Egyptian I.D.'s. They could be forged. He would claim a Western conspiracy against him."

"There might be a third possibility," Crimmins stated. "Suppose the pilots actually were bonafide Egyptians with Zoser. And suppose Gadhafy is a partner of Sempher, and he actually gave the planes to Zoser. We know that Gadhafy hates the Mubarak government and is really using Sempher to keep Egypt off-guard. If that's the case, Sempher has to be stopped right now before he can cause the government further instability. With Zoser at his throat and Gadhafy waiting on the sidelines to pick up the pieces, Mubarak doesn't stand much of a chance. We might have far more than one madman to fear...we now might have two."

They left the dead men lying in the sand, but took

their personal possessions, meaning to turn them over to the proper authorities. However, before they returned to Cairo, Loring had the pilot circle the oasis again. Perhaps the aftermath of the air battle caused it, but Loring felt his sense of observation was sharper now, more intense.

"Yes, that's the place. I can make out the cleft in the rock wall. How could I ever forget it?"

The pilot went on to Cairo alone, stating he would have Bradshaw contact them after getting his report. It was a serious threesome who returned to the Mena House. As the three of them got on the elevator to go to their room, a strange man edged up to Loring.

"I'm Sam...Bradshaw sent me. There's one of us on your floor and in the lobby lounge, and the gardener below your window is from the agency as well. We'll be around even if you don't see us. Bradshaw said to tell you that the riots are to start today, at noon. Just two hours from now. He says he has things under control, and you better stay where you are...don't go into the city. The final phase of 'Operation Amun' is ready to begin."

Chapter 25

Shortly before noon Tahrir Square was jammed with mobs of local people going about their business as well as curious tourists, all milling about in wild disorder. The confusion and hesitant movements of the many tourists were no more out of place than the actions of most visitors in numerous other strange and exotic settings. They wanted to see everything in the shortest possible time. The residents, on the other hand, usually crossed and recrossed the busy Square with normal regularity, set on avoiding contact with the strangers.

The uncertain and haphazard behavior of the local Cairo residents in the Square this day presaged a break in their routine. An unusual event was anticipated by watching eyes on the fringe of the babble. Shops and booths were open for the usual tourist business, but the shopkeepers were apprehensive and nervous. Tradesmen kept vigil, their eyes skirting around the Square, waiting expectantly. Even the blare of horns coming from stalled traffic sounded ominous in the late morning heat and bustle. Mule carts veered in all directions, the animals' braying added to the chaos. The situation in Tahrir Square was not quite normal.

Abdullah El-Zed was in his position. He had arrived at the Square to survey the entire area several minutes ahead of the scheduled hour. He quickly spotted many of the men he had handpicked for the task ahead.

They appeared ready. When El-Zed determined all

was in order, he moved to the center of the Square, the spot he had chosen in advance for his role in the coming operation. From there he could watch the entire place just by turning his body. Conversely, from this selected spot, he could be seen from all quarters. At exactly twelve o'clock, El-Zed raised both his arms over his head as though in pious supplication, and slowly turned a full three hundred and sixty degrees. It was the signal for the trouble to begin.

Suddenly, there was a shout of anger from the north end of the Square, all but lost in the normal street noises. Then, another shout, followed by pushing and scuffling. The fighting grew, spilling over to other contiguous groups, both Christian and Moslem. The melee spread like ripples in a pond, engulfing all of those it came in contact with. At first, it was only a mob reflex but it quickly deteriorated into the destructive riot that was so carefully planned.

El-Zed watched the spotty fights develop in various sectors of the Square, confident his men would skillfully involve more and more people until the entire Square was a bloody battlefield. When Tahrir Square could no longer contain the mobs, the riot would naturally spread outward to meet combatants rushing out from his next stop...El Khalili Bazaar. He would have preferred to remain in the Square to watch his handiwork but he had to leave to be at his next assigned position in time to give the signal.

He climbed into his waiting car and drove down El Bustan Road toward El Khalili. He noticed the nondescript Volvo sedan as it pulled into the flow of traffic behind him but it had no significance for him.

El-Zed approached El Khalili Bazaar. His was a mission, a job for which he was being well paid. He had no interest in the motive or morality of his work. Money had its own morality, its own code of ethics. He was long past believing in man's ideals or politics. His life of borderline poverty instilled in him nothing but greed. He was mentally spending the wages Yamani promised and savoring the anticipated charms of the black Salah. His vivid imagination saw her supine on his bed waiting for him, her long tapered legs wide apart. His reverie was interrupted by the shop of the weaver, his next command position.

The Khalili was a maze of streets and alleys connecting shops and stalls with one leading into the other. The layout of the area was unique in that a tourist could enter one shop and not be required to go back out into the hot street. One could traverse the entire block of shops in relative comfort, seeking any mercantile bargain.

The smells and babble emanating from this mecca of Egyptian tourism drifted well beyond the actual confines of the bazaar, mingling with the other noises and smells of Cairo. The Khalili still reflected the damage sustained during the earlier riots and fires, but that was considered an inconvenience at worst. It was business as usual.

The corner intersection where El-Zed stationed himself was one of the three places which afforded a commanding sightline to the most obscure and remote reaches of the bazaar. His timing was precise. At one o'clock sharp, he raised his arms above his head and turned the full circle as he had done in Tahrir Square. The results were the same. Skirmishes broke out between local Moslems and Christians with the tourists being ignored for the most part. Blows were exchanged and wrestling in the dusty streets escalated. People gathered in shop doorways, in the streets and alleys, all urging one group or another to look for an advantage. As expected, knives appeared, the bright afternoon sun glittering off the burnished blades.

El-Zed was satisfied with the progress of the riot. More and more people were becoming involved and the entire

Khalili would soon be up in bloody arms. With a final smug glance at his doing, he left his position to make his way to Kalawun Mosque for the third riot, a mere three blocks away.

He positioned himself in the sunbaked courtyard of Kalawun Mosque. It was fifteen minutes before two o'clock.

At two o'clock, El-Zed raised his arms and began his pirouette as he had done before. Out of the corner of his eye he noticed two men rushing toward him. From the looks of them, it was plain to see they were after him. He knew who they were...the police.

Apprehensively, he began to run, not bothering to glance behind him. He would not be taken by the police this way. This was all too easy, he thought. The two men waiting for him knew exactly where he'd be. It was a betrayal. It had to be and but one person outside of himself knew his exact timetable...Achmed Yamani.

Eluding the stupid police would be no problem. They were not aware of how many avenues of escape were known to El-Zed. He quickly mingled with the throngs of the devout Moslems in the courtyard and slipped out the service gateway, rushing to his car parked two blocks away. Yamani had to be confronted, made to pay dearly for this betrayal.

"That son of a pig will not see the setting sun this day!" El-Zed shouted to the wind as he powered his car away from the mosque and the aborted capture.

The two men calmly climbed into their Volvo sedan as though they had all the time in the world.

"I'm certain he'll head back to Yamani's place, Captain Habib." Peter Bradshaw sat behind the wheel, heading back toward Old Cairo. "We can pick him up there with Yamani as well. The President now has enough evidence to go after Zoser."

"You are correct, Mr. Bradshaw. My orders are clear. Once we take Yamani and El-Zed into custody, I am to gather an armed force and arrest Kurt Sempher on charges of treason and espionage. Do you wish to accompany me on the kill, as you Europeans say?"

"I wouldn't miss it for the world. But there are three others I want along." Bradshaw was thinking of Loring, Merrick and Crimmins, the three who did so much to make it all happen.

"But of course. Especially Mr. Loring. From what I understand, he is the only person in Egypt still alive who can identify Sempher. No one else has seen him." Captain Habib kept his dark eyes on the heavy traffic surrounding them.

"Please hurry, Mr. Bradshaw."

The Volvo screeched to the curb in front of Yamani's house in Old Cairo. Bradshaw and Habib rushed into the place, pushing aside the crying women who were grouped at the foot of the stairs. When questioned, one terrified woman pointed up the stairway, directing them to Yamani's study. Bradshaw bounded up the stairs, two at a time, with Habib one step behind, his gun out, ready to shoot.

When they slammed through the door of Yamani's study, the sight that greeted them was not totally unexpected. Achmed Yamani would lead no more uprisings. He was sprawled on the floor of his study, a curved dagger protruding from his massive chest. Blood was seeping through his silk shirt saturating the rich Persian carpet. Abdullah El-Zed was crouched over the body, his hands bloodied, still cursing the inert body on the floor.

"The son of a pig betrayed me. May he rot in hell!"

Captain Habib raised his gun and fired. The single blast from the .45 opened El-Zed's head from the crown down to his chin. The Arab dropped on top of the still form of Yamani.

"A clear case of self defense, if ever I saw one," Bradshaw said as Habib holstered his gun. Turning abruptly, the two men left the house, leaving behind the moans and cries of Yamani's harem.

El-Zed had no way of knowing that his instigated riot had been stopped at almost the exact time he left Tahrir Square. Even had he remained to watch the fighting for a few more minutes, he would not have believed it could happen, everything had been too well planned.

As it was, right after he left, Father Yosef from the Coptic Abu Serga Church and Imam Abdul Mosishe of Ahmed Ibn Tulum Mosque linked arms and forced their way into the midst of the rioters. Angry shouts and insults greeted them when they were recognized for what they were. Each of these holy men took turns in admonishing the combatants in spite of the threats from all quarters. They called on the fighters to cease their blood lust under pain of dire consequences.

It was impossible to make out the words they spoke beyond a few yards from the fighting, but the effect was immediate. The fighting stopped, slowly at first, then more rapidly. The noise which now filled the Square was a wave of praise and glory to God, to Allah, and to man, replacing the cries of anger and hate. Father Yosef and Imam Abdul Mosishe left Tahrir Square, their arms still linked in friendship.

As El-Zed turned on the crowded street, heading toward Kalawun Mosque and his second riot, he hadn't picked up on the two men who left the bazaar behind him. He hadn't seen the intrusion of the two clerics, arms linked, who waded into the center of the fierce fighting. The milling rioters continued their pushing and shouting, knives being waved aloft in search of soft flesh.

The holy men appeared unafraid and stood their ground, admonishing the fighters with words of caution, love, and salvation. As in Tahrir Square, the riot was gradually quelled by the action and intervention of the two clerics. One was a Lutheran minister and the other was a Moslem qadi. The singing, chanting and general feeling of brotherhood cascading through El Khalili could not be heard by Abdullah El-Zed.

"Loring? Bradshaw here. How was your excursion in the desert this morning? Our pilot friend gave me his report. A bit dicey, wasn't it?"

"Peter! So glad you called. Have you heard the news about the riots? I wonder how they pulled that one off, those priests and imam, I mean?"

"It was something the Pope worked out. I'll tell you all about it later. Loring, Yamani's dead. Operation Amun is finished. Mubarak's ordered the army to take Sempher now that he has enough evidence. They want you along to make the identification. I never realized until now how vulnerable you were, being the only one who could identify him. Be ready to go the first thing in the morning."

"I'm not the only one left, Peter. There's still the Menefee, don't forget. We're all going in the morning...me, Bert and Marc. We all have a stake in this. We'll be ready."

When Loring hung up he joined his friends across the room. "That was Bradshaw. He says Yamani is dead and that Operation Amun is a thing of the past. We're going in with the army in the morning to get Sempher. This is what we've all waited for."

"Good show!" Marc shouted. 'Any idea where Josh might be?"

"I think he is out in the desert, with Sempher." Crimmins continued to harbor his suspicions of Claridge. "With the riots aborted, with Amun finished, Sempher is on the edge ready to fall. Claridge could be making a deal with Zoser."

"I don't think he would be that foolish," Loring said. "Josh knows too much about Zoser to make any deal with Sempher. He knows Sempher would kill him the first chance he gets. Claridge is around someplace but not with Sempher."

The assault team gathered by the Pyramids before the eastern sky was awake. Myriads of stars appeared as pinpoints of light against the inky sky. They were so close overhead in the desert that one was tempted to reach up and grasp a handful. Yet with the dawn came their release, one by one, until the gray dawn welcomed the fire of Amun. This day, however, the stage was not empty when Amun made his entrance. The engines of war were waiting in the wings.

The army unit was composed of sixty men and officers. Huddled on the fringe, a somber quartet spoke together in whispers, not eager to take up the gauntlet of force. Loring, Merrick, Crimmins and Peter Bradshaw were being briefed by Captain Habib. Under no circumstances were they to take an active part in storming the caverns. They were included as observers only. The army would do what fighting was necessary.

"I don't envy Habib's position," Loring said, trying

to be understanding. "He has a responsibility to his superiors to get Sempher with minimum casualties but he's being hampered by us getting in his way. If we hadn't planned and dreamed of this chance, I'd let Habib go on without us."

"Derek, you know none of us actually likes this, but we have to go through with it." Merrick was being as logical as he could. He was obviously eager to go, yet intelligent enough to realize this was out of their league.

"I would gladly pass, thank you, if MI 6 didn't expect me to see it through. I'll admit it, I'm a bit of a coward." Bradshaw was honest. His eyes reflected his fear, close to terror.

"Regardless of any consequences, I'm committed to this. You all know why." Crimmins was being his normally stubborn self.

The landing pad adjacent to the pyramid compound was cluttered with equipment and arms. Each man, with a full combat pack, fell silent as the hour for takeoff approached. The gear was loaded aboard the U.S.-made gunship helicopters, and the men squeezed in as space allowed. The choppers rose slowly into the lightening sky, then turned and flew toward El Fayoum.

The morning sun was streaking across the desert floor when the assault force reached El Fayoum. Two of the planes veered to the north where their contingents were to take and force entry at the Lake Qaroun approach. The other choppers hovered at the south end, near the oasis, and waited for the north group to land. The plan called for a coordinated attack, with a separate group hitting each end of the caverns at the same time. Once on the ground, men and equipment erupted from the helicopters, prepared for an immediate assault. Crimmins and Loring were part of the south group and Merrick was with Bradshaw to the north. Word was passed and the assault was started.

Group South approached the stone escarpment which spanned a narrow ravine. The depression in the desert floor was the telltale sign of an abandoned river bed. A narrow slit in the rock face revealed a dark and seemingly unguarded passageway beyond. The opening was barely wide enough for a man to pass through. Captain Habib called for Loring, asking him how much of the cave detail he recalled.

"As soon as you're inside, the passageway turns gradually until you come to an intersection. From what I remember, I was forced to go straight ahead, not taking either branch of the joining passage. If the Brotherhood has guards posted they could pick us off, one by one, at that intersection."

The military mind had the simple solution...blast your way in. A bazooka shell widened the opening to allow several men through at a time. When the smoke and rubble settled, Habib led his men into the labyrinth. Loring and Crimmins followed at a distance. Derek shivered when he entered the cave, remembering the smoking torches bracketed to the walls and the chanting Brotherhood. He remembered Nadia. The Brotherhood was not there this time. The hooded figures must be further back, deeper into the passageways and possibly grouped around Sempher.

The troops leading the attack rounded up remnants and stragglers of the hooded Brethren who offered no resistance. No shots were fired and there was no shouting or running amok. None of the prisoners said a word. They merely stood in groups, waiting for the order to leave. Suddenly, as though by a silent signal, a weird chant came from the mass of cowled figures, a chant which invoked the wrath of Zozer upon the intruder.

Habib commanded the chant to stop, demanded the

quick surrender of Sempher and the Brotherhood. There was no change in the attitude of the prisoners. The chant became louder, and more vengeful. Habib detached some men to search the passages and to take into custody anyone they found.

Loring suggested to Habib that they go on ahead to the altar and throne room beyond. If Sempher was still in the caverns, the throne room would be the likely place for him to be. Habib agreed and they left the resentful captives under guard and proceeded further into the passage Loring remembered so painfully. In the widened chamber, the stained and cold stone altar stood as a beacon for Loring's loss.

"This is where it happened, isn't it?" Crimmins threw his arm around Loring's shoulders, steadying his friend who was hesitant to go on.

"Yes. They murdered Nadia on that obscene altar. I warned Sempher I would come back and kill him. Let's get on with it."

Captain Habib led the way further into the complex, accompanied by three armed soldiers. Loring and Crimmins lagged behind, leaving the search entirely in the hands of Habib. When the group approached a sharp intersection, Loring called ahead to Habib.

"The throne room is at the end of the left passageway, Captain, about fifty yards. Be careful of a trap. Sempher won't be easy to get."

The sight that greeted them when they entered the throne room startled all but Loring. Habib and his men stood immobile in amazement at the recreated splendor of the Third Dynasty replica.

Crimmins gazed around the room, his eyes wide with undisguised appreciation. "Blimey, I didn't think it was possible," he uttered under his breath. "The man is a bloody genius."

"Only the best for our Pharaoh...all that his money can buy," Loring said, appreciating the awe of the men at their first glimpse of what Sempher created. He let his own eyes circle the room...the gold-encrusted throne, marble floor, carved and painted walls. A slight movement from the far side made them realize they were not alone. On a pillowed couch against the far wall, Josh Claridge lay partially hidden in deep shadows. He was still and quiet as though asleep.

"Josh, what the hell are you doing?" Loring hurried to the couch, only to stop short when Claridge held up his hand weakly.

"Mr. Loring, do you know this man?" Habib had Claridge under his gun.

"Yes, he's part of the Menefee society, sworn enemies of Zoser." Loring swung around to Claridge, pain and confusion reflected in his eyes. "Why, Josh? For Christ's sake, why?"

Claridge made no attempt to get up from the couch. His labored breathing signaled his weakness.

"Your guns won't be necessary, Captain. I'm not going anywhere. My little friend here saw to that."

Claridge let his hand stray to the dark side of the couch. A venomous cobra was snuggled against his body, coiled and still. A pitiful smile crossed Claridge's lips.

"I'm sorry, Derek. The temptation was too strong. I never would have hurt you, or Bert. It just happened. When our man on the inside reported to me that Sempher was dead...."

"Sempher is dead?" Loring and Crimmins both shouted.

"Yes, he died a few days ago. Heart attack. I already knew that when I met with you at the museum. I knew all about the plan, and decided to go ahead with it. This Brotherhood is powerless without a strong leader and Yamani would have ruined it." Claridge's voice faltered. After a moment, he continued.

"It was all so easy. I came here and told the brothers I was the new leader and that I would give them the power to restructure Egypt. What I didn't count on was the complete failure of the riots, thanks to the Pope. We never realized how strong formalized religion was." He coughed up some phlegm and blood. Everyone watched in silence.

"The timing was bad, Derek. If 'Amun' succeeded, you would have been powerless to take this place. The army would have been busy elsewhere. Since it failed, everything was lost. I took the easy way out, the same as Cleopatra. I let this slimy snake feast on my arm."

"What about the Menefee?" Crimmins asked. "Are they finished as well?"

"Most likely. There are a few scattered groups around, but with no central control or leadership, they can't do much. Besides, now that the Zozer Brotherhood is destroyed, there's no further need for the Menefee."

Claridge's breathing was becoming more labored, his voice weaker. His end was near. At that moment, Merrick and Bradshaw rushed into the room. Troopers led the way with a timid, pregnant girl following. When Marc looked at the dying Claridge, his shoulders stooped and his voice broke.

"You were right all along, Bert."

"Only partly, Marc. It's no consolation for me."

Claridge made one final effort. "Don't think too badly of me. I was just one more weak bastard in this world."

Joshua Claridge died, his face and body contorted with pain. Everyone watched in horror, silently, as he writhed in his last convulsion. After a while, the girl spoke.

"What about me?"

"Miss Yamani," Crimmins answered, "your father is dead. You won't be blamed for any of this. Dr. Nashtoi asked us to bring you to him. He said he would take care of you."

Loring put it to her directly. "Nara, were you here about five weeks ago when I was brought in with another woman?"

"Yes, I was here. I remember seeing you and the woman being taken to the altar."

"Do you know what happened?"

"The woman was killed on the altar in the old way. You were taken out into the desert to die slowly in the old way. How did you survive? No one ever survives the desert death."

"Never mind about me. Think carefully, Nara. What happened to the woman? I saw her killed, but I don't know what they did with her afterward. Do you know?"

Before Nara could answer, Crimmins turned to Loring and said, "Derek, let it go. What good will it do to resurrect it all again?"

"Bert, I have to know. I want to be at peace. Nara, what happened?"

"When the ritual was over, they took her body and left it in the desert sand outside the caves. It was halfway to the oasis."

"The bastards!" Loring was shaking. "You mean they just dumped her body and left her to the desert?"

"Yes, but I buried her secretly when I was alone."

"Will you take me to where you buried her?"

"Yes."

They left the throne room then, leaving the mop up work to Habib and his men. The captain called to Nara as they were leaving. "We will need you to show us where Sempher is buried, miss. Don't be gone too long."

The girl led them out into the desert to the oasis. There, beside a palm tree, she pointed to a crude mastaba, an oblong cairn of stones partially covered over by the drifting sand.

"I pulled her here at night and buried her. The jackals would have gotten to her. It was all I could do."

Loring didn't move toward the grave. He couldn't bear to look upon the remains of his love. Crimmins stood apart with tears in his eyes, remembering the young, vibrant woman he considered a daughter. Merrick and Bradshaw did nothing, each silent in his own thoughts. Finally, Loring forced himself to the heap of stones, looking at it as though he might see his lovely Nadia as she once was. He had to do it, heaven help him!

He dropped to his knees and pushed aside some of the stones and sand. Whitened and clean bones were gradually uncovered. He gathered a few, and tenderly placed them inside his shirt. He left the rest covered by the desert. He faced his friends.

"I'll have these cremated and take the ashes back to Hawaii with me. Nadia once told me she knew she would never see the islands. This way, at least, she can be a part of the place that means so much to me. And she can remain a part of this place, too, where our love blossomed and we became as one with each other."

"Bloody ghoulish, if you ask me." Bradshaw didn't fully understand it all. Crimmins and Merrick did. They kept whatever thoughts they had to themselves.

It was time to return to Cairo and put the final stamp on the Zoser affair. It was only eleven o'clock when the helicopters left El Fayoum. The hottest part of the day was still to come.

Chapter 26

A military entourage drove to Saqqara in two Jeeps. Nara and Loring rode in the lead vehicle with Captain Habib who was in a hurry to have this entire matter over and done with. By the time he returned to Cairo from El Fayoum the army had been placed on war alert, and Habib didn't want any possible combat orders delayed by this excursion to Saqqara.

Habib was a fighting officer, not a paper shuffler, and the prospect of being involved in the coming conflict with Libya set his blood pounding through his veins. Still, he was compelled to curtail his personal desires long enough to complete this official assignment.

Loring and Nara were silent during the trip. They had been engrossed in their own thoughts ever since Captain Habib left them at the museum on the way back from El Fayoum. Loring wanted to inform Dr. Nashtoi of the end of Zoser and to leave Nara in his care.

He was concerned that Nara Yamani was so complaisant and indecisive. The knowledge of her father's death had no visible effect on her. She seemed to accept the news indifferently, as though he was a stranger with no attachment to her. The fact she was carrying Sempher's child seemed to have no special impact on her, either, beyond the normal maternal feelings. Nara Yamani was indeed a lost woman, Loring thought, neither knowing nor caring as to her future.

The museum curator was overjoyed at the news coming from El Fayoum. He was finally able to explain to Loring about the burden he had been carrying for so long. Working with the Menefee to destroy the Brotherhood had cut deep into his soul. He was out of his element with intrigue and killing. His life was complete only by pursuing a scholar's role. Now, with Loring's account of the Fayoum episode, he visibly brightened.

"Doctor, the army is coming back for Nara and me in an hour. Nara has to lead us to Sempher's tomb and I have to make a positive identification of the body. He was mummified, you know. Poor Nara had to witness the whole thing. But there is something I wish you would do for me." Loring pointed to the bundle he had with him.

"With Nara's help, I found the grave where Nadia was buried. I have a few of her bones here which I retrieved from the sand. Could you have these cremated for me secretly to avoid long explanations and permits. I want to take some of Nadia's ashes back to Hawaii for burial. I realize this is an odd request, perhaps even illegal, but will you do this for me and for Nadia? She thought very highly of you."

Nashtoi opened the small package Loring handed him. There in the folds of the wrapping were the few whitened bones Derek took from beneath the stone cairn. Nashtoi faced Loring.

"There will be no problem," he said. "I would do it even if there was. It can be done right here. They shall be ready by the time you return from Saqqara."

"It'll mean a lot to me, Doctor."

"Now, what are we to do about you, young lady?" Nashtoi turned to Nara, lovingly. "Will you stay here with me? My wife and I will take good care of you, and when your baby is born, you can decide where you wish to go. I have friends who will see to your welfare."

"Thank you, Doctor. Your offer is generous. I must accept for I have no other place to go."

"Good! Then it is all arranged. I shall inform Mrs. Nashtoi to prepare our guest room. Since you have other things to do with the army, now, I'll be here when you return."

The old Egyptian appeared years younger and was smiling as Loring and Nara left to meet Captain Habib.

As they approached the environs of Memphis, Loring broke his silence. "What do you intend doing with the tourists at Saqqara, Captain?"

"No disrespect, Mr. Loring, but give us some credit for seeing the difficulties with the tourists. For what we have to do, it would be poor public relations to have the foreigners getting in the way, pointing their Polaroids and Canons at everything in sight. We sent some men on ahead to close the place down. We won't have any distractions from tourists."

Passing slowly through the dusty streets of Memphis, Loring could not help but wonder how or why the residents stayed on. Their lives had to be totally empty of all happiness. The vast desert was driving them out. It was as certain as the sun rising each day in the east that the days of Memphis were numbered.

A pitiful few inhabitants stood in forlorn clumps, vacantly watching the army vehicles treading a slow path through the few obstinate goats intent on defecating in the dirty road. They gave no indication this caravan was in any way different than any of the others which continually passed through. These people were beyond caring any longer. The gods had fated them for extinction, a total erasure from the scroll of history. They were resigned.

At the turnoff leading north to the compound of Zozer's Stepped Pyramid, the army trucks lurched ahead in a rush to end their journey. Nara directed the driver to the ruins of the forgotten pyramid at the far end of the burial compound. They drove as far as they could in the scattered rubble of stone and sand, then stopped. The men left their Jeeps and approached the heaps of stone.

Then Nara pointed out the stones that hid the entrance—hid it so completely she was compelled to remove some of the rocks herself to reveal the dark passage beyond. The army men went to work where Nara pointed and the hidden entrance to an underground chamber was exposed. Habib led his men through the opening, and into a dark and silent world of stone and sand. They heaved and pushed at the large rock which sealed the burial chamber. It required the combined efforts of the entire company to turn aside the stone which concealed the tomb.

Light from the army torches bounced off the walls of the chamber, glancing across the elaborate decoration of the walls and ceiling. The army men were all young and not fully aware of their heritage. They stood in awe at the shimmering splendor of the tomb. Habib had lanterns lit, their yellow glow producing an eerie dimension to the scene.

All eyes were drawn to the ornate and glittering sarcophagus set in the center of the chamber. On top were the decomposing remains of the priest, Zumab. The stench of death was overpowering in the restricted confines of the tomb, and Habib pushed the corpse closer to the door where the air was circulating. He turned to Nara.

"Is this it?"

"Yes, Captain," Nara replied. "The mummy is inside the inner coffin."

"Wait, Habib," Loring said. "Please give me a few minutes to examine the sarcophagus...professional curiosity."

"Very well, Loring. But hurry it up. The stench is overpowering and we have a schedule to keep."

Loring walked around the pewter sarcophagus, studying the rich gold ornamentation, begrudgingly giving credit to Sempher's authenticity. He appreciated the gold and ebony death mask delicately fashioned in the ancient manner. Even though the man had been greedy, ambitious, mean and amoral, Sempher certainly knew his history and art.

However, the inconsistency of the tomb caused Loring to wonder. Sempher was completely wrapped in the traditions of Zozer, pharaoh of the Third Dynasty. Then why, with unlimited wealth at his disposal, had Sempher gone to such lengths to make his tomb a replica of that of Ramses VI, who was part of the Twentieth Dynasty? Was it because Ramses tomb was so richly decorated that it would give Sempher a feeling of greatness to know he might spend eternity in the reflected glory of Ramses, or was it because Sempher hadn't dare construct a pyramid for himself for fear of drawing attention to himself? Loring knew he would never find the answer in Egypt. Better to let the reason remain dead with Sempher.

Habib's men removed the heavy lid of the pewter sarcophagus uncovering the inner cedar coffin. They lifted it out and placed it on the sandy floor of the chamber where the dowels were knocked out. The coffin lid was slid aside and the mummy of Kurt Sempher was taken out in silence. The men acted uncertain as to how they should handle the linen-wrapped body. Was Sempher actually a king? Habib made the decision for them when he ordered the body taken out into the open, quickly.

"We don't have all day. Take it out and let's get on with our job."

The bright desert sun poured its rays down on the group standing around the mummy. Loring took a curved dagger from Habib and started to uncover the head. He carefully cut away the linen wrappings only from the head and neck of the body, leaving the rest of the mummy intact. For what he had to do, identify the remains, all he needed was an examination of the head. With each layer of cloth he cut away, Loring was impressed with the precision taken in duplicating the ancient art. There had been no haste, no hurrying to get an unpleasant task finished and done with. Each layer had the resin and gum spread evenly to assure complete adhesion.

At last it was done. A contorted and withered head was revealed. Loring had studied many mummy remains during his years in museums and digs, but his hands were shaking now that he was actually feeling the leather skin clinging to the sightless skull gazing up into the sun.

He was amazed at how exacting the process had been. He noticed the small bruises below the eye sockets, evidence that the brain had been removed through the nasal passages. There were no other marks on the head, no cuts or other signs of trauma. The eyes had been removed during the actual mummification process to rid the body of extraneous organs which would decay. Loring recalled that when he saw Sempher in Zurich, the man had bulging, protruding eyes. The empty sockets showed depressions around the bridge of the nose which could have exerted pressure on the eyeballs to give them a swollen appearance.

The cheeks were less than full, still with sparse remains of the beard stubble Sempher must have had when he died. The hair on the head was thin and short, while the gray eyebrows were bushy and full as Loring remembered from the Zurich meeting. He had been correct then in assuming Sempher shaved his head. With a deep sense of relief, almost euphoria, Loring turned to Habib.

"This was definitely Kurt Sempher."

"Very well. My orders are clear. You will make it official for the record. Here, take this form and fill in the particulars while we dispose of this thing." Habib signaled his men, who brought up some equipment from one of the Jeeps. Loring retired into the shadows of the ruined tomb and began to write.

I attest that I am a citizen of the United States, and affirm that the mummified remains uncovered at Saqqara, Republic of Egypt this date are those of Kurt Sempher.

I further declare that Kurt Sempher was the sole leader of an organization known as Zoser International and known as the Zozer Brotherhood, who aspired for the violent overthrow of the present legal government of the Republic of Egypt.

I witnessed the murder of Nadia Shepherd, a citizen of Great Britain, by the hand of Kurt Sempher while the same Nadia Shepherd was in the service of Her Majesty's government of the United Kingdom.

Derek Loring

"This should satisfy the damned bureaucrats for the time being," Loring said to himself. Later, he'd write a report that would shake up a lot of people.

He looked toward the cluster of army men grouped around the mummy. Captain Habib gave a stern order. "Get on with it."

The flame thrower spewed liquid fire over the mummy, engulfing it in searing flames. The mass burned furiously for a short while, then died down and smoldered until only gray-white ashes remained. Habib did not wait for the ashes to cool before he had his men scatter them over the sand.

"The old bastard is still buried here at Saqqara, but no one will ever know it. There will be no cult worship of this obscenity."

Habib collected his men, leaving two behind to guard the tomb. "The army will send someone to permanently seal it for all time," Habib said, as he motioned for Loring and the girl to get back in the Jeep. It was time to head back to Cairo.

Loring handed Habib the statement he had written. The Egyptian read it and grunted his approval.

"Your work here is now finished, Loring. I wish you a safe journey back to America. President Mubarak would have preferred to thank you personally for what you and your friends have done for Egypt, but unfortunately he has pressing matters with Gadhafy to settle first. He hopes you understand. Also, he has expressed his appreciation to your President by a personal letter."

"I understand perfectly, Captain. All I want is to gather my things and leave quietly. If you would please drop me and the girl at the museum, I'll get out of your hair and let you get back to your war."

The two army vehicles drove down Kubry El-Giza, the wide boulevard leading past the Great Pyramids, the Mena House and over the Nile into downtown Cairo. Loring and Habib shook hands when they parted company at the museum entrance. Loring paused, then said, "Be careful, my friend. Keep your head down."

Dr. Nashtoi was waiting for them. Loring told him of the mummy, the tomb, his identification of Sempher, and the incineration of the body. Now, he thought, Nashtoi can get back to his love, unfettered by politics and intrigue. He was happy for the curator.

Nashtoi handed Loring a box, carefully wrapped in papyrus and sealed with a wax impression of the Egyptian state seal.

"This will get it out of the country without trouble. I put the ashes in a canopic jar as I believed you would want. We can never thank you enough for all you endured for us."

"I did what I had to, Doctor. So did Nadia. Thank you for your kindness and understanding." Then he turned to the girl. "Nara, try to forget the past. Make a new life for yourself and your child. Dr. Nashtoi will take good care of you."

"Goodbye, Mr. Loring. May the blessings of Osiris and Isis guide your path." There were tears in Nara's eyes as she kissed his cheek.

Loring left the quiet and musty museum, and took a cab back to the Mena House to meet Merrick and Crimmins. When he arrived, Merrick asked if he would mind having dinner first.

"Not at all. The food here is decent however it's expensive. But what the hell, I still have my fee from Zoser, and we deserve a night on the town."

Before they had a chance to leave their room, a knock on the door startled them. Peter Bradshaw stood there, very proper and official. With him were two other men, strangers.

"Derek, these men want to talk with the three of you. John Caine and Paul Soloman, CIA. Gentlemen, this is Derek Loring, and over there by the window are Marc Merrick and Bert Crimmins. Do you want me to leave?"

"No, Bradshaw, you might as well stay. What we have to say concerns you, too." The man called Caine spoke. "Mr. Loring, the agency felt you were entitled to an explanation as to why it appeared your country, and Britain, left you fellows on your own. Actually you were not...alone, that is. We did have you fairly well covered, but damn it all, you did do some unexpected things."

"Such as?" Loring asked, perplexed.

"We've been on to Zoser since before Istanbul. Political coups and assassinations were its stock in trade. We worked with MI 6 there, and it was your untimely abduction which blew it. We had Wells dead to rights, but he slipped away. People at the agency felt that Zoser would contact you when the time was right, when Sempher was to make his final play for power."

"I still don't know what you're driving at."

"When you took this assignment you let your personal feelings get in the way. Shepherd kept us up to date on what you were after. She was trying to make up for Istanbul. But we had another problem. Gadhafy. His terrorists were all over, and we had to stop him before he launched an attack on Syria and Israel. He wants control of the Arab world. We were spread thin, and MI 6 was just as sparse as we were. Unfortunately, when you got your evidence against Zoser and wanted us to get active, we were putting out a lot of other Arab fires."

"Go on. What's the bottom line?"

"MI 6 felt that your operation was in their ballpark and jurisdiction...we didn't. Then Hopkins called in the KGB in a sincere effort to back your play, but now the Kremlin expects payment which we are not prepared to make. You three have created more havoc in intelligence circles than you can imagine. But, luckily, it all turned out okay."

"Okay, my ass!" Loring was furious. "If you were so goddamned efficient, where were you when Nadia and I were taken off that plane? Where were you when she was killed? Where were your able and efficient agents when Marc's car was bombed, nearly killing the three of us? Where were you when Operation Amun was started with the riots? Don't you dare talk to me, to us, about how thin you were spread. That's plain crap. Why don't you admit you blew it and why you bastards will continue to blow it, time after time?"

"Now, fellows, calm down." Bradshaw interrupted. "MI 6 helped you all it could. We couldn't order you to do anything...it had to be strictly your own show. As it was, we nearly didn't get the riots stopped soon enough. Yamani did his work too well. If we got in the picture too soon, Zoser would still be alive and well, biding its time to strike again."

"But what about the law?" Crimmins spoke, now, "Murder, kidnapping, treason, espionage...all were apparently given sanction by your agencies. We were trying to stop Zoser by lawful means, not that we always succeeded, but we respected the law. Now you come here after the game is over and tell us that what we did, and the way we did it, got in you way. I don't believe our society is ready for your kind of justification."

Agent Soloman took up the argument. "Your kind always flaunt the law. But when you're in real trouble, you come crawling to the government looking for help. Sometimes, I wonder why we bother."

"That's it! You can all get the hell out of here." Loring and Merrick stood together, ready to throw the agents out. "We heard your explanations and don't buy them. You made your duty call, placated the poor civilians. Now, you can go back to your world of shadows. We don't want any part of that world. Now, get out before we throw you out. We've a plane to catch."

The three friends had difficulty calming down after the others finally left. Their thoughts of a quiet farewell dinner left with the agents. All they wanted now was to get to the airport as soon as they could. Merrick said it best, in the taxi. "In one way they were right. We did what we started out to do, and we did it our way. What little help the CIA and MI 6 gave us was just whatever served their own interests. I don't know about you chaps, but I have a clear conscience about this."

"Well said, Marc," Crimmins replied. "My mind is at ease, finally. I don't have any more self-recriminations about Wells. He was part of what's wrong with the world. Too bad there are so many more out there like him."

Loring looked at his two companions, half wishing they could stay together. But it could not be. He knew he would have to leave them soon and return to Hawaii. He was destined to travel his world alone, doing what he had to, and when he had to do it. He tucked the papyrus-wrapped box under his arm and stepped from the taxi. Come on, Nadia, he said to himself, it's time to go home.

Epilogue

It was doubtful Priory Farm would ever be as it once was before the Zozer Brotherhood intruded on the lives of those who found the farm a haven from strife. In only a few weeks the tranquillity of Priory Farm was totally disrupted by the intrigue and killings which had gone hand in hand with that evil cult.

Veronica and Marc found themselves influenced by a discontent thoroughly foreign to their character. In the past, their lives had been orderly, not regimented or severe, but generally predictable and routine. That was gone. The loss of friends, however, was the most tragic aftermath. Ron Menefee and Joshua Claridge were both dead. It was strange. Ron died defending a principle, and Josh died denying that principle. Nadia Shepherd was a dear friend by association with Derek. She, too, was dead. Bert Crimmins was so close to being lost, but an inner strength surfaced during the Egypt experience which brought him back. And what about Derek Loring? Was he gone from their lives, despondent and grieving, wrapping himself in the torment of his dreams?

Marc had come home early from the bank. His help and sacrifice for the government earned him a directorship in the bank, an event which normally would have been cause for celebration. Marc accepted the promotion and the brief notoriety with subdued grace and thanks. The truth was he really didn't care. While Derek was at the farm, Marc was excited and outgoing, reliving the entire episode. Now that Loring was gone, Merrick retreated more and more into himself, almost locking out Veronica.

He was standing at the gate, the one leading to the church, with Briget at his side. He was gazing over the hills and woods of Surrey, looking far beyond the horizon. He saw, not the green fields and dappled foliage, but the hot and arid desert sprawling eternally toward the west from Cairo. He didn't hear the larks and cardinals trilling in the trees. Instead, he heard the ominous chant of the Brotherhood echoing throughout the ancient caverns of El Fayoum.

The desert was calling but Marc knew he could never answer, never heed the call to adventure again. It will soon pass, he told himself, and become only a memory. Until then, he would squeeze every drop of excitement from the adventure. He felt he was entitled to it.

Bert Crimmins stood by the window of his new office. His resignation had not been formally accepted and now, as Deputy Superintendent of Scotland Yard, he felt his life was once more on track. His part in the defeat of the Zozer Brotherhood earned him a commendation and a letter of appreciation from Queen Elizabeth.

Although his star was once again soaring in the heavens, Bert was not content. He had a modicum of respect, but these periods of daydreaming he experienced consumed a large part of his days. He found his mind wandering whenever he was not actively involved in the Yard business, whenever he was alone. These daydreams started right after Loring left England, and seemed to get more vivid with each passing day.

Bert looked over the stretches of London from his window. In the distance he could see the towers of the Parliament buildings but they didn't register in his view.

He saw instead, the dunes of the Sahara beyond the Pyramids. He saw the caverns of El Fayoum snaking through the rock and desert sand. He relived the painful death of Josh Claridge, the deadly cobra nestled silently beside him. He heard the babble of Cairo, its many tongues and dialects streaming up to his window obliterating the street traffic of London.

Bert realized this disturbing period was merely the result of heightened excitement generated by his brush with death, but he so wished it would stop. The call of the desert was loud and persistent, keeping him trapped within himself and interfering with his duties. How long could he ignore the call, the summons to return to the heat and spell of El Fayoum?

As he did with regularity when this feeling seeped into his soul, he abruptly turned away from the window to immerse himself in the routine paperwork accumulating on his desk. He forced himself to deal with the here and now, pushing the desert deeper into his past. Bert Crimmins knew with certainty that the beckoning desert would always be in his mind.

Derek Loring lounged on his lanai which faced the broad Pacific. In the west the sun was beginning its final plunge into the sea to end another day of dreams, sorrow and loneliness. The sky was streaked with vivid hues of red, orange and purple as the sun descended and the colors reflected in the gentle swell of the tide.

On a rattan table beside him, in a canopic jar with a cover resembling the god, Anubis, the ashes of Nadia were commanding his thoughts. He knew it was time to put the woman he loved in life to rest. Her death in Egypt, impaled on that obscene altar, did not take her from him. He brought the ashes home to keep her beside him, but the emptiness and sadness he experienced every time he handled the jar made him conclude he had to let her go. Her memory would be the legacy he inherited from her. That would be enough.

Loring steered a small boat out toward the reef where the swelling tide broke in gentle white water. He allowed the craft to drift with the sea, the world around him darkening fast with the disappearance of the sun. It was time.

His eyes misted over as he uncovered the jar. He slowly poured out the ashes with finality and reluctant purpose. They floated on the surface, clumping together in small inanimate islands, drifting with the tide. He whispered his last farewell, letting the words scatter on the breeze. Then he gazed at the black horizon. Amun died in the western sea, drawing the soul of Nadia Shepherd with it. He heard a sea bird in the distance. It's mournful cry floated on the trade wind.

It was finished. Derek headed the boat toward the white beach, dropping the alabaster jar into the sea. All traces of Nadia were erased, except those that would always dwell in his heart...and at El Fayoum.